HOUR OF the ROSE

Christina Skye

AVON BOOKS NEW YORK

To my mother

This is a work of fiction. Names, characters, places, and incidents either are the product of the author's imagination or are used fictitiously. Any resemblance to actual events, locales, organizations, or persons, living or dead, is entirely coincidental and beyond the intent of either the author or the publisher.

AVON BOOKS, INC.
1350 Avenue of the Americas
New York, New York 10019

Copyright © 1994 by Roberta Helmer
Inside cover author photograph by Bill Morris Studio
Published by arrangement with the author
Visit our website at http://www.AvonBooks.com
Library of Congress Catalog Card Number: 93-90653
ISBN: 0-380-77385-6

All rights reserved, which includes the right to reproduce this book or portions thereof in any form whatsoever except as provided by the U.S. Copyright Law. For information address Avon Books, Inc.

First Avon Books Printing: April 1994

AVON TRADEMARK REG. U.S. PAT. OFF. AND IN OTHER COUNTRIES, MARCA REGISTRADA, HECHO EN U.S.A.

Printed in the U.S.A.

WCD 10 9 8 7 6 5 4 3

If you purchased this book without a cover, you should be aware that this book is stolen property. It was reported as "unsold and destroyed" to the publisher, and neither the author nor the publisher has received any payment for this "stripped book."

WITH DEEPEST THANKS:

to Helen Woolverton for so generously sharing her
wealth of Medieval expertise;

to Christina Lynn Whited for all the "special stuff" that made
Kelly come so vibrantly alive;

to Earl Martin for intriguing details on firearms and calibers
and infrared scopes;

to Barbara Harkins for impressive aplomb under looming
deadlines;

and to Ellen Fuscellaro for her thoughtful suggestions
throughout.

Prologue

The great feline sat motionless on the parapet, his body a slash of shadow against the rising moon. Below him the granite walls of Draycott Abbey stood silent, impassive. Coldly vigilant.

Waiting.

Just as the great cat waited.

A cloud danced before the moon. Somewhere in the deep woods a small animal cried out and made a reckless dash for safety.

But the night held no safety, as the creature's tormented cry revealed, drifting on the cool, still air.

The cat's ears pricked forward. Slitted amber eyes probed the darkness.

There was no whisper beyond the breeze ruffling the heavy centifolia roses at the abbey's ancient base. No noise but the gurgle of the moat's silver waters, ever restless, ever changing, like the fortunes of the warriors who had fought to hold these lands for twenty generations and more.

Far out on the rolling downs, past the black

reeds of the Witch's Pool, past the sharp face of the cliff known as Lyon's Leap, a sound rent the air, bell-like, unforgettable, the fine clang of purest gold.

The cat eased forward and began to purr.

He raised his head and sent a low, plaintive cry to the moon.

To the night. To the shadow that called to him from inside the abbey.

The centuries made no difference. Gideon had obeyed before and would obey again. Some laws had no rules, no limits, no bounds, nor anything that mortals knew as months, days, or years.

And so it was for the love between cat and master, ghost and friend.

The leaves tossed. Deep in the night a church bell rang twelve clear strokes—and then one more, faint and haunting. Ineffably sad.

And on that sound, a shadow stepped from a portrait in the Long Gallery. Empty space shuddered and gave way to broad shoulders and a chiselled jaw. To black velvet and white lace cuffs that danced in an unseen wind.

To the brooding features of the eighth Viscount Draycott, the abbey's ghostly guardian, who now materialized on the abbey's parapets, his dark eyes burning.

He was a man who had died two hundred years before.

His face was hard, too strong for common beauty. Like the abbey's weathered granite, it was marked by years of war and callous betrayal. The hands were powerful—yet exquisite in their care as they eased over Gideon's sleek gray fur.

Guardians, these two had been. Together for decades. Nay, for centuries. And guardians they would be, through dangers yet unseen.

The cat's black-slitted eyes gleamed in the moonlight. His cocked head held a question for the figure standing before him.

"You felt it too, did you, old friend?" The Draycott ghost stared out over the parapets, studying the abbey's hills and fields, a patchwork of black and silver in the moonlight. "Something not as it should be. Something out *there*." The proud, sensual lips frowned. "Whether man or beast or dark intent, I cannot say. And that strange, haunting sound . . ."

Again it came, the feeling that something was wrong.

The cat eased up onto black-tipped paws. He crooned a question deep in his throat.

"Nicholas? Draycott's twelfth viscount is well, never fear. At this moment he lies sound in his bed." The ghost laughed dryly. "Though not asleep."

The cat's gray tail twitched.

"His wife? Beside him, I should imagine." The full lips curved. "Like her devoted husband, not sleeping either." He turned away, his face cast into hard profile. Half was bathed with cool silver light; the other brooded featureless, trapped in a darkness and a distance that no human mind could comprehend.

The ghost of Draycott Abbey cast out his spectral, sentient net. Past tree and stone he searched, over rich green earth and fragrant roses he knew bud by brilliant bud.

He felt it instantly.

Danger.

It mocked him, an affront to every solemn vow that kept him locked in this ancient place.

Phantom lace fluttered in a phantom breeze. Gideon meowed as the long-dead eighth viscount turned and began to pace the cold stones. "Full well have I loved this abbey, Gideon. Through war and strife, through the sway of kings and traitors have I guarded these weathered walls." He frowned. Deep lines scored his brow and cheeks. "But this danger is different, stranger than any we have known before." He peered out into the midnight black of hill and tree.

And saw a woman whose hair streamed red-gold in a cloud, her eyes wide with fear. Behind her were lights, ten times ten, and a hatred that coiled through the ancient air like smoke.

Her hand stretched out to him. Her eyes held a wild plea for help.

Frowning, Adrian moved into the glowing vision, fighting to reach her.

But not of this time she was, perhaps not even of this world.

And then she vanished as quickly as she had come, leaving behind only the dry scrape of dead leaves on cold stone.

"I've lost her, Gideon." The black-clad figure cursed harshly.

The great cat meowed, brushing against his master's booted feet.

High overhead a shooting star flamed over the dark hills, a pinpoint of silver against the velvet sky.

Then the light went out.

And in its passing something cold and faceless, an evil long centuries old, crept forward in silence toward the sleeping abbey.

Chapter 1

"*F*orget it, Miles. Not this time."

The woman turned from the window of her adobe house, her shoulder-length hair russet in the sunlight. Her face was pale, tight with strain. Somehow it made the clarity of her turquoise eyes all the more striking. "This time you'll just have to find someone else."

"Come on, Kelly. You're the best there is and you know it."

"I'm also the *tiredest* there is." Kelly Hamilton sighed. "You must know how busy I am here. We've just found evidence of pit dwellings at level two and the first team has gone in after a cache of pots and grave goods that appears to be in pristine condition. On top of that our funding proposals are due next week, and I haven't even begun to—"

"The pots will wait, Kelly. So will the homesites. They've waited a thousand years already, haven't they?" Slender and blond haired, Miles O'Halloran looked like a slightly rumpled academic. As he smiled at Kelly, his soft gray eyes took on a sleepy quality.

But Kelly knew his mind was razor-sharp beneath that genial English veneer. Only this time neither his arguments nor his affability was going to sway her.

Because she wasn't going back.

Not for any reason.

"Even bureaucrats can be staved off, Kelly. Deadlines can be delayed. Unless . . ." His eyes narrowed. "I don't suppose this has anything to do with that last job you did for us."

Kelly's fingers tensed as she brushed a fine veil of dust from a magnificent black and white Anasazi pot.

Miles frowned. "Accidents can happen, you know. There's no reason to blame yourself for that girl's death."

At his words, Kelly Hamilton went completely still. "I told you never to discuss that." She turned, her face hard. "*Never*, Miles. That was one of my conditions if I agreed to help you."

"Oh, come on, Kelly. No one here knows anything about your work with us. Your secret is quite safe, I assure you."

"For how long?"

"As long as it matters. I gave you my word on that."

Kelly looked around at her adobe room. Pine floors ran bare from one baked-earth wall to the other. The last rays of sunlight spilled through the skylight, gilding a row of hand-split beams that had come from an old Spanish mission.

The room's few furnishings were magnificent and intensely personal. Muted blankets in shades of purple and magenta handwoven by one of her friends. A peach linen sofa with bent twig frame and arms. And of course the artifacts Kelly loved so well: a beautiful terra-cotta Hopi burial pot with rich, flaring curves. A set of antique Kachina dolls and a fine contemporary Nativity set carved in polished redwood.

Kelly sighed. The desert wind spilled through the room, ruffling the dried flowers hung from the ceiling. Bowls of lavender, verbena, and sage perfumed the air from sun-washed sills.

She breathed in the rich scents. This place had been her haven since the fall that had nearly taken her life. Since she'd discovered her strange gift.

And if word about her singular "talents" got out, she would lose it all—her house, her job, and her reputation as an up-and-coming star of New World archeology.

She wasn't about to let that happen.

"The answer's still no, Miles." She stared out at the graduate students just visible in the distance laboring over a wind-swept canyon full of Anasazi ruins. "There are already enough rumors circulating about me." The slender archeologist laughed bleakly. "And in this case the truth would be much stranger than *any* rumor."

"That's why we need you, Kelly. You're *unique*. This will be the very last time, I promise you."

Kelly looked down at a sharply indented flint arrowhead and thought idly about using it. "Right, Miles. That's exactly what you said the last time—and the time before that."

"This time it's true," the Englishman said urgently.

"I can't. I'm through."

"You can. In fact, you *have* to."

Kelly's brow rose. "Is that a threat?"

"No, damn it, of course not. It's just a fact. We need you to do this. And *you* need to do it."

"What I need are a few dozen skilled field-workers and approval on my grant application." She sighed. "Go back to Washington, Miles. Go back to your careful men in careful suits and your careful meetings where you sit around discussing the latest developments in satellite reconnaissance data, armament stockpiling, and terrorist infiltration."

"Kelly, you—"

"No, don't say it. I know I'm not supposed to know that sort of thing. I'm just supposed to come up with raw information when your other intelligence sources don't work out. And it was good for a while, I don't deny that. For a time I did need to bury myself in a mission, in anything that would convince me that this— this *gift* of mine was good and honorable. But no more. You see, I'm tired of the odds on working miracles, Miles. And that *is* what you come to me for, isn't it? For miracles."

Frowning, Miles picked up a mint-condition stone chopping tool and ran it slowly over his fingers. "I suppose you might say that. But you've done it for us before, Kelly. Time and again. And as far as the people I represent, I've always been honest with you. This matter is unofficial, something that comes directly through me. I only give you cases where lives are in jeopardy—things I know you'd believe in. Not that I can discuss them, of course."

"Of course." Kelly gave a bitter laugh. "Your world is just as closed-minded as mine. You know, we're every bit as primitive and super-stitious as our medieval brethren. It's just that *they* were honest about it, while we hide behind mumbo jumbo like statistical probability, psionic energy, and magnetic resonances."

Wistfully she studied the distant line of hills, red-gold in the brilliance of a setting Arizona sun. "Nothing ever changes, I guess."

"I could see to it that you get the things you need here. Workers. Money."

"Just like that?" The fatigue in Kelly's voice took on an edge of bitterness.

"*Just* like that." Miles's face turned hard. "Power has its uses, after all. And I think you've earned that much from us, after the help you've given us in the last few years."

"I'm sorry, Miles. I'm not going to jeopardize the new life I've made for myself here and the archeology career I've worked so hard to establish."

"Damn it, Kelly, this one is *important*!"

"Aren't they all?"

"What's happened to you?" Miles gestured at the stark red hills. "All you seem to care about is *that*. Good Lord, it's nothing but a shadow world. An ugly pile of dirt and stone."

"You're wrong, Miles," Kelly said softly. "It's beautiful, in its way. Just as beautiful as England. But—England is finished. I won't be going back there, not ever. After the accident, I thought I'd never work again. But when I came here, I found something new to love. I found hope and beauty, Miles. And it was all because of those strange, stark hills you're so quick to call ugly."

"I do believe you're gushing, Kelly Hamilton."

Kelly smiled at the hard, chipped flints in her fingers. "Maybe. If so, I'm entitled. I've learned to take my beauty where I find it. All of which adds up to a *no*. I can't leave."

"You actually *like* this place?" O'Halloran frowned. "Damned unsettling, if you ask me. It must be all those ruined walls and dusty graves.

I half-expect the ghost of some vengeful warrior to sneak up behind me at any moment."

"Maybe that makes *you* psychic too, Miles."

"Things would be a damned sight easier if I were, believe me."

Kelly smiled, but her hand slid to her waist. Abruptly her strong, slender fingers tensed.

"You okay?"

"Of course I'm okay," she said carelessly. "As okay as a person can be working shorthanded from dawn to dusk with amateurs who can't tell pre-Cambrian soil from night soil. I'll be even better when you get out of my hair and let me finish."

But the man beside her wasn't fooled, not for a second. "Something's wrong, isn't it? Damn it, Kelly, why haven't you—"

"I'm fine, Miles. This is just a bug I caught down in Mexico last month."

O'Halloran looked unconvinced. "Whatever it is, you're working too hard. You deserve better than this." He put up a hand when Kelly tried to interrupt. "No, hear me out, Kelly. I don't want to see you get hurt. I can do things to help you out here. Just tell me what you need. Money? You've got it. Equipment? Name the brand and give me quantities." Miles's gray eyes took on a sudden intensity. "I mean it, Kelly. You name it, and it's *yours*."

Kelly shook her head. "You really are the limit, Miles. First ultimatums, now wild promises." She crossed her arms atop her chest. "Okay, what about workers? *Experienced* workers. How would you get that?"

"Does that mean you'll go?"

"It means I want to know how you'll get workers."

The Englishman cursed softly. "Did anybody ever tell you that you're the most stubborn, the most pigheaded—"

"A thousand times, Miles, and in about twenty different languages."

But Kelly studied him, unable to fight down her excitement. With a dozen workers she could finish excavating the present level in record time without any sacrifice of quality. She knew there were some extraordinary pieces down there just waiting to be unearthed, but so far she'd been hampered by lack of funds and manpower.

If Miles could change that, she owed it to herself to hear him out.

The Englishman hesitated. Probably deciding how he was going to hide this on his agency expense reports, Kelly thought.

"As it happens, I have two or three school chums who are working in the Southwest right now. I imagine with the right incentives I could persuade them to assist you."

"Browbeat them, you mean."

"Let's say *convince*. With an indecent amount of money and a few choice publishing offers." He turned guileless eyes on Kelly. "Do I look like a Mafia enforcer, after all?"

Kelly snorted. "You look like a distinguished but slightly forgetful Oxford don, Miles, and you know it! Half your danger is in that innocuous manner you cultivate so well."

Sighing, she turned and studied the rapidly setting sun. The saguaro cactuses were in silhouette, their long shadows black scars across the earth.

Wearily Kelly brushed back a lock of sun-warmed hair. "I messed up once for you, Miles. Isn't that enough?"

"You couldn't have known—"

"Ah, but I *should* have," she said bitterly. "After all, that's my job, isn't it? Predicting. Reading tea leaves. Peering into crystal balls. In fact, if you ask me nicely, I might just dig out my tarot cards and—"

"*Stop it, Kelly.* You're a woman with incredible skills—skills we've only just begun to tap. You've got no bloody right to go around feeling sorry for yourself because of a mistake you had no way of preventing. When are you going to put it behind you and get on with your life?"

Kelly turned, her eyes bleak. The darkness there was answer enough.

Miles cursed softly. "Listen to me, Kelly. Five years ago you lived. You lived after an accident that would have killed most others. Yes, your body was pretty badly bashed up, but you *lived.* It had to be for a reason—especially considering what happened when you came out of that coma. Considering the *things* you were able to do."

Kelly's jaw tensed. She studied the fast-creeping shadows, not wanting to think about that horrible day in England five years before. Not wanting to remember how her dreams had come crashing to an end in a black wall of pain where she had faced her own death.

When she'd awakened after two months in a coma, she was different. Able to see things that other people couldn't. Things that weren't anywhere nearby.

Even now she didn't know how it worked, this skill of hers, though the experts had seen it often enough to have a phrase for it.

Remote viewing, they called it. The ability to describe a place—*any* place—simply from map coordinates. Terrain, structures, hidden rooms, and human occupants, Kelly could see them all.

Usually.

But the name didn't make the process any easier to explain. Nor did the words ease Kelly's fear when it happened. Even now her whole being rebelled, shrinking back from the thought of that chasm she must cross, a gateway to churning shadows and restless energy where everyday rules and logic were swept inexorably away.

Kelly's fingers twisted around a button on her white shirt. "Go away, Miles. Just—leave me alone," she whispered, her eyes locked upon the hills glowing blood-red in the setting sun. "Let me do the work I love and put all those other things out of my mind."

"I can't do that, Kelly. You're too good at all those *other* things. And right now we need you very badly on a job back in England. It won't be onerous. In fact, I almost envy you. England's beautiful this time of year. You remember what it's like, don't you? It's been five years since you studied there, but you can't have spent your whole time there in a book."

Remember? How could she ever forget?

She swallowed, trying not to think about green hedgerows flecked with summer rain. About mornings full of dew and wild roses. About mist that clung to neat rolling lawns too green to be real.

And again came the memory of old stones and weathered towers, of the Norman ruins she had once loved—but could never face again.

Suddenly she began to pick up Miles's anxiety. It flowed over her in acrid waves, thick as smoking sage. Along with it, Kelly sensed eagerness, a hint of fear, and utter dedication. There was no doubt that Miles was certain what he was doing was right.

Kelly only wished she could be that certain.

Sight. That was what her mother and her mother's mother would have called this gift she had been given.

Only it wasn't a gift, Kelly knew. It was nothing but a curse. A cruel thing that ripped her wild-eyed and trembling from sleep.

And it was working now.

Because deep in her bones Kelly had known that Miles would come today. She'd had all the usual twinges. She'd been dropping things all day, making mistakes, lapsing suddenly forgetful in the middle of a lecture to a crew of graduate students.

Only one thing made Kelly Hamilton do that.

A job. Another urgent call from Miles, drawing her into the netherworld she hated and feared.

And yet was secretly fascinated by.

That fascination made her reach out now, in spite of logic and prudence. "Where is it this time?" she asked slowly.

O'Halloran's eyes narrowed. "*You* tell me."

Kelly heard the challenge in his voice. "You want to see if I've still got what it takes?" She angled her head and studied the dried lavender hanging in bundles from the split-log ceiling. "Okay, how's this? It's—it's somewhere in green forests. Between gray walls and silver water. With roses. Roses everywhere—pink and peach and scarlet." She looked at Miles, her eyes the same pure azure as the desert sky. "A castle, I think. Dro—no, Dray. *Dray*—something . . ."

The man before her blanched faintly. "And you say you *don't* read crystal balls? You did that *cold*, Kelly. With no maps, no coordinates, no nothing. Good God, sometimes you scare even *me*."

With a tense gesture Kelly smoothed one of the handwoven blankets hanging on the unpainted wall. "It just happens that way sometimes. Not often, but sometimes. I can no more control it than I can predict where or when it will happen. I don't do straight psychic work, you know. I don't seem to have the control for that. Only with the maps, with the focus of coordinates." She shrugged. "And I'll let you in on a little secret, Miles. Sometimes I scare myself."

"Why should you be afraid of seeing what others can't? A lot of people would kill to have that kind of talent, Kelly."

"Some people would kill to get *rid* of it," she said flatly.

Miles studied her intently. "Odd, I've never considered it that way before—as if it were an intrusion. But you do pick up on things. I saw something in your file about—"

"Not often. Like now, there's more, I'm sure of it. I'm getting a sense of danger, of something pressing down. A boulder? Or something symbolic. Like—betrayal perhaps." She stared out at the magnificent Arizona hillside, watching purple shadows war with the last red rays of sunlight on the harsh cliffs. "But I can't focus on it, not without maps and coordinates. And not always then . . ."

No answer. Miles was chewing his lip, squinting at the floor.

"Miles? Does any of this make any sense?"

"Sense? By God, you're nothing short of a bloody marvel. I knew I was right to hold out for you! As a matter of fact, you've given me more in a few minutes than all our so-called *experts* have given us in two weeks. Did you see anything else?"

Kelly frowned. "Colors. Weight." She had a sudden keen sense of something hidden—buried, maybe. Though the room was warm, she found herself shivering. "What's the place called?"

Miles studied her with barely suppressed excitement. "Draycott Abbey. A granite Jacobean moat house with crenelated roofs and twisting chimneys. Something right out of a Constable painting, believe me. It was built on the site of an old Cistercian abbey, I believe. What else did you get?"

"Bits and pieces, mostly. Sunlight. Peace. Swans on a pond—or some small lagoon."

"That's the moat. Lord, but you're good! What else?"

Something angry and sharp gathered in Kelly's throat. *What was she doing? She'd sworn not to let them pull her into this again.*

But something about those images tugged at her. Something about that kind of peace and timelessness spoke directly to her heart, hinting at the answers to questions that had haunted her for five years now.

So instead of turning away, she took a deep breath and stared at Miles over her locked fingers. "Happiness—great happiness. But at the same time great pain. A hidden pain that feels like it stretches back for centuries." She gave Miles a crooked smile. "Not much help for assessing military targets, am I?"

"More than you know," Miles said grimly.

He moved to the door. A man who looked big enough to bench press a Harley Davidson was standing outside, his face hidden behind wraparound sunglasses. Miles said something quiet, and the man disappeared.

This is how it begins, Kelly thought. *A visit, a phone call, and suddenly I'm back in again—whether I want to be or not.*

"What's so important about this place in England?"

As soon as she spoke, Kelly realized she'd blundered. She was supposed to offer impressions, give descriptions of anything she picked up that might be important.

But she wasn't supposed to *ask* questions. Not *ever*.

Maybe it was time she started.

"Well?"

Miles gave her a sharp look. "You know I can't answer that, Kelly. I can only say that it will save lives in a distant part of the world. A whole bloody *lot* of lives."

Kelly watched a clump of sage leaves quiver in the hot still air. "What kind of operation is it this time, Miles?"

"Not military, if that's what you're worried about. Lord, Kelly, I shouldn't even be talking about this with you. This is so secret I'm not even supposed to *think* about it. But we're in trouble and nothing else has worked, so—" He cursed softly. "Look, this time it's anti-drug. And there are some *major* governments involved, believe me. But no more questions," he added flatly.

Kelly felt some of the tension ebb from her. She had to be certain it wasn't some kind of military

assault, something that caused death rather than
averted it. She had sworn never to be involved
in that sort of work. "But if it's not military,
then—"

"Sorry, Kelly, but I've told you too much
already." Miles turned as the Harley Davidson
man returned. A look passed between them.

The man in the sunglasses handed Miles something, then disappeared, closing the door carefully behind him.

Kelly tried to tell herself she didn't care what
that look had meant. That she didn't care what
Miles was holding in his hands.

But it was a lie. She did care.

For some reason she already cared about *anything* that concerned that peaceful castle she had
glimpsed surrounded by a silver moat. Maybe
because it reminded her of all the issues she'd left
unresolved when she'd left England and come to
Arizona.

Maybe because it was time to face her past,
so that she could finally look toward a future
unclouded by regret.

Miles cleared his throat, looking suddenly uncomfortable. "The abbey's present owner, the
twelfth Viscount Draycott, is cooperating closely with us. You'll have the run of the estate
plus access to whatever information he's come
up with. Unfortunately, there's not much. And
I might as well tell you that the place is—
well, supposed to be haunted. People tell all
kinds of stories about a lonely figure who
walks the battlements. About a cat who seems
to appear and disappear at will from an old
portrait. It's even said that when the village
church bells ring thirteen times, the ghost of
a long-dead Draycott ancestor comes to life

and stalks the abbey grounds, terrorizing anyone foolish enough to invade his domain. Not
that there's any truth to the stories," he added
quickly.

"Ghostbusting, Miles?" Kelly laughed dryly.
"That's hardly my line."

Miles lifted an unmarked envelope. Inside was
a tight scroll of densely printed paper. "No, but
this *is*."

It was a map.

Kelly didn't move as she stared down at the
tangles of green that meant woodlands, at the
snaking pink contour lines, at the black single
hatching that meant chalk pits and the double
hatching that meant sand pits.

The margin read "Sussex." An ordnance survey map, no doubt.

The letters began to blur. For a moment yellow
bled into red and green. Her palms went clammy
and she heard a faint, distant whine.

Panic gripped her. *Don't take it*, a voice of cau-
tion urged. *You know what will happen when you
touch it. When you breathe deep and focus on those
dancing lines.*

But even in the fear, there was a spark of
deadly fascination. It called to her, urging her
on, promising her the answers to a thousand
questions that still haunted her five years after
her fall—and her strange endowment with unexplained skills.

"I don't want to do this, Miles." It was only
partly true, but Kelly had to say it.

"I know you don't. But I need you. Go on,
Kelly, take it. As an archeologist, you'll find it
fascinating. There are some amazing Norman
ruins in that part of England."

Then somehow she was reaching out.

And the map began to whisper. Of secrets. Of betrayals and deaths that had taken place centuries before.

Kelly closed her eyes. Slowly her fingers opened, flush to those cunning little lines and colors. Somewhere down the hall the clock with the carved malachite face and the delicate silver hands clicked once, then began to chime softly.

Kelly took a deep breath. She stilled herself and reached out to those green puddles and snaking red lines.

Breathing.

Being.

Going deep and letting her mind drift, floating along those thin pink curves.

Until they filled her mind. Until she *became* them.

The humming came first. For a moment she felt blinding fear. And then it was there inside her. *The knowing*. As if she were part of that distant place.

"Okay, here it is, Miles. It—it's intense this time." Her voice tightened. "This place—it rushes up and surrounds me. Old and proud. Very powerful."

As she spoke, Kelly touched the map lightly, tracing trails of energy. Sifting through the phosphorescent waves of sensation. "It's alive with color and light. I see green and silver. Crimson, too. Flowers—*roses*. And I see love here, love passed down for centuries. But there is something else, something cold." She paused, her brow lined. "Something ancient that has waited long to taste its revenge . . ."

Fear tightened Kelly's stomach. "Those soil samples from the abbey are going to prove very interesting. I think you'll find they contain metal fragments. Very old ones. Something tells me they're genuine."

"Genuine?"

"Scandinavian origin, most likely. Iron and gilt bronze. Possibly some sort of decorative hilt or scabbard mounts."

"Oh, grand. All we need is a horde of treasure hunters descending on the place."

Outside in the gathering darkness a crow flew low, screeching harshly. The chime of distant bells seemed to drift on the wind.

But Kelly didn't hear.

She was already a continent away, climbing green hills where summer lay white and pink upon budding hedgerows.

"I'm seeing some sort of lines. The marks of ancient structures. Perhaps some sort of old Norman wall." Abruptly she stiffened.

"What is it, Kelly?"

Her fingers skated delicately over the paper, searching for something.

"Damn it, Kelly, talk to me."

"I'm getting something specific. I—I felt it. What you're looking for—an urn, isn't it?"

Miles's face went pale. "Jesus Holy God."

"It's there all right, Miles." Kelly swallowed, trying to pull back from that other world that caught at her, claiming her a little more each time.

But each time the deadly fascination grew, making it harder for her to leave. Each time the temptation grew greater to drift, to let go of everything she was and slide away into all that streaming light and restless, energy.

One day Kelly knew she might not make it *back* at all.

Miles cursed softly. "Urn? I never mentioned what we were looking for."

Kelly took a ragged breath. Her eyes blinked open and she gave Miles a lopsided smile. "When I'm good, I'm *very* good, Miles. It's definitely an urn. Probably solid gold." Abruptly her hands stilled on the map. "Unfortunately, that's the *good* news."

The Englishman's eyes narrowed. Kelly noticed that he didn't seem to be surprised. She found herself wondering what *other* things he was holding back from her.

"What's the bad news?"

"You—or should I say we?—have to find this urn soon."

"You're sure, Kelly? No room for error?"

"No, of course I'm not sure. It's not like the skies open up and angelic voices sing in my ear." Kelly shivered suddenly, feeling the pull of that other place, feeling the chaotic streams of energy tug at her still.

"So how long do we have?"

"I can't be sure, Miles." She dragged unsteady fingers through her hair. "Maybe a month—maybe a week."

"In that case, you'd better get going. A plane is waiting for you at Flagstaff. After that you'll catch a commercial flight from Dallas. I'll give you a file with everything else you need to know."

And there'll be darned little in it, Kelly thought. It was always like that. They preferred her to go in cold, to see what she could pick up purely by her own skill.

She felt pain gnaw at her solar plexus. She locked her jaw, fighting the slow, burning waves that came too often lately.

"You'll have to be damned careful, Kelly." Miles studied her face. "There's a whole lot more than you know riding on that urn."

Then he reached out and squeezed her hand. Just once, swift and hard.

His fingers felt cold.

Kelly thought hers probably felt the same.

Chapter 2

*T*en years.
    It might as well have been a lifetime. To two innocent boys, born to a world of privilege and endless possibilities, ten years *was* a lifetime.

But it had passed. Life had changed, and not necessarily for the better.

Commander Mikhail Burke's dark eyes narrowed as he looked out over the boundaries of his Sussex estate and across at Draycott Abbey's neighboring forests.

So near and yet so very far away. And today no one called him Mikhail, only Michael.

The tall ex-Royal Marine Commando eased back in his saddle, trying to brush off the feeling that he was being watched.

Just nerves, fool.

Too many years in the wrong kind of work. There's no one watching you here. Not now, at least, while he was remanded on official leave.

For the record, anyway.

The black-clad rider laughed. It was a sharp, bitter sound. Beneath him the great black horse stirred uneasily.

"I don't suppose we can put it off any longer. Shall we take the long way? Past the old Roman camp?"

The horse danced skittishly, ears pricked forward as if listening to something in the sad sigh of the wind.

"Uneasy, you great brute?" Burke's face hardened. "So am I, if the truth be told. Strange place, Draycott. Bloody strange place," he mused. "And always was. If Nicholas hadn't been my best friend . . ."

His hands tensed, gathering the reins.

Had been, but wasn't now. And there was no time to waste wishing he could change the past.

"Now is now and Nicholas needs me, whether he likes it or not. So we'd better get on with it."

They shot forward through the trees toward the ancient wooded landmark known as Lyon's Hill. Just beyond, a deep chasm ran the length of Draycott lands.

Laughing recklessly, Burke bent forward and took the narrow gorge at a gallop.

"Commander Burke? Do come in."

Marston, Lord Draycott's imperturbable butler, held open the massive oak door of the gate house and greeted Burke as if it were perfectly normal for him to come calling.

As if it hadn't been ten years since Michael Burke had darkened the abbey's doorway. As if there hadn't been a horrible row, a knockdown brawl that had left two friends deadly enemies.

Burke's jaw hardened as he stared at the beautiful forecourt between the gate house and the main house. At the weathered stone walls bright with damask roses.

So beautiful.

So *deadly*. For a man might go to unnatural lengths to acquire such beauty.

Burke felt a sense of uneasiness as he followed Marston inside, past gilt-framed paintings and centuries-old tapestries. And then the peace of the place crept over him, just as it always had when he was a boy.

He forced those memories away, too. This was work, only work, he told himself grimly.

He *almost* believed it.

Somewhere in the rear of the great house a phone rang, and Marston went off to answer it. Burke waited, looking around and feeling the years roll away.

Suddenly he was eight again, hanging on his mother's hand as he caught his first glimpse of Draycott Abbey. His English had been accented with his mother's native Russian then, and the great house had awed him, but he'd been game enough when introduced to the viscount's son, young Nicholas.

From that day forth the two boys had been steadfast friends, wandering heedless and happy over the green hills and forests. They had fought a hundred wars, bested a thousand imaginary foes in those green woods, neither expecting that fate would have the final laugh and leave them enemies.

Even then Michael had loved and feared this ancient place and he discovered that the passage of time had only heightened those feelings.

But this was no time for memories. Work had summoned him back to the abbey, work that would require the cold-eyed professional rather than the wide-eyed boy.

"That was for you, Commander. I took the liberty of informing his lordship, the viscount, that you had arrived. He is . . . desirous of speaking with you." The butler hesitated slightly. "I trust that's not a problem?"

So Marston *did* remember that blazing row. Burke sighed and gave a quick nod. "Of course not. Lead on, Marston."

Down the portrait-lined corridor they went, past the mahogany stairs leading up to the Long Gallery. Past the beautiful pink salon with its crimson velvet curtains overlooking the moat.

Past the alcove where Nicholas and Michael had exchanged their first boyish insults, which had led to their first fistfight.

Burke almost expected to see two youthful red faces glaring at him as he crossed the corridor.

But there was nothing there, of course.

Only ghosts. Only memories.

In the end, the two were exactly the same, weren't they?

"You can take it in here, Commander." Marston held open the door to a chintz-filled study.

Burke crossed the room slowly. Where did one begin repairing a ten-year rift? How did one go about patching up a decade of buried anger and bitter misunderstanding?

"Marston? Is that you?" The voice on the other end of the telephone was tinny, but Burke would have recognized it anywhere. Nicholas sounded just the same, except for a certain tenseness that hadn't been in his voice before.

Burke held the receiver, his jaw hard.

"Hello? Marston, did you get Burke?"

"*Nicholas.*" One word. One simple word. And yet it was so hard to say, with so many emotions bound up inside it.

"Burke? Is that you?"

"I'm here, Nicholas."

Silence fell, cold and awkward. Somewhere in the magnificent old house a door closed softly.

"God, it seems like forever, Mikhail." Nicholas Draycott used the proper Russian pronunciation that Michael's mother would have wished him to use. Through her blood Burke's ancestry stretched back to Russian royalty. And that blood, as she had so often reminded her son, was bluer than any Windsor upstart's.

"Ten years. *Too* damned long, Misha."

Michael's fingers tensed on the receiver. He did not answer. It was dangerous to open the doors on ten years' worth of memories. On unresolved anger and painful secrets.

"So, nothing's really changed, has it? You're not going to talk about what happened. Not even now."

"It's better if we don't." Some things made going back impossible, Burke thought grimly.

Losing your mother to your best friend's father had to be one of them.

"Better for *whom*?"

"For both of us, I'd say."

Again a silence.

"Your mother?" Nicholas hesitated. "She is . . . well?"

Burke kept his voice impassive. "She's fine. She summers in Cumbria and winters in Ibiza. Jaunts about the world more often than I do, I think."

"Ah, yes, that job of yours. Something dreadfully clandestine, I suppose."

Burke said nothing.

"Stupid of me to mention it."

"Not stupid, Nicholas. Just—well, you know I can't discuss it." And that just about exhausted their conversational choices, Burke thought. All the *safe* ones, at least.

Which meant it was time to get down to business.

"I heard. About what happened to you in Thailand."

Draycott gave a dry laugh. "It's over. That's the best thing I can say. I've forgotten almost everything. Maybe that's just as well."

Burke studied the bright, flower-strewn room. "The abbey looks beautiful, by the way. Seeing it again makes me terribly jealous."

"All my wife's doing, I assure you. Kacey loves the house as much as I do. She's forever poking about some ancient portrait, trying to stave off damp rot or a thousand nasty kinds of depredation. If there's any Draycott art collection left, it's purely thanks to her. She even found a pair of Sargent canvases hidden in an attic. The woman's an utter miracle."

"She's also drop-dead gorgeous, if half the rumors I hear are true."

Nicholas laughed. "True, all of them. I wish you could meet her, but the baby's due any day. There have been some complications, so I thought it best to bring her here to London for a few tests."

Burke frowned. "Nothing serious, I hope?"

"Supposedly not. Kacey thinks they're all making a great fuss about nothing."

Michael felt a surge of jealousy at the tenderness that warmed Nicholas's voice. Then he thought about how Nicholas had looked the last time he'd seen him.

It had begun when he was handed a new assignment, something involving a half-mad, half-genius druglord named Trang. From his base in northern Thailand Trang was making a lot of people filthy rich.

And a lot of people in London damned uncomfortable.

He had also been holding an English diplomatic attaché captive there, an Englishman named Nicholas Draycott.

Burke frowned, dragging himself back to the present. "You were saying—about those tests?"

"The doctors say not to worry. You know how these Harley Street fellows are. Anything to hook you up to expensive machines and make you agonize over the results, so you won't scream highway robbery when they hand you the bill."

But Michael heard the anxiety in his friend's voice. On the rosewood side table he saw a gilt-framed photograph of a woman with hair the texture of finest silk and a smile that warmed every corner of the room.

Burke's jaw hardened. "Let them do their job. I'm sure your wife's in the best of hands."

"She'd bloody well better be," Draycott said grimly. "You can be certain that Kacey is the *only* thing that would keep me away from the abbey. Especially at a time like this, when I'm just starting to remember about that urn." Burke heard the creak of a door opening. "Hold on a moment, Michael."

The receiver was covered, and Burke heard the sound of muffled laughter.

Once again the ex-Royal Marine felt a stab of jealousy, but he crushed it ruthlessly. Nicholas Draycott was more than entitled to his happiness. After the hell he'd endured as a captive for fourteen months, he was entitled to just about *anything* he wanted.

And Burke should know. He had helped plan

the rescue operation. He'd been one of the men who had parachuted in to rescue Nicholas from that living hell. He knew he'd never forget the way his friend had looked when they pulled him from the underground cell where he'd been held.

Only Nicholas didn't know that. His memories of that nightmare experience were dim and at the time it had seemed a good idea to keep it that way. The specialists in London had all agreed it would be best for Nicholas to pull a temporary veil over those long, harsh months of captivity.

Now Nicholas had begun to heal. And though other memories had returned, the memories of his time in captivity hadn't come back. The consensus was that the pain would have been too great for him to bear.

Burke frowned, hoping Nicholas never remembered. Sometimes he wished *he* could forget like that . . .

"Sorry, Michael, Kacey had a question. But didn't I read something about you recently? Caught quite indelicately with a Swedish film star. Birgit something or other. And in a limousine right outside Harrods no less!"

Burke gave himself a shake, realizing that Nicholas was talking about one of the more reckless females his name had been linked with in the last six months.

He managed a laugh. "All lies, I assure you. The tabloids wouldn't know a piece of truth if it hit them dead between the eyes. Which is something *I've* longed to do often enough."

"So there are no matrimonial prospects looming on the horizon? No long-legged stunners hungry for a drafty old wreck in Sussex and one of the most eminent titles in all of Britain?"

"Apparently not. I'm afraid I must not be good marriage material after all."

To Nicholas's credit, he did not ask any of the dangerous questions he was itching to ask. Instead he cleared his voice and moved on to safer ground. "Listen, Michael, I haven't got much time. Kacey's got to go in for another checkup in a few minutes."

"Then get going. There's absolutely nothing to worry about here. I'll take care of everything."

"I know you will. That's what makes me so bloody angry." Draycott cursed softly. "You know as well as I do that it should be *me* there, sweating this thing out, taking all those risks. Not you."

Burke made his voice very cool. "What risks? You've misplaced an urn full of microfilm somewhere on the grounds and I'm going to find it for you. It's nothing, Nicholas. *Less* than nothing. Believe me, I take more risks just crossing Park Lane at rush hour."

"You're the same bloody liar you always were, aren't you?" The viscount hesitated. "Did you hear that my memory was starting to come back?"

"Someone from Special Branch phoned me last week. They said that you'd requested me particularly. You could have contacted me yourself, you know." Burke couldn't keep an edge of anger from his voice.

"I *didn't* know. We haven't exactly been on the best of terms for the last ten years, remember?"

No, we haven't, have we? Burke thought grimly. *Not since I discovered my childhood was based on a lie. Not since I found out my mother was in love with your father and always had been.*

"I remember," he said slowly. And then, "So

how did it happen? When did your memory start coming back?"

"About two weeks ago. At first it was just bits and pieces about Bhanlai and the camp. Then some things about the rescue, but all jumbled. The funny thing is, I almost thought I remembered seeing *you* there."

"Damned strange how the mind works." Burke decided it was hardly the time for sensitive explanations about what had happened in Thailand. "You've remembered nothing else since?"

"Afraid not. Bloody mess, isn't it? I wake up one day and discover I've brought out a priceless Thai urn carrying a list of every key political and commercial contact that Trang ever made. Smugglers, arms dealers, and drug runners—they're all in there. And you know the real irony? Trang saw to it that *I* was programmed to bury the thing somewhere safe here in England where he could retrieve it when he got around to it. In a place where no one would find it, right here on Draycott soil."

Burke bit down an oath. He'd been hoping Nicholas would have remembered more by now, once the floodgates had opened.

No such luck, Misha. This one's going to go the hard way.

"I called Ross as soon as I was certain. I kept the shovel and the soil samples that were on it. There was quite a lot of thick clay. Unfortunately, about half of Draycott's soil is clay. Still, I thought the samples might prove useful."

"Every little bit helps." Michael wished there were a whole lot more. Frowning, he fingered the photograph of the smiling viscountess. "What does your wife know about all this?"

"Only the minimum, though the Fleet Street

tabloids had a field day when I got back from Bhanlai. Kacey was in the States then, thank goodness. Oh, she knows I was over there in captivity. She knows I escaped. That's about the extent of it. And I want to keep it that way, Michael. She's—she's got enough to worry about without adding my problems to it." Nicholas's voice tightened. "Damn it, man, I'd drive down right now and help you tear up every inch of the abbey if it weren't for Kacey. Not that I think it would help very much."

"It *wouldn't* help, Nicholas, believe me. I know this place just as well as you do, remember? I was right beside you when you explored the Witch's Pool and Lyon's Leap and all those moss-covered Norman ruins. Damned unsafe they were too. Besides, this is work, and I always work alone." He made his voice utterly cool.

Utterly professional.

"Damn you, Misha. If I thought for a moment you were lying to me and there was the slightest chance of my helping you with this, I'd come back right now. But I just can't remember anything else about burying that bloody urn. And believe me, I've tried."

"Stow it, Nicky." The old nickname came easily to Michael's tongue, even after ten years. "The best thing for you to do is concentrate on taking care of that beautiful wife of yours and getting the silver spoon ready for Draycott's next heir."

"So you don't think it was just a dream?" Nicholas said slowly.

"Afraid not. Trang was crazy, but brilliant. This is *exactly* the sort of thing he'd dream up."

"I was hoping I was wrong. That the whole thing might be just another nightmare . . ."

Burke knew how much it cost Nicholas to say

that. There must have been plenty of nightmares after those hellish months in Bhanlai. But nightmares were better than facing the pain of real memories, weren't they?

Burke watched a swan glide across the moat. "You're sure it's here? That you buried it somewhere on Draycott land?"

"I'm not *sure* of anything, Misha. It just broke through, out of that black wreck in my mind." Draycott laughed shortly. "All I get are odd chunks spewed back at me, flotsam and jetsam of the months I spent in Thailand. Kacey says it's better that way. Maybe she's right."

"She *is* right. If it's meant to come, it will. Don't waste your energy worrying about it."

"I hate you when you're right, Misha. And I've had a lot of practice hating you. Even when we were boys, you were usually right."

"So why fight me now?"

"Because it doesn't *feel* right, that's why!" Burke heard a clicking noise as Nicholas shifted the phone. "I'm looking out at Hyde Park in full bloom and I can't help asking myself what the devil I'm doing here in London." He sighed. "And Kacey's been so bloody good about everything. First we had to cut short our honeymoon in Venice after the death of her friend from the States. The woman's ex-husband had tracked her to England and shot her. Terrible business. It was weeks before Kacey could even talk about it. Now *this*." Nicholas muttered a curse. "So much pain and so much dying. And I'm afraid there's going to be more, because something tells me that damn urn is booby-trapped, Misha. Don't ask me why, but I can feel it."

Michael smiled grimly. "No worry. Booby traps are my specialty, remember? And my own estate is right over the hill, in case you've forgotten. If Draycott blows so does Edgehill, which gives me a damned good incentive. Now get your pregnant wife over to the doctor and leave me to my work."

This time the hardness in his voice said it all clearly: *It's not personal, Nicky.*

Now it's business. All business.

"Very well. Since you're such a bloody competent bastard, I'll leave everything in your hands." He cleared his throat. "Thank you, Misha. I owe you for this. Especially considering how bloody awful things have been between us. Your mother—then the fight and all."

"Go see to your wife, Nicky. We'll talk. We'll talk a lot—when this is all over. Meanwhile you should know that no thanks are necessary."

Both men fell silent. Each was hoping that the ten-year rift was finally on the mend.

"So what are you waiting for, Nicky? Get *going!*"

"I'm going, I'm going. By the way, say hello to the abbey ghost—assuming that you see him. Of course, you *won't*, since only the pure at heart can see Draycott's special guardian."

"I guess that leaves *me* out," Burke said dryly. "You too, come to think of it."

Nicholas chuckled softly. "You might be surprised about that, my friend."

And then, before Michael could say anything more, the receiver clicked off.

"Did you do it?" The voice might have come from two miles away or two thousand. "Is everything in place?"

"All arranged. Ready to be activated tomorrow."

"You're close enough?"

A sharp laugh. "No problem. We could listen to a pair of ants screwing on the kitchen sink if you wanted."

"Excellent." A pause. The sound of rustling paper. "What about Burke?"

"What about him? He's looking but he hasn't found *nada* yet. When he does, we'll know it. We've got the whole house bugged, along with the telephone."

"What about the girl?"

"She changed her schedule. Not due in till tomorrow."

"Another bloody complication. I don't like that."

"You want me to—"

Harsh laughter filled the air. "Oh, I'd like nothing better! But we can't, unfortunately. Not yet. It would raise—a great many questions."

"Why not move things up? Give me free rein for two hours and I could—"

"You could ruin *everything*, that's what you could do! I've got too much invested to risk losing it all now."

"But you said—"

"I said *my* way. In *my* time. Understand?"

A low curse. "Understood."

"Good. Make sure you do."

For a moment the line crackled.

Then it fell away into dead silence.

Chapter 3

*H*eathrow Airport was mobbed.

Kelly squeezed into a narrow phone booth and squinted down at the piece of paper Miles had given her just before she'd left. She dialed quickly and heard a series of clicks as the call was rerouted.

A man answered. She gave her name, then waited through another series of clicks.

While she waited, Kelly wondered what Miles's office looked like. She was thinking idly about trying to image it in her mind, when a voice barked to life out of the transatlantic static.

"Kelly? Are you all right?"

Kelly smiled a little, hearing the urgency in Miles O'Halloran's voice. "Relax, Miles, I'm fine. The flight was a little rough, but nothing I won't be able to sleep off." Smiling wryly, Kelly looked down at her hands. They were still trembling from the jerky descent they'd made through unexpected turbulence.

"Don't tell me you've come up with something already?"

"I'm good, but not *that* good, Miles. I'll need to see the place first. No, this is something else."

She twisted slightly on the wooden seat, trying to find a more comfortable position as she pondered something that had bothered her all through the long flight. "I just want to clarify the story I'm to use over here. I take it that no one in England knows what I'm really doing. That I'm supposed to locate the urn using my—my odd little gift." She said the last word grimly.

"Correct."

She hesitated. "Why don't you just tell them?"

Silence. The sound of a chair squeaking. "A fair question, Kelly. But I'm not at all sure I'm able to answer it."

Able meant *allowed*, Kelly knew. "Fair questions deserve fair answers. Besides, I don't want to have any surprises that might backfire. I need to know what the story is, Miles, and I need to know *why*."

The Englishman sighed. "Very well. We need that urn, Kelly. If we find it before our U.K. counterparts do, we'll have a better bargaining chip for getting something else that is very important to us."

Kelly traced a circle on the smooth plastic receiver, thinking about contour lines and slope colorings. "I don't suppose that something else might just be hidden inside the urn?"

"I'm not about to answer that and you know it." Miles's tone warned her that there were boundaries he could not cross and that Kelly had just reached one.

"But this man Burke is looking for the urn and so am I. That might present a real problem."

"Not if you find it first." Miles's voice was cold.

"Are you telling me to lie, Miles?"

"I'm telling you to find that urn and then call me. Immediately."

Kelly's throat went tight. "Isn't that illegal?"

"Not in the slightest."

"What about unethical?"

"I suppose that depends on whom you're talking to."

She frowned. "How about horribly Machiavellian then?"

"Sorry, love. No one said the world was a nice or fair sort of place. Trang certainly wasn't a nice or fair sort of guy," Miles added grimly. "But I'm glad you checked in with me because something has come up. We got an analysis back on those soil samples that the viscount made. You were dead right. Badly corroded iron and gilt bronze. Under x-ray at the British Museum laboratory they revealed extensive gold inlays. Sword mounts, just as you predicted. The experts say they may be Scandinavian, not that they look like much under that ugly green corrosion."

"Few things do after being buried in the earth for nine hundred years."

"At least it gives us a perfect reason for your visit. Simply put, you're there to locate the rest of the sword. And you'll have references from all the right places, believe me."

It would be a good cover, Kelly knew. Except for one small fact.

She hadn't practiced continental archeology for nearly five years.

"Then I'll need to see Professor Bullock-Powell before I go down to the abbey. After all, it's been a long time since I've worked out of North America. If anyone probes too deeply, I'm going to mess up. And this man Burke who's working at the abbey doesn't sound like the type to miss anything."

No answer.

"Miles? Are you still there?"

"I'm here, Kelly. It's just that—well, the people at S.I.S. aren't going to like it."

"S.I.S.?"

"The British Secret Information Service. Used to be called MI-6. They're not thrilled about anyone being at the site but their man, Burke. We had to push hard to get you in, and they want you out as fast as possible."

"So? Hold them off."

"Can't. It seems that the P. of W. has taken a personal interest in the recovery of this sword. National cultural treasure and all that."

"P. of W.? Plain English please, Miles."

"His Royal Highness, the Prince of Wales. Fits right in with his ideas about preservation of cultural heritage. That's a key thing with him these days."

"At least he wants to preserve his country's past," Kelly said, thinking about the pot hunters who were obliterating all hope of archeologic records across the Southwest. "You can't just pull rank?"

"On the Prince of Wales?" Miles asked dryly.

Kelly stared at a shop selling magazines and newspapers opposite the phone booth. Charles's aquiline features gazed back at her from at least two dozen different publications. "I can see where that could be a problem. But I still need the time."

"Then . . . you've got it."

"I knew you had a heart under all that tweed, Miles. What about the viscount? Has he remembered anything more?"

"Nothing. He's consented to undergo hypnosis and some experimental mood-enhancing drugs. But not until after his wife's had her baby." Miles sounded bitter. "So for now we're left with one great big blank."

"This warlord, Trang, who was mentioned in your file. He's definitely dead?"

"You mean could he surface and come after the urn himself? Not unless he's the next avatar of Vishnu. And believe me, Kelly, the man was no candidate for sainthood. No, we've traced everything and there's nothing to suggest that Trang didn't die in that explosion when Nicholas Draycott was rescued."

"Why do I get the feeling that you're not convinced about that?"

Miles sighed. "I don't know, Kelly. Something doesn't fit. And I'm getting a backside full of flack with this one. Meanwhile, the prince's intense interest isn't helping anything. Just find me that urn, okay?"

Kelly was picking up Miles's fear very clearly now.

And very few things could scare Miles O'Halloran.

She frowned out at the passing crowds of travellers, at the laughing children and their harried parents. "Is this urn really so important?"

"Very important. And don't even think about trying to put those red-hot brain cells of yours to work on what's inside the urn. Believe me, it will be a whole lot safer for you if you *don't* know."

"In that case, I won't try. Just see to the arrangements with Professor Bullock-Powell, won't you? I have a feeling that's going to be important, Miles."

"Consider it done. Don't ask me how I'm going to explain it to the S.I.S. though."

"You'll manage. You always do. And Miles, one more thing. No welcoming committee when I get to the abbey, okay? I want to do this quietly, to pick up all the leads I can without a lot of distraction or excess static to clutter things up."

"Static? Is *that* how you think of the rest of us fellow humans?"

Kelly frowned. When she was working, anything could become a distraction. "Just see to it, Miles. No bands, okay? No red carpet. And no security force. I know what I'm doing."

The man on the other end of the line muttered something beneath his breath. "It will be more dangerous this way, Kelly. I wanted someone there to keep an eye on you."

"I'll manage."

"You've never done anything like *this* before."

"I'll still manage."

"Okay, Kelly, but I damned well don't have to like it. Not a bit. Just watch yourself. And if there are problems, I'm sending someone in after you—whether you like it or not."

"I don't expect you'll have to, Miles. Alone is how I work best."

It should be, Kelly thought, as she hung up the receiver. She'd had a whole lot of practice working alone.

Sir Cedric Bullock-Powell had silver hair, a long, distinguished face, and clever, faintly sad eyes.

He was sitting with steepled fingers, staring at Kelly from behind a desk bristling with artifacts. Sunlight speared through the faded velvet curtains, brightening a study crammed with artifacts garnered over a lifetime of excavation.

"I can't quite believe it's you, Kelly. How long has it been? Three years? Four?"

"Five." Kelly drew a tight breath. "Five years."

"You never told me why you left. In fact you never told me anything at all about what happened that night. Whatever I knew about the accident, I had to read in the papers, just like everyone else. Afterward I waited for you to come back to the site, but you never did."

"Things . . . changed."

"What things? You were just beginning to come up with some significant results in your topographical dating. You could have gone on to any university in Britain. What happened to make you change your mind?"

Pain happened. Betrayal happened.

She looked at the books stacked in a precarious pile. "I just had to leave. The reasons aren't important now."

"No? I think they are. You were in a coma for a long time after the accident. I came to see you twice, but they said it made your pulse go sky-high. I was told politely but firmly not to come again."

"I—I never knew."

"I wondered if you did." The professor's eyes narrowed. "Everyone missed you, you know. My son in particular." There was a question in his voice.

Kelly ignored it.

"At one time, I even thought that you and he . . ."

She pushed to her feet and turned away, her hands locked over her chest. "As I said, things change."

"You always had a talent for making stone and dust come alive. It's a rare gift, you know. You shouldn't waste it."

"Waste it? We *do* have universities in the States, you know. You might have heard of Harvard? Yale? Princeton? Right now New World archeology is in the middle of some pretty earthshaking discoveries." She smiled faintly. "No pun intended."

The old scholar simply shook his head.

You old fossil, Kelly thought, remembering his cantankerousness and biases. But there was a fondness in the memories too. "Will you help me or not?"

"A refresher course? You want me to cover five years of research in two hours? Impossible and you know it."

Kelly's eyes snapped. "I've kept up with the journals. We wouldn't exactly be starting from scratch. You were a darned good teacher, after all."

The professor frowned. "I've been told to extend you every courtesy, Kelly. I have been told this by people in offices so secret they don't even have names. I have not been told why. Only that it concerns the discovery of what may turn out to be pieces of a priceless sword on a private site in Sussex." His bushy brows knitted. "I don't suppose you're going to enlighten me, are you?"

"Isn't the discovery of a possible Norman sword in datable soil reason enough?"

"For you to return after five years, without a word? No."

"I'm afraid it has to be."

His brows rose. They had been close once. Her respect for him had been boundless. Cedric had never been able to shake the idea that he had done something to destroy that respect.

God help him if he knew what, though.

He rubbed his forehead irritably. "I was told that you have only this afternoon. I hope you are still a quick study, Kelly. You used to be— it's one of the reasons I was sorry to lose you."

She seemed to hesitate, her shoulder to the light slanting through the curtains. "I was sorry to go."

"Then why—"

Her eyes hardened. Her chin rose.

Cedric Bullock-Powell sighed and pushed to his feet, motioning Kelly to follow him next door.

She remembered this room well. Open journals littered a long worktable where artifacts spilled from boxes and glass-topped cases. The most fragile pieces rested in small, many-drawered chests, swathed in acid-free paper.

"As a matter of fact, I've followed your discoveries about scot-price and water burial for swords. They are intriguing."

England's premier archeologist turned, one silver brow arched. "Perhaps there may be some hope for you after all, my dear." His mouth twisted with the faintest hint of a smile. He pointed to an intricate drawing of a sword tacked on the far wall.

"Single-edged hacking sword. Anglo-Saxon."

"Composition?"

"Iron with gold inlay."

"Origin?" he asked curtly.

"Sutton Hoo."

The professor's smile grew a bit larger. "Probable dating?"

"Seventh century."

"Not good enough, Kelly."

"624 or 625, according to Haroldson's latest article. But then you never did like Haroldson very much, did you?"

The old man was smiling clearly now. "Acceptable. But everyone knows the big things. It's the little things that set an amateur apart from a professional."

He turned to lift a straw-lined crate from the cluttered floor. "Well, don't just stand there gawking. Help me lift these votive sculptures up onto the table. Then, my dear, we'll see what you *really* know."

"Hold up, fellow."

Black against the purple twilight, Michael Burke fought to hold his restive mount steady. A crisp wind ruffled his hair and tugged at his black sweater.

The valleys were fast filling up with mist. Burke sniffed the air. Clear and cold. Rain before morning.

In truth, he was as restless as his horse. He'd been told—no *ordered*—to cooperate with some pushy American archeologist who was coming down tomorrow to investigate a possible Norman burial site on Draycott land. Even the prince of Wales was interested in the results.

Burke cursed fluently.

Beneath him Nero danced. Lightning snaked over the dark, thickly timbered hills.

Let him come, Burke thought grimly. Let a whole troupe of archeologists and the prince himself come. He'd send them all packing soon enough.

His gloved fingers loosened on the reins. The horse pranced. And then the great legs lifted, plunging over the green earth.

Dark and savage as the night, Burke's laughter drifted back on the wind.

Chapter 4

"You sure as how you're expected, miss?"
The driver of the out-of-date Mini that
passed for Long Milton's only taxicab looked
worried. "This in't no sort of place to be wandering about alone, you know. Especially not on
a night like this."

Lightning arced over the road as he spoke.
Kelly fingered the envelope carrying Professor
Bullock-Powell's letter of recommendation. In the
end he'd given her a glowing endorsement, along
with a suitably high-handed explanation of why
she would be doing the survey work at Draycott
Abbey instead of himself.

Kelly hoped the deception would work. After
all, it had been five years since she'd worked on
an English site. Five years since—

"You awright, miss?"

Ruthlessly, she drove down the harsh memories. "Fine, really. I'm expected." Not until tomorrow however. That would give her several hours
tonight to walk the grounds undisturbed and see
what initial impressions she could pick up. Then

and only then would she present herself at the abbey's front gate.

The driver's eyes narrowed in the rearview mirror. "Don't mean to pry, y'understand, but people do say as how this place is—well, odd. That there be lights and such. I've even heard it said that—" He sniffed. "Ah, well, no business of mine. That'll be five pounds six, miss."

As they came to a stop, Kelly squinted down at the pile of coins on her palm. After a moment she shoved the whole handful forward, leaving it to the driver to sort out.

"Now then, that's a deal too much, miss! Just take two of these and three of these, I will. Best if you're more careful about that in future."

"Ah, but you have a very honest face." *And your daughter is going to give birth to that baby any minute now, so you'd better hurry home.*

Kelly smiled and pocketed the unused coins. That's the way the awareness came sometimes, swift and uncomplicated. Most of the time, it didn't, however. "Well, I'd better be off. You must be anxious to get going."

The driver scratched his head. "True enough. My daughter is down to hospital at Hastings. Expecting my first grandchild, I am," he added proudly.

"Congratulations." Kelly feigned surprise as she opened the door and stepped out into the chill wind. Somewhere in the hills above the abbey an owl hooted long and shrill.

"You sure you'll be awright, miss?" The driver frowned. "Maybe you'd better come back to the village with me. The Boar's Head is comfortable enough and not like to be filled. You can come back in the morning, when it's light."

Kelly shook her head. "I'll be fine, really I will. But thanks for your concern. And take care of that elbow of yours. With the storm coming it will be bothering you."

"Elbow? Now how would you happen to know about my—"

But Kelly was already crossing the lawn. She gave the driver a last, cheery wave, then turned and began her climb toward the abbey.

She saw it first by moonlight. It was as vast and proud as anything she'd ever seen.

Her boots whispered over the long grass as she moved closer. She wasn't sure *what* she'd expected, but it certainly wasn't this. She put down her suitcase and stared about her.

Gray granite walls climbed sheer for sixty feet up to stone parapets surmounted with snapping pennants. The Long Gallery glittered silver behind a bank of thousands of tiny leaded panes.

Now *this*, she thought wryly, is a *castle*.

A chill wind swept over the single-story gate house, tossing Kelly's russet hair about her slender shoulders. Absently, she swept the long strands back, transfixed by the structure before her.

The scent of roses drifted on the damp air. Kelly closed her eyes and breathed in the rich, heady fragrance, transported to a grander age.

Off in the distance came the high, shrill cry of a hawk, circling in lonely gyres above the dark forest. The sound made Kelly shiver and thrust her hands deep into her green suede jacket.

Forget how old it is. Forget how beautiful it is.

But Kelly couldn't drag her gaze from the weathered gate house, from the silver sweep of the moat and the exquisite mullioned windows above.

Something about them tugged at her, disturbed her.

She pulled her jacket tighter. "Okay, so you're nice. All right, *more* than nice. You're *fantastic!*"

A prickle shot down her spine. She whirled about, studying the dark trees behind her. "Hello? Is . . . is someone there?"

For a moment she thought she saw the bushes part and what might have been a fox or a badger slink into the forest.

Or it might have been a cat. A sleek gray cat.

But there was no answer, of course. There was no sound but the wind, sighing over the mortared parapets. No answer but the faint whoosh of the moat, gurgling in the moonlight.

No answer but the restless night, curling dark and chill around her.

At the end of the moat, Kelly sat down on her suitcase and studied the abbey. In the last hour she'd looked at it from every side. She'd paced the damp earth, run her hands over weathered stone, and poked at the bordering yew hedges.

And she'd gotten *nothing*. Not a single clue. All she'd felt was an ancient beauty and a shimmering network of memories that danced about her like fine mist.

Exhausted, she let her head sink onto her hands. Across the grass, moonlight pooled up like pale frost.

And in that moment Draycott's beauty reached out to her. First in voices. Then in colors and distant laughter . . .

As she watched, the great walls changed. Granite glimmered and melted, replaced by rough-hewn walls raised around a high earthwork.

Closing her eyes, Kelly sat back.

The images took her.

The stone keep rose, rough and hasty, crowning the new embankment. Water glinted from the deep ditch surrounding it. A few thatched huts huddled in the protective shadow of the wooden palisade. In a few months there would be twice that many.

Suddenly a shout rent the air. The massive gates of the castle creaked open and a man rode through. A man in chain-mail hauberk and crimson overtunic.

His face was harsh. His eyes glittered with silent fury.

Lyon of St. Vaux cursed, driven by thoughts of revenge.

Tall and broad-shouldered, the Norman knight sat his great black destrier. His eyes narrowed against the setting sun as he surveyed the lush fields of oats and rye and barley.

His fields. Won with his own blood, spilled in years of battle.

The Norman's face was harsh, but pride found its mark there too. He took a keen pleasure in the changes he had wrought here in five scant years, all in the service of William, his king.

But today regret warred with pride. Today he felt the old restlessness, tinged with thoughts of home. It was all so different here, all so far from the rich fields of Normandy and Anjou . . .

Beneath him the great destrier danced skittishly. "Doucement, my beauty. This is our home now. All the dreaming in the world cannot change that."

Across the valley two mounted warriors pounded into view, sunlight flashing off their beaten silver helms. They were coming fast, Lyon saw. More prob-

lems with the wretched Saxons, no doubt.

Vainly, the conquered people continued to wage their shadow war, striking from fen and forest whenever they had the chance.

St. Vaux's face hardened. Even here, beneath his very nose, a Saxon woman was said to raise bonfires by night, calling forth the pagan spirits of forest and glen to smote the Norman invaders.

But not for long, par Dieu!

The Norman's eyes snapped with fury. The wench would soon learn the folly of spinning her dark spells on his land! Aye, all of these rebel Saxons would!

For this land was given to him to be held in fealty to William, and hold it he would. Neither Saxon nor Norman nor demon of hell itself would obstruct him in that duty.

Nor would William find anything to cavil at in his vassal's work.

Grim faced, St. Vaux spurred his black horse forward as the riders approached. "Well, what is it, Gilbert? More of these hobgoblins that unnerve our horses and unseat our valiant warriors?"

"Not spirits, my liege. 'Tis flesh and blood this time." The knight looked uncomfortable. " 'Tis . . . the woman."

"She who weaves her dark spells to mislead the witless country folk?"

"Aye, the one they call Aislann. Hugh FitzRolland has her pinned down in the forest by the old Roman track."

St. Vaux's face went very hard, as hard as the iron-gray waves that swept the rocky shore where he'd come squalling into the world and taken his first faltering steps. "Then let us proceed, my dear Gilbert, and watch me well. This day you will see how a Norman breaks the spirit of these God-cursed peasants who seek to defy us."

*   *   *

Kelly snapped back to reality with a shudder.

Overhead a driving wind shrieked through the black trees. Lightning forked across the distant hills.

She frowned, tugging her jacket closed. How much time had passed since she'd stopped to rest?

She had just hefted her suitcase and stood up when she heard the low drone of a motor coming from the gravel road that run up to the abbey.

A moment later twin headlights cut through the darkness. A gray Land Rover lumbered up the hill and came to an abrupt halt beside her.

The passenger door swung open. A man's dark features appeared, half-hidden by shadow.

"Well? Why didn't you bloody wait at the corner, like I told you?"

Chapter 5

*K*elly frowned, clutching her suitcase. It would make a pitiful weapon, but it was all she had.

"Get in, damn it." The man made no move to help her. "Donnelly sent you, I suppose."

Kelly blinked. "Donnelly?"

"Never mind. Just get in. It's going to storm any minute."

Feeling a powerful sense of reluctance, Kelly slid into the car and wedged her case at her feet.

The Land Rover's motor kicked in with a roar and the big car swung back onto the drive. All the while, Kelly studied the man at the wheel.

She couldn't see much in the dim moonlight, but what she did see was enough to give her pause.

Blazing eyes. High cheekbones slanting against a granite face. Big hands in black gloves that gripped the wheel with competence and a barely leashed energy.

She decided the silence had gone on long enough. "I'm Kelly Hamilton."

The black-haired driver, studied her face, then shrugged.

"It's customary to answer in kind." Kelly's voice was tight with anger. She was bone-tired after a day of travelling and five hours of sparring with Professor Bullock-Powell.

All right, tough guy. The ball's in your court.

Her chin rose and she looked straight ahead, paying no attention to the man seated beside her.

But the effort cost her something.

Because she was getting all sorts of energy bleed from him, energy that seemed to hover around him in churning clouds. Though most of it was blurred, Kelly picked up three things loud and clear.

Pain. Irritation. And a fierce force of will.

Grimly she set her mental defenses in place. It was something she had learned to do well in the last five years. Otherwise she found herself picking up snatches of the private agonies and interior battles of every stranger who passed her in the street.

She'd been careful never to tell Miles that, of course. It was hard enough for her to deal with the demands of focused imaging through the medium of a map.

But Kelly couldn't seal off the power of *this* man. It was too raw, too immediate. And somehow her eyes refused to leave the long black-clad fingers curved tensely around the Land Rover's steering wheel.

They slammed over the rutted gravel road, going far too fast for comfort or safety. At the top of the hill, her silent driver rammed the clutch into second and took a hairpin turn so fast that Kelly went flying against the door.

Something told her he'd done it on purpose.

Kelly felt her own anger kick in. "Nice road," she said sweetly as the Land Rover jolted up out of another pothole. The chassis groaned, then rattled loudly. "Great car," she added as the rattle turned to an earsplitting whine.

The black eyes swung to her face. "Take up your complaints with the boys in London, Hayley."

"The name's Kelly, not Hayley. And I'm not complaining."

Once again Kelly felt the lash of those cold eyes. "Not yet, but you will." The man's mouth hardened. "Why didn't they send a man this time? And why an American?"

This time? Swiftly Kelly reprised her conversation with Miles. *Had there been another archeologist sent down to survey the abbey?* Blast it, she couldn't remember.

She decided to bluff it out. "I'm American, all right, but you'll find nothing at fault with my scholarship. Nor with my technique."

The black eyes narrowed. "I'll reserve judgment until I've seen you in action, Lacey."

"The name is Kelly. *Kelly Hamilton.*"

No answer.

Kelly fought down a rush of anger. *Relax*, she told herself sharply. *The man is just trying to goad you, to see how far he can push before you crack. Just sit back and relax while you enjoy him for what he is: a classic textbook case of full-blown English male chauvinism.*

They bucked and pitched along the uneven drive. "Do you always drive like this?"

"Something wrong with the way I drive?"

"Nothing at all. As long as your insurance is up to date." She sniffed. "Fortunately, mine is."

"Just what I need, a woman who thinks she's a wit."

"Just what *I* need, a man who's forgotten the meaning of the word," Kelly returned sweetly.

Muttering, her dark-haired driver rammed the gearshift into second and took another turn on two wheels. Again she was sent flying, only this time it was against his side. For one blinding moment she felt her breast cradled against his arm before she struggled back to her seat.

Anger was pouring off him in waves now.

Gears crashed on metal. The Land Rover grated to an abrupt halt as lightning cut across the indigo sky.

Black eyes met blazing turquoise. Out of the corner of her eye Kelly saw the man's gloved fingers clench and unclench against the wheel.

"Let's get a few things straight, shall we, Ms. Hamilton?" The barely suppressed fury in his voice was unmistakable now. It caught Kelly right in the stomach.

"I'm listening."

"Good. Simply put, you're here because I was overruled. I don't want you here. I don't *need* you here." His lip quirked slightly. "Not that I wouldn't enjoy exploring our . . . mutual interests . . . at some other time. But this is work, so let's just get it over before we shred each other into little pieces, shall we?"

Kelly's brow rose. "My, what a lovely speech. I bet you say that to *all* the girls."

"You didn't hear a thing I said, did you?"

"Oh, I heard. Every nasty word. And for the record I don't care to be here any more than you do. So you keep to your side and I'll keep to mine. Deal?"

The dark eyes took on an indefinable heat. "Deal."

Then it hit her.

Burke. The word exploded into her mind. This had to be the man Miles had warned her about. *Ex-Royal Marine Commando and one helluva tough customer.* Who else would be prowling about the abbey at this time of night?

The puzzle pieces slid home with a click. Yes, Kelly thought, studying those angular, chiselled features, Miles's description had been perfect.

Too bad the *man* wasn't.

The Rover roared back to life and lurched over the pitted drive.

"How about slowing down? I'd like to keep my neck and my body attached, if you don't mind. Quaint of me, I know, but there it is."

The ex-soldier's lips curved slightly. "It would be a shame to do anything else. Considering how well they go together." Dark eyes slid over Kelly's jacket, measuring the soft curves beneath. "Everything else seems in commendable shape, too. On second thought, maybe I'll bend my own rule. Doing anything later, Ms. Hamilton?"

Kelly's hesitation was only momentary. "Before or after I break your jaw?"

The man at the wheel gave a crack of dark laughter that seemed to startle him as much as her. It was a rich sound, full of life, entirely different from what she'd expected from this tense-faced, hard-talking stranger.

Somehow she couldn't help but find it appealing.

That realization made her frown.

"Afraid of something, Ms. Hamilton?"

She sat forward. "What makes you say that?"

"The way your jaw just went tense. And I notice you haven't answered my question."

"That's right, I haven't." *Blast it, the man was too observant by half! She'd have to remember to be* careful around him. She couldn't let him catch on to her real reason for being here.

Beside her Michael Burke laughed softly.

He'd expected a lot of things, but not a beauty like this one. Not an American and definitely not a woman with such fire in her eyes. "I'll admit one thing. You're the best they've sent me yet."

Kelly didn't answer. She didn't trust herself to talk while her heart was pounding double time. Meanwhile, she couldn't seem to block the energy that was pouring off Burke in restless waves. It muddied her concentration and left her strangely breathless.

It's also doing odd things to your pulse, a mocking voice pointed out.

How was she ever going to stand working here without murdering the man?

At that moment the abbey loomed up before her. Weathered granite walls blotted out the indigo sky, overpowering her with their sheer bulk. Kelly felt the building's age and vast power settle around her. She sat forward, watching the moat lap silver around the abbey's stone flanks. Light broke and spilled, tumbling back into shadow.

It was restless, relentless, beautiful.

And it was unspeakably dangerous . . .

The intuition burst upon her without warning. With it came a tension that rode straight up the back of her neck.

Betrayal, she thought, reaching out, trying to focus and define that first inchoate impression. When she did, darkness struck her, utter and absolute. It was almost as if a door had been slammed in her face.

Kelly gasped at the force of that darkness.

Burke heard her soft, telltale hiss and glanced across at her, his jaw tense.

Wondering why the hell she bothered him so much.

She wasn't a raving beauty. Her hair was thick and shiny, true, but in the dark he couldn't even see its color. Her mouth looked interesting, generous but firm. Maybe a bit *too* firm.

The rest of her? Burke frowned. The sweater she wore beneath her suede jacket molded her skin and hinted at some interesting curves, but who could say?

He forced his eyes away. What was he doing? This was a professional visit and nothing more, no matter how the woman tried to goad him. Donnelly's idea, no doubt. He knew Burke liked his women spirited.

He ground the car to a halt that sent his passenger pitching toward the dashboard.

"You have a real way with gears, Ace." Burke watched her eye the battered dashboard and interior with palpable dislike. "Why don't you get a real car and leave this heap in a junk pile where it belongs?"

Burke thought about the Land Rover's high-performance four-wheel drive, its fully floating axle shafts and four-channel antilock brakes. In the last few years he'd added a few of his own special modifications: quartz-iodine headlights for crystal-clear night driving under any conditions, bulletproof windows, and two-inch reinforced steel seat frames.

Heap of junk? This car had saved his life on three continents and the chassis had the bullet holes to prove it.

He shrugged. "A real heap of junk all right. But it suits me fine the way it is."

"That figures." The American made something that sounded like a snort. "How do we get inside?"

"Right this way." Burke jerked open his door. "Mind where you step, Miss Hamilton. Legend has it that this place is haunted."

"Oh, that must be a *big* draw for the tourists."

Burke smiled faintly. "Scared?"

"Don't count on it, Englishman."

Silently, Burke slid to his full six-plus feet and set off for the rose-covered gate house, leaving Kelly to fetch her suitcase by herself.

"I'd advise you not to dawdle, my dear," he called back over his shoulder. "You never know *what* might be waiting for you out there in the shadows."

Chapter 6

*B*urke shoved open the broad oak door of the gate house and watched expressionlessly as Kelly struggled through with her suitcase. He wasn't about to make this any bloody easier for the woman!

She knew the arrangements, after all.

Frowning, Burke swung the great door closed and secured it with a bolt of solid steel.

"Nice security system you've got here," Kelly muttered. "Very advanced."

"What electronics can beat this? Built to withstand outlaws, rebels, and highwaymen. Even a siege or two." A few more steps brought them to a narrow stone bridge that led across the glinting moat to a quiet courtyard.

The scent of roses lay heavy in the air. Pale blooms trembled on dark green vines. Something about those roses tugged at Kelly's senses.

Something fragile and very old.

"Coming, Ms. Hamilton?"

Shaking her head, Kelly followed. And still the feeling lingered. Something important, or her own fantasies running riot in this ancient place?

A white-haired butler in sober gray flannels met them at the inner door. Kelly blinked at his lime-green running shoes.

"Thank you, Marston."

"I've left out chicken Kiev and a Grand Marnier soufflé, Commander." The butler smiled faintly. "I believe those are your favorites."

"Now I see why Nicky is terrified someone will lure you away from him."

Marston gave a pleased smile. "I'm delighted to hear it. Not that I would consider leaving Lord Draycott, of course." His eyes flickered over the rust-haired woman half-hidden behind Burke's broad shoulders. "Shall I take the young lady's luggage out to the gate house before I go?"

"No need. It will go upstairs, not to the gate house. *If* she stays. And if she does, she can see to her own things."

If she stays! Kelly shot Burke a look that was pure acid, but the man seemed utterly oblivious. So that was his game. Make things as rocky as possible in hopes that she would turn tail and run.

Any thought Kelly might have had of leaving was summarily dismissed at that moment.

The butler frowned. "But surely—"

"Good night, Marston." His words were clearly an order this time.

"Very well, Commander." The butler's expensive rubber treads crunched away over the polished wooden floors leading toward the rear of the abbey.

"Commander? What kind of commander?"

"This way, Miss Hamilton."

"You didn't answer my question."

"That's right. I didn't, did I?"

Kelly ground her teeth. "Are you always this rude?"

"I suppose that depends on how much my leg is bothering me," the Englishman said harshly. "So let's get this over with. We'll use the study."

Tense with anger, Kelly followed, wishing devoutly that she had packed fewer textbooks.

And maybe one or two more dresses? a sly voice asked. *Michael Burke is an extremely attractive man, after all.*

She grimaced and focused her attention on the portraits lining the silk-covered walls. Men with faces like Roman statues. Women with eyes that seemed to look off into some sad, distant past.

At the far end of the corridor, Burke stopped. His eyes were hooded as he pushed open the door to a book-lined study warm with gilt frames, good prints, and bright chintz curtains. Here, too, roses scented the air, lush in crystal vases scattered about the room.

The peace of it reached out and wrapped around Kelly, soft as an Arizona twilight.

What love there was in this room, she thought. Love old and new. Love tested in bitter trials, in years of torment and separation.

Something told her that a love like that would not fade with the end of mere mortal life.

"I trust this will do?"

Kelly barely heard him. She was too busy trying to focus on the room's myriad energy trails.

She closed her eyes, picking up something else. Something chill and diffuse, of an intensity she had never felt before.

It felt almost like . . . *sadness.*

She shivered, feeling a prickling at her neck.

"Cold, Miss Hamilton?"

"Cold?" His scrutiny was unnerving.

"Yes, cold. As in pale. As in shivering."

"I'm not cold. And what makes you think I'm s-shivering?" She cleared her throat. "If you don't mind, may we get right down to work? I've several letters for you here. References. Charts. A list of the equipment I'll be bringing in. I suppose Viscount Draycott told you about—"

His bitter laugh cut her off. "References? What use would *they* be? And the only equipment you'll be needing here, Ms. Hamilton, is your own two hands." His eyes narrowed on Kelly's hair as she moved beneath a wall sconce. "So it is red," he said softly.

"What?"

"Your hair—it's red. Auburn, actually." Abruptly the Englishman frowned and turned away.

Only then did Kelly realize what he was doing.

He was stripping off his gloves. A moment later his black turtleneck followed.

Kelly's eyes widened in disbelief.

But the man paid no attention. He pitched the sweater onto a black Chinese lacquer screen, then reached down to his pants. Every movement was quick and practiced.

Kelly's heart took a nosedive in her chest. Her eyes locked on the white bandages revealed with the shedding of his turtleneck. "Wh—what are you *doing*?"

"Please, Miss Hamilton." Burke's voice was hard, laced with weariness. "We can dispense with the pleasantries. It's very late and we're both tired." He freed his zipper and shoved down the dark corduroy pants. "Let's just get this over with, shall we?"

Kelly swallowed audibly. A queer humming attacked her blood as she watched his powerful bronze thighs bunch beneath white briefs.

And then she saw the fine tracery of lines, silver scars that snaked across his outer thigh and disappeared beneath the fine white cotton.

My God, she thought dimly, *his leg must have been shattered and then sewn back together.*

"Are you just going to stand there and stare?"

Kelly felt her face turn hot. He was all man. All lean strength.

All arrogance and danger.

And despite every instinct and expectation, Kelly couldn't pull her gaze away from that rugged, battered body.

She cleared her throat. "I'm afraid there's been some sort of misunderstanding."

Burke's hands went still at his sides. "I told Donnelly not to send you, but he insisted. Now that you're here, Ms. Hamilton, you're going to finish what you were sent to do."

Kelly blinked. *Who was Donnelly? Not one of Miles's people, certainly. But if not, then who?*

"My dear young woman," Burke said harshly, "I know that you're very attractive and that most of your patients are probably delighted to dispense with the medical exam and get right to your other, er, *services. I* am not so inclined, however. So get yourself over here and finish."

"Finish?" Kelly's lips seemed frozen in place.

"Examining my hip." Burke's eyes darkened. "And the bloody metal pins that are just barely holding it together."

So that was it. In spite of her irritation, Kelly felt her breath wedge in her throat. And in that unguarded second she caught a slashing glimpse of pain, pain that went on and on . . .

His pain.

The pain of a shattered body knocked fifty feet from a burning car and then laboriously sewn back together, inch by agonizing inch.

She tried to block out the force of those memories, tried to resurrect her guard.

Too late. For some reason, she couldn't. Maybe she'd been too slow. Or maybe she'd worn herself thin with the stress of travelling and almost two days without sleep.

"Damn it, get on with it! Or are you so anxious to have me down on the sofa that you're ready to forget about the rest." Burke's leg shifted. Kelly saw him wince. "I suppose you can make a tidy living that way."

Kelly dropped her case and gestured sharply. "On the sofa. Facedown," she snapped.

Surprise darkened Burke's slate-gray eyes. "Facedown? Isn't that a little unorthodox?"

"Now who's stalling?" Kelly's voice was taut with fury.

After a moment Burke shrugged, then eased down on the leather sofa. Kelly noticed that he frowned when he lifted his right leg from the floor.

Up close the tracery of stitches was even more chilling. Her fingers began to tremble. What in God's name was she doing?

The lean thighs bunched and tensed. The sight left Kelly oddly breathless. "Mr. Burke—" She cleared her throat. "There's been a mistake. You see, I'm not actually—"

Her "patient" sat up abruptly. Soft white cloth stretched taut over sleek bronze muscles.

Dear God, the man was tall. And his shoulders were nothing short of beautiful.

Kelly stiffened. *What's the matter with you?*

You've seen a man before. A man wearing a lot less than this one.

Not in a long time though. And never one who looked like this.

Burke was staring at her, his arm draped tensely across the leather sofa. "Ms. Hamilton," he said. Slow. Patient. The way one would talk to a not-very-bright child. "I would greatly appreciate it if you would pull yourself together. There is no need to be squeamish. I am well able to put up with a little more pain, I assure you."

A little more pain.

The flat way he said those words made Kelly wince as if he'd struck her.

This man did know pain. He'd known pain for a very long time. If the scars on his legs didn't prove that, then the harsh lines about his mouth did. Still, that was no business of *hers*, was it?

"Well, Miss Hamilton?"

She was going to murder Miles for getting her into this, Kelly thought. She scanned the room swiftly, looking for some avenue of escape, but found none.

Where was a butler when you needed him? she thought wildly. "Now listen to *me*, Mr.— Mr. Blasted Commander Burke. I assume you're the man that Viscount Draycott left in charge here. But you've obviously got *me* confused with someone entirely different."

Burke eased back against the couch and treated her to an icy stare. Kelly's gaze flashed to the powerful shoulders, to the broad chest darkened by sleek black hair.

"Are you quite through staring?"

His blunt question horrified Kelly. Her hands tensed to fists. Every moment she grew more overwhelmed by Burke's churning emotions and the dark power of the house itself.

Burke shot to his feet. The next second Kelly was pinned flat against the silk moiré wall.

"You're not from London, are you? God, you're not even from T. and R."

Kelly swallowed. "T. and R.?"

"Therapy and rehabilitation. And Donnelly didn't send you either."

His eyes weren't black at all, Kelly thought blankly. Up close like this she could see every detail of them. They were cold and clear, the brooding gray of wintry seas, flecked with a faint hint of gold.

Grand, she thought. She was trapped in a deserted house in the middle of nowhere, pinned to the wall by an angry stranger who might as well have been naked.

Angrily, she shoved at the hands locked beside her head. "That's right. I'm not from London! I'm not from R. and T., or whatever you call it. I came about the sword. Viscount Draycott has agreed to—"

Burke didn't budge. "Sword?"

"Of course the sword! I'm the archeologist Professor Bullock-Powell recommended."

Burke obviously wasn't buying any of this. "Then why didn't you tell me sooner? Too busy enjoying the view?"

Kelly heard the sensual taunt in his voice.

"I—I tried. How was I to know you'd make the bird-brained assumption that I was someone else? Besides, you were having too much fun being furious at me to listen." She wrenched at his grip, driving her hip forward, only to freeze when the movement rocked their bodies together.

Torso to torso. Thigh to straining thigh.

She gasped, feeling his heat, feeling his hardness.

Her voice came in a breathless rush. "Let go of me! You—you don't believe a word I've said!"

"You're right, I don't. But somehow I'm not sure that it matters anymore." His gaze slid dark and hot over her heaving breasts, outlined perfectly against her angora sweater. "Actually, I'm beginning to think you're *exactly* what the doctor ordered."

"Damn it, you can't just—"

"Can't I?" He laughed softly. "Just watch me."

Kelly swallowed. And then his rage was gone. Hunger burned in his eyes instead.

His fingers loosened slightly, slid to the wall, and curved over her own. Slowly, inexorably they twined through hers.

Kelly gasped at the intimacy of that gesture. It was a gesture meant for lovers, a gesture for people who had stripped themselves bare in an act of stunning intimacy.

Why was he doing such a thing? And to *her*, a complete stranger?

An image came to her then, sharp and swift and hotly erotic. She saw their bodies coupled in love, legs entwined, thigh to thigh as he slid inside her.

The hot, sweet fantasy made her face go crimson.

The man beside her cursed low and fiercely. "Damn it, can't you stop that."

"S-stop what?"

"Blushing?"

Blushing? Since when was that a treasonable offense? "Now you listen to me, Mr.—Mr.—"

"Burke." He eased the word softly against her cheek. Against her neck. Against her damnably sensitive earlobe. "Michael Burke. My friends call me Misha."

"That leaves *me* out!"

"Why? I've always thought a woman should know the name of a man she's about to sleep with."

"In your *dreams*, Englishman. Now 1—let me go!"

He didn't. Their fingers were still entwined. The gentle friction of his calloused palms was insistent and intensely erotic.

"I'll bet you make love with the same finesse you drive that car of yours!"

His smile was solid-gold challenge. "Want to find out, Kelly Hamilton?"

"Not in a month of Sundays! Not in a thousand years!"

His eyes fell, measuring the pulse pounding at her throat. Surveying the jerky rise and fall of the soft breasts outlined against her sweater. "Nice," he said softly, investing the word with a host of erotic undercurrents. "And you're lying."

Kelly felt her sweater draw tight against her chest, felt the sensitive crests thrust taut against the soft wool. She knew *he* saw them too.

Damn the man! And damn her body for turning traitor on her!

"Who sent you?" he muttered thickly. "Anderson? O'Reilly? They told me they were going to do it, but I didn't believe them."

Kelly tried to talk, but she was having trouble even breathing. And with every second of contact she felt the chaos of Burke's thoughts more keenly.

Anger.

Suspicion.

Desire.

They warred with each other, rushing over her in waves so fierce that she could almost touch them.

Burke's eyes smoldered. His leg moved, inched slowly between hers, all heat and muscle.

All granite and male. And Kelly hadn't known a man's touch, not in a very long time.

"You're a sight, Kelly Hamilton." His voice was low and rough. Even its roughness was persuasive. "I didn't know women still blushed like that." He laughed bitterly. "Hell, the women I know *never* blushed like that . . ."

His eyes slid over the curves outlined against her sweater. "And all that softness. Hidden and sweet. Just here . . ."

Kelly watched his hand, willing herself to block it and turn away, to escape before it was too late.

But she didn't. There was a tension in his eyes, a raw hunger in his touch that both frightened and fascinated her. And it felt in some way—

Familiar. That was the only word for it.

Burke's breath hissed through locked lips. "God, how soft are you?" And then his fingers eased down to cover those intriguing curves.

Slowly.

Gently.

As if he were touching the most precious thing on earth.

"N-no. You can't—" Even as Kelly spoke, the fire touched her. A breathy little sound fluttered from her throat.

The sound made Burke freeze. His fingers stilled. What in the hell was he doing?

He scowled as she shoved hard at his chest. "Steady, Ms. Hamilton. There are two of us here. And *both* of us were liking what I was doing."

Kelly winced as if he'd struck her. "L-let me go."

Burke didn't move. "I'm not so sure I can, Red. There's something about you—something about *us*, together like this. For something that's all wrong, it feels damnably good." His eyes hardened. "I want to know why."

Kelly wrenched free and spun toward the door. She had to get away from here. Tonight. Right *now*. She couldn't take another second of this bizarre house and its wrenching beauty.

Nor could she bear this man, who was just as unsettling as the abbey.

She'd call it off. Miles could find someone else to do his sleuthing.

Blindly, she searched for her suitcase. "Listen, this was all a—a mistake. You don't understand and—oh, God, I can't explain it to you. But I'll see that they send someone else. Just as soon as possible." She was babbling and she didn't even care. "Blast it, where did I put my suitcase?"

"Where are you going?"

Finally Kelly found the case, half-hidden behind the chintz sofa. Ignoring Burke, she caught the handle and moved unsteadily toward the door.

Somehow, without the slightest sound, he'd crossed the room. He was only inches away from her now.

She could feel the heat of his body. She could taste the roil of his emotions.

Anger.

Shock.

Uncertainty.

And along with them she felt his driving need to understand, to know what in heaven was happening to him.

"Ms. Hamilton—Kelly. If Donnelly didn't send you, then who did?"

Kelly's fingers bunched low over her abdomen. "As I told you, I'm an archeologist. Not that it matters, because I'm getting *out* of here. And I mean to make a point of never seeing you or this house again!"

She stalked through the door and out to the restless shadows in the corridor.

Past the priceless portraits.

Past the three-hundred-year-old Chinese imperial porcelain.

Through the most beautiful house she had ever seen. And in her turmoil Kelly saw none of it.

Outside the lightning snaked closer. She'd have to hurry if she wanted to make it into town before the storm broke.

Michael Burke swore long and fluently, watching the slender shoulders stiffen and disappear down the corridor.

What in God's name was going on here? If Donnelly hadn't sent her and she wasn't the paid female companionship that his old Commando friends had threatened to foist upon him, then who in bloody hell *was* the woman?

He speared his fingers through his long hair. The movement brought a sudden, painful memory of how incredibly soft she had felt beneath his hands. Lord, she had even smelled good. Like desert wind and sun-dried sage.

Grimly Burke seized his trousers and jerked them on, then subjected his sweater to the same angry treatment. No one had told him the archeologist was coming tonight. Nor that the scholar was a *woman*. A man was bad enough, considering the risks involved if Nicholas's worries about the urn being booby-trapped were true.

But there was no way Burke would stand for a *woman* being quartered here under those circumstances.

Outside the study, prongs of lightning forked through the sky. Burke heard the first slap of rain against the windows. In a minute or two, the woman would be soaked!

Ignoring the pain at his hip, he jammed on his shoes and went out after her. Someone had to rescue her, after all. And tonight he was the only hero Draycott Abbey had to offer.

In his haste to be off, he didn't see the faint glimmering that lit the room in his wake.

Chapter 7

She was struggling up the hill with her suitcase, squinting against the rain, when Burke caught up with her.

He tried to call out, but the wind hurled his words away.

He caught her and pulled her around to face him. "Look, let's get one thing straight. You can't go wandering off, not in this storm. It's fifteen kilometers to the village and you'll never make it in the dark. There are a ridge and two cliffs blocking your way."

"Falling over a cliff and breaking my neck would be *infinitely* preferable to spending another minute in *your* company!"

Burke smothered a curse. "Come back inside and dry off. I'll have Marston bring some tea. Then we'll sort this whole bloody thing out from the beginning."

Kelly shook her head angrily. "There's nothing to sort out, believe me. It was a mistake, pure and simple. And now I'm leaving."

"You can't go."

"Oh, no? Just watch me."

Burke's jaw tightened as he watched her struggle up the hill, slipping on the rain-streaked grass.

He'd have to carry her back. Otherwise there was no telling *what* sort of trouble she'd get into.

Just as Burke was forming this resolution, Kelly slipped on a patch of mud. Soil and rock gave way with a gurgle and sent her sliding to her knees. Her suitcase flew from her fingers and landed against a rock, lingerie and textbooks disgorged in a crazy tangle at Burke's feet.

The Englishman bent with leisurely grace and lifted a frothy undergarment from the pile. White lace and impudent peach ribbons dangled from his fingers. "Interesting. Is this standard issue for archeologists these days?" He studied the fine satin straps. "Hell, even rehabilitation therapists dress more practically than *this*."

"Give me that, you cretin! And God help anyone who'd have to rehabilitate *you!*" Sputtering furiously, Kelly lunged for the undergarment.

She missed and landed flat on her backside in three inches of mud.

"At least this sort of *uniform* might get a man up and moving again." Burke's black brow quirked as he freed another provocative garment from the pile.

Lavender satin fluttered in the wind, draped against his hard fingers. "Nice," he said softly, his eyes on Kelly's face. "Very nice."

"Put those back!"

"Somehow I don't think you're in any position to be giving orders."

"Oh, no?" Without stopping to think, Kelly lashed out with her moccasined foot and caught him dead in the calf. His startled half-shout was balm to her ears. So was his expression of surprise. But what happened next was not quite so enjoyable.

He tumbled down on top of her, camisole and half-slip forgotten as he hit the mud and pinned her to the ground.

Kelly felt him shudder, felt his whole body stiffen with the pain of impact.

Too late she remembered the scars crisscrossing his leg. *Good Lord, what had she done?* "Are you—" She shoved her wet hair from her face and touched his shoulder. "Did I—"

His mouth was rigid with pain. "No, I'm just fine, Ms. Hamilton. I'm bloody marvelous, in fact." His arms were taut at his sides.

Kelly bit her lip. What had gotten into her?

Then the instinct for self-preservation kicked in. The man was finally immobile. Now was the perfect time for her to—

"Oh, no you don't!" Hard fingers circled Kelly's wrist even before she'd struggled halfway to her feet.

Rain licked at her face. She twisted wildly, driving one foot against the slick grass, fighting to work free of Burke's thigh.

But the movement only drove them closer. *Unbearably* close.

Rain pounded over them, hissing against the dark earth.

Burke stared down at Kelly's face. "We'll both get dry a lot faster if you answer my questions. For the last time, who sent you? And why did you come tonight rather than tomorrow?"

In answer, his captive wrenched one hand free and took an angry swing at his jaw.

Burke smiled darkly. "In that case, it's going to be a long wet night, Red."

"Don't call me that! My name is Kelly Hamilton. *Professor* Hamilton, to you! And in answer to your surly question, Professor Bullock-Powell sent me to locate an artifact buried on Draycott land. A very *valuable* artifact. Heavily corroded, of course, but priceless. Especially if it's the double-edged sword that I expect it to be."

Burke cursed softly. "So you really are an archeologist."

"Why so surprised? Because I'm a woman or because I'm an American?"

"Neither," he said bluntly. "Because you're so damned beautiful."

Kelly was startled by his backhanded tribute, but she wasn't about to be sidetracked. "I'm sorry if that's a problem for you. I suppose a man like you finds it impossible—"

"Hold on a minute, Professor. A man like me? Just what the hell is *that* supposed to mean?"

"Exactly what I said, Mr. Burke. A man like *you*: big, strong, and a one-hundred-percent throwback to some nasty neolithic cave dweller. A man who no doubt finds it impossible to believe that a mere *woman* might be capable of a project requiring any sort of intelligence."

Burke gave her the ghost of a grin. "That's one big chip you've got on your shoulder."

"Maybe working with men like *you* put it there."

"Ouch," Burke said softly.

Kelly shivered as rain trickled down her neck. If they didn't get out of this rain soon, they were both going to end up with pneumonia. She sighed. "Look, if I show you a letter of reference, will you believe me then?"

"I might."

Muttering, Kelly reached for her pocket and dug deep, searching for Professor Bullock-Powell's scrawled letter of introduction.

Burke scowled down at her, at the mane of wild auburn hair, at the rain-streaked suede jacket, at the butter-soft angora sweater that hugged her soft curves.

Every last damned one of them.

Rain beat down on his back and head, but he couldn't take his eyes away. In the rain that fluffy thing she was wearing had turned transparent. He tried to ignore how perfectly it teased her shadowed nipples into tight little buds.

"I put it right in my back pocket," Kelly muttered. "But now everything's so blasted wet—" She twisted her head, trying to see behind her.

Against his will, against every shred of common sense, Burke found himself leaning closer. His eyes followed the curve of her hip, the softness of her waist. He wondered how she'd feel if he moved a little higher and—

Kelly's elbow jabbed his rib. "Just help me g-get the blasted letter!"

"Stop fighting so I can! Otherwise we'll both—"

He never finished.

The next moment a shot whined out of the woods behind them and cracked harshly off the abbey's granite walls.

Chapter 8

"*Get down!*"

Burke moved at the same moment, shoving her beneath him and protecting her with his body.

"Tell me that wasn't a gun I heard." Her voice was a raw whisper.

"I wish I could, but I'd be a liar," Burke muttered.

Kelly could hear his heart pounding. Somehow that made her feel better. What didn't make her feel better was his body going taut, nerves stretched razor-sharp as he awaited a movement from the darkness.

None came.

"If they're going to make a move, it will be soon, while they've got fear in their favor."

"F-fear?" Kelly squeaked. "Wh-who's afraid?"

Burke squeezed her wrist. "That's the spirit, Red."

Around them the rain pelted down in big noisy drops that pinged across the flagstones in front of the gate house and drummed against the rich, black earth.

Kelly's teeth began to chatter. *From cold,* she told herself, *not fear.* But she was intensely grateful for Burke's warmth and the comforting strength of his body atop hers.

And then she felt a faint prickling at her neck.

Danger. She touched it, read it clearly, felt cold hatred probe them from the darkness.

She focused on the dark trails of emotion, trying to trace its source. *There.* She found it just beyond the first line of trees.

But *who?* And why?

She reached out, challenging the shadows, courting the cold silence.

And found nothing. Had the man gone, or was her insight failing? Kelly blinked back tears, wishing for the thousandth time that her visions came clearer—or not at all.

Above her Burke shifted slightly. "When I tell you, run for the house. But not until I give the word. First I'll try for that yew hedge by the moat. If I draw fire, then stay put. And stay *down,* no matter what happens."

"But how could anyone see to fire in this ink soup?" she rasped.

"Because they'll probably be using an infrared scope and laser sights."

Kelly swallowed. *Draw fire . . . infrared scope.*

The cold, expressionless way Burke said those words made her shiver. So he really was one of *them,* one of the men from that same shadow world Miles lived in.

Burke went on tautly. "If there's no repeat fire, then I'll head for the edge of the bridge. I want you to go for the gate house at the same time. By then they'll be watching *me,* not you. At least they'd *better* be," he added grimly.

"But—"

"No more questions. The lecture's over, Professor. Now get ready to move."

Kelly bit back her fear as she felt Burke tense. He slammed to his feet and pounded zigzag style toward a scrubby black hedge.

He made it. There was no answering movement from the darkness.

His arm rose. She saw him gesture sharply. Time to go . . .

Squinting against the rain, Kelly stumbled to her feet and made for the door to the gate house. At the threshold she turned, peering back into the darkness.

Burke had already disappeared.

It was twenty minutes before he returned. His sleeve was ripped, his pants were streaked with mud, and his face was pale with strain.

A fire was already blazing and tea steamed on a side table, compliments of the impassive Marston. The butler hadn't asked Kelly where Burke was and Kelly hadn't seen fit to tell him. What was she supposed to say, that they'd narrowly escaped assassination outside the gate house?

Burke watched her from the doorway, his hands thrust in his pockets. "Are you all right?"

Kelly nodded, feeling her throat go tight.

Burke moved stiffly toward the snapping flames. He draped one arm along the mantel and reached out with the other to the fire.

He protected you with his body, Kelly thought. He didn't think twice about it. Maybe she had the man figured all wrong.

"Did you find anything?"

Burke frowned down at the fire. "It was just

a hunter. He must have strayed from the public lands on the far side of the valley. Probably drunk."

"A hunter? Drunk or not, why would a hunter—"

Burke turned. His face was hard, ridged with strain.

Kelly read it in his eyes. *He's lying. But why? And what else doesn't he want me to know?*

One thing was certain, she wouldn't find out by asking. With shaky fingers she shoved her damp hair from her face. "Thank you—for protecting me out there. After all that, I know this must sound rather silly, but—well, I *do* have letters." She held up a sodden pair of envelopes.

"Look, Ms. Hamilton—Kelly—it's late." Burke brought a muddy hand up to massage his neck. "We'll discuss all that in the morning." Kelly saw one hand ease down to his hip as he reached behind the curtain and pushed at something on the wall.

"You found something out there, didn't you?"

He didn't answer. Firelight cast his face into harsh silhouette.

"You rang, Commander?" Marston appeared in the doorway.

"See Ms. Hamilton to her room, will you Marston?" Burke's face was unreadable.

Kelly noticed that neither of them mentioned the small matter of a gunshot fired at point-blank range on what was supposed to be private property.

"You're not going to tell me, are you?"

Burke merely nodded to the butler, then turned back to the fire, careful to avoid looking at her.

But in that unguarded moment Kelly had seen his face. His eyes were hard, the lines of exhaustion about his cheeks and mouth very pronounced.

"Will that be all, Commander?"

"Quite, Marston, thank you. I'll close up down here."

So that was it. No answers were to be given. She would get nothing more from Michael Burke this night.

As she followed Marston out into the hall, Kelly chanced one last look at her host.

He was standing before the fire, his shoulders rigid, his expression veiled.

He was furious, she could read that much.

But he was also afraid.

Mikhail Augustus Sergei Burke, Viscount Dunwell and Marquess of Sefton, stared blindly into the fire. Loneliness scraped at him like tiny claws rasping on slate.

And regret . . .

It always began this way. First the snap of a twig in the darkness, then the whine of a sniper's bullet from some shadowed corner.

Only now he wasn't alone. Now there was a woman who shared his danger. And that made Michael Burke blazingly angry.

It also made him frightened. He knew what could happen to people who got caught in the middle, even innocent people.

Especially innocent people.

He'd also felt a strange reluctance to lie to her. She was *different*, this woman. She was smart and stubborn and brave. A lot of people would have been in hysterics after such an experience, but not her. A woman like that deserved to know why she had been shot at.

But Burke couldn't tell her. And that gnawed

at him, because for the first time in a very long time he felt like telling the truth, the *whole* truth, and rules be damned.

He laughed bitterly. *Hunter indeed.* He'd gotten one clear glimpse of a heel print in the mud. It had come from an expensive lug-soled climbing boot. Whoever had taken the shot had been careful about keeping to grass that would hide his tracks. That implied a clear professionalism about the attack.

Was it one of Michael's old enemies, someone from a dozen shadowy criminal organizations or a hired marksman sent by a seething third-world dictator determined to pay Burke back for his meddling? Or was it one of Trang's hirelings come to complete his dead employer's transaction?

Every instinct warned Burke that this had to do with the urn. That was the worst scenario, after all, and Burke's experience had always been that the worst thing that could happen did happen.

That meant things would start getting nasty fast. He would have to keep a close watch on the russet-haired archeologist. Meanwhile he was bothered by the certain knowledge that he had been unforgivably careless out there in the night. His anger and recklessness had nearly cost Kelly and himself their lives. Whoever had taken that shot might have cut both of them down while they stood arguing.

Yes, he would have to keep a damned close watch on the woman.

But not for long. He meant to see that Kelly Hamilton was gone by the morning. It was too bloody dangerous to have any amateurs wandering around Draycott Abbey.

Scowling, he rubbed the knot of muscles throbbing at his neck, wondering where in heaven Nicholas had buried the wretched urn. He had already crisscrossed the abbey grounds, checking all the obvious hiding places—and then some not-so-obvious ones.

The results had been less than thrilling. Metal sweeps and infrared scans had been equally fruitless so far. Tomorrow he planned to try out a state-of-the-art portable sonar scanner on loan from some old friends in the Royal Marines anti-terrorist unit.

But something was whispering to him that time was already running out.

He stared into the fire, feeling hope slide through his fingers like cold, dry sand. He couldn't fail. Not at the first favor his best friend had asked of him in ten years.

Only Nicholas wasn't his friend. Friendship had died on the day the two had discovered they were something far closer. After years of secrecy and deception, the truth had finally emerged as Nicholas's father lay dying.

Half-brothers.

How Burke had tried to fight that knowledge. How he had burned with fury when he'd heard the words.

Even now, ten years later, he still couldn't understand a passion of that sort, so fierce that it could rip through two families and uproot a dozen lives.

Maybe because he'd never known that kind of love himself.

Burke stared into the fire, his face grim. Oh, he'd heard the stories about the ghosts of long-dead lovers said to walk the abbey halls. He knew all the legends about the thirteen bells and the brooding portrait in the Long Gallery.

But only those pure and true of heart could hear the soft, lilting laughter or smell the scent of phantom roses.

Burke knew that left him out. His heart was no candidate for purity or truth. Sometimes he wondered if he even had a heart left. What had he to fear from shadows or roses or rooms that seemed to glitter with odd, hidden lights?

Besides, he had a job to do. Nicholas was counting on him to find that urn. If not, the people in London would eventually send down their own team and *they* would tear the abbey apart stone by stone to find what they wanted.

Burke couldn't let that happen. In some sense, the abbey was part of *his* blood, even though it had come on the wrong side of the blanket.

He walked to the window and stared out over the moat. The storm had passed and the moon was rising, full and silver, over the sleeping hills.

At Burke's side the curtains fluttered softly. The air seemed to stir and shimmer.

He stiffened. For a moment he sensed someone—*something*—behind him in the darkness.

Then he shrugged and turned back to the fire.

There was nothing there, of course. There never was. Only shadows. Only an old house with too many secrets.

A dim gleam lit the room, just beyond the range of the firelight. The man before the window did not notice, his eyes locked on the fire.

The light rose, twisting upward in swirls and sparks and bright eddies.

Until once again Adrian Draycott stood, grim faced, beneath the tinkling chandelier.

Blast it, what was going on here?

First the viscount and his laughing wife had decamped for London. Now this insolent *upstart* moved in and made himself at home! Truly, it was the outside of enough!

Adrian Draycott's phantom eyes lit with angry sparks. Perhaps he would just have to send this fellow Burke about his business. Yes, one good jolt of demonic laughter, one blast of spectral energy and the irritating man would be gone for good.

The man's fear came through to Adrian then. He read it well, though the man tried to control it.

Keen black eyes narrowed on Michael Burke's rigid back. *So he, too, had picked up on the danger to the abbey. From some sort of burial relic?*

He frowned, thinking again about the woman who had called to him on the parapets. He had seen her again and once more she seemed to reach out to him, trying to find her way home. Something about her had stirred a memory he could not trace.

The resident ghost of Draycott Abbey cursed softly, then broke into bitter laughter. No need for such care, after all. This man Burke wouldn't hear him.

Only the current Viscount Draycott was accorded that right—along with a few others, and then only under exceptional circumstances and by means Adrian himself did not quite understand.

The door creaked slightly. A sleek gray shape padded over the polished floor.

The man before the window heard the sound and turned, his slate eyes narrowing as he saw the great gray cat. He bent down slowly and slid his powerful hands along the cat's warm fur.

Unseen, unheard, Adrian Draycott watched those strong, capable hands and wondered if his instincts were correct. Was this indeed the only man who could save his beloved abbey from destruction?

And what of the other one, the woman with hair like fine burgundy and eyes like the Aegean sea in spring? Eyes that saw too much?

The room chilled with the force of his anger. *Damn and blast, when would he find the key to this new danger confronting his abbey?*

Chapter 9

"If you will follow me, Miss Hamilton, your room is this way."

"In a house as beautiful as this, I'll follow you anywhere, Marston." Kelly was pleased that she managed a real smile.

"Your room is just beneath the Long Gallery and overlooks the Witch's Pool."

"Maybe I *won't* be following you anywhere. That sounds like a bad place to get much sleep."

The butler chuckled. "Oh, nothing so unpleasant as it sounds. Three generations of Draycotts have slept in that room. It is a very pleasant place, actually, and the pool is quite charming."

Kelly had to fight an urge to pinch herself as she followed him up the massive stairway, passing two Tintorettos, a Caravaggio, and a breathtaking Whistler *Nocturne*. Everywhere the air was redolent with the scent of lemon oil and roses. She had visited manor houses before during her years in England, but never one as magnificent as *this*.

In spite of the gunshot she found she was looking forward to the visit.

They passed a cut-crystal bowl full of white blooms. "The viscount and his wife must like roses. They seem to be everywhere."

"We have many old roses here at the abbey. At last count there were some thirty varieties, I believe. They are something of a Draycott specialty." The butler seemed to hesitate. "An early ancestor brought many back with him from the Holy Land after the Crusades. They were meant to be a gift for his wife."

Kelly barely heard. She stopped on the landing, her breath catching. There before her, framed between a pair of massive Sargent portraits, sat a pair of superb Anasazi burial bowls.

"Hardly your usual Sussex find," she murmured. The bowls were in mint condition, their smooth flaring rims a study in balance and grace. She knew an American collector who would pay seven figures for a bowl like this.

She was impressed, all right. A further inspection only added to her admiration. "Nice," she pronounced softly. "*Very* nice."

"They were acquired by the late viscount. He was held to be something of a connoisseur."

"He'd *have* to be to come up with two beauties like this." Kelly frowned. "They ought to be behind glass, however."

"I shall inform her ladyship. She has taken on the care of the abbey's vast collection. Very capably, I might add." Marston shook his head. "But I fear that there are a great many objects here in need of restoration."

Kelly studied the paintings. "These two are magnificent. Sargents, aren't they?"

Marston moved closer and gave one of the portraits an infinitesimal touch to straighten it. "Among his finest. This one is the wife of the tenth viscount." He pointed to a long-necked beauty with luminous eyes and ebony hair. "The other is her sister. At the time they sat for these paintings, they were the focus of a great deal of gossip. It seems that rumor was split as to whether her ladyship's sister was having an affair with Sargent or with her brother-in-law." The butler's lips curved slightly. "In the end it was decided that she was probably involved with both men."

Kelly couldn't help but smile at this bit of outrageousness. She sensed that Marston was testing her. "Isn't that carrying family loyalty just a little too far?"

The butler's eyes glinted. "Not in the slightest. By all accounts the three were the very best of friends, and continued to be so until their deaths. Extraordinary people, the Draycotts. If you are interested, there are a number of books about them in the library."

"Oh, I'm interested all right. One never knows what details will turn out to be important, especially if the texts go back very far. Even family hearsay can prove useful. I can use all the help I can get to pinpoint the location of this sword that the viscount seems to have stumbled upon."

Marston's head crooked for a moment and his expression grew serious. "I hope you will be successful. It would be a discovery of significance for the family."

"You really do care about them, don't you?" It was far too forthright, but Kelly didn't care. She was fascinated with the bond she felt. Something told her that understanding that bond would help her grasp the rest of this puzzle Miles had handed her.

The butler inclined his head. "It has been my pleasure to be here at the abbey for twenty years.

I do not believe I have regretted a single minute of that time. The Draycotts can be arrogant and utterly ruthless, of course, but they are unfailingly charming while they are about it. Perhaps that is why they win the loyalty of all who are privileged to know them."

Kelly's eyes narrowed. "And Commander Burke?"

A shadow seemed to cross Marston's face. "His lordship could provide you with family stories at least as interesting as these, I suspect."

"His *lordship*?"

"The commander is a marquess in his own right, although he chooses to be addressed by his military title. His estate adjoins Draycott Abbey several miles to the north." The butler studied her face for a moment. "You would enjoy a visit to Edgehill, I think. There are several Norman ruins on the way. You might find them helpful with your search."

"If I stay," Kelly said flatly. "It's not every day that I get shot at, you know."

The butler's face went absolutely expressionless. Clearly he was not going to enlighten her as to any suspicions he might have.

"I see. That's every bit as much as Commander Burke told me. I take it this sort of thing doesn't happen here every day."

"I really could not say, miss." He stopped before a lovely room furnished in rose damask. A black Chinese lacquerware screen gleamed between two matching brass-handled lacquer chests. "This is your room. There is a bell beside the fireplace. Please ring if you require anything."

She needed explanations, not a bell. Blast both the men! They were about as garrulous as a pair of corpses. "Maybe I should sleep with my mace tonight, just in case someone tries to shoot me again."

"I am certain that will not be necessary, miss. As long as Commander Burke is about, you may feel quite safe."

Great. A mad gunman outside, and a collection of priceless art inside. Factor in a sullen marquis turned Royal Navy Commando who might have stepped right out of a profile in *Guns and Ammo* magazine.

The scenario didn't hold much promise for a comfortable night.

He was also a man who faced danger without complaint. A man who protected you with his own body without a second thought, a nagging voice reminded her.

Kelly sighed. Right at that moment she didn't feel at all safe. But she did feel curiosity and a strange sort of exhilaration.

She only wondered what this bizarre old house was going to offer up for an encore.

Two hours later, with a long hot soak and a cup of Marston's best herbal tea behind her, Kelly was feeling more the thing. She was distinctly enjoying the feel of the damask coverlet and crisp white bedlinens monogrammed in discreet white stitches with the Draycott crest.

Before her on the bed were assembled three maps of Sussex, Professor Bullock-Powell's last monograph on Norman weaponry, and a slim parchment volume entitled *Chronicles of the Family Draycotte*. This last book she had found standing against her pillow when she'd emerged from her bath.

Marston's doing, no doubt. Deuced efficient, these English butlers.

Kelly folded away the maps and studied the fragile, leather-bound volume. Her fingers cupped the embossed cover lovingly.

She opened the first page, savoring an exquisite illuminated "D" that covered the entire sheet, then moved on to the first entry.

To my children and their children's children, the handwritten inscription began, flowing bold and black across the parchment. *May they love this house as much as I have done.*

Kelly couldn't help but smile. More Draycott arrogance, she thought. But she supposed that a family who owned a Caravaggio, two Tintorettos, and a Whistler and could trace its garden back nine hundred years was entitled to a certain amount of arrogance.

She turned the page and read on.

On this day of Our Lord, the 21st of June, 1262 is born a son. We shall name him William, after the Conqueror who led us to these shores. Meanwhile there is much work to be done. The Witch's Pool must be drained and the gardens extended. The first builders have arrived from London to repair the forecourt and the old moat. The workers will be quartered at Lyon's Hill, where our stone will be quarried.

Kelly frowned.

Lyon's Hill.

Something about those words tugged at her mind. She meant to explore the feeling further, but sleep seemed to have overtaken her, gentle as the breeze ghosting through the damask curtains . . .

A moment later the old book slid forgotten to the monogrammed coverlet.

*   *   *

The hounds were barking wildly.

A rider charged up the hill toward the yew forest. Immediately two men in chain mail dropped to bended knee. The closer one grabbed the reins of the great black destrier.

The rider was Lyon of St. Vaux. He jumped down, his voice raw with anger. "Where is the woman?"

"In the woods, seigneur. She kicked Hugh and fled up the hill into the forest. He's just gone in after her."

A frown crossed Lyon's face. How was this possible? Hugh was one of his very best men. How had the wench managed to catch him unaware?

Lyon's fingers touched the great scabbard that hung at his side. For a moment he felt a faint tingling across his neck, and with it a raw sense of foreboding.

It was as if this moment had been waiting for him, as if his whole future hung trembling on the weight of what he did next.

Pure nonsense, he told himself. It was simply the effect of this strange forest, where darkness reigned even at the height of day. Where foxes cried in the dead of night and queer lights danced in restless circles.

And then the Norman remembered his dream, a dream that had plagued him for weeks on end. He had seen himself dying far from home, in a land full of strangers.

Unmourned and unmissed.

Cursing, Lyon shoved down that dark stab of warning. After all, what was one wretched female against him, the scourge of Saracen and Saxon alike?

St. Vaux had no time for fireside gossip or heathen superstitions. The demons he feared were real and *entirely physical. They carried heavy broadswords and shields.*

He was certainly not about to admit fear for a slip of a girl whom the heathen Saxons called a witch. Looking around, he saw his men were watching him. Their faces were hard and there was a tension about their jaws.

Lyon saw that they would not meet his eyes.

So that was how things stood. Any more mistakes with the girl and they would begin to doubt his ability to lead. That would be fatal, soon leading to chaos and revolt.

His fingers tightened on the hilt of his broadsword. A vast emerald glinted at the beaten silver pommel, circled by a sunburst of garnets.

The sword had been passed down among the St. Vaux men for five generations. No one knew exactly where the weapon had come from or how the first St. Vaux had come to possess it.

Lyon's father swore that the great blade had saved his life more than once, humming a warning as an assassin approached.

It was Lyon's most precious possession.

He smiled, fingering the golden crossguard. As long as he had his sword, all would be well.

And now he would find the wench and make her yield to him, by God. She would do it right here, before all his men, to set their fears at rest. And then Lyon would bind her hands and toss her in with the other rebels until he decided what to do with her.

His face was like stone as he strode up the hill, waving away two knights who hastened to his aid. His eyes were locked on the faint wisp of red of Hugh's tunic, just visible between the dense yews.

Impatiently, the Norman tossed away his cloak and

metal helmet. His hauberk was next to go.

If he would fight a woman, he would do it as a man ought, without tools or any weapon save his wit and skill. For in truth St. Vaux was skilled on three continents as a masterful lover who pleasured his women well. No scrap of a female would stand long before him.

The red of Hugh's tunic vanished in the darkness of the great yew wood. A chill wind played over Lyon's skin, ruffling his hair.

Silence descended, but it held no hint of peace about it.

No, this was a cold, unnatural silence. A silence that spoke of ghosts and charms and the powers of the dark.

Cursing, Lyon strode on, ignoring the twigs that snapped and clawed at his face. He had had enough of Saxon superstitions. Enough of the eerie dreams that had plagued him ever since he'd set foot on this foreign shore.

He hastened his steps, anxious to have the business done with. A few minutes sufficed to bring him deep into the woods. His boots of soft leather crunched over dry grass and fallen leaves. Hearing a sharp sound to his left, he drew his sword and spun about.

"Nothing but a bitch hare, you fool," he muttered as a small white shape darted off into the foliage. On Lyon strode, his fingers tense on the hilt of his sword.

And then he heard a high, keening cry. His stride lengthened, and he broke into a run.

He came upon them in a bower of ferns and wild roses. Hugh had the woman pinned to the ground with his dagger raised above her neck.

"Stop, fool! I ordered that she was not to be killed. That will only increase her hold over the other Saxons!"

Lyon said the words without knowing why. He had given no such order, of course. Before this moment he had had little care for whether the wench lived or died, as long as her influence over the populace was broken.

But now, looking at the slender thighs that twisted and strained against the green forest floor, Lyon felt heat rage through his loins—a heat such as he had never felt before. And her hair—

By the Holy Mother, it was long and full, the texture of finest Damascus silk . . .

His fingers tightened on his sword. "Enough, Hugh. Let her go and stand aside."

Suddenly it was as if Lyon had split into two people. One part of him, the cold-blooded soldier, marvelled at this order, which was so lacking in logic and good sense.

But the other, the full-blooded man, glared down at his most trusted knight, hating Hugh for feeling the pleasure of her supple, half-naked body beneath him. For feeling the sweet heat of her breath against his neck . . .

His fingers clenched. "Now, man! Or you'll feel the kiss of my blade."

Frowning, Hugh FitzRolland came to his feet. Almost immediately the girl stumbled to her knees and began to inch backwards toward the heart of the forest.

"You are dismissed, Hugh." It was a flat order. Lyon did not even deign to turn his head as he gave it.

Hugh's footsteps whispered over the leaves as he disappeared back down the hill.

Suddenly the forest seemed to still. The air hung heavy, dark with foreboding.

Lyon felt sweat bead his brow and naked chest. Tension gripped him, and with it came the hot, sweet *ache of desire, a desire more keen than any he had ever known before.*

"Give me your name, Saxon." His voice was hard as the local flint.

The girl's eyes glinted, wild and savage as the foxes that Lyon hunted through these wild fields.

"Your name, I said!" Desire made him blind, made his fingers tighten on his sword.

Her face paled, but still she did not answer him. Instead she pushed slowly to her feet, her simple gown falling in a cloud of petal-green around her slender body. Her grace, even then, was an awesome thing, and Lyon marvelled at it.

But tame her, he would. And after he tamed her, by God, he would—

He strode closer. "You do not deign to answer, wench? Not to me, who is your seigneur and righteous lord?"

At his words her glorious green eyes filled with anger. "Righteous?" she spat. "What do you and your kind know of righteousness? Of mercy? All around you the country lies in dread. Villages ring with the pleas of starving children, and you hear it not." She came to her full height of scant five feet. "I spit on your righteousness, Norman!" Though she was dwarfed by the great warrior before her, she gave no sign of fear.

She was utterly magnificent, Lyon thought dimly. But her words had stabbed his pride, and no warrior possessed pride like a St. Vaux. "Doucement, ma fille. Else you shall taste the edge of my sword." His voice dropped, low and dark. "Once again, I'll ask you your name. And I expect an answer this time."

"But you'll not have one. You and the Norman dogs that lap at your feet deserve no such fealty!"

Lyon's fingers wrapped strong and tense around the hilt of his sword. Anger whipped through him like a blood-red storm. He had been three weeks from home, plodding through spring-muddied roads and dodging rebel arrows from one end of Sussex to the other.

His old hip wound was aching and his joints were weary from twenty straight hours in the saddle.

And now this frail, arrogant slip of a female had the utter temerity to stare in his face and hiss curses.

But he'd teach her a lesson, by God. One she'd never forget!

He strode over the thick leaves stretched in a carpet of brown and gold. His eyes, icy silver, never left her face.

The woman did not retreat, much to his surprise. He had fully expected her to.

"So you think yourself brave, Saxon? Will you face my blade with the same fire?"

He saw her shoulders quiver, saw her small chin rise defiantly as she faced his wrath.

"Well met, Aislann of Milton." He laughed dryly as he saw her start at his words. So his spies had been right. The description they'd given fit her well. And he could see from her shock that this truly was her name.

So this was the Saxon woman he'd been seeking all these months.

He came to a halt while they were yet two strides apart. Slowly he raised his sword, watching for any sign of fear.

None came. Her face, though pale, was rigid and set, her small hands clenched to fists.

"You may claim the battle, but you will not claim the war, Saxon."

"We shall see, Norman dog," she answered tensely.

Lyon's blade rose high, glinting in a bar of sunlight that lanced the thick green canopy overhead.

The emerald on the weapon's hilt flashed. A bolt of green seemed to fly out, travelling straight to the girl's heart.

With a wild cry Lyon spun the blade, circling it low in ever-widening gyres.

Even then she did not move or flinch.

And her stubbornness infuriated him.

Without a word he drove the great blade slashing earthward, light arcing off its thick polished shaft.

Her head rose, defiant even beneath this slashing blow. Lyon knew he would never forget that sight: her grim lips, her furious green eyes. Her slender shoulders, stiff with determination.

Her wild beauty and silent defiance.

He cried out in fury. Only by dint of all his vast skill and strength did he halt his thrust a scant inch from her shoulder.

Then the weapon rose until cold steel kissed her cheek and carved one tiny curl free.

It wafted downward, falling upon her breast, which Lyon saw was trembling slightly.

So she was not as brave as she pretended, the Norman thought. The knowledge brought him pleasure—and something far darker. Something bittersweet and sharp as the mead he'd drunk at William's table four weeks before.

Bah, what care had he for a Saxon's feeling! Especially such a wayward witch as this!

Suddenly he found himself lifting the fallen curl from her sweetly trembling chest.

It was still warm from her body.

Lyon stiffened. He felt an urge to throw it from him, to turn and run from the fate that seemed to gather before him, cold and threatening as the mist that drifted up from the forest floor.

At the same time, he knew an ache, a tormenting need to run his hands over that heated skin. To feel the soft swell of her breast and the sweet thrust of her nipples against his palm.

He muttered a curse, then flung the lock of hair aside, as if it had burned him.

Abruptly the silence around them was shattered. Somewhere down the hill came the crash of shrubbery and the bellow of a boar.

Then Lyon heard the wild cry of a man in mortal pain.

It was Hugh.

Chapter 10

She awoke before dawn, damask against her wrist, linen beneath her cheek. She sat up slowly, listening to a clock chime somewhere in the abbey.

Five o'clock.

Sighing, Kelly wondered what was happening back at the dig and what kind of havoc her cat was causing at home.

She shoved back the covers, then frowned. Her head ached. Her lip was tender. Bitten in her sleep? But it was neither of those things that made Kelly go very still.

It was the memories. Harsh shouts and blood dotting her fingers. The thunder of hooves and the glint of a great blade.

The room began to spin. Kelly stumbled to her feet. The curtains billowed out as the window sprang open, driven by the wind.

A wind rich with wood smoke and thyme.

She locked her hands across her chest, trying to ignore the wild thunder of her heart. Just a dream, she told herself sternly, but in truth she knew it was something far more.

A *vision*. An image flung out from that other place where time did not exist and thoughts were real. The place she feared but could never stop being attracted to.

She looked down and saw that her fingers were clenched around the leather-bound Draycott chronicle. She dropped it as if burned.

"G-go away. You're just a dream. Just some half-forgotten memory stirred up like dust in an old room. I didn't come here to dredge up the past. Not mine or anyone else's!"

But a voice whispered that it would not be nearly so simple to forget *this* dream.

Breakfast was scones and an omelette with raspberry sauce and fresh mint sprigs eaten in a sun-drenched alcove overlooking the moat. Marston hovered, ever helpful but ever impassive, dispensing clotted cream and butter in tiny wedges the shape of the Draycott crest.

By the time Kelly finished a very fine cup of Earl Grey tea, she had begun to forget her bizarre dreams of the night before. "Thank you for lending me the book about the Draycott family, Marston. It was quite fascinating."

"Book?" The butler's brow rose.

"The *Chronicles of the Family Draycotte*. I found it by my pillow."

The servant rearranged a silver plate and smoothed a thick linen napkin. "I am delighted to be thought of assistance, but the book did not come from me, miss."

"Oh. I thought . . ." Kelly frowned. "It must have been Commander Burke in that case."

"Perhaps, but I seem to recall that that particular book disappeared some months ago. His lordship meant to show it to his wife, but had no luck in finding it." He looked up at Kelly. "And you say it was lying on your pillow?"

Kelly nodded.

The butler started to say something, then turned away to assemble the tea things. "The viscount will be most pleased to see it again, I am sure."

He doesn't believe me, Kelly thought. Her eyes narrowed. "Are there other books of this sort in the abbey's library, Marston?"

"Several dozen, I should imagine. They were placed in a special case after the viscountess found that the pages were damaged with mildew. If you like, I shall ask Commander Burke to show them to you, as he is familiar with their contents."

"He is very much at home here, I see."

"His lordship and the commander have been friends since they were boys. Commander Burke knows this house nearly as well as Viscount Draycott does. It was a great relief to the viscount that his friend was able to be here while he and his wife are in London."

"And what exactly *are* his duties here? Besides frightening off crazed hunters, of course."

Marston studied a spot several inches above Kelly's head. "I believe it would be best if you asked the commander that, Miss Hamilton."

The man was turning obscure on her again, Kelly thought irritably. "I'll ask if I see him. But first I'm going to take a walk around the grounds. I thought I'd have a look at the Norman ruins near Lyon's Hill."

Marston nodded. "It is an impressive spot. If it would be useful, there is a map of that area locked in a chest in the study. It is only a small thing, but it is carefully rendered and very old.

His lordship thought you might be interested in it."

"I would indeed." Old maps often carried forgotten place names that might give a clue to the sword's location. And intuition told Kelly that where she found the sword, she would also find the urn.

"In that case I shall bring it along to you. Perhaps you might also like a hamper to take on your walk. Would cold chicken *en croûte*, a pâté, and fresh strawberries be satisfactory?"

"Satisfactory? Ah, Marston, with all these attentions you'll turn my head. I may never want to go home."

The butler smiled, but there was no mistaking the frown that continued to darken his forehead as he carried the glinting Georgian silver teapot from the room.

"Kelly?"

"Come on in."

Burke pushed open the door and blinked. The reorganized bedroom looked like a World War II command center. Maps stretched across every available tabletop, anchored down with vases and Venetian glass paperweights. Nearby archeology texts rose from the floor in shaky stacks and dotted the rumpled bed.

"Where's the war?"

Kelly did not smile. She shoved back a strand of russet hair and tapped at a green-hatched ordnance survey map. "Here. And here, I suspect."

"I thought you said you were leaving."

"I changed my mind." She shrugged. Graceful. Stubborn. "There's too much work to be done here."

Burke frowned. On the nearest map he made

out Draycott's rolling acres, their hills marked by concentric curves. Most of those green curves were now dotted with red crosses. "Very interesting. Counting casualties?"

Kelly did not look amused. "Those are probable locations for the sword site, based on a comparison of geologic formation and stratigraphy. One of those spots will match the earth found clinging to those Norman sword fittings that Viscount Draycott dug up. At least, we think it's Norman. Professor Bullock-Powell believes there's a good chance it might have belonged to William the Conqueror himself." She tapped the map lightly. "I've cross-referenced all the likely sites. As you can see, most are located near the area called Lyon's Hill. I plan to take a walk there this afternoon."

Burke leaned closer, studying the map. "There must be fifty crosses there."

"Closer to sixty."

"That will take days—weeks even."

Kelly shrugged. "Nobody said it would be easy." She pulled another map onto the table. Far more detailed, this one showed underlying geological formations. The red crosses clustered near three major formations where chalk beds gave way to hard limestone outcroppings.

Burke recognized those formations. There were similar ones running over onto Edgehill land. "So the soil had limestone in it?"

Kelly's brow rose. "You're familiar with maps like these?"

"I've used them a time or two." Burke had used them *more* than a few times, as it happened. But that had been in the mountains of northern Thailand and the jungles of Colombia.

Never in his own backyard.

He leaned closer, studying the colored bands, fascinated in spite of himself. Mentally he matched the crosses with familiar Draycott landmarks. The woman was bloody good, he thought, awed.

Swiftly he checked off places that might be suitable spots for hiding an urn. None seemed promising.

As Burke studied the map, he almost regretted that he couldn't let her project continue. But with the urn at stake, there could be no question of that.

Frowning, he traced a yellow ridge running between two green layers of Downsland chalk. "Winklestone," he murmured.

"I beg your pardon?"

"That's what my old nanny always called it. It's a hard local limestone, much used for stonework and interiors in this area. But Nicholas— that's Viscount Draycott—and I chiefly liked it because it was full of fossil remains."

"Winklestone," Kelly repeated slowly. "It's a lovely name. I'll remember it." Her head cocked as she studied him. "For an amateur you're very sharp at reading maps, Commander Burke."

Her face was pale and she had faint blue circles beneath her eyes, Burke noticed. For some reason that made him angry. "So what do you do next?"

"I think of some way to narrow the search." Kelly gnawed at her lip. She tipped a lampshade, angling the light so that she could see better. Her finger moved idly back and forth over the lower corner of the map. "Some early maps of the area might help. Family chronicles, too, just in case there's a mention of any legends about the sword."

If Burke had had any doubts about her skill, they dissipated at that moment. "Pretty damned thorough, aren't you?"

The American stood up and rubbed her neck. "I try to be, Commander." Her lips curved.

Her eyes were glinting, Burke noticed. And they were the *damndest* shade of turquoise. "Even when your host is being singularly unpleasant?"

"Oh, you weren't *singularly* unpleasant."

He felt a grin snake across his face. "One of these days that tongue of yours is going to get you into a lot of trouble, Red."

"I keep hoping, Englishman."

Warmth curled through him. Standing near her like this, he felt like smiling back. Hell, he felt like doing a lot more than *smiling* at the woman. And maybe the knowledge of that attraction bothered him more than anything else.

Burke knew that when things got personal, it was easy to make mistakes. Deadly mistakes.

He stepped back and angled his shoulder against the wall. "Those maps aren't entirely current, you know."

"I suspected not. I've sent for more recent ones. You know, remote satellite images. Infrared details." She frowned. "Sorry. I must be boring you."

"Utterly," he said with a faint smile.

Her cheeks flushed. She looked away, searching through the papers on the table beside her.

"By the way, Marston tells me you found the Draycott chronicles. Nicholas has been looking for that book for nearly a year."

"Don't thank me. *I* didn't find it. As I told Marston," she continued firmly, "I merely came across it propped on my pillow." Her eyes narrowed. "A nice little joke, Commander. I'm sure the tourists enjoy that sort of thing."

"It's no joke, Miss Hamilton. It wasn't me and it wasn't Marston. Whoever put that book in your room had to get past some damned sophisticated security to do it." He looked down at the maps, toying with a green-swirled paperweight. Two intruders in one night was too high for coincidence.

Frowning, he plunged the glass oval back onto the table and let the map snap closed. "Get packed. I'm taking you into the village right after lunch."

"Now wait just a minute. You can't come in here and—"

"I can, my dear Ms. Hamilton, and I just have. You are leaving and that is quite final."

"If it's about the letters, I have them right here. They'll tell you everything you need to—"

He cut her off curtly. "I have no need for any letters."

"But last night, you said—"

"Forget about the letters, Professor. You're not staying. This research of yours will just have to wait."

Kelly's eyes glinted with fury. "*Why?*"

"Because that's the way it is."

"No, that's *not* the way it is. I happen to have a personal letter of invitation from Viscount Draycott offering me the run of the abbey until that sword is found. I also have a reference from the finest archeologist alive in England today and a rather nice little note from someone else who's very interested in the results of my research." Her brow rose. "Aren't you going to ask who it is?" When Burke didn't answer, she crossed her arms over her chest and glared at him. "No matter, I'll tell you anyway. You might know him—he's the heir to the British throne."

"Very impressive ammunition, Ms. Hamilton. However, you're still not staying." His jaw hardened. "I don't care if you have a personal recommendation from the pope himself, you're still leaving."

"Like *hell* I am! I'm desolated if having a woman working at the abbey makes you uncomfortable, but that's *your* problem. I'm here and I'm staying."

Burke almost changed his mind at that moment. She was so determined, so alive and full of righteous fury and stubbornness, that he wished he could agree. But he couldn't.

"Get packed. I'll send Marston up for your case in thirty minutes."

Kelly's fingers went taut against the edge of the black lacquer table. "What's the matter, Mr. Burke? Feeling cramped?"

Maybe it was because of this strange old house. Or maybe it was because of the exasperating female before him. For whatever reason, Burke found his control slipping fast. "Just take my word for it, the timing's all wrong."

"This has to do with that gunshot from the woods last night."

Burke's eyes narrowed. "That was just a drunken hunter, as I already told you."

Her head cocked as she studied him. Burke had a strange feeling that she was looking right through him, measuring all his secrets. Impossible, of course, but the feeling left him slightly shaken.

"I suppose English hunters always go around taking shots at people on their own doorsteps."

Burke merely shrugged.

"Listen, Commander, I may be an American, but I'm not a complete fool."

"Nobody said you were."

"Then don't treat me like one. If you recall, I was in line for that bullet too. I think that entitles me to a better explanation than the rubbish you just handed me!"

"Well, you're not going to get one, Professor. Not from me." He strode to the door, then turned back, his eyes unreadable. "I'll be up in thirty minutes. Be ready."

As Burke walked down the hall to the study, he thought he heard the American mutter something that sounded like, "Bring the queen with you next time and just maybe I will."

He almost smiled.

Hardness. Eyes of cold slate flecked with amber. Arms that were as tense and rigid as Draycott's implacable granite walls.

That's what Kelly thought as she watched Michael Burke stalk from her room.

She thought of angry pride. Of bitterness and too many years of pain. Yes, all those things made the man.

But what was that to her? Her life was already too complicated as it was. She looked down, studying the map beneath her fingers. She caressed its cool plastic surface, seeking energy trails, lingering traces of feeling.

Nothing came. Nothing but unfocused sensory static.

The lapse left Kelly bereft, angry, and very confused. What was happening to her here?

She pushed to her feet and wrenched on her coat and shoes. Enough with pointless speculation! She had work to do, serious work. And as Miles always said, if one door doesn't open, then go try another.

That was exactly what Kelly meant to do. Pacing Draycott's fields and hills might just trigger some burst of intuition.

It was rather ironic, Kelly thought, but she might well find that Norman sword in the process. For some reason she had a feeling it was very near.

Almost as near as her own heartbeat.

The operator put Burke through almost immediately. He should have been gratified, but he was too irritated to notice.

"Ross here."

Burke was too keyed up for preliminaries. "I want her out, Ross."

There was a dry laugh. "Commander Burke, I presume?"

"Of course it is. And don't try to change the subject, you silver-tongued, overpaid bureaucrat."

"Compliments, Commander?"

"That was no compliment. And either she goes or I do."

There was a moment's silence. "Very well. I trust you have enjoyed your stay at the abbey."

"Now listen to *me*, Ross. I'm not going to—"

"No, you listen to me, Commander. This archeologist is all we have. She and those soil samples." Ross paused. "Unless you've come up with anything helpful?"

"You bloody well know that I haven't."

"Fine. Then Miss Hamilton will have to stay."

"Damn it, haven't you been able to find anything more from the other end, over in Thailand? What about Trang's old cronies?"

"Absolutely nothing. No one seems to know anything about an urn."

"Or they're not saying."

"That, unfortunately, is another possibility."

Burke stared at the sun glinting off an old sundial by the bridge. Once again he felt a nagging jab of intuition. Of overlooking something right at the end of his nose. "What about Nicholas?"

"He has remembered nothing new. Of course, with the viscountess due to deliver at any hour, the man is predictably distracted."

Burke made a hard sound. He stared out through the mullioned windows, out over the shining moat, feeling Draycott's strange, haunting beauty seep into his very soul. But experience had taught him that beautiful things were usually very dangerous. "Can't you postpone this business with the sword? Just until we've found the urn?"

"Impossible. We're getting pressure from the very highest levels on this. Right from the palace, in fact. That sword will be a find of international importance. Whatever government agency oversees that success will corner a great deal of goodwill, if you understand me."

"I understand you," Burke growled. He was no stranger to that sort of branch politics. "Then here are my conditions. Accept them or else."

"Or else what?"

"Get yourself another man."

"That would hardly be advisable, Commander. You know Draycott Abbey better than anyone else in the service."

"Then that doesn't leave you much choice, does it?"

Ross gave a long-suffering sigh. "You drive

a hard bargain, Commander. Very well, name your terms."

"First, I want everyone else kept away from the abbey. That means neighbors, friends, visiting tourists, and building inspectors. Anyone trying to come in or out is to be stopped on sight and questioned personally by you."

"Very well. Am I to assume that this is connected with the shots fired outside the abbey last night?"

"You don't miss much, do you?"

"That's what the overburdened English middle class pays me for, Commander. You might have called me sooner, you know."

"What difference would it have made? The fellow was gone by the time I got Kelly inside. I found a print, however. I'll need an overnight analysis."

"Of course. Meanwhile, I've already assigned an extra cordon around the abbey, as well as several men to the village. Just in case someone comes asking questions."

"Oh, grand. You S.I.S. types will stick out in Long Milford like a herd of water buffalo in Regent Park."

"Thank you for your vote of confidence," Ross said dryly. "Do you want someone posted inside the abbey? As a servant, perhaps?"

Burke laughed grimly. "You don't know Marston if you think he'd let his position here be usurped. But there's no need. Not yet, at least. No, next I want two portable sonar scanners and the latest satellite reconnaissance for this part of Sussex."

Ross's answer was a little slower this time. "On their way. Do you have something specific in mind?"

"Let's wait and see before I say more."

"Anything else?"

"I want to know everything you have on this archeologist who's been assigned to look for the sword."

"There's not a great deal, I'm afraid. Oh, we have the usual professional details. Seven academic awards for teaching and two for publication. Twenty-two articles to date. Up for tenure twice in Arizona and denied twice. Something to do with departmental politics. She's been away from medieval studies for several years."

Burke went very still. That intuition became a scream. "Away?"

"She was up at Oxford until about five years ago. Had a fine career ahead of her. Professor Bullock-Powell still speaks most highly of her. She was a former student of his."

"Sounds like you found a lot to me," Burke said dryly.

"Nothing that counts. Nor does it explain why you might be suspicious about the woman. And you *are* suspicious, aren't you?"

"Come on, Ross, can't a fellow have a few secrets?"

"Not in this business, Commander."

Ross was right, of course. Maybe that's what made Burke so angry. "Find out all you can. I want to know everything about her. Who her kindergarten teacher was. Whether she likes her spaghetti soft or *al dente*. *Everything*, no matter how trivial it might seem."

Ross's pause was just a shade too long. Burke heard the tap of a pencil at the other end of the line. "That kind of information could take some time, Commander."

"We don't have time, Ross. And I just can't

shake the feeling that—" Burke smothered a curse. "Don't ask me why. Just do it."

"It would help if you were more specific."

"No." *Not yet*, Burke thought grimly. Not until he could figure out what it was about Kelly Hamilton that bothered him so.

Other than the palpable sensual attraction he felt whenever she was in the same county, that is.

"If you prefer, I could have her removed. The professor must have someone else who—"

"*No.*" The word came out sharper than Burke intended. He frowned at the abbey's rose-covered walls. "If someone has to be here, it might as well be her."

"Does it strike you that the lady might have reasons of her own—reasons other than archeology—for being there?"

Oh, yes, it strikes me, Burke thought. *In fact I've thought of nothing else since I first set eyes on her.* "I've considered the possibility."

"I see," Ross said slowly. He hesitated before continuing. "There is one thing, actually. Ms. Hamilton's recent work has been with Meso-American archeology—Anasazi sites in particular. Before that, as I mentioned, she worked here in Britain with Professor Bullock-Powell."

"What happened?"

"That's just it. I'm not sure. The professor's being damned tight about the subject. It might be important or it might be wholly irrelevant, but I thought you should know—in view of your concerns."

"Try the local papers. You'd be amazed how much finds its way into print, most of it lies, of course. Still, there might be the stray grain of truth."

"I'll get on it."

Footsteps sounded outside the door, followed by a low tap.

Burke frowned. "Sorry, Ross, but someone's outside. I'll have to go. Just see what you can come up with."

"Consider it done, Commander."

Chapter 11

Kelly sat back against a sun-warmed stone and wiped dust from her cheek. At her feet were two maps and the Draycott family chronicle. Beside the old book lay Marston's opened hamper, with her salad of fresh greens and herbs half-eaten.

Overhead a hawk circled lazily above the wooded valley. To the east the ivy-covered ruins of a Norman castle thrust up from a tangle of vines, like Sleeping Beauty's enchanted bower. Around the walls lay the ghostly tracks of ancient fields once tilled by medieval peasants. Their narrow furrows, once lush with wheat, barley, oats, and rye, were still visible as shadows against the fertile Sussex soil.

And what of the lord and knight to whom the village owed its allegiance?

To the north Kelly could just make out the steep face of the gorge known locally as Lyon's Leap. Here, so legend had it, a Norman warrior had galloped to his death, pursued by a force of Saxon rebels. Even now, Marston had related with relish, the warrior's ghost was said to gallop along the cliffs on moonless nights, calling the name of his beloved, whom he would never see again.

Kelly shivered a little, though the sun felt hot upon her shoulders. She would tackle Lyon's Leap next, but she didn't feel ready yet. Not while she was still haunted by wisps of troubled dreams and images of a stern-faced warrior wielding a mighty sword.

Meanwhile, the maps were doing nothing at all for her. She was off, terribly off. The gift she had scorned and cursed for five years suddenly seemed to be denied her.

Was it this place? she wondered. Or was it simply *her*?

She stared down at the ordnance survey map. For a moment she smiled, savoring the thought of Burke's fury when he returned and found her gone.

Then she put the arrogant Englishman out of her mind. She had managed to learn one thing, at least. According to an old map in the Draycott chronicles, this land had not belonged to the Draycotts at all, but to the neighboring estate. For two hundred years the families of St. Vaux and Draycott had warred over this fertile valley until finally a boundary had been fixed, just to the south of the cliffs. That line continued east, running along the slope where Kelly now stood. Lower still, it struck dead through the center of the Norman ruin.

Why did she feel there was some significance to that fact?

Brushing back a russet curl, she sank onto the grassy slope and looked over the valley. Sunlight clung to the twisting silver ribbon of a stream.

Sheep dotted the lower fields, and beyond that thatched cottages peeked from a copse.

Beautiful, she thought. Timeless.

Home.

The image seized her with shocking force. Kelly gasped, dragging in the fresh country air. Air that felt like *home*.

Utter nonsense! Draycott Abbey meant nothing to her. Her home was the red-rock cliffs of Arizona, where the sky stretched blue and clear forever.

And yet. And yet . . .

Above the trees a kestrel floated in lazy circles. *Kee-lee kee-lee*, its clear, high call echoed over the quiet valley.

Emptying her thoughts, Kelly reached out, seeking any detail or fragment of impression.

She had once tried to explain to Miles how her imaging worked. At first it was a little like trying to see in the dark, she'd explained. And then the closing off and the retreat deep within. Only there, in the silence away from the clamor of the outer world, did the visions swell and flow. Usually they came slowly, the way waves rippled out from a pebble dropped into a quiet pool.

But today there was nothing, subtle or otherwise. She was alone, blind in a way she hadn't been blind in five years, since the accident and recovery that had left her with an unwelcome gift.

She shoved to her feet, glaring at the maps as if they were somehow to blame.

So try it another way, a voice whispered. *Turn it inside out and see what you come up with that way.*

Hands clenched, Kelly stood at the ridge of the hill and listened, reaching out for images

that seemed to dance just beyond the edge of
her awareness.

The sword? The urn?

Or was it something far more dangerous than
both?

Overhead the kestrel cried shrilly. A bead
of sweat trickled down between her shoulder
blades.

Suddenly she saw water, cool and deep,
spilling silver over malachite-green. The image
caught at her, held her. It wasn't much to go on,
but it was all she had.

Sighing, Kelly rolled up her maps and tucked
them into her backpack. She would find the
stream she could see glinting at the far end
of the valley. On her way she meant to take
a closer look at those ruined Norman walls.
If nothing else, they would make a fine place
to finish Marston's picnic lunch, she decided.

Fifteen minutes later Kelly dropped her hamper, maps, and books and stood in silent awe
before the remains of the old Norman castle.
Weathered with age, green-dappled with lichen,
the walls sang of an older age full of high magic
and great heroes.

Once these walls would have rung with the
stamp of hooves and the shout of knights on
their way to do battle for their king. The songs
were still there, Kelly thought, pushing past a
thorned spray of blackberries and a smaller plant
bright with tiny purple flowers.

She opened her hands over the sun-warmed
granite. It was *coming*. She could feel the tension race through her. Beneath her hands the
hot stone seemed to hum, somehow alive,

whispering the long-forgotten secrets of this ancient place.

Kelly frowned. Was she on Draycott land or St. Vaux land now? Here, ringed by the great stone walls, it was difficult to tell. Following the ruined granite east, she felt a thorn dig into her skirt, pulling her to a halt. She bent down to free the tiny spine, and suddenly a shadow passed over her. Something cold pricked at her neck.

Some ancient instinct urged her to flee back to the safety of the sunlit slopes above.

And then all peace was torn from her.

The vision was upon her before she knew it, jolting through her like a high desert storm. White-faced, she clung to the granite wall, fighting to hold the buffeting power at bay.

But she was helpless before such strength and cruel clarity.

Out of time, the visions came. Out of an ancient past full of beauty and cruelty. It was as if they had waited, safe inside the shadow of these ruins, for the day that Kelly finally stumbled across them.

And as she staggered to her knees, Kelly realized that the images flooding through her head were more *real* than any dream, more dangerous than any threat that she had ever known before.

Lyon swung about and ran toward Hugh, his captive forgotten. God's blood, boars were unpredictable at any time, and their tusks could inflict terrible damage.

Hugh was lying pale and still just by the edge of the forest. His leg, swollen and blood-streaked, was propped upon a fallen log.

The boar had vanished.

*The wounded Norman vassal gave a wan smile.
"Sorry, Lyon. It came from those shrubs. Gored right
through my cursed leg, the devil d-did."*

Lyon studied the terrible wound. A great gash of
flesh had been torn away and blood oozed in thick
pools.

Even as Lyon bellowed for his men, he was bending
low, wrapping his fallen cloak around Hugh's cold
body. He pressed a wedge of linen against the wound
to stanch the flow of blood.

"He is—hurt sore, your man?" Aislann was staring down at the fallen knight.

Lyon did not turn. "Aye, he is hurt. Hurt most
foul."

Aislann frowned. "He has lost much blood. If you
wish, I will tend him."

This time Lyon did turn. His face was granite, his
eyes shot through with fury. "You? Do you think I
would turn even my dogs over to your tender wrath?
Be gone, witch. I only pray that you plague us no
more."

Aislann stared at him uncertainly. The knight was
no friend of hers, nor was his vassal.

But still she stood and still she felt the gnawing
guilt grow inside her. For the man had been hurt
because of her. Aislann had planned it this way. She
knew well that the boar and his mate haunted this
part of the forest. Now, with a young brood, the boar
was more dangerous than ever.

She frowned down at the Norman overlord. "I will
not hurt him, if that is your fear. My skill is for
healing, not harm. I swear it by the name of our Holy
Mother."

Lyon's hands tightened. So she was a Christian
after all. At least she pretended to be. He tensed as
Hugh gave a convulsive shudder. "Be gone, witch!"

A trio of knights appeared. "Make a sledge," Lyon growled.

Behind him came the soft crunch of grass. Only with great effort did Lyon keep from turning.

When silence fell behind him, he knew that the Saxon had gone.

For some reason the thought left him cold. The forest seemed to close in on him.

"Hurry up, you fools! His lifeblood drains away while you blunder about! And send someone to follow the Saxon. I don't wish to lose her after all this time."

They settled Hugh before the fire in Lyon's own solar. Lyon sent a man for the priest and a lay healer from Hastings.

Meanwhile Lyon waited, pacing impatiently. He shouted twice at his chamberlain and even raised his voice to the priest, who looked stern and shook his head.

The afternoon passed. Hugh grew ever weaker.

As twilight closed around the great hall, locking it in cold shadows, St. Vaux stared long into the crackling fire. In the flames he seemed to see the glint of red hair, the flash of green-gold eyes.

It was all prattle, of course. All those tales about her strange skill were no more than the babbling of fearful old women.

But Lyon decided that for Hugh's sake he must try.

He came abruptly to his feet and dragged his great black cloak over his mail hauberk, then strode to the door, calling for his horse.

Twilight darkened the hills as St. Vaux galloped toward the small thatched cottage at the far side of the village. He had ordered his men to hold Aislann there until he decided what to do with her.

Shoving open the door, he saw the Saxon bent before the fire, stirring a steaming pot. Lyon caught the tang of rosemary and lavender, along with spices he did not know the names of.

His stomach twisted. He realized he had not eaten since Hugh had fallen in the middle of the day. Now it was evening.

But hunger was the last thing on Lyon's mind. He filled the doorway, all hardness and shadow. "I need you at the bailey," he said harshly.

He watched the Saxon spin about, startled. Her face was gilt in the firelight, her hair a cloud of red and gold.

Desire stabbed at his loins. Lyon saw the pallet of hay and fragrant herbs behind her and had to fight a raw urge to shove her down and bury himself deep inside her. For a moment he was blind with the need to catch her wild moans with his mouth. To tease her velvet skin until she arched against him, mad with a passion as wild as his own.

It cost him much to force down the urge.

"Now, wench! Have you not ears in your Saxon head?"

"I have ears, Norman. I have also heart and head in this body of mine. You did not need my help before. When I offered, you scorned me and then clapped me here like a caged vixen cub. Why should I help you now?"

Lyon pounded across the dirt floor and seized her shoulders. "Because I command it, woman! Because you are mine to order as I will!"

"I am no man's slave," Aislann hissed. "I answer only to my heart and to my Maker."

The Norman's lips hardened. "But your Maker is not here now, Saxon. Here and now it is I who hold you, I who touch you." His eyes darkened. "And it is I who hold your fate in my fingers."

Sweet God, he could almost feel her heartbeat and the gentle thrust of her maiden's breasts. It would be unforgettable heat and drenching softness when he drove deep inside her.

He swallowed painfully. "Stop tempting me, witch, lest I shove you down and take you here and now, with my men to watch from the doorway."

He heard her breath catch. In the end it was that sound of fear that made him release her and jerk away. "Get whatever things you need. Then you will ride with me, for the night is dark and there are wolves in these woods."

"They will not harm me," Aislann said flatly. In her eyes glinted a cold challenge.

Once again Lyon felt the urge to cross himself as if before the forces of darkness. What if she were in truth a witch? "Fine words, wench, but I've seen what the wolves leave behind. 'Tis no pretty sight, I assure you. Now hasten!"

Her hands clenched at her waist. "I will not set one foot outside with you, Norman. Nor will I help you. Not unless you grant me one boon."

"You dare to lay conditions on your service?"

"Your imprisonment has made me value my services higher, Norman."

St. Vaux felt fury lick at his blood. "By all the Saints, do you think to bargain with me?"

"Your man must fare very ill or you would not have come," Aislann said calmly. "And that means that the others you have engaged to help him have all failed." Her green eyes flashed. "With that the case, I think you have little choice but to bargain with me."

"What price, curse you?" Lyon grated through clenched lips.

"The freedom of my betrothed. He is falsely accused of poaching from the Royal Wood and is being held at Hastings, under sentence of blinding."

Lyon's eyes blazed, raking her slender form. Jealousy lashed him like the bite of an adder. "And what is this miserable creature's name?"

"Aelfric of Pevensey," Aislann said with quiet dignity. "He already carries the wounds of your men and will die without treatment."

Lyon's eyes narrowed. "How do you know of his condition?"

"I have my ways."

Once again the Norman knight felt a shiver work down his spine. Her eyes were huge, filled with fires that spoke of unnatural sources.

He shrugged. If she truly had such power, then she would be made to use them in aid of his wounded knight. "Aelfric of Pevensey," he repeated icily. His eyes raked her face. "Have you lain with him, my lady?" His term of address was chosen to mock her now. "Has the Saxon sampled the sweetness of your willing young body?"

Aislann's face flamed. "Have you respect for nothing, Norman dog?"

Lyon's hands clenched convulsively. Damn, how he hated her. And how keenly he wanted her. The thought of another man's hands on her breasts, his manhood driving inside her, made Lyon's vision blur with rage. "Not for the likes of you, Saxon. And you still do not answer my question."

"Nor will I. 'Tis no business of yours."

"I prefer to know what manner of scum I release from William's gaols."

"He is not scum," Aislann said hotly. "He is the son of Hereward himself." Abruptly she bit her tongue.

Never should she have mentioned Aelfric's connection to Hereward, the fiery Saxon rebel who continued to resist the Norman might.

St. Vaux smiled slowly. "Indeed. You interest me vastly, ma belle. The son of Hereward the Wake is your betrothed?"

"N-no, not that Hereward. He has disappeared into the fens to the north. Aelfric is no relation to that one, I assure you."

Lyon ran his finger along her pale cheek and brushed the arch of her lips.

They were trembling.

Aye, he would make them tremble. He would make her cry out in wonder and joy when he—

"He must be much a man to hold your fealty so deeply," he growled. "Very well, witch. I shall do what I can, but only out of regard for Hugh, who is my best knight and oldest friend. One day and one night, I give you. But if I fail and this man Aelfric is not to be freed, I shall be back for you. And then you will put your skills to healing Hugh or suffer my lash."

Aislann's chin rose. "Come then, Norman. If you return without Aelfric, you will find my refusal remains the same."

Lyon's eyes hardened, shot through with red sparks from the firelight. "Oh, you may count on my coming back, Saxon. And God help you if you try to resist me then."

Kelly dug at the hot granite, fighting the sights and sounds of a world that had disappeared nine hundred years before.

She failed. On the colors raced and plunged, hot in her veins and razor-sharp. On the sounds rang out, as if part of her own hearing.

Until they became *her* sensations, *her* emotions.

In some strange way she witnessed the whole scene as both spectator and participant. In the odd, merged perspective of a dream, she was man, woman and wild, silent forest.

And Kelly realized this was only the beginning.

Chapter 12

*A*s he had promised, Lyon gave her one day and one night. Now, as she was gathering herbs beneath the twining roses of the great oak, Aislann felt the first nudge of alarm.

The Norman. He was coming, just as he'd promised.

She spun about. Rose petals, mint leaves, and vervain were crushed in her fingers as she surveyed the great forest that swept unbroken all the way to the southern cliffs.

She saw nothing unusual. Sunlight filtered through the great green canopy and the air was noisy with bright wings and birdsong.

But there was a hint of crimson just beyond the river. Her eyes narrowed.

Again came the flash of color, nearer this time.

Then Aislann remembered. Crimson was St. Vaux's color, conferred upon him by William the Barbarian in honor of his bloody victory at Senlac Hill.

Then it must be so. Truly it was Lyon of St. Vaux. He was coming for her, just as he had sworn.

With a ragged cry she turned and ran toward the cottage.

* * *

The Norman spurred his great horse on. God's blood! He'd meant to catch her unaware. Now it was too late.

St. Vaux cursed darkly as his prey fled across the thick grass. He urged his destrier forward and nearly caught her beneath a rose that twined around the great oak tree.

But she was swift as a woodland fox and knew every corner of concealment. She ducked behind a thorn-studded thicket before Lyon knew it, leaving him nothing to show for his efforts but stinging fingers.

"Come out. Saxon. You only fuel my anger by these games."

"'Tis hardly a game, Norman." Her voice came tight and angry from the far side of the shrubs. "Have you brought your men along to help you?" she asked bitterly.

"I need no help, Aislann. Not with one small slip of a vixen like you."

"We shall see about that."

Lyon heard the sound of scuffling. Some instinct made him look up just as two owls darted from the foliage. Furious at being disturbed, they shot straight for his head.

Cursing, St. Vaux brought his destrier around and made for the other side of the shrubbery.

She was already halfway to the cottage.

With a wild cry he charged after her. "I'll have you, Aislann! Hugh grows white and pale from his wound and by God you'll tend him. You cannot hope to escape me!"

She ducked through a row of yew shrubs just as he would have caught her.

Lyon cursed. The opening was too small for his horse. But alone . . .

He leaped down and plunged through after her.

And found himself stumbling knee-deep into a pool of mud. A black-nosed hog squished toward him, snorting with curiosity. St. Vaux struggled to his feet and looked down at his mud-stained chausses and hauberk.

He would thrash the wench! By God, he would turn her over his knee and flay her white bottom soundly when he caught her!

If he caught her, Lyon thought ruefully.

She was nearly at the cottage.

He turned and gave a high, shrill whistle. Instantly, the black steed circled to his side in response to the call.

Lyon was mounted in a second and at Aislann's heels in three more. "Give it up, woman. I'll see you're not harmed if you cease your struggling."

"Save your speeches, Norman pig! Your promises are worth less than the mud that coats your fine leather boots! I would not trust you even if—"

But her last words were cut off as St. Vaux plunged low, caught her waist, and swept her up before him. "I told you I'd be back for you."

"But without Aelfric. He'll die in that foul place!"

"His crime was witnessed. Poaching from the King's Wood. 'Tis the King's Law and even I have no say in such a matter, Saxon."

"You lie!"

"Hugh is dying. You will come, wench. I'll not have his blood on my conscience."

"I will not."

"Damn it, woman, I have done what I can for Aelfric. He was given blankets and visited by a healer."

Aislann blinked. "I don't trust you, Norman. Put me down or I'll—"

He pulled her against him and crossed his hands

atop her chest, holding her still. "Or you'll do what? Send your curses down upon me? Cast the evil eye over me as you did upon the old crone in the village?"

" 'Tis a lie! I did no such thing. It was merely the ale sickness. The woman would not give it up, though I warned her often how it would be if she did not."

Lyon's lips curved. "Ah. So you are not a witch after all."

"Of course I am n—" Aislann swallowed, then jerked at his imprisoning hands, kicking wildly. "In truth, I am a witch! I am!"

"In that case, little vixen, you may use your magic to win back Hugh's health. And after that, since you have such fire, perhaps I'll let you turn it upon me."

"Upon you? Gladly! With eye of newt and gall of snake I'll turn you into a toad! No, into a wart upon a pig's back. 'Tis all you deserve!"

Lyon threw back his head and laughed. The sun burned warm upon his face and the woman in his arms was fire itself.

Yes, the wench felt good. He would tame her, and then he'd bed her. After that he'd woo her. It was an odd way to go about the business, to be sure, but it seemed the little hellion left him no other choice.

For he would have her. In his arms and in his bed. With all her fire loosed on him and him alone. Of that there was no question.

Before him, Aislann locked her lips in cold fury. She did not utter another word as Lyon held her close and plunged from the forest.

Lyon slid off his mount with Aislann still caught in his arms. He threw his reins to a waiting page and strode through the bailey. "How fares Hugh?"

he demanded of the bearded chamberlain who came out to await his orders.

"He weakens, my lord. Ever more by the hour. And just a few minutes ago . . ."

"What? Out with it, man!"

"He began to cough up blood, seigneur."

Lyon swore grimly. He caught Aislann's arm and dragged her along behind him. As St. Vaux strode past, a cluster of Norman ladies giggled sharply.

"He is insatiable," one woman hissed. "He will ride her well, then toss her back where she belongs."

"And where is that?" the woman's companion asked mockingly.

"Why, in the sty with the rest of the pigs, of course."

Their laughter jabbed at Aislann like tiny knives.

"Come, my lady. Your work begins."

Conscious of the mass of eyes upon her, Aislann raised her chin proudly. "You need not wrench my arm from my shoulder, Norman. Then I will be of no use to you."

Lyon gave her a dark look. "In that case make haste. I have no time for dallying." He held up a woven bag. "Your herbs are here. Water has already been prepared and put at the boil."

"How efficient you are, Norman."

Lyon's eyes raked her lips. "Efficient and more, Saxon, as you shall see. Now move."

Aislann followed him through the crowded bailey, past frowning knights and their hard-eyed ladies, her chin upturned. Even the mud-splattered Saxons stared at her with mute hostility.

Aislann felt the force of their scrutiny. Villein, cottager, and serf watched her with sullen eyes as they went about their labor in the newly built stone keep. By being here she betrayed her own people. Aislann knew they would never forgive her for that. Aelfric had counted her as his woman, and he was the secret leader of those who hoped to drive the Norman invaders from these shores.

Not that the brutish St. Vaux knew that.

The Saxons had feared her before, even while they came to her in the dead of night, asking her help to cure their coughing children or unhealed wounds. Aye, they came to her cottage, but they did not like to. And because of their fear, they were halfway to hating her.

This would take them the rest of the way.

Aislann sighed. She could not change what she was. No more, she supposed, could the broad-chested warrior beside her change what he was.

The thought sobered her. She felt herself wondering, just for a moment, what sort of village he came from. What sort of family. Did he miss them now and then?

Aislann drove the thought from her mind. She had a healing to concentrate on. If Hugh FitzRolland died, St. Vaux would never believe it was because his illness was beyond curing. The blame would be all for her, Aislann knew.

In that case she might never leave this bailey again.

Not alive, at least.

The knight was lying in the great solar. Smoke drifted around the room from a fire banked in one corner. Above it a cauldron bubbled noisily, slung on iron poles.

The room was clean at least, Aislann saw. No mud. No dirty rushes. No animals living in the corner. And the shutters of painted wood were thrown open to the sun and fresh winds.

A good beginning, she decided.

She knelt by the bed and studied her patient's face. He was pale, his lips tinged with blue.

Aislann raised the coverlet and studied the jagged wound at the man's calf. The skin was stretched taut and flecked with angry yellow spots.

"Well?" Beside her the great Norman paced restlessly. "Will he live?"

Aislann slowly lowered the cover. "There is a possibility, Norman, but it is not large. I shall not spin you any witch's tales. His wound is bad and that brings his fevers. His leg might have to be taken off."

Lyon's face went very hard. "No. He would rather die whole than live as half a man."

Aislann's eyebrow rose. "You give yourself the right to make such a decision for him?"

"It is what Hugh would wish," Lyon said flatly. "Just as I would wish the same." He challenged her, his eyes hard as slate.

Aislann sighed. "Let us hope, in that case, that it will not be necessary." She opened her bag and began arranging small bundles of herbs upon the bed. "I shall need basins and a supply of freshly washed linen. And someone to keep the fire going at all times."

"You shall have them," the Norman said simply. As he strode from the room, he was already shouting orders to his chamberlain.

Aislann cleaned the knight's wound carefully and laid on a layer of crushed parsley. To that she added last fall's reddest rose hips and garlic cut to a smooth paste. As she worked, the Norman stood beside her, saying nothing as he handed her whatever bowls or utensils she required.

His frown grew as Hugh began to toss and mutter restlessly. "He grows worse, Saxon." His tone was accusing.

"It is not necessarily a bad sign. The wound must flow before he can heal."

Lyon did not challenge her, not then or even later when she had the wounded knight lifted from the bed so she could wash him and have the linens replaced.

"I have heard the Saracens follow such practices," he said thoughtfully several hours later as the sun glowed golden through the open shutters.

Aislann slanted him a challenging look. "Do you now charge that I am Saracen as well as a witch?"

He gave her the merest hint of a smile. "Nay, Aislann. To be Saxon is enough of a charge against you." He looked back at his sleeping friend. "Besides, Hugh seems to rest better now. Perhaps in this case the Infidel's way is best."

With a sigh Aislann sat back in the carved three-footed chair that Lyon had brought up for her. She studied Hugh's face and nodded. "He is improving. His color is better and his breathing grows more peaceful."

Lyon studied her, seeing the fatigue in her slumped shoulders, the pallor in her face.

Muttering darkly, he fetched a goatskin pouch from the bed and carried it to her. "Drink," he ordered flatly.

Her brow rose.

"I need you well to tend my knight. You have not eaten or drunk in all the hours you've been here."

Aislann realized it was true. She slanted her head and swallowed the rich wine Lyon held up to her, coughing as it burned down her throat. "What—what is it?"

"The fruits of my fields, back home in Normandy." For a moment his eyes lifted to the window. "You should smell the black earth there in spring, when the vines begin to send up their first shoots. And again in the fall, when the grapes hang dark and heavy upon the vine." Bitterness crossed his face.

"You miss it?"

He turned and stared out the window. "Aye, I miss it. It was my home for fifteen years. The village was full of sun and the harvests always rich. Not like your cursed land," he said curtly. Then his eyes narrowed. "But perhaps this is not your land. You speak differently from the other Saxons."

"My mother was from the north. My name is from her own people."

Lyon's eyes were unreadable. "She chose well."

Suddenly the door was thrown open. A tall, sallow-faced man of aristocratic demeanor strode into the room. "What is the meaning of this sacrilege?" He glared at Aislann. "Where is St. Vaux?"

The Norman moved away from the shadows at the far wall. "I am here, Bishop. But I do not believe I requested your attendance."

"No, you did not. And it is all the influence of that one, that tool of the devil!" He raised a crucifix studded with rubies and pearls and shook it at Aislann.

A shorter man entered the room, timid in a threadbare habit and bare feet. "Aislann?" His face creased in a smile as he saw the slender woman beside the bed. "Oh, my daughter, is it truly you?"

Aislann kissed his hand. "So it is."

"You know this—this daughter of Satan?"

At the bishop's abuse, the village chaplain rose to his full height, which was still considerably less than five feet. "Know her? I was present at her birth and again at her baptism. I know her as well as my own mother." The sturdy friar's eyes glowed. "And a good deal better than I know you, Your Grace."

Lyon's lips slanted into a smile. "So you are a baptized Christian." He chuckled. "So much for all that talk of spells and witchery."

" 'Tis not talk!" the bishop said sharply. "I order her from this room and from this keep, St. Vaux. She brings the stench of evil to everything she touches."

Lyon moved closer. His fingers gripped his sword. "This keep that you speak of is my keep. And it is mine to command. I advise you to remember that."

"But the woman is—"

"I command. And she shall stay until I decide otherwise."

The bishop's face turned white with fury. "Very well, St. Vaux. You make your choice clear. If your soul burns in hell for this piece of recklessness, so be it. I wash my hands of you." With that he strode to the door, his heavy crucifix slapping at his thighs.

The chaplain gave Aislann one last hug. "Be careful, my daughter," he whispered. "There are those who would do you harm." His eyes rose to Lyon's face. "Take care of her," he ordered, his voice surprisingly firm. "By bringing her here, you have only added to her danger. She is feared now by Norman and Saxon alike. Had you eyes, you would have seen it before."

An angry shout rang from the hall. The chaplain sighed. "Such haste, always such haste. I fear it will bring the man to a bad end."

Shaking his head, the bald man hurried from the room.

Lyon was frowning as he crossed the crowded bailey.

The manor court had been longer and more bitter than usual this day. Everyone seemed to have some grievance to bring forward—Norman and Saxon alike. Two brothers had quarrelled over the rights to a singularly ugly pig. Two sisters had fought over the size of their dowries. The northern fields were unequally divided. The southern fields were too poor to tax.

On and on it went.

Lyon's neck ached. He was tired. He was frustrated. He was angry.

This was not the work he would have chosen for himself. He was a knight, after all, a warrior trained in hard combat. To win land was his skill—but to hold it?

That, Lyon had discovered, required skills that he was not sure he possessed.

As he climbed to the great keep, he looked out at the surrounding countryside. His fields stretched rich and green as far as his eyes could see.

In spite of the sight Lyon couldn't shake a feeling of creeping danger.

He was at the top of the stairs when he heard the low groans. The rustling of linens. He stiffened as the groans grew deeper. By God, he would kill Hugh!

He charged through the door to the solar with sword drawn, light flashing off the grooved tang. "By heaven, if you touch her again, I'll—" Lyon froze.

Hugh was hot with fever, struggling to rise from the bed, and Aislann was fighting to keep him down.

Not the intimate scene Lyon had envisioned.

Not the sleek, hot parrying of thighs that he had expected.

Was he possessed by demons? St. Vaux thought as he went to help Aislann. Would this woman never give him an instant's peace?

"Why didn't you call for help?"

"I was just going to."

"When did he turn this way?"

"Only a few minutes ago. But in truth I don't understand it! He's done so well until now."

Between them they forced the sweat-soaked knight back upon the bed. With trembling fingers Aislann caught up a fresh wad of linen and dried Hugh's chest and forehead.

"The wound is much better. The swelling is nearly

gone and the edges have begun to mend. And now this . . ." The Saxon sat back with a sigh. "Truly, my lord, I do not understand it."

Lyon went very still.

My lord. For the first time she had given him his proper address. And it had come artless and unrealized, as she worried over her patient.

He revelled in the sound, feeling it warm the dark, stony corners of his heart, a heart that had been too long at war and was uneasy in the ways of peace.

My Lord. How he savored the words.

Then Lyon smiled slightly, brought back to reality when he realized that Aislann did not even realize what she'd said.

He moved closer. His hand brushed hers as he felt Hugh's forehead.

She did not pull away, he noted.

And then his thoughts were all for Hugh. "God's blood, the man is burning. He's as bad as he was before you came." Frowning, Lyon studied Hugh's thigh. It was just as Aislann had said. The wound was clear, pinkish-red, with no sign of taint or swelling.

His heart turned cold. Perhaps it was true after all. Perhaps she was no more to be trusted than any of the other sullen Saxons who worked for him by day and plotted against him by night.

"I will ask you direct, Aislann of Milton. Did you tend my man fair or did you give him bitter herbs to harm him?"

Aislann's face went pale. "I have tended him just as I vowed, Norman. He has had only my best herbs and truest care. He should have been well by now!"

Their eyes locked. Steely gray plumbed furious emerald. Lyon felt the danger of the decision he must make now. Around him the jaws of a metal trap were closing tight. One mistake, one misstep and they would both be lost . . .

"*Do you give your word on the Holy Book, Saxon?*"

"*I do.*"

"*And you have no knowledge of what ails him?*"

"*None.*" The Saxon frowned. Her hands went to her waist.

"*Aislann?*" Lyon's eyes narrowed. "*What is it?*"

The woman swayed forward. Her breath seemed to desert her.

Lyon cursed and braced her with his arms as she began to fall.

Her face was ash-pale. "*The cauldron. I—I drank of it, as is my custom. I meant to be sure it was ready for Hugh.*"

A spasm went through her. She whimpered, digging her fingers into her stomach.

Lyon caught her up against his chest and ran to the door, bellowing for the chamberlain.

Aislann shuddered again, her eyes wide and glazed with pain. "*I fear—it is poison, my lord.*"

Lyon felt fury pound through him. Poison? Who would dare, here within his own keep? "*Steady, ma petite. We'll have you well. My chamberlain will fetch sharp cider, whey, and mustard from the castle stores. They will purge you.*"

The Norman could only pray that it would be soon enough.

He watched. It was what he did best.

No one could see him here, hidden in the shadows where the granite ridge rose from the valley floor. Yet from here he could see everything that took place in the ruins or to the north where Draycott's cliffs rose like a line of great gray teeth.

He watched the woman cry out and clutch at the ruined walls. He smiled to see it. The smile grew broader as he saw her sway and fall at the foot of the ruins.

When he was certain that she would not get up, he slid silently from his hiding place and began to work his way toward her.

In his carefully gloved hands was a plant. A plant with dull green leaves and tiny purple flowers.

Chapter 13

*K*elly awoke slowly to the dull sound of thunder in her head. Her lips were dry and her face felt hot. The images had waned but were not forgotten. Even now she felt the Saxon woman's fear and pain as if it were her own.

She pushed slowly to her feet, feeling her legs shake. What did the vision mean? Was it merely some savage piece of history witnessed by these stones and passed on to her in a chance moment of clairvoyance?

Sighing, she shook a leaf from her skirt and looked about her. The hamper lay askew against a boulder, thermos and salad tumbled onto the grass. The rumbling in Kelly's stomach reminded her she'd eaten next to nothing since breakfast.

With fingers that weren't quite steady she found the thermos and took a long drink. She frowned, thinking the lemonade had tasted better earlier. Still, it was all she had.

She was just about to take another drink when she heard a rustling in the brambles behind her.

She tensed.

It was only a cat. A great gray cat with amber eyes and black-tipped paws. It slid through the vines and ghosted about her skirt, shoving at her leg.

"Out exploring too, are you?" Kelly sank down against the boulder and slid her hand over the cat's sun-warmed fur.

The gray head arched. A low purr rolled through the air.

Kelly took a deep breath, reassuring herself that everything was normal. This was the twentieth century all right. An airplane shrieked overhead and somewhere beyond the woods a car backfired.

Yes, she'd take global warming and nuclear contamination any day in place of the arrogance of a Norman knight and the treachery of castle politics.

Here in the twentieth century she was safe. No one stalked her here. No one hissed oaths at her here. No one here stared at her as if they wished she were dead.

But her throat ached and somehow the fear would not leave. Her fingers shook as they eased over the cat's sleek body. What she needed was more of Marston's famous lemonade, Kelly told herself.

She reached toward the thermos.

In a blur of gray fur, the cat sprang against her hand and knocked the thermos to the ground. Legs stiff, eyes glinting, he blocked the long silver canister and hissed.

Then Kelly saw them. Dull green, the leaves spilled from the thermos onto the grass.

She felt her stomach tighten. A wave of pain slashed through her.

She remembered she had seen those leaves

beneath a berry vine before she'd touched the ruined walls.

And now Kelly remembered where she had seen those leaves before that. Tracking local flora was one of her hobbies. She had once seen a woodcut of those leaves in an old book of herbs at the British Museum.

Now it looked as if the hobby had saved her life.

For she, just like the Saxon, had been poisoned with mandrake leaves. And somehow this strange, great cat had known it.

Before the knowledge could sink in, the cat twisted about and faced the ruins. Shrill cries poured from its throat.

"What—what is it?" Kelly whispered.

And then the knowledge was in her mind as surely as if a voice had spoken.

Run. We cannot help you here. You must find your own way back to Draycott lands.

A thousand questions sprang to her lips.

Again the deep voice rang out, harsher this time. *Go! Before it is too late.*

Kelly hesitated. The cat was pitted before the ruins, tail rigid, teeth bared. Hiss after shrill hiss filled the quiet air.

That was the last thing Kelly saw before she turned and ran toward the sunny ridge to the north.

She might have made her way in safety except for the stones half-hidden in the long grass. She stumbled on the first, crying out in pain. And on the second she tripped, tossed forward.

Her hands reached out in vain. Seconds later her head struck the ground.

She cried out as Aislann's world swept back around her.

* * *

By evening it was done.

The sharp cider and mustard did their painful work as purgatives. Hugh and Aislann, though both weak, were resting peacefully.

Now the door of the solar was guarded by Lyon's chamberlain and his two strongest men. Nothing was to be taken in or out without St. Vaux's express consent.

Lyon now meant to find the one who had betrayed him.

For three hours he had the castle searched from bailey to keep. No stone, no corner was left unsearched. Wardrobes were turned inside out and the food stores scrutinized. Dovecote and dairy were ransacked. Even the animals were shooed outside the gates so that Lyon could complete his task. Finally, hard by the bailey's north wall, the Norman found what he'd been looking for.

What he'd been desperately hoping he wouldn't find.

It grew on chalky soil, half-hidden by a tangle of berry vines. Its leaves were dull green, with soft hair. Small flowers, dark purple, hung like bells from the foliage.

Lyon cursed harshly.

Dwale. His own people called it deuil for the grief it caused all who touched it. But here in Sussex it was known as mandrake, the Devil's plant. One root carried enough poison to fog a man's brain and leach the life from his limbs.

Lyon bent down and examined the plant more closely, careful not to touch the leaves. Fury shot through him as he tasted the bitterness of betrayal. So the traitor was here in the castle. He `looked at the serfs and villeins going about their work, trying to keep their curious eyes off the Norman lord who was turning out his castle from top to bottom.

Was the traitor among them even now?

For some reason being an outsider had never weighed so heavily on Lyon before. Even his own knights were studying him curiously. No doubt the presence of the flame-haired Saxon made them uncomfortable.

A movement down the hill caught his eye and he pushed to his feet. "Ho, boy. What are you about there?"

"Tending the pigs, m'lord." He was a squirmy creature, more dirt than skin, but his blue-gray eyes were keen.

"Come here then."

The boy did not move.

"Come, boy. I won't harm you."

Slowly the child scuffed toward the great golden-haired Norman.

"What is your name?"

"Cynric, m'lord."

"A bold name. What is your job?"

"I do tend the pigs, m'lord."

Lyon bent forward. "Come you here and look at this, Cynric."

The boy knelt beside Lyon and stared down at the plant beside the knight's hand.

"Have you ever seen such leaves before, boy?"

"No, m'lord." There was a note of fear in his voice. Lyon frowned, wondering if the boy spoke the truth.

"That is, I water the pigs here at the pool most every day, but never have I seen flowers like that before."

Lyon stared down at the noxious leaves. He knew the plant had not been here long. He had walked every inch of ground from bailey to keep before choosing this site. He had meant his castle to hold and grow, to occupy a key spot overlooking a strategic valley pass, and he had chosen his spot well.

No, there had been no mandrake here when Lyon's castle had been built. Whoever had done this had been at the work only recently, for the poison-bearing flowers and leaves were still fairly small.

That was probably the only thing that had saved Hugh's life. And Aislann's.

Lyon's eyes went icy. "Tell me this, boy, and here's a coin in it for you. Have you seen anyone here, anyone at all who did not belong by the springs where the pigs come to water?"

The boy sat back. His grimy hands tugged uneasily at his dusty leggings. "Just one, m'lord."

Lyon felt tension grip him. "Give me the name."

"I'll not feel the bite of your lash, m'lord?" The boy's expression was wary. "Mayhap the name be . . . Norman."

Lyon's fingers clenched. Sweet God, it was one of his own people? "Nay, my lad. Not even if the name be Norman. But if you lie or give me less than the whole truth, you will have cause to regret it."

The boy Cynric rocked back on his heels. Crossing his hands on his scrawny chest, he studied Lyon. Finally he nodded. "Very well, then, m'lord, since I have your word on it. An' I've seen how your word is kept. Aye, it was her what done it. Her with the jet-black hair and the flashing jewels. Her what sings her songs for your knights by firelight. The lady Vivienne."

Lyon found her laughing with her ladies in her fine timber house just beyond the castle walls. They were examining some new crates of silks just arrived from London.

"Out!" Lyon thundered, sending the ladies scattering like colorful birds.

Vivienne. His dead brother's wife.

Lyon felt an icy rage as the slender woman stared at him, a faint smile upon her beautiful face. "And to what do I owe the rare pleasure of your company, my lord of St. Vaux? It has been bestowed upon me so rarely, after all."

Lyon felt his rage burst into full flame. He gripped his fingers tight to keep from strangling her. He would have to be clever to get the truth, he realized.

He strode to the window and fingered its rich tapestry. "You are comfortable here, my lady?"

"Tolerably."

"You have decorated your house well. My compliments."

She shrugged. "It is hardly the grandeur of my husband's castle in Rouen."

Her green eyes glittered. Strange, Lyon had never noticed before just how cold they were. "But things are vastly different here, Vivienne. It is a conquered land, and peace must be bought for a price. We are yet fighting to hold it."

The Norman beauty stood up abruptly and tossed down her embroidery. "So I have heard. Again and again, until I grow sick to death of hearing it! Saxons this and Saxons that. Harvest this and harvest that. Pardieu—what care have I for a miserable pack of heathen dogs?"

Abruptly her shoulders went stiff. She drew a sharp breath and composed herself. "But how remiss of me. Surely I may bring you wine or mead, my lord. Have you eaten?"

Lyon's eyes went very cold. "I shall not take wine at your table, Vivienne, nor food of any sort." The warrior slowly moved closer. His gaze held hers, like a predator entrancing his prey. "No, not today nor any other. Because of this." His hands slid beneath his surcoat and emerged with a small bag of leaves and roots. He threw down the wet clump.

It landed on her pristine embroidery, leaving behind a trail of green slime.

Vivienne's face paled.

"You have nothing to say? No clever explanations to give me?"

"I—I know not what you mean, my lord." She looked down and adjusted her skirts. When she looked up, her lips were softly curved, her face luminously beautiful once more.

Unblemished and unflawed, that face was a thing of great beauty. Lyon had always thought it so, even when his brother was alive. For years he had lusted after his brother's wife. So deep was that fever that Lyon had gone away on pilgrimage to escape the dishonoring passion in his blood.

A passion that the Lady Vivienne had been careful to incite whenever she could.

Lyon could see that now, too.

"Oh, no? Where have I seen such herbs before, I asked myself? Not perhaps in your gardens at Rouen? Do I not recall your maid laughing as I saw a pair of rodents lying dead after they had trespassed upon your peace once too often?"

Vivienne's beautiful brow arched. "I do not understand you, my lord. I know nothing of rodents or poison. And as for this . . ." She waved her fingers gracefully at the sodden mass in her lap. "It is simply some native root. Why do you trouble me about it?"

"Give it up, Vivienne. You were seen. Did you think you could pocket your prize all unnoticed?"

"Who saw me?" she hissed.

At that moment Lyon saw the full corruption of her soul. It left him shaken, sickened. My God, he thought, to think that once I loved her!

"The name does not matter. For the crime you have committed, that of plotting to kill my knight, I have

every right to order your death. I could see you hanged from the roadside tomorrow."

Her fingers clenched and unclenched upon her jeweled girdle. *"I will not beg before you, Lyon. Not before my husband's snivelling, raw-boned younger brother. I shall not soil my pride in such a way!"*

"I see." Lyon did see. All too clearly. The years of cunning and cool manipulation. The careful flirting and the veneer of righteousness. She had simply been trying to keep him interested in the event he proved of some use to her after the death of her husband.

"Nay, upon second thought hanging would be too good for you, my lady. But you will go from this place and you will take nothing but the clothes upon your back. A boat will be waiting at the river. You will sail to the coldest isle of Brittany. Perhaps the good sisters of Sainte-Marie will be able to drill some piety and remorse into that icy heart of yours. I shall see that you are given their most austere cell in encouragement of that end."

Vivienne sprang to her feet, her green eyes flashing. *"You foul swine! Do you think I care what you order? Do you think I have no friends who will see to my safety? Why William himself will laugh when I tell him what you've done! Ah, but then you were ever a blind fool, Lyon."*

Lyon turned to the door, sickened, unwilling to hear more. *"You have three hours, my lady. Do not be late for the boat lest you discover that I have come to regret my leniency."*

As Vivienne and her ladies boarded the vessel that would carry them to London, a trio of sullen faces watched from the forest. The leader's eyes missed nothing. After the boat moved away, the company gave up their anxious silence.

"What means this, Aelfric?" one of the men asked.

"Why has he rid himself of his brother's wife?"

"What need has he to plow her?" another Saxon called angrily. "Now he has the flame-haired Aislann to warm his bed!"

Aelfric spun about and grasped the man's tunic. "One more word and I rip the tongue from your throat, Celwyn!"

His two companions went very quiet.

Aelfric, meanwhile, stared at the fast-retreating boat. "Aye, Aislann has whored herself for the Norman bastard. No doubt she likes the fineness of his bed more than the coarse straw she'd share with me." His eyes hardened. "But not for long. She'll have to leave the castle someday, and when she does, I'll be waiting."

The Saxon's hands clenched and unclenched jerkily. "And on that day I'll pin her down and plow her in the pigsty, for all to see. I'll take her in the dirt and filth where she belongs. After that I'll shave her head and leave the hair hanging on the castle gates, bright and glossy. Right where the Norman pig can see it!"

"Ms. Hamilton?"

There was no answer.

Frowning, Burke pushed open the door. He stared at the empty room. He stared at the clothes still hanging in the closet. At the books still stacked on the bed.

Hearing a noise, he swung around to find Marston studying him with barely concealed interest. "May I help you, Commander?"

"Ms. Hamilton—where did she go?"

"I believe she was planning to explore the Norman ruins near Lyon's Leap."

Burke cursed fluently. A call to London had kept him longer than planned. "How long ago did she leave?"

"About an hour." Marston frowned. "I believe she was planning to be out for some time, so I prepared her a lunch hamper. I trust that is not a problem?"

"It bloody well *is* a problem. The woman was to leave. As a matter of fact, I wish *you* would go too, Marston, but I know it's useless to hope you will."

Marston's brow rose. "Quite useless, I assure you. I have been in the service of two viscounts here at the abbey and I do not propose to let a little tiff about a buried sword drive me away from my duties now."

Rather more than a little tiff, Burke thought grimly. "Very well. Pack up her things. I want her ready to go. And keep your eyes open. If you see anything odd—anything at all—use that walkie-talkie I left you."

Chapter 14

*F*rom the distant hills came the tinkling of sheep bells and a faint, high whine.

Kelly sat up slowly.

Her legs were shaking. Her throat was raw, as if she'd been crying.

Slowly the terror faded, washed away by the rush of the wind and the heat of the summer sun on her shoulders.

By the time she was wide awake, Kelly was already wondering if it had all been just a dream. Shaking her head, she pushed to her feet.

Get a grip, Hamilton. It's the urn that counts, not this medieval pomp and pageantry.

Brushing a twig from her hair, she stared down at the cool gray walls enveloped by dense brambles. Even in the full heat of midday there was a coldness about the place that made it uninviting.

But the danger, if true danger it was and not simply her reliving of some ancient tragedy, now seemed to have passed. Here at the crest of the hill, warmed by the sun, Kelly felt an odd sense of peace creep through her. She had the feeling something was still down there, something that would answer questions she was almost afraid to ask.

Just as clearly she knew that if she left now, without seeing this mystery through to the end, she would never be whole again.

All of which meant she had to go back.

Down to that dark circle of stones that both fascinated and repelled her. Down to the shadows that licked at the hot granite until the walls seemed to shiver and dance.

Right now, in fact, she was standing on the ridge that she had marked on her map. Intuition whispered that both urn and sword were buried somewhere in this very limestone.

Her chin rose. It was there, the answer she needed. All she had to do was be brave enough to seize it.

"I told you to be ready to leave and I meant it."

Kelly squinted up into the sun as hard fingers gripped her shoulders.

With his back to the light, Burke's face might have been carved from stone. *Caught between a rock and a hard place, Hamilton*, she thought grimly. "And *I* told you I'm staying. Now I suggest you let me go or I'll—"

Burke's eyes narrowed. He ran a finger over her forehead. Though he was gentle, Kelly winced. "What happened?"

"An accident. I tripped while I was exploring down there." She nodded at the ruins below them.

Burke cursed darkly. "Damn it, you can't just go blundering about. There are burial mounds all over these cliffs and those Norman walls are unstable. You might have been crushed."

"But I wasn't, was I? Dilapidated structures happen to be my specialty, if you recall. Now if you'll just step aside, I'd like to—"

Frowning, Burke turned over her wrist. Already a bruise darkened the pale skin. "I suppose this was another *accident?*"

"How did you guess?"

Burke's jaw went very hard. "I want to know what happened down there, Professor."

"I told you, I tripped."

"Try again."

For a moment weariness slumped Kelly's shoulders. Her gaze slid to the dark stones. "You wouldn't believe it if I told you," she said softly.

"Why don't you try me?"

For a wild moment Kelly thought about how it would go. *First the walls began to hum. Then I had a dream about people who have been dead maybe nine hundred years. Then came the best part. I felt myself getting poisoned. Only it wasn't a dream. Because there were the same kind of leaves in my thermos.*

Yes, a truly convincing story.

"Look, I have to get my maps before they're ruined."

Without warning, static hissed behind them. Cursing softly, Burke reached into his back pocket, tugged out a small receiver, and jabbed at a button on its side. "Burke here."

The other voice was scratchy against a faint electronic hum. "Picked up an intruder, Commander. Down in alpha-five sector. Two men in pursuit. Instructions?"

"Just get the damned man. Then bring him up to the house."

Burke shoved the receiver back in his pocket and watched Kelly's face. "You were saying, Ms. Hamilton?"

So there *had* been someone down there, Kelly thought wildly. Someone who had watched her when she fell. Someone who had slipped the mandrake into her thermos.

The knowledge left her shaken, feeling somehow violated and unclean.

"Make it the truth this time."

"Let go of me and I might consider it," she snapped.

Burke looked down and frowned when he saw his hands still wrapped around her wrists. "I didn't realize . . ." He couldn't seem to look away from the pale skin and the bruise that mottled the underside of her wrist. "You can see the danger now, can't you? This is exactly why you can't stay here any longer."

"All I *see*, Mr. Burke, is that you make a good dictator." Kelly jerked her hands free and glared at him. "I'm getting my maps. *Now*. If you'd like to come along, fine. Otherwise, you can stay here and watch."

A few seconds later she heard footsteps behind her. And though she was loath to admit it, she was glad for his company when she felt the shadows of the ruined walls brush over her.

At that same moment a gust of wind snapped one of Kelly's maps up into the air. They both went for it at the same moment and their heads bumped right over the black line that ran down the center of Sussex.

"Ooow!"

"Bloody hell!"

Burke caught the paper first. With unsteady fingers he twisted it to a tight scroll.

Then he frowned. Kelly was still bent over, her hands at her forehead.

"Kelly? Are you all right?"

She wasn't. The danger was there again, all around her, pressing down on her like tons of cold granite. The Norman ruins? Or something closer, something she couldn't make out?

She shook her head, fighting the fear until she managed to work her way back to some semblance of calm. "I—I'm fine. Just some pain in my head. I must have hit it harder than I thought." She stood up and pressed a steadying hand against the wall.

Burke frowned, but didn't argue. Without a word he snagged another of her maps, then reached over her shoulders and secured it against the granite wall. Kelly felt the warmth of his chest behind her.

"Th-thank—" She stopped, cleared her throat. "Thank you," she managed coolly. "Now if you don't mind—"

He paid no attention, opening his fingers and studying the map.

"I've g-got work to do, Commander."

"So do I, Professor."

As he spoke Kelly felt his thigh slide across her hip. She swayed, lost in sensation, feeling for a moment as if someone had pulled the ground out from under her.

Suddenly Burke's gloved fingers settled at one corner of the map. "What's this?"

"What's w-what?" *Great. Now my speech is going.*

"This blue network of lines." Burke pointed to the upper corner of the map.

"That is a narrow, diffuse limestone stream-bed. Shale underlayer, most likely. The limestone layer begins mid-stream, then branches east off Draycott property." There. She'd managed to sound halfway competent at least.

"Anything that matches the soil samples from the sword fittings?"

"Close but nothing conclusive, I'm afraid."

Abruptly his fingers tensed. "Wait a minute—did you say there was a shale layer beneath the limestone? If so, then the stream could be fairly unstable, couldn't it?"

Almost as unstable as my pulse right now, Kelly thought wildly. "If there were an earthquake, yes. Even some sort of focused tremor might make the stream change its course. Why?"

"That's almost at Edgehill," Burke said slowly.

"Edgehill?"

"My estate. We border Draycott to the north." He studied her, his expression unreadable. "Maybe you'd like to visit. We have our fair share of ruins on the other side of Lyon's Leap, you know."

Kelly blinked.

My estate. How easily the words rolled off his tongue. But to Kelly there was nothing smooth about them. To her they stood for a million miles of separation, uncrossable miles forged of years of wealth and privilege and birth.

Lord Burke. My estate. They might as well have been born in two different times.

The sooner she got that worked into her thick head, the better.

"I'm sure it's lovely, Lord Burke, but I'm afraid I won't have time. Unless I hurry, I'm going to lose my shot at that sword."

Michael's eyes narrowed. "Would that bother you a great deal, Red? If you lost your shot at this sword?"

Kelly nodded, her jaw tense. It wasn't entirely true, of course. She was beginning to think that spending time with Michael Burke was more important than finding the sword or Miles's urn.

And that kind of vulnerability scared her speechless.

"I see."

"I'm glad."

"*Hmmm.*" They were so close that the low murmur started at his chest and crossed right up her spine. The sensation made Kelly shiver.

Burke frowned. "Cold, Red?"

"Not in the slightest. But I *would* like to finish here."

Burke started to say something, then tensed. A moment later Kelly heard the low hum of a motor.

"That must be the Land Rover. Let's gather the rest of this stuff and get you out of here." With a fluid economy of motion, the Englishman gathered up the contents of Marston's hamper, caught the last of Kelly's maps, and then slung them under one arm. "I'll admit one thing. You've lasted longer than I thought you would. But now it's over. You're going to the village and catching the next train to London. Maybe when these 'accidents' stop you can come back and try again," he said flatly.

Kelly had different ideas.

The man in the Land Rover looked tired and worried. As they jolted back to the abbey, he and Burke spoke only a few words—due to Kelly's presence, no doubt—but the tension in the air was unmistakable.

Outside the gate house, Burke strode off to pick up her suitcase and stow it in the back of the Land Rover. Then he turned away to speak with the other man.

They appeared to be arguing.

Kelly inched closer, trying to listen. A few moments later she was sorry she had.

The intruder had slipped past their net and disappeared somewhere to the north of the cliffs. Burke was furious. He jerked out the receiver and told someone on the other end exactly what he thought about his ineptness. Since he was staring at Kelly as he said this, Kelly knew she was the next topic of conversation.

She was right.

"The woman goes, Ross. She's not trained for this, damn it. She'll only be in the way. And I bloody well can't guarantee to protect her if you can't keep the area secure."

Kelly couldn't make out the specifics of the other man's answer. All she could read was the fury that hardened Burke's features as he listened. A moment later he jammed the receiver back into his pocket and stalked around to the driver's seat.

"It looks like you've got friends in high places, Red. But this isn't over, not by a longshot. I'm going to get you out of here if it's the last thing I do."

He drove fast but well. Kelly found her eyes drawn often to the strong fingers on the wheel, easing the Land Rover over bumpy roads and past century-old stone walls.

Moody. Unpredictable. She pondered the description in the file that Miles had given her. The words fit, of course. But there was far more to the man than that. The folder hadn't mentioned that he was also intense and scrupulous about doing whatever he considered to be his duty.

"Do you want to know how it happened?"

"I beg your pardon?"

"Those scars you saw last night." He gave her a searching look. "It was a car accident. Petrol ignited. I was trying to drag someone out. A woman."

Kelly blanched, seeing the scene all too clearly. The flames, the scorching wall of heat. The fear and the rage.

Most of all the pain . . .

"Did you . . . succeed?"

"No." It was a dead sound. "And that's why I want you to leave. Innocent people tend to get hurt when they're around me, and my conscience is just about as full as it can get."

Kelly heard the guilt that tightened his voice. "Who was she?"

"She was going to be my wife. Only we never made it that far."

"And you think it was your fault."

Burke downshifted sharply and took a turn that left gravel spinning. "No." He scowled over the wheel. "I *know* it was."

"Accidents happen, Commander."

"In my line of work, Miss Hamilton, even the accidents aren't accidents. Now they're happening here." He looked across at her. "Frankly, that scares the hell out of me."

She appreciated his honesty, especially since she knew it cost him to admit a thing like that. "You love this place, don't you? Just like Marston."

"I suppose I do. Only natural, considering that I almost grew up here." His jaw tightened. "I owe it to Nicholas Draycott to see that the abbey is kept safe." His brow crooked as he saw her staring at him. "What now?"

"I was just thinking about the abbey. How beautiful it is. And how I get the strange sense that it has a life and a will of its own."

"So you've felt that, have you?" Burke nodded slowly. "It's always affected me that way, too. You seem to have a pretty keen intuition, Red."

Kelly shrugged.

"Don't want to talk about it?"

"No."

He slowed the Land Rover just before fields gave way to neat stone fences and cobblestoned streets. From beneath his seat he pulled a canteen, which he used to douse a strip of linen. Frowning, he bent close and cleaned Kelly's forehead.

The gentleness of his movements made her breath catch.

"Better?" His voice was low—and far too close.

Kelly had trouble meeting his eyes. "Much." She swallowed and tried to move away, only to feel the tense curve of Burke's fingers on her shoulder.

"Do you have these 'accidents' often?"

Kelly shrugged, not trusting herself to speak.

"What if I told you I'd done some checking of my own, Professor? I know that you work too hard and your students love you. Also that you studied in England but left abruptly. Tell me why."

His eyes were iron gray flecked with veins of amber. They reminded Kelly of the sword she was searching for, a thing of power and great beauty. But like the sword, they carried an element of danger.

She looked away, concentrating on a row of finely preserved Georgian houses set around a neat village green. "No."

"I'm going to find out. It's merely a matter of time."

"Why does it matter? You said I'm not staying."

"I said I *want* you to leave. I'm not sure I have enough power to make it happen. That's why I want to know about that gap in your past."

"You're welcome to search, Commander."

Burke's hands tightened on the wheel. "Oh, you can count on my doing just that."

It was a nice little town, Kelly thought as Burke maneuvered around several farm trucks, past a row of Georgian town houses, and down a narrow cobblestone lane. The streets held a sprinkling of people this sunny afternoon, but none of them seemed in any particular hurry. Nor did they seem overly curious about anyone around them.

Long Milton. Yes, a cozy place, she decided. The sort of place where people respected each other's privacy.

"He's parked *where*?" The wife of Long Milton's baker stood before the library's bay window, staring at the town librarian.

"Outside the Crown. In that battered Land Rover of his. With a *female*." The last word was pronounced with dramatic emphasis.

"A real looker, is she? All chichi like?"

"Couldn't see her proper."

"It's been far too long since the lad's come into the village." Maryanne Jervis, the baker's wife, had strong feelings on the subject. "It's good for business, don't y'know? Brings publicity for Long Milton. Gives the place cachet like." She pronounced the "t" firmly. "I think we should do all we can to see he comes back soon."

"I don't think his lordship will like it, Maryanne." The librarian shook her head. "The man doesn't care for people meddling in his affairs."

"Rubbish! I've known his lordship since he was in small clothes. He won't see it as meddling. Now hurry along. We need to have a word with Bess over at the Crown before he gets there."

"*We*?" her friend said faintly.

"We," Maryanne said firmly, moving off toward the local pub.

Down the street the village postman slowed his steps and tipped his hat to the owner of Long Milton's only seafood shop. "Just like I told you. Parked outside the Crown, he is. And with an American! Can you credit that?"

"American?" There was a note of awe in the shopkeeper's voice. "Haven't had a Yank in the pub since—oh, the far side of six months. Now what would an American be wanting with—"

"It's not the pub she's interested in, lackwit! It's *him*. Our lordship. About time someone pinned him down, that's what I say. Maybe this'll keep him closer to home in future."

"I don't know. Since his father's died, Lord Burke hasn't seemed much interested in Edgehill. Besides, he's always seemed an independent sort."

The postman gave his friend a knowing smile. "That's what they *all* seem like, Wilson, my boy. But only until the female of the species gets at 'em." He turned and headed for the Crown. "I feel in the mood for a pint. You coming?"

Chapter 15

*T*he Crown was Kelly's perfect idea of a tradi-
tional English pub.

Ivy curled about the latticed windows and
cobblestones covered the courtyard. A plump
ginger cat with five squirming kittens sat nap-
ping on the windowsill beneath a weathered
pub sign.

Peace. Confound it, there it was again . . .

"Why are we stopping here?"

"I've got to meet someone." Michael studied
a man in very new looking tweeds and nodded
faintly. "Come on," he ordered.

"Aye, aye, Sergeant," she snapped as Michael
led the way into the pub. "Next you'll tell me
I'm supposed to play a game of darts while I
wait."

"Darts? Don't even whisper such heresy. This
is Sussex, girl! We play frog-in-the-hole here!"

"Frog-in-the-hole? I'm afraid even to ask."

As Burke took her elbow and steered her into
the shadowed pub, Kelly felt two dozen pairs of
eyes swing about and lock onto her face.

The conversations did not still, nor did anyone

move, but Kelly felt their curiosity like a physical probing.

A plump woman with hair an improbable shade of bluish-gray hailed Burke from behind the counter. "Is that yourself, Lord Burke? Why, it's been five years if it's a day. Bless me, I'm surprised I still recognize you!"

"That long is it, Bess?"

The woman's green eyes twinkled. "No matter. Just see you don't stay away so long next time. You know I always keep a tankard for you here at the Crown. So what will it be, your lordship?"

"Once was quite enough, Bess."

"Ah, well, in that case, Michael it is."

"Much better. I'll have a pint of Dogbolter, thanks."

"What about for you, love?" The woman smiled expectantly at Kelly. "Mild, bitter, strong ale, or stout?"

"I haven't the slightest idea," Kelly said faintly. "I take it Dogbolter wouldn't do?"

The woman laughed. "Not for *you*, love. It's got a bit of a bite, you understand."

Burke laughed. "An understatement if I've ever heard one. Better give her some of your Sussex Mild, Bess."

"So I will, your lor—er, Michael."

Burke steered Kelly to an alcove booth facing the street. They edged past friends and neighbors Michael had known since birth, sharing a few words, but never stopping for long.

"Is it always this crowded?" Kelly whispered, after bumping over five sets of knees and finally managing to wedge into the booth.

"Not usually," Burke said thoughtfully. He nodded to the mayor, who stood nursing a pint at the counter. Beside the mayor stood the postman, the baker, and the owner of the Long Milton seafood store.

Burke frowned as the realization dawned.

Most of Long Milton was crowded inside the pub at this moment and now Burke knew why. They were waiting to get a glimpse of the first woman he'd ever brought to the Crown.

He wasn't sure whether to smile or curse.

A moment later Bess returned, tray and ale in hand. "Have you ever been to Long Milton before, my dear?"

Kelly shook her head. "I've not been so lucky, I'm afraid."

"Ah, now here's a lady who knows the good things in life, Michael, my boy. But you must understand that we're not to be confused with any of the other Miltons, Miss Hamilton. No matter what you hear about Upper Milton, Little Milton, Milton-in-the-Vale, and Milton-upon-Trent, not a one of them can compare with Long Milton, I assure you."

Burke winked at Kelly. "She's pulling your leg. She considers you fair game because you're an American."

"So I gathered." Kelly's eyes twinkled. "I expect it was hard when you heard that you'd lost the Colonies?"

"Lost the Colonies? When?" Bess's eyes rounded. "Bless me, I've got a son in Virginia and a nephew in Dallas. If we'd lost the war, believe me, they'd have told me." She winked at Kelly. "I hear we've had a spot of trouble collecting taxes on that last shipment of tea, though."

Kelly nodded gravely. "So I've heard. And George III's not doing too well these days either."

Bess smiled at Burke over Kelly's head. "I like this one, Michael. Got a sense of humor, she has."

"Yes, she quite does, doesn't she?"

Abruptly Bess clapped her big, capable hands together. "But what am I about? You two must be fair to famished. My Tom's just taking the sticky buns from the oven. They always were your favorite, Michael. Unless your tastes have gone all refined and sophisticated these days?"

Kelly had the sense that the woman was questioning things much deeper than Burke's taste in food.

Michael sat back slowly. "I don't believe they have, Bess."

"I'm plenty glad to hear it, lad."

After she bustled off, Burke drained his glass and stood up. "I'll be back shortly. I'd prefer if you stayed inside until I get back. Just in case."

Just in case.

Kelly thought about the clump of leaves in the thermos and the intruder who had escaped Burke's net. She looked around at the smiling faces in the pub. Any one of them could have come up from the abbey just before she and Michael arrived.

She looked up at Burke and nodded. "I'll stay."

Inspector Ross was waiting for Burke in a large room at the George Inn, which the service had taken over until the urn was found.

Tall and sixty-ish, Gerald Ross looked like the queen's equerry and in fact was the equerry's brother. He was just putting down the telephone when Burke strode in.

He nodded at the receiver. "That was the prince of Wales. Just checking on the status of the sword." Ross said a few carefully chosen oaths and waved Burke to a seat. "Tell me more about the intruder at the abbey this morning."

"Nothing to tell. He managed to get away, damn him. But not before he tried to poison Kelly. Don't you see that this changes everything? We're obviously dealing with a professional here. How can I keep this woman safe?"

Ross smiled faintly. "In my considered opinion, Commander, the very safest place that Miss Hamilton can be right now is next to you."

"I'm good but I'm not that good, Ross. Especially when the woman's too headstrong by half and hasn't any idea of the danger she's running."

"You certainly don't expect me to tell her, do you?" Ross steepled his fingers. "She was chosen by our American counterparts because of her skill and familiarity with this period and the Sussex area. Professor Bullock-Powell backed up their choice. But the Americans assured me that the woman would be told nothing about the sword's connection to Trang's urn."

"So she thinks she's out on your average, everyday archeological dig." Burke shook his head. "Not exactly sporting, Ross."

"That's what *you're* here for, my boy. To keep an eye on her so that she can finish her work. Now go and do it. Unless you want me to pull the plug on the whole thing and send in the demolition boys to find the urn."

"You can't," Burke growled. "They'd have Draycott's fields plowed up and the abbey in pieces inside of a day."

"Yes, they do tend to be untidy," Ross said coolly. "On the other hand, they are quite efficient."

"I'll stay," Burke snapped. "But have some more men posted around Lyon's Leap. There's a limestone ridge running through there and it might just be the source of those soil samples. I doubt it's an accident that the intruder was seen in that area." Burke frowned at Ross. "Anything more on why Miss Hamilton left England five years ago?"

Ross stared at Burke over steepled fingers. "She was in an accident at a site in Norfolk. She was working with Professor Bullock-Powell at the time. His son found her lying unconscious." Ross's eyes narrowed. "Nasty concussion. Four broken ribs. She was in a coma for two months, I believe."

Burke took a slow breath, thinking about that kind of pain. It was a pain he knew from firsthand experience. "What happened then?"

"She left the hospital and went back to the States. A year later she was finishing an advanced program at Harvard. Two years later she was teaching in Arizona."

Burke frowned. Why hadn't she wanted him to know about the accident? Was she just an intensely private person or did it have some other significance?

He pushed to his feet. "Keep digging, Ross." As he walked back toward the Crown, Burke prayed that it wouldn't be another dead end.

Two counties away Professor Bullock-Powell stood staring at the chaos of his work room.

Books were shredded, tables dumped, and priceless artifacts scattered everywhere over the wooden floor. Every drawer had been opened and overturned.

Fifty years of meticulous research now lay strewn about the room like so much flotsam in a storm's wake.

The old man pulled the crumpled fragment of an Anglo-Saxon helmet from beneath a pile of papers, his eyes blurring. Who would *do* such a thing? His books and accession notes had value only to a fellow academic, while the antiquities he kept here would be instantly traceable, hence of little cash value in the black market that traded in such things.

The scholar stood up slowly, his legs unsteady. He couldn't even say for sure what had been taken, not until he'd brought some order to the place.

He ran a hand across his forehead and sighed. They'd even taken the box with his excavation records and field notes. Dear Lord, how could he begin to replace that kind of information? For years his assistant had been badgering him to make a computer transcription, but the old scholar had resisted. Computers made him nervous, he'd said glibly.

Now he wished he'd paid more attention.

At least the ancient Norman shield was untouched. He drew the teardrop-shaped artifact reverently from its case and studied the wood and leather face. Thank heavens they hadn't gotten *this*. The shield had fascinated him ever since he'd discovered it forty-five years before in a quiet Sussex valley. It was an exquisite artifact, but to him it had always felt like something more.

It felt as if it had been shaped to fit his own hand—almost as if it had once belonged to him.

But that was impossible, of course. This particular shield was centuries old and might have been carried on Senlac Hill at the Battle of Hastings itself.

Muttering, he laid the shield carefully back in its case. Even then the uneasiness did not leave him. With it came a sense of guilt for some task contracted for but never finished.

He stared at his office. In addition to the chaos to be sorted through, there were articles to finish, objects to be vetted for the museum. Scholarly requests to be answered.

But this guilt was different. It loomed from a mistake far more serious. He could never sense what, except that it seemed to have something to do with his former student, Kelly Hamilton.

And then he remembered the scabbard mount.

He ran to the neighboring room and unlocked the dusty cupboard he kept intending to replace with something more secure.

The velvet-lined box was lying just where he'd left it. Carefully he pulled it out and opened it.

The mount glittered golden in the sunlight, gilt bronze worked in an intricate filigree of animal motifs. He suspected the mount and the sword it belonged to were at least twelve hundred years old.

If she were very lucky indeed, Kelly might find the sword that belonged with this breathtaking ornament.

The old scholar slid the fragile piece away, imagining the beauty of such a set with scabbard and weapon restored. Men might well kill to possess such a prize. Probably they had done so already, as the sword passed down from generation to generation.

As for its owner, the professor had found very few records. The area where the mount was found had been held by a Norman knight named St. Vaux who had come to England with William of Normandy. The man was said to have carried a magnificent sword that had been in his family for generations. But the warrior appeared to have disappeared late in the eleventh century, and of his sword there was no further mention.

Hardly surprising, the professor thought. The country had been in turmoil after the conquest, with lands wrestled from one strong man to the next.

But the gleaming scabbard mount seemed to haunt the professor. It was important, somehow he sensed that. If only he could figure out why . . .

"Ready to go?"

Kelly looked up with a start. "Back already?" She sat before a plate carrying the outline of four sticky buns. "Bess said to tell you she'd wrap some up fresh for you. She wanted them to be nice and hot." Kelly crooked a brow. "Some sort of local *noblesse oblige*?"

"Absolutely. What value is a title if it can't get one warm sticky buns whenever one wishes?"

But Burke's expression was shuttered as he steered Kelly through the packed pub and out into the afternoon sunlight.

"From the look on your face, I'd guess that you were overruled, Commander Burke."

"Right again, Professor. It's left me in a bloody mood, I warn you. So let's get several things straight before we go back to the abbey. First of all, you're my responsibility now. While you're at Draycott Abbey you do what I tell you when I tell you."

Kelly didn't like the sound of that at all. "Maybe I don't want to be your responsibility, Commander. Maybe, just maybe, I can take care of myself."

Burke studied the cut on her forehead. "Like you did this morning at the ruins?"

"A few bruises." She shrugged. "I get more than that every day at a dig."

"Sorry, Miss Hamilton, but this is not your everyday dig. And while you're here you're my responsibility, whether you like it or not. That's what men do, don't you know? Protect women."

"You really are a throwback."

A faint smile played over Burke's mouth. "A throwback to what?"

Kelly shook her head. "That's what I'm still trying to figure out." Abruptly she had a vision of a warrior in chain mail and a crimson tunic. A man with eyes that had seen too much death and had known too little love. A man who could make a woman feel totally secure in the warm grip of his arms.

She pushed the thought away, shivering, as two carrot-headed boys came running over to Burke.

"Hey, Tommy, look who's here. It's the commander, it is! Halloooo, Com-mand-er!"

"Well now, who have we here? James Carrow, I see. And you too, Tommy. Why are you two hanging about the Crown?"

"Waiting for our da," the pair said in unison. "He stopped in for a pint."

The smaller boy, his cheeks covered with freckles, inched closer to Burke. "Begging your pardon, Commander, but would you tell us again about that raid in Malaysia? The time the helicopter stalled and you had to jump out under enemy fire."

Burke's face went very hard. "We'd better save that for another time, Jamie."

"Oh, *please*, Commander! We've got a bet laid on it, see? Tommy says you got wounded then, but I says no, that it was the next day, when they found you and dragged you back to—"

"Not now, Jamie."

"Aw, leave him alone, Jamie. Sorry, Commander. My brother don't mean nothing by it. You know how kids can be." Tommy Carrow, all of twelve, gave his brother a good-natured cuff on the arm. "Come on, silly. Can't you see the commander wants to be alone with his lady friend?"

Burke did not move as the two boys charged off down the street. "I'll go around and get the Rover," he said tightly, then disappeared around the corner.

Kelly's eyes locked on the hard line of Burke's back. Was he favoring his right leg slightly or did she merely imagine it? And what about the raid the boys had described? It was obviously a tale told and retold in the village. The tale of a local hero.

She was still thinking about what made a man show that kind of heroism when she heard the hiss of tires behind her. A car swung out of a cobbled alley into the half-shadows. The motor whined and then the car slammed between the narrow walls and shot out into the road.

Straight toward her.

Its grill was polished silver. Somehow Kelly couldn't take her eyes away from those gleaming lines. Not even when she heard the thud of tires crashing over the uneven cobblestones.

She was going to die. Here and now. Tossed off that shining black hood. She could taste death— *her* death—all around her.

That realization drove air back into her lungs and energy back into her shaking legs.

Gasping, she spun about. To her right stretched a row of narrow, half-timbered shops built out to the street. Then she saw the single window, opened to catch the afternoon breeze.

Kelly closed her eyes and plunged headlong through the fluttering curtains. Behind her came the roar of a motor. Something burned across her ankle.

A moment later a car exploded past her in a blur of black.

Chapter 16

*B*urke found Kelly shivering on the polished floor, her knees caught tight to her chest. Her white face only made the terror in her eyes more stark.

"Thank God," he muttered as he slid through the window and knelt beside her. "I heard a car. What happened?"

"The car." Kelly whispered the words. "Oh, God, Michael, it almost—"

"I'm here, Kelly. Right here." His arm circled her shoulders and he eased her against his chest. "It's over."

But it wasn't over, not for Kelly. Her heart was hammering and her knees were shaking worse than ever. "He—he came out of nowhere. He must have seen me, but he didn't even slow down."

"Don't, Kelly. It's over now." Burke eased a strand of russet hair from her forehead. "Probably two teenagers on some sort of lark. Try to forget it."

At that moment laughter echoed down the street. Burke cursed softly. "We'll have to go out the back way. Someone's coming." He pulled her to her feet. "Can you make it?"

Numbly, Kelly nodded. Somehow her feet moved and her body followed, but all the time her mind was a thousand miles away.

She realized she was very lucky to be alive.

What if she hadn't seen that window? What if next time there *wasn't* any window?

She stood motionless, feeling the hiss of the wind, smelling roses and mint from somewhere in the tiny backyard garden. Down the alley, gravel skittered over cobblestone.

Again she sensed danger closing in around her. "Kelly?"

She looked at Burke, finding it hard to focus. The sun slanted through his hair, casting up glints of blue and bronze amid the jet-black strands. His eyes were shadowed, tense with worry. His mouth—

Dear Lord, his mouth was hard. Full. She wondered what it would taste like against hers.

Slowly she ran one finger over Burke's upper lip.

He cursed softly. "I don't think this is a good idea, Red."

Kelly didn't hear. Her head slanted back. Her thumb eased along the hard line where his lips met.

"In fact," Burke continued hoarsely, "this is a bloody *bad* idea."

"I agree," she said numbly. "So w-what are you waiting for?"

For one unguarded moment heat swept through Burke's eyes. Even then he didn't move. "What is it about you, Red?" His voice thickened. "And God help me, what is it about *me*? Why do I want to break every rule in the book when I'm around you?"

Burke felt desire jolt through him at that moment, while her lips trembled. He'd been terrified before and he'd be terrified again, but it would never be as bad as the panic he'd felt when he saw the car rocket out of that alley.

Nor would he ever forget the sight of Kelly, white-faced and trembling on the wooden floor.

He'd been so *sure* he'd lost her . . .

His fingers slid over her spine. She felt like cool, clear water, like rain on a smooth spring lake, and Burke explored the currents of her, measured the secret flow of her, all in raw, aching silence.

Because Burke knew those same flows and currents. Only right now they were pulsing through his blood, screaming through his head.

Flooding into his heart. The heart he'd long thought impenetrable.

He'd almost lost her. Even now the thought left him shaken.

His fingers found the softness of her hip, eased open, guided her against him. He met trembling flesh and hunger as fierce as his own. When Kelly moaned, his breath caught with the ache of that sweet, yielding sound.

She was warm and soft and he wanted to feel her everywhere. Right now.

His hands were at the buttons of her sweater before he knew it. Two slid open. Her neck was bared. The soft curve of her breast spilled free, filling his fingers.

Kelly's head fell back. She closed her eyes and pressed closer.

With a low, inchoate groan, Burke bent forward and released the flimsy lace that bound her, molding one budded nipple with his lips.

She tasted like citron and damask roses. Desire overpowered him.

Her hands dug into his shoulders. "Michael, please—"

"Kelly—dear God, we can't do this."

But even as he said it, Burke couldn't keep his hands from cupping her hips and pulling her against him. From tonguing the rich, sweet curve of her breast.

When she shuddered, Burke felt the movement in every bone of his body.

It shocked him. Terrified him. Enflamed him.

He knew that he could take her, right then and there. Up against the weathered bricks, with nothing held back and no second thoughts. It would be swift and raw and inexpressibly good between them, now while the adrenaline and sour taste of death still throbbed through their veins.

Danger was the best aphrodisiac. Burke knew that well from his experiences in Turkey and Thailand—sometimes even in London.

But what happened afterwards, when their blood cooled and their pulses finally slowed? That Burke also knew. Afterward she would hate him for taking advantage of her vulnerability.

He couldn't chance it.

But sweet heaven, it wasn't going to be easy. He wanted her. He more than wanted her. His hands tensed, cupping her hips.

Vainly he fought to pull his eyes away from the naked curve of her breast and the thrust of her nipples.

Somewhere down the alley a door squeaked open. A cat gave a low, sad yowl.

Burke froze. He forced himself away from Kelly and drew a ragged breath.

What in the name of heaven was he doing?

He looked at her face, watching the russet lashes flutter against her cheeks. He looked at the satin skin framed by her open sweater.

They were in the middle of an alley, seconds away from total, blinding intimacy. Sweet God, what was he thinking of?

Slowly Burke reached down and tugged her sweater back in place. With unsteady fingers he began shoving the tiny buttons closed.

Her hair drifted around his hands, thwarting his progress, teasing him with scent and heat and softness.

With every touch, he tasted desire, raw and reckless as it had never been before. But now his desire was sharpened by an almost painful sense of protectiveness. Burke realized that the very last thing he wanted to do was hurt this woman, whom he sensed had been hurt too much.

If he stayed here a second longer, he feared he'd do just that.

He smoothed her sweater in place. "Come on, Kelly."

She blinked like a sleeper coming awake. "Where—are we going?"

"Home." Burke tugged off his suede jacket and slipped it around her shoulders. "Before I do anything else monumentally stupid."

His face was grim as he steered her to the mouth of the alley, where the Land Rover waited.

By the time they had reached the abbey, Kelly's mortification had set in with a vengeance.

His momentary slip had revealed his emotions precisely. He thought of his brief moment of contact with her as something *monumentally stupid.*

That realization left her with a storm of emotions that wavered between laughter, fury, and excruciating regret.

As soon as they came to a halt, Kelly jumped out and began searching blindly for her fallen maps. "Th-thanks for your help. I—I'd better be going. I've got maps to cover. Quadrants to check. Data to record . . ."

She was rambling, but she couldn't help it. How *could* she have been such a fool to fall apart like that? Being afraid, even being hysterical, was one thing, but turning to putty in Michael Burke's arms was utterly inexcusable.

Burke stood behind her. "It's not settled, Kelly. Not nearly." His hands opened over her forearms. He caught her gently and turned her resistant body around to face him.

Their thighs brushed. His breath feathered over her cheeks.

Abruptly Kelly felt the telltale hardness at his groin.

She felt as if the earth had just gone seismic beneath her feet. "W-what are you doing?"

"I'm telling you something important. And I'm showing you, too. Because the truth is that I want you badly. I've wanted you since the first second I laid eyes on you. And that kind of truth seems damned important right now, Kelly. Maybe because I nearly lost you in that alley. Or maybe because I haven't shared the truth enough with the people I . . . care about."

The people he cared about? Kelly caught a ragged breath. "Oh," she said weakly.

Burke's naked fingers slid down and opened

over hers. " 'Oh.' Is that all you're going to say, Red? How about something more concrete, like *'I hate you.'* Or *'Thank you.'* Or *'Get lost, Englishman.'* " His eyes were strangely vulnerable. "Right now anything would be preferable to 'Oh.' "

"Th-thank you," she said weakly. *I care about you, too,* she added mutely. But she wasn't about to say it aloud. Other men had taught her that vulnerability was to be hidden at all costs.

It was a lesson she'd never forget.

Burke studied her face. "Concrete, but still not what I was hoping to hear."

"I could have said *'I hate you.'* "

Burke's lips quirked. "I guess I'll give up while I'm ahead. But from now on when you go out, I go out with you. And at night you sleep in my room, where I can keep an eye on you."

Kelly's heart did a jerky little dance. "No way. That's a very bad idea."

His eyes were flint-dark, uncompromising. "Right now, I'm half inclined to agree with you. But I'm damned well going to keep you safe, even if it makes you uncomfortable."

Uncomfortable? The word didn't begin to describe what she was feeling.

Run, the tiny part of Kelly's brain that was still logical screamed. *Flee. Disappear.*

Her eyes met his. She seemed to zoom into freefall, drowning in hunger and gray-gold heat.

Run? How could she? Her knees were roughly the consistency of half-cooked marshmallows. "No problem. We're going to act like two mature, responsible people, of course. W-we're going to do our jobs like sensible professionals. How hard can it be?"

"Painfully hard," Burke said grimly. "In fact,

I'm beginning to learn new meanings for the word."

Kelly felt the heat of his body and realized he was talking about something much more specific than their situation.

Her face took on a wash of color.

"Right again, Professor," Burke said hoarsely. "Which leaves us no better off than before."

Kelly's chin rose. "We are two mature adults, Commander. We are quite capable of respecting each other's privacy. I am sure we will be able to reach a satisfactory working arrangement."

"Kelly?"

Looking at Burke's dark smile, Kelly felt a moment of misgiving. "Yes?"

"I've never reached a nice working arrangement with *anyone*," Burke said softly. "And I doubt that I'm going to start today. Especially not with a woman who is as stubborn and smart and damnably desirable as *you* are." Then he grated something not nearly so polite. "Now let's go inside and get you cleaned up before Marston suffers a cardiac arrest."

The sun spilled beyond the woods in a glory of gold and crimson.

Slowly darkness settled over the abbey's weathered walls. Somewhere in the distance a bell began to chime.

Twelve times, and then once more.

As the last peal receded, fog crept from the valley and inched toward the sleeping abbey, white tendrils outstretched like ghostly fingers.

Kelly did not see, caught in restless dreams. Nor did Burke see, where he sat before the library fire, nursing a whiskey that offered burn but no warmth.

Only the great gray cat noticed, his amber eyes turned to the night. Beside him a black-clad figure turned to pace the lonely parapets, brow furrowed, lost in thought.

Chapter 17

Sleep was not going to come fast, Burke thought grimly. *If* it came at all, which he doubted.

Not with Kelly Hamilton lying four feet away, clad in a wisp of nothing that didn't hide a single sleek curve from his heated imagination.

He cursed silently and swung to his side, trying to find a position that wouldn't irritate his throbbing hip.

He didn't find one.

And the other pain wasn't helping either. Like a hot sweet cloud, it played through his blood, stirring fantasies he hadn't known in years. And *she* was in every one of them.

Grimly, Burke twisted to his other side and pounded his pillow into a wad beneath his head, reviewing the cause of his insomnia.

First he had offered her the bed. God knows, he'd slept on things a lot worse than an over-stuffed sofa.

But the American was having none of it. She had frowned, then disappeared into the adjoining bathroom, returning a few minutes later draped in a lacy thing that did nothing to cool Burke's overheated body but did *everything* for the perfect curves betrayed by the soft satin.

Burke had cursed softly and headed for the bed. Anything to erase the memory of those sweet shadows of breast and thigh that were driving him slowly insane.

She could take the couch, Burke conceded hoarsely, wanting her under the covers and out of his line of vision as soon as possible.

Then, having gotten the couch, she wanted the curtains open.

He wanted them closed. Just in case someone with an infrared scope tried something clever. He hadn't told her that, of course. Instead he claimed he never slept with the curtains open.

They had argued over that one for a full five minutes. This time Burke was adamant and Kelly had finally conceded.

Or at least he thought she had.

But now Kelly sat up slowly, frowning at him from the sofa. He heard the rustle of linen and satin. "I—I wish you could leave it open. I don't like sleeping in the dark." She said the words very softly.

Burke stared at the dark shadow of her hair on the pillow, at the pale oval of her face. He forced his voice to be casual. "Care to be more specific about that, Red?"

"No." She twisted away. "I don't."

Burke studied the stiff line of her back, wondering what was behind that revealing admission. Wondering everything there was to know about Kelly Hamilton.

"You can tell me about it, you know."

Silence. And then, very soft, "Not about this, I can't."

Burke cursed softly. She was a woman with too many questions about her, none of which she wanted to answer. Meanwhile, the window had to be closed. "It's a question of security, Kelly. With this open neither of us will be safe. But I suppose a candle wouldn't do any harm." Moments later a soft glow filled the room. Burke eased back on the bed.

More rustling of linens. "It's . . . because someone out there might have a gun, isn't it? One of those laser things you mentioned before."

She was sharp, Burke thought. Maybe she was too sharp for her own good. "That's one of the reasons," he said guardedly.

"I . . . understand."

"Sorry, Red," he said flatly. He lay that way a long time, hands behind his head, watching shadows from the candle flicker over the wall.

When he turned back, Kelly was asleep.

Or at least he thought she was. Then she pushed to one elbow, her eyes dark and slumberous.

"Michael?" she murmured sleepily, hugging the lavender-scented pillow to her chest.

"What, Red?"

"Why do you do this kind of work if you dislike it so much?"

Once again she got right to the heart of things. Burke laughed grimly, trying to hide his discomfiture. "Is it so bloody obvious?"

"Not to everyone. To me, yes. Maybe because sometimes I don't like all the things I have to do either."

Burke started to ask what there was not to like about digging up old pots and dusty bones and priceless swords, but he decided not to. He wasn't up to a deep philosophical discussion right now.

"Go to sleep, Professor. I'll tell you some other time. Sometime when I'm not so—" *Unsettled by your beauty. So reckless with wanting to take you into my arms and show you how paradise feels.*

"So tired," he finished hoarsely.

Silence. But not for long.

"I'm *not*, you know. Crazy, I mean."

His dry chuckle filled the silence, surprising them both. "I never thought you were, Red. That *I* was, maybe, but never you. Now *go to sleep.*"

With a final, sleepy smile, she did just that.

But just as Michael had feared, *he* was far longer in finding the same comfort.

He watched the abbey lights go out one by one. No one could see him here, not even the clever officers ringing Draycott's fertile hills. As usual they overestimated their talents. Since they could see no one, they were certain that no one could see them.

But they were wrong. He could see their every move from his hideaway. With his infrared sight he knew when they fanned out and when they stopped for tea from their thermoses and when they changed shift. By now he even knew half their names.

Yes, he was wonderfully efficient. He'd always been that way. Except when he heard the voices and his head began to ache. It had happened that morning when they'd nearly caught him.

Now the voices were coming again.

Cursing softly, he inched back into his hideaway. The pain was near. Already he could feel it. With every heartbeat the darkness rose inside him.

He shuddered, locking his fingers against his head and his back against the cold stone alcove, trying to make the voices stop.

Finally he won. The pain began to recede. But by the time it was over, his fingers were shaking and he was covered with sweat.

Up on the hill a faint glow emanated from one of the abbey's windows. He stared at it, hatred burning in his eyes, and thought of how he'd make them pay.

Particularly the woman.

Chapter 18

*K*elly dreamed of wood smoke and roses that night. Tossing on the sofa, she saw thatched huts and herbs steaming in a great iron cauldron. She saw eyes that followed her from faces filled with anger and distrust.

Most of all, she saw a grim-faced Norman warrior and a red-haired Saxon beauty—a beauty who felt like *her*.

After the poison had been expelled from Hugh's body, he grew stronger by the hour. He was still weak, but his skin was slowly regaining its ruddy hue. And his appetite, always before like that of a bear, had returned with a vengeance.

Aislann despaired of keeping him well when he ate to such excess.

She was scolding him roundly one morning after watching him drain three bowls of herb and partridge stew. "Enough, my lord! Any more and you'll sicken from surfeit."

"Nay, my appetite has been too long denied. Do you not know that a man begins to sicken when he is not given what he needs most?"

Aislann tried hard to suppress a grin, for the man was a rascal and no mistake. His body was crossed with scars, but he had a kind heart. During the course of his illness she'd come to care for him sincerely.

They were bent close over the bed, Aislann fighting for control of a warm loaf of bread that Hugh was threatening to consume whole, when a sound from the threshold caught them up short.

Perhaps it was surprise that made Aislann look guilty.

Perhaps it was the shock of seeing Lyon's eyes, black with fury, his face iron-hard.

"Stand back from the wench, Hugh!" As St. Vaux stalked closer, he slid his sword from its scabbard. Sunlight glinted off the bright forged blade.

"Lyon? What are you doing?"

"Enough, Aislann. Get back from him or I'll have his head from his neck where he lies!"

"Are you mad? We were just—"

"I can see well enough what you were doing. Hugh's reputation with women is well earned."

At this, the wounded knight shoved awkwardly to his feet, dressed only in a loose tunic. "Lyon, what maggot has worked its way into your brain now? The woman was only trying to keep me from consuming any more of that fine bread she's been all morning at making in the kitchens." Abruptly his eyes narrowed. He saw the fury that gripped his friend's frame. "Ah," he said slowly. "I see. So it is true."

Aislann turned, frowning. "What is true? I don't understand—"

"Enough!" Lyon roared. "Take your garments and be gone, FitzRolland. You're obviously fit enough to be about an honest day's work. You'll not lie about wasting your strength tossing up maidens' skirts."

*Hugh caught up his cloak slowly. As he came abreast
of his friend and lord, he stopped. "You're wrong, you
know. Utterly wrong."*

"Go!" Lyon roared.

*Hugh trod angrily from the room. Silence fell over
the solar. A mote of dust danced across the floor and
floated about Aislann's skirts while sunlight glinted
off the blade still clenched in Lyon's fingers.*

*The Norman took a step closer. His point levelled
at Aislann's breast. "Did you find his body enticing,
Saxon? Did you hunger to hold him between your
white thighs? Perhaps your puny Aelfric does not
give you what you need."*

*Aislann's face flushed red with fury. "You toad!
You stinking—"*

*"Enough talk. I've seen your passion for Hugh.
Now I shall taste it for myself."*

"Not while I yet live!"

*His blade fell low. Flat-edged, it snagged her sash.
"Stop, Lyon. It was not what you think!"*

*Lyon jerked again, tugging the sash down her slen-
der waist. "FitzRolland was a notorious skirt-chaser
long ere he came to England, Saxon. Do not take it
as a mark of beauty, for he would have anything in
skirts. In a few more minutes you would have been
naked and panting. But now it's me you'll pant for,
Saxon. Me you'll spread your thighs to."*

*"Never!" Aislann cried. Grabbing up her skirts,
she shot for the door.*

*Lyon caught her halfway. He circled her waist,
hefted her high, and carried her to the bed. The next
moment he tossed her down and fell beside her.*

*His hands were at his chausses before he knew
it. Leather and wool went flying. A moment later
Aislann's skirts were shoved above her thrashing legs
and her undertunic torn cleanly in two.*

Her belly was flat, soft as silk, and her breasts pushed high in a curve of ivory and rose as she twisted beneath him.

Lyon felt lust pour like poisoned wine through his veins. It had been that way since the first second he'd set eyes upon her.

His manhood rose, hard and desperate. Desire screamed through him. Take her. Ride her and be done with it!

But Lyon could not forget her eyes.

Wild, they were. Haunted, with a blend of fury and fear. They caught him, held him, made him remember that he did not want her this way.

He wanted her smiling, laughing as he had seen her with Hugh only moments before.

In God's name, why had she never smiled or laughed with him that way?

"By St. Mary and St. Cuthbert, do you see what you've done to me, witch? Do you feel how my weakness for you invades my loins even now? Do you see how it drives me, so foul that it causes me to draw my sword upon my dearest friend and truest knight? What manner of witch are you?"

Aislann's face went white.

Lyon pulled away and knelt above her. Aislann forced her eyes away from him. "I am no witch!" she hissed. "I am only Aislann."

"Ah, but being Aislann might be dangerous enough," Lyon said, so softly she could barely hear him.

For a moment sadness swept his face.

Then, catching up his sword from the floor where he had dropped it, the Norman turned and strode from the room.

After that Aislann saw St. Vaux only seldom. He was careful to be out whenever it was time

*for her to walk to the kitchens for her meals or
see to some posset for Hugh.*

*She had moved to sleep with the other women
serving at the castle. Their looks had been harsh
with disapproval, Aislann noticed.*

*Sometimes she heard Lyon's thundered commands
or the heat of his anger vented on a knight
who had been slow to do his bidding. Otherwise, she saw almost nothing of the Norman lord.
Although Aislann knew it was for the best, it goaded
her.*

*But soon he would have to release her. There was
no possible reason for her to stay now that Hugh
was well enough to resume his duties. In fact,
Aislann wondered why Lyon had not sent her away
already.*

*The only reason for his delay was the one
she least wanted to face—that he was biding his
time until he would summon her to his bed.*

A spark popped in the fireplace. Silver light
poured through the room. Somewhere in the
night a bird cried shrilly.

Kelly lurched upright. Her eyes were filled
with panic. "Let me go!" Her hands twisted in
the air as she struggled with invisible foes that
moved only in her dreams.

At her soft moan, Burke lurched to his
feet, knocking over a chair and two stacks of
books in his haste to reach her. Smothering a
curse, he bent beside her and touched her face.
"Kelly?"

She continued to twist, her eyes fixed blind on
another place and time. "No—it wasn't like that.
You—you don't understand!"

"Hush, Kelly. It's a dream. Nothing but a bad
dream." Michael caught her thrashing hands and

pushed them to her chest, afraid she might harm herself.

Kelly tensed at his touch, her face going pale. "Stop! I won't, do you hear?" A ragged sound escaped her lips.

"Kelly? Damn it, what's wrong?" As he spoke, Burke slid a tangle of hair from her face.

Kelly shuddered. The wildness in her eyes began to fade. "Burke? Is that y-you?"

"No one else, Red." He slid down beside her and pulled her against his chest, easing his hands deep into her hair. "Want to tell me why you were screaming?"

"S-screaming?"

He gave her a wry smile. "Loud enough to wake the dead."

To wake the dead. Maybe he was closer than he knew, Kelly thought grimly. "I don't know. A . . . dream, I think."

She closed her eyes and reached out into the night, out into the drifting fog and the restless silence that danced just beyond the abbey's walls.

Nothing. And yet—*something* . . .

She gnawed her lip, trying to read the darkness and sift through the conflicting energy she read in the fog.

"These dreams come often, do they?"

"Often enough." Even now, Kelly felt the reality of that other world wash over her. It had all been wrenchingly real. The smells, the pain, even the fear. She still half-expected to hear Lyon's hard feet on the stairs and his shouts echoing through the hall.

But that was impossible.

It was nine hundred years since the Battle of

Hastings and centuries since the last Norman knight had been laid in his grave.

Which meant either that she was crazy or that somehow this beautiful, bizarre house was challenging laws of nature, space, and time, propelling her back into a world that had long since turned to dust.

And it appeared that Kelly had no control over how or when it happened.

She made a soft sound of protest at the thought. Frowning, Burke slid his thumb across her cheek.

Something hard and naked swam through his eyes. "You're afraid of me."

"No, you're wrong. It's just—" She drew a ragged breath and locked her hands. She had to make him understand that it wasn't him she was afraid of. "It's all these things that have been happening. I—I'm jumpy, that's all."

"I told you it was dangerous, damn it."

"So you did. I'm not blaming you."

Burke cursed softly. "No? Well I am, Red. I knew how things would be from the beginning. I should have gotten you out of here while I could." His hands slid through her hair. "Now it's too late."

"You couldn't get me out now even if you wanted to," Kelly said flatly. She thought about the dreams that felt like memories. No, she wasn't *about* to leave until she had her answers.

She studied Burke's hands, noting a fine line of scars across one wrist. Gently she ran her thumb across a faint silver mark. "What about you? This kind of thing must be old hat for you. And don't tell me you got those reading maps, Englishman."

"I didn't."

"So how did you get them?"

Burke didn't answer. He started to pull away, but Kelly's fingers tightened.

Suddenly she thought of her own body, bones shattered after her fall. The stitches had been neat and contained, but they were there, just the same.

She could feel them right now.

Maybe that was why she reacted the way she did. Maybe it was the effect of this strange, beautiful house, where love spilled everywhere like a shimmering golden mantle.

Or maybe it was the pain and regret she felt bleeding from Burke like a dark cloud.

Without thinking, she opened her hand, covering his wrist.

Burke stiffened. "Don't, Red."

"Why not?"

"Just—because."

Kelly's brow rose. "Afraid, Commander?"

Anger flared in his face. "Afraid? You're damned right I'm afraid. And *you* should be too. You don't know a single bloody thing about me."

Her head cocked. "Do I have reason to be afraid of you?"

Burke looked down. Her fingers were still curved around his hand. Somehow the sight seemed to fascinate him.

"I'm not sure," he said slowly.

Close to him like this, Kelly noticed that his eyes were alight with tiny specks of amber. Once again she thought of the Norman sword, buried in darkness, waiting to sing with light once more.

"*I* am." Her face was very serious. "You *are* a throwback, you know. You're a man of decision and honor. You do what's right first and ask questions later. Not politically correct in this day and age, but it has its appeal nonetheless."

Kelly moved, lifting her hand to the hard planes of his face. At the movement her gown slipped from her shoulder, revealing a curve of creamy skin and the shadow of one upthrust nipple.

Burke cursed softly.

He shoved to his feet, aroused muscle protesting every inch of the way. His control was slipping fast and he knew he had to get away before he did something they'd both regret.

But when he turned back Kelly was looking at him. Staring as if she couldn't stop. As if she were fascinated by the shape and texture of his mouth and every other part of his body.

"Don't, Kelly." His voice was harsh. "Don't look at me like that—like you want what I have to offer. Like you're feeling the same heat I am. Damn it, you'll only get hurt."

She gave an odd shake of her head. "Maybe I don't believe that, Michael. Maybe . . . maybe it wouldn't matter if I did."

She pulled him down to her.

He resisted for one microsecond, measuring her eyes. But all he saw reflected there was honesty and an awed sense of wonder. Finally, with a groan he let himself go.

He fell into the kiss, the way he'd been wanting to do ever since he'd seen her standing by the road to Draycott Abbey, bedraggled and angry and drop-dead gorgeous.

And what started as a kiss ended in a journey of texture and physical rebirth that took him deep as the ocean, far away as the steaming jungles of Thailand. He was reborn in the heat of her, in the sweetness of her body flowing over him like fine aged whiskey. She burned him—and left him thirstier than before.

He drove his fingers into her hair, his body on fire. His lips opened, hard and hungry, and he groaned out her name when her tongue answered, feathered hotly over his.

Born over. Suddenly young and yet achingly old. Capable of every feat of raw male strength but utterly vulnerable to her slightest touch.

"Michael." Her voice was slumberous, soft with passion. The sound sent sparks of desire jolting through muscles he couldn't even name.

"Kelly, don't. I can't do this. *We can't do this.*" His words ended in a groan. He bent closer to claim her mouth with lip and teeth. When his tongue slid over her, his hands shook.

And then, as he watched, she inched the silk from her shoulder until it hissed into a sensuous pool about her waist.

He was lost in the beauty of her, drowning in the honesty of what she was offering.

"Kelly, you don't have to—"

"I want you, Michael. Don't ask me to apologize or explain it. Right now I don't want to explain anything. I just want to feel your hands upon me, your mouth against me everywhere."

Burke cursed, laid low by a hot wave of desire. "Not this way, Kelly. Damn it, not now. Not while all the questions are still there. It's just adrenaline talking."

Kelly made a ragged sound of protest.

Burke caught her shoulders and crushed her to his chest. He felt as much as heard the wild little sound that escaped her lips. His fingers, almost of their own will, slid beneath the wild tangle of her russet hair and curved over her breast.

"Soft. Hot. God, Kelly, you're killing me."

"What if I don't care whether it's adrenaline I'm feeling? Just once, that's all I want. Just one kiss. What harm can there be in that?"

Burke knew exactly what harm. With the way he was feeling, one kiss would never be enough.

And then, while a bell pealed faintly somewhere out over the downs, Burke cursed and pulled away. The muscles outlined upon his locked arms told Kelly that it cost him a great deal.

Before she could tense or protest or turn away, he hushed her with his mouth. With the stroke of his strong hands on her neck. With the gossamer touch of his tongue on the needy crest of her breast.

Then he set her away from him. "It's the adrenaline, Red. Fear makes a person do crazy things."

Their eyes met. Kelly watched silver light play over the hard muscles at Burke's chest, unaware of the way that same light lit her own soft curves.

But Burke saw. He *felt* it until he wanted to shout with the pain of wanting her. "When it happens, I want it real between us. And I want just the two of us in this bed when we make love, not some specter lurking over your shoulder."

"One thing I'll say for you, you're smooth with your rejections, Englishman."

Burke answered with a laugh that was just as unsteady as her smile. "Hell no, Yank. That was no rejection. It was a definite 'some other time.' Because at any other time, Kelly, I'd be buried deep inside you right now and we'd both be halfway to heaven."

He frowned down at his hands. The scars shone

fine and silver in the moonlight. "But not tonight, Red. I've seen what adrenaline can do to a person. I know the way it turns you inside out, makes you think and do things you'd never consider when you were sane. I don't want that for you. For *us*. Do you understand, Kelly? I want this to be more than just a few hours of reckless pleasure. I don't want you to wake up and look at yourself in the mirror tomorrow, wishing it had never happened. Hating me because it did."

"I wouldn't—"

"Maybe not. But I'm bloody well not about to take the chance."

"Michael? What are you—"

"I'm taking you to bed," he growled. The next second Kelly was caught up in his arms and moving across the room. "And then, my brilliant, bullheaded beauty, we are *both* going to get some much needed rest."

True to his word, Burke put her down and chastely tugged the lavender-scented sheets over her shoulders.

In the sudden silence the room seemed very small. Very hot. Excruciatingly intimate.

And Burke's thoughts were anything but chaste.

When he lay down beside her, he was careful to keep a full six inches between them.

Just as he expected, the distance didn't do the slightest damned bit of good.

"We must help them, you know." The voice drifted for a moment, then focused near a dense tangle of crimson centifolia roses.

The eyes came first, then glowing cheeks, slender arms.

"Of course we must." This voice was deeper.

Very grim. It hovered over the moat and swept through the rustling leaves of the climbing roses that dotted Draycott Abbey's granite walls. "But how? And what in the name of heaven are we fighting?"

The next moment this voice, too, took shape. Adrian Draycott stared out at the drifting mist, his dark eyes snapping. "I've searched this whole castle and found nothing. But the vision came to me again last night. Her hand reached out. And God help me I could do nothing!"

The woman he had always loved moved closer, light sliding into shadow. "We'll just have to keep trying."

"Oh, that I mean to do, my heart." Adrian's voice hardened, tossed out over the windswept mist. "For I'll not have these ancient walls taken from me. I fought to build them. I fought to *hold* them." He shook his fist. "And hold them I always will!"

The figure beside him slid closer until their brightness mingled. The Draycott ghost turned, a crooked smile on his lips. "I am inclined to the grandiose, I fear. My apologies."

"But you are at your most magnificent then, I assure you, Adrian."

"You flatter me too well, my heart."

"I merely give you the truth."

"The truth?" He cupped her cheek. "The truth is that you manipulate me shamelessly."

"I . . . support you. Encourage you." Her eyes glinted. "*Adore* you."

"If only there were time for us to sample some of that . . . encouragement." Frowning, Adrian looked north to Lyon's Leap, where mist trailed over the cliffs that bounded Draycott's acres. "But there is no time. I hear her again, outside in the mist. I must help her find her way home."

"But how? And who *is* she?"

"No questions, my love," the figure beside her said grimly. Soon his shoulders were wreathed in light.

Chapter 19

W hen Kelly awoke, Burke was gone.

She ran her fingers slowly over his side of the bed. *Cold.* He'd been gone for some time.

And then she saw the note, tucked just beneath the edge of her pillow.

Take the day off, Red. If that sword has waited nine hundred years, it can wait a few days more.

I'll be back around mid-afternoon. Ask Marston to serve your lunch out on the terrace overlooking the moat. It's glorious this time of year.

He didn't sign it.

Then Kelly saw the P.S., slanting hard and angular across the back of the sheet.

By the way, I like that satin thing even more when you're inside it. Even though you do snore. Just a little.

Kelly flushed. Her hands went to the minuscule straps of fine silk that hugged her shoulders. Even now one of the straps slid low, exposing the smooth curve of her upper breast.

Heat shot through her as she remembered tossing restlessly and coming half awake in the night, only to feel his hard hand cupping her waist or his thigh straddling her leg.

Even now her skin carried the texture and scent of him.

Blast it, what was she doing? Muttering, she slipped on a white angora turtleneck and a soft floral challis skirt.

She had work to do. Whether Michael Burke liked it or not, she was going to do it.

It took Kelly a while to find the card Miles had left her. She frowned, turning the simple white sheet over and over in her fingers, thinking about his final counsel. "If you need anything, just call. Someone will find me, day or night. Remember, there's no need for you to go through this all alone."

The tension in her stomach grew.

She picked up the receiver and began to dial.

"And I'm going to need a more current geological breakdown of this part of Sussex. Something showing shale and limestone formations in particular."

"Already on its way. You should have it—" Kelly heard the rustling of papers. "Let's say before noon."

"Thanks, Miles. You're a lifesaver."

"You sure you're all right?"

Kelly rubbed the knotted muscles at her forehead, trying to ignore a gnawing sense of danger. "Of course," she lied smoothly. "But I'm afraid I haven't turned up anything definite about the—"

Miles cut her off. "I understand," he said curtly. "No need for details, Kelly. Not on an unsecured line."

An unsecured line. Kelly felt something cold dig

into her chest. Those three little words reminded her just how serious the task facing her was.

"I see."

"You *sure* you're all right, Kelly?"

She sighed, looking out at the roses clustered beside the moat. She thought about the intuition she'd had yesterday involving water. At first she'd thought the urn might be buried in the river or even in the moat. But the image might have been a clue to something entirely different, something that was connected with water or simply *near* water.

She couldn't be sure. And until she knew for certain what the image meant, Kelly decided not to mention it to Miles. "I'll manage."

"Kelly?"

"Still here."

"This man Burke. Is there anything—odd about him?"

"Odd in what way?" she asked carefully.

"Moody. Unpredictable. Anything."

Both descriptions fit the man, Kelly thought grimly. But for some reason she found herself reluctant to discuss Michael Burke with Miles. "Nothing in particular. Why?"

"The man has rather a nasty reputation, I'm afraid. I didn't know the extent of it before or I'd have told you sooner. It seems he's got quite a history of causing trouble. A while back there was some sort of problem over in Thailand. He took matters into his own hands rather than following orders. Nearly got everyone killed. He also ignored every rule in the book and got involved with the daughter of a high Colombian official. A woman he was supposed to be protecting. Very *personally* involved, if you know what I mean."

Kelly felt a raw burning in her stomach. Yes,

she knew exactly what Miles meant. Cooped up with Michael Burke, week after week, night after steamy night, what woman could *resist* getting personally involved, she thought bleakly.

"Kelly? Are you there?"

No, I'm dying, Miles. In bits and tiny pieces. And I'm hating myself for being too stupid to see what was happening until it was too late.

Kelly raised her chin. "I'm here, Miles. Anything else I ought to know about Mr. Big Bad Burke?"

"Only that he's a loose cannon. A lot of people were glad to see him put out of commission in the aftermath of that Colombian business."

"Is that where he got . . . the scars?" Kelly heard the words from a great distance, almost as if a complete stranger were talking.

Silence. "So you know about that." Another silence. "I hope you're not—well, that you're keeping your distance with this one, Kelly. Damn it, the man's *way* out of your league."

Kelly thought for a moment about the unsecured line, then decided that was Miles's problem. "Tell me how it happened, Miles."

Miles sighed. "He's gotten to you, hasn't he? I can hear it in your voice."

"Nothing I can't handle. Just tell me the rest."

"You're too stubborn for your own good sometimes, Hamilton. Okay, I'll tell you. But the case is still under investigation and you're to forget everything I'm about to tell you. Got that?"

She didn't. She hated all this secrecy. But she only nodded. "I hear, Miles. Loud and clear." So much for the unsecured line. Apparently only the urn demanded secrecy.

"It seems that the woman he'd been working

with in Colombia was spirited out of the country, possibly with Commander Burke's help. At any rate, she turned up in London about fourteen months ago, with a new name, a new face, a new identity. And she moved in with Burke."

Kelly went very still. Outside the window the roses blurred into streaks of red and orange. "Go on, Miles."

"She thought she was safe, but it turned out to be a mistake. A big mistake. Because people were still watching her. Very unpleasant people. One day Burke went out for an errand and she slipped down to leave a surprise for him in his car. That one little trip saved his life. She took the blast of the bomb that had been left there for Burke."

Pain. Clawing darkness. Kelly felt it engulf her.

"Kelly? You still there?"

"Go on."

Miles hesitated. "You sure you want to hear the rest?"

"Tell me."

"Burke tried to save her from the inferno. He was badly hurt and has been a long time recovering, so I hear."

Wrong, Kelly thought. *He's still not healed. He carries that guilt around with him every waking minute. He swims in it like a dark pool, and I see it clinging to him whenever I look at him. No, something like that wouldn't heal easily.* "Thanks for telling me, Miles," she said very carefully. Trying to ignore the tears streaking down her face.

"Are you *okay*, Hamilton? Because if you aren't, I'll have someone else sent over to—"

"I'm fine, Miles. Absolutely fine."

"Then stay that way. In the meantime, watch

out for Burke and just—oh, damn it, just *be careful.*"

Kelly picked up the undercurrent of fear in his voice. "Don't worry about me. I'll be fine, really. Talk to you soon."

She stood for a long time after Miles hung up, telephone in hand, staring out the window. Ignoring her tears, she watched a swan cut through the moat's glowing waters. The smooth silver wake drifted out and then spent itself against the dark banks of the moat.

"Miss Hamilton?"

She spun about, brushing at her cheeks. "Y-yes?"

It was the clean-faced officer who'd accompanied them back to the abbey in Burke's Land Rover. "These just came for you." He held out a cardboard cylinder.

Kelly made out Professor Bullock-Powell's ornate script. He had promised to send her anything he could find about this part of Sussex right after the conquest. "Thank you—er, I don't believe I know your name."

"Herrington, miss. James Herrington."

"Thank you, Mr. Herrington. By the way, have you seen Commander Burke today?"

"He was going to the northeastern part of the grounds to have a look at that limestone and shale streambed. Can I give him a message?"

"No, I'll do that myself, thank you."

"But you can't, miss. That is . . ." He rubbed his jaw, looking distinctly uncomfortable.

Kelly's brow rose. "And why can't I, Mr. Herrington?"

"The commander left strict orders that you were to stay here in the abbey, where it is safe. Until he returns, that is."

"Oh he did, did he?" Kelly shook her head at Burke's unalloyed arrogance. The man had an ego roughly the size of Montana. "Well, that won't be necessary, Mr. Herrington. Commander Burke wanted to have a look at these maps, too. I believe I'll just take them along to him myself," she added blithely.

"But Miss Hamilton—"

"Have a lovely day, Mr. Herrington."

Kelly didn't look back as she moved toward the door. She wasn't about to spend the rest of her stay at the abbey under house arrest! And the pang of guilt she felt at disobeying Burke's order soon vanished when she heard Herrington following her at a discreet distance.

Seated in his office five floors above Constitution Avenue, Miles O'Halloran was in the midst of what promised to be a lousy day.

He glared out at the rain-slick street.

He hated rain. It always left him edgy, reminding him of how badly they'd botched everything in Thailand the day Nicholas Draycott was rescued.

It had been raining then, too. Great gray sheets that banked in off the South China Sea and cut their visibility until they almost missed the tiny airstrip half-hidden by the jungle.

Damn the rain. It always agitated him and put him off stride. It also reminded him that the urn had slipped through their fingers again.

Frowning, he toyed with the paperweight beside his telephone, rethinking the conversation with Kelly. Things weren't going smoothly over there, he could hear it in her voice. There had been too many unexplained accidents. He had his ways of seeing the reports his British counterparts would have liked to deny him. He knew about the intruder who'd gotten away and the car that had nearly run Kelly down in Long Milton.

Cursing, he glanced up at the clock, calculating the time in southern England. He jerked up the phone and began to dial, only to replace the receiver mid-number.

This was hardly something to delegate to someone else. Not with Kelly already in place and weeks of planning completed.

Definitely not with a loose cannon like Michael Burke involved.

This time, little as he liked the risk of exposure, Miles would have to go over and sort things out himself.

He stared at the paperweight shoved to the side of his desk. It was just a silly little tourist trinket made of molded plastic and cheap silver paint, nothing that warranted a second glance. But something about it nagged at him.

For the first time Miles noticed it was a castle. A castle that had roughly the same proportions as Draycott Abbey.

He held it for a long time, turning it idly, thinking about rain and the urn and Kelly, before he finally put it down.

Kelly was dusty and parched by the time she saw the jagged line of pine trees bordering the lower edge of the stream. From the shadows came low gurgling. Even the sound made her feel cooler.

A thick layer of pine needles muffled her footsteps as she moved toward the river bank. Above her rose sheer granite walls topped by the gnarled roots of an ancient oak that dominated the crest of the cliffs.

It hit her then. She shuddered as she realized where she was standing.

Lyon's Leap.

The place where the ghost of a long-dead knight was said to ride on moonless nights. Kelly knew that knight. She had seen him in her dreams.

Now she began to feel the weight of the place, heavy with treachery and betrayal. It grew around her, whispering to her, tugging at memories. She reached out, trying to focus on the source of that dark betrayal.

But almost instantly some instinct made her draw back. Frowning, she told herself it didn't matter. Nothing should matter except finding Miles's urn.

Kelly pulled off her pack and let herself slide to the bottom of the hill, thinking about how good it would feel to strip off her shoes and dunk her feet in the stream.

Maybe even more than her feet.

And then she saw him.

She froze, pulse pounding, breath knotted in her throat. It couldn't be, but it was.

He was stretched across a sunny boulder, bronze knees to bronze chest, surveying the cool green river.

And there was no mistaking the fact that he was utterly naked.

Chapter 20

*H*er heart did a crazy dance.

What was ex-Royal Marine Commando Michael Burke doing stretched bare-bottomed plain as day by the river?

Kelly caught a ragged breath as he raked his wet hair back from his face. She watched the motion knot muscles along his calf and shoulder. She watched his chest ripple, dusted with dark hair that narrowed below, where he—

She jerked her gaze away, feeling her cheeks flush. She shouldn't be here. She *couldn't* be watching him like this. It was inexcusable. It was totally reprehensible.

And yet she couldn't turn away. Her feet, sinking into the damp mud by the river, might just as well have been trapped in cement.

She was still standing, frozen, when he came slowly to his feet. Kelly's face flamed as she saw the full sweep of his naked bronzed body.

It was the body of an athlete. Or a man who stayed alive by being faster and stronger than his attackers.

He strode to the edge of the river and paused, then eased to a crouch. Every motion was slow and deliberate.

Kelly realized it was pain that made him move so. With a dark fascination she watched as he scooped a handful of warm mud along his hip and outer thigh.

Kelly tasted his pain then, as deep and raw as if it were her own. When he lay back and let the warm mud do its work, she felt that too. Hands clasped behind his head, face turned to the sun, Burke found a sort of peace then and Kelly read every wave and stir of that peace as she stood with the wind ruffling her hair.

She realized then that she was seeing Burke as he really was, with all his pain bared and his fierce strength revealed.

A throwback all right.

Abruptly she went very still. She felt the brush of something faint and cold. Something too slight to be the wind.

And as she watched, the scene before her seemed to shimmer and blur. The trees darkened and the stream seemed to take a different course through the valley.

She stiffened, trying to fight the vision, trying to hold back the sounds and colors welling up out of some long distant past.

Her heart began to pound. Snatches of dreams danced through her mind.

Shouting.

Hoofbeats.

Voices heard in the night.

It was all waiting for her.

Breathless, she stumbled to her feet and clambered up the bank, raining gravel and pebbles down behind her. Tears were blurring her vision by the time she reached the top of the rocky bank.

But she wasn't fast enough. As she stumbled into the forest, the visions overtook her.

It was the third week since Aislann had come to the castle. The sky was clear and the air sweet with lavender and mint as she went out to fetch water from the little spring near the north wall of the bailey.

As she bent to the pool, Aislann heard a low whisper.

"Are you the one called Aislann?" A thin, sandy-haired boy with scrawny knees and a ragged tunic stood before her. "Are you she who tends the wounded knight?" the lad continued, after looking warily about.

Aislann nodded. "I am. Why do you seek me?"

"I carry a message for you. It comes from . . . Aelfric."

The name sent a prickle between Aislann's shoulders. It was a name she had sworn to honor and obey. The name of the man she was betrothed to.

A man she had never liked and certainly did not love.

She suppressed a shudder. "What has Aelfric to say to me?"

"He bids you wait for him at midday beyond the castle walls where the river curves north. He says to tell the Norman that you need more herbs. He can scarcely deny your request after the care you've given his best knight."

Aislann's eyes darkened. Again the orders, the cold commands, things she had hoped she'd escaped forever. Aelfric had been uncomfortable with her abilities and had turned from her, though never formally breaking their troth. Then he had fled north, refusing to pledge his fealty to St. Vaux.

She sighed. It appeared their parting was not to be so simple. "I—I have no time to see him." She turned to go, but the boy caught her hand.

"He says that your sister fares ill in the village. He says . . ." The boy looked away. "He says it will fare worse for her if you do not come as he orders."

Suddenly it was all so clear. Aislann saw exactly what would happen to her younger sister if she disobeyed the arrogant Saxon who was to be her husband.

"Very well. Tell Aelfric I shall be there. But I cannot vouch for the time, since I have no control over the Norman's wishes. He answers only to himself."

"I shall tell Aelfric." The boy went very still, studying her intently. "My lady?"

"Yes, little one?"

His answer came soft. "Go careful with Aelfric."

Aislann waited to approach Lyon. Only when he sat full from his meal, surrounded by seneschal, armorer, and bailiff, intent in conversation, did she steal forward into the great hall.

At first no one noticed her.

She cleared her throat and stepped closer.

St. Vaux looked up slowly. His eyes measured her from head to toe. "Yes, Saxon?"

"I would have your permission to go outside the gates, my lord. I require more herbs, you see."

Lyon's gaze was dark, unreadable. "And where might these herbs be found, Saxon?" From his tone, he could have been a complete stranger to her.

"By the deepest part of the river."

The other men fell silent. Aislann felt their gaze flicker from herself to Lyon.

They wonder what is between us, *she thought.* And they wish he will be rid of me before I bring any more trouble to the castle.

She could hear their thoughts as if they had spoken. So it was with her sometimes, though she had been careful to tell no one but her mother of her strange gift. She had found it safer not to speak of such things.

Now, looking at Lyon's granite face, Aislann tried to use her strange skill again.

And found nothing. His heart and mind were closed to her, locked and barred like the castle's great gate.

Still she knew she had picked her time well. St. Vaux could hardly refuse such a simple request, not when made in public like this. To refuse would have betrayed a weakness he could not allow himself to show.

The Norman knew that she had picked her time well, too. His fingers tensed upon the gleaming sword his armorer was showing him.

"So be it, wench. Go about your business. But be gone no more than one hour. Otherwise I shall assume that you have run away and I'll set my dogs upon you."

His tone was totally impersonal. A moment later he turned back to his armorer and began discussing the heft of his new sword, as if Aislann did not exist.

His treatment left her burning, furious. She would show this oafish Norman! She would stand for his arrogance no more than Aelfric's!

For answer she bent low, giving the Norman a deep and exaggerated curtsey. His men broke into low laughter at the sight.

But Lyon's bronze face showed no mark of humor. And the tension in his broad shoulders told her that she would pay dearly for that bit of impertinence upon her return.

*   *   *

She left the castle warily. Despite her fears she saw no one following her and began to think that Lyon must have taken her at her word.

She held her basket tensely as she moved off through fields heavy with oats and barley where villagers were busy at their work.

None approached her. None called her name. When she walked through the crowded fields, a pathway formed before her.

It was all done in silence.

And it was so utterly damning that it made Aislann's heart twist in her chest. But she only held her head up higher and clutched her basket close.

It had been bad before, of course. The villagers had always feared her. But since Aislann had come to the castle to tend Hugh FitzRolland, their hostility had grown far worse.

The river was but a short walk. A pair of jays chattered shrilly and dived over Aislann's head in a blue-white flash of wings as she topped the hill and made her way to the bank.

The reeds were thick here. Geese meandered in the shallows, paddling slowly, while an occasional carp jumped up and split the sunlit waters.

Many times Aislann had come here with her mother to gather herbs and learn the skills of her mother's people to the north. Exactly where that was, Aislann had never learned. Her father had been uncomfortable discussing how her mother had come to Sussex.

She had listened to everything her mother had to teach about flowers and petals carefully picked at the moment of greatest power, then dried carefully and well. Now her mother was dead, and

the flowers were all Aislann had to remember
her by.

Aislann sighed as she lifted her skirts and
waded into the water. Since she was here, she
might as well be about her task. In truth, her
herbs were low and she would soon need more. She
was just bending down to pluck a handful of violets
when a twig snapped up the bank.

Aislann stood up slowly.

A long shadow fell beside her, drifted close, then
bled black into hers.

"So you've come, my beauty." Aelfric's voice was
deeper after his weeks at Hastings.

"You left me little choice," Aislann said sharply.
She saw that his face was harder, his frame bony and
awkward after his captivity. She wondered that she
had ever thought him handsome or kind. "Besides,
what you told the boy was true. I do need more herbs.
Now that I'm here, perhaps you'll tell me why you
summoned me so urgently."

A faint smile played over Aelfric's lips as two other
men slipped out of the forest shadows.

Aislann struggled to hide her fear. "Well, Aelfric?
The Norman gave me only thirty minutes. He said
if I were gone longer, he would set his dogs upon
me."

Aelfric threw back his head and gave a harsh bray
of laughter. "Is this how you soften the man's heart,
Aislann? Methinks his hours between your legs have
left him sour-tempered!"

Aislann's eyes flashed. "I have been to the castle to
tend his knight who was wounded by a boar. I have
done nothing else there, Aelfric. There is nothing that
I need be ashamed of."

Aelfric strode toward her, his eyes cold. Aislann
wondered suddenly if there wasn't a hint of madness
burning there.

"Ah, but what else would I expect you to tell me, my sweet betrothed?" He caught a strand of her flame-red hair and toyed with it gently. "What else would you say to the man you were supposed to wed? Would you tell him you were soiled, tainted by the lust of his worst enemy?"

Aislann took a step backward. "I have nothing to lie about. My help for Hugh FitzRolland was the thing that bought you your health."

"So the terms were laid so clear, were they? How many nights did he claim you for his bed, whore? Two? Three? Twenty? Did you pant for him? Did you welcome him eagerly, the way you never welcomed me?" Aelfric's face hardened. "Never once did you care to let me taste the pleasures of your body before we were wed. Yes, I see now how you have paid for my health. But I'm sure you never thought I would escape."

"I bought nothing with my body. It is a lie!" Aislann caught her herbs to her chest, a weak weapon before his fury.

"Is it, my sweet?" Aelfric laughed coldly. "We shall soon find out, if so. For I mean to have you, Aislann. Here, as I should have done all those weeks ago. You would have been mine already had not William and his swine driven us from our lands."

Aislann went sheet-white. "Not this way, Aelfric! It is wrong! You cannot—"

"Silence!" With one hand he motioned to his companions. "Guard the banks. Watch for any Normans that St. Vaux might send out after his whore." Aelfric's hand went to his coarse tunic. "Guard well and when I am done, you may sample the slut, too."

Aislann did not wait to hear more. She turned and ran up the bank. In the distance she could see the gates of the castle, but now they looked far distant.

Her herbs fell forgotten, her basket kicked into the water, as she caught up her skirts and ran with every ounce of her strength.

But Aelfric's legs were longer. He captured her easily and threw her down onto the muddy bank, his body crushing hers. "Here I shall have you, witch. Here with the mud beneath us. It is only right, since we are both fouled by the Norman's betrayal."

His eyes glittered, full of madness. He wrenched off his tunic and tossed his club to the ground.

Aislann struggled, clawing desperately at his face, but she was no match for his strength. "You cannot do this, Aelfric! It is against the pact by which our families bound us!"

"You broke that pact the day you went to St. Vaux's castle. Maybe you broke it even before," Aelfric added harshly. He brought his hand down across her mouth. "Enough of your wailing!"

Aislann caught a wild breath and bit him.

"You'll pay for that, wench!" Cursing, Aelfric kneed apart her thighs.

Blindly, Aislann filled her hands with mud and threw it full in her captor's face. With a roar, Aelfric staggered back, clawing at his eyes in agony. With every movement the fine grains of sand were driven deeper.

Aislann stumbled to her feet, knowing she would have only seconds to escape. She kept to the reeds, moving fast, running blindly, unaware of her direction or the rocks that cut her feet. Unaware of the way her torn chemise gaped free.

Her heart was hammering in her chest and her throat was raw when she heard the thunder of footsteps somewhere up the bank.

A hard, calloused hand caught her wrist.

She hurled herself forward. "No! Let me go!"

"Aislann, stop!"

It was Lyon. She cried out and fell against his chest. The Norman's fingers slid into her hair as he held her tightly.

And then she felt his body go rigid.

Slowly he put her behind him.

Aelfric stood frozen, caught in a wild charge up the bank, his clothing all awry. He stared dumbly at the huge Norman.

"I see how profitably you have spent your time since your escape, Aelfric," Lyon growled. "Is this where the valor of Saxon men is spent—terrorizing defenseless Saxon women?"

Aelfric's hand went to his club, but it was gone, flung away and forgotten in his lust to possess Aislann. His fists opened and closed in impotent fury. "Aye, Norman. A Saxon knows full well how to reward betrayal. Especially that of a woman!"

Lyon moved closer. His hand went to his sword.

Aelfric paled and took a step backward.

"Your fear is a stench upon the wind, Saxon, but I shall not stoop to behead you as I would choose. Your blood would only tarnish my blade." With that, Lyon threw off his sword and cloak. His feet moved wide. "Face me instead of her. Face me and prove you're a man and not the dog you appear!"

With a wild growl Aelfric charged. The Norman parried him easily, caught his leg, and tossed him down upon the bank.

But Aelfric had learned his own tricks in the squalor of the Norman jail at Hastings. He bit Lyon's calf, making him stumble, then leaped forward and seized Lyon's sword.

Cursing, the Norman rolled to the side just as the mighty blade crashed down against the mud. Again the blade fell, and this time Lyon escaped by mere inches. All the time he waited, watching for his chance to strike back.

It came a second later. The Saxon, fueled by fury, slipped on the muddy bank and lost his balance. Lyon went in low and hard. He caught Aelfric at the knee and sent him flying backward onto the bank. The Norman's sword went flying into the water.

Lyon's fingers circled Aelfric's throat. "Tell me one reason why I shouldn't kill you right now, swine!"

"Because I've only done what you've done. I've lusted to ride the wench as you did. She's a witch, can't you see? She betrays any man who looks upon her, trapping him in a spell he can never escape. She's done it even to you, Norman!" Aelfric gave a shrill, laugh.

Slowly Lyon came to his feet. He stared down in disgust at the Saxon squirming in the mud. "I cast you from my hands forever, Aelfric. Should you ever have the stupidity to set foot here again, I swear I will not repeat my leniency."

Aelfric stumbled to his feet, eager to escape, but Lyon caught him up short. "One more thing. See that no more of your foul lies are spread about Aislann. If I hear of such, I'll track you down, no matter where you hide. Then I'll hack the tongue from between your teeth, I swear it. Now go!"

Aelfric did not need a second order. He lurched past the Norman, then grabbed up his tunic and club. A moment later he melted back into the darkness of the woods.

On the edge of the river, Aislann stood watching, her heart turned to stone. She did not move, not even when Lyon caught up his cloak and set it about her shoulders.

"Did he hurt you, Aislann? Did he harm you before I . . ."

"No." Her voice was raw. "He—he didn't. You came before—" Her eyes closed for a moment and Lyon saw a shudder run through her. Her chemise

was ripped and her soft, white skin lay bare to his anxious gaze.

But all Lyon could see was the terror in her eyes and the red welts along her neck and arms. Fury rode him, fury and fear, for he knew how close he'd come to losing her just now. The Saxon was clearly mad. Lyon could only rage at himself for not having seen it sooner.

And his stupidity had left Aislann a clear target for Aelfric's wrath. Nothing could change that fact.

Aislann's hands moved restlessly atop her waist. "I—I think I should like to go back now, my lord." Her chin was high despite the tremor in her lips and her voice held the stubborn pride that he had come to know so well. The sound made his lips curve.

"And I shall take you, my beauty. But not with your bodice gaping. Otherwise we'll leave a path of wagging tongues all across the bailey. They'll think that we—" He did not finish, but bent down to pin his cloak over her torn garment.

Color stained Aislann's pale cheeks.

"Come," Lyon said gruffly. "I'll help you scrub off some of that mud." He caught Aislann up and carried her into the water. Little silver eddies played about them as he took the edge of his cloak, dipped it in the water, and used it to scrub Aislann's arms.

She watched him numbly, her eyes wide.

Lyon gave her a reassuring smile as he set about her other arm. "You mustn't expect me to blanch, you know. I have four sisters and I daresay I can do the job nearly as well as you can, my lady."

Aislann swallowed, unable to believe that any of this was happening.

First had come the horror of Aelfric's attack. Now Lyon stood beside her, speaking gently while his fingers moved over her skin. She'd never imagined this side of him, slow and thorough, inching through her

hair and coaxing free the tangles earned in her struggle with Aelfric. She saw him smile as he scrubbed a
spot of dirt from her cheek.

Aislann felt something twist inside her, something
soft and inexplicably warm. Like a seed buried deep,
it edged upward toward light and heat. As she stood
with Lyon's hands upon her, that seed opened its
petals to the sun and burst into full flower.

Her heart began to pound.

St. Vaux saw and understood. Even before she did,
perhaps. The sight of her desire was like hot coals, like
joy poured full into his weathered heart.

But he knew he could not touch her, not while she
trembled with the memory of the Saxon's violence.
Lyon wanted it different between them. He wanted
her to remember only heat and pleasure when he took
her against him.

Instead of catching her close as he yearned to do, he
sat back on his heels and collected a handful of clean
moss to soothe the welts at her shoulders. That done,
he smoothed her chemise and straightened his cloak.

"There," he said gruffly. "Though it would hardly
suffice for court dress, it will do well enough here at
the castle to shield you from prying eyes. After all,
you went off to gather herbs, and no one will expect
you to return pristine from such a task. Now let's see
if we can't find that basket of yours before it—"

He stopped abruptly. Damn it, he was prattling on
like an old woman!

Aislann's fingers cut him off, tense upon his fore-
arm. "Why, Lyon? Why do you turn away?"

He looked away, her beauty a torment.

"It is because you are afraid of me, isn't it? Because
of what Aelfric said." Aislann's eyes misted with
tears when Lyon did not speak. She stumbled blindly
toward the river.

He caught her in the reeds, calf-deep in the cool water. "Never did I believe the man's foul lies."

"You must. Everyone believes that—that I am a witch."

By heaven, was ever a man so tasked! Lyon fought for sanity, even as the white curve of her breast tormented him from beneath her torn chemise, shredding his sanity even further. "Hold still, woman."

Aislann shrugged off his hand. "Liar! I—I can see it in your eyes!"

"I have no belief that you're a witch, Aislann!"

Aislann went very still. "You . . . don't?"

"By all that is sacred, woman, I see that you have powers, yes. You have skills that others lack. But these are things of good, not evil. 'Tis not the powers of darkness that work through you. I have seen those other skills before, in Acre and Sicily and Damascus. What you do is nothing like that, do you hear me, Aislann?"

She gave a ragged sob. Her head slid down against his chest while hot tears filled her cheeks. Lyon's words had soothed a fear she had kept long buried.

They harrowed her, these visions she could not control—these knowings glimpsed in firelight or candle flame. How else could she explain her ability to look into a person's face and see his illness—and its source?

She had not asked for the sight. Lately she had begun praying that it be taken from her.

But now, feeling Lyon's arms around her, Aislann knew it was true. Her gifts were meant only for good.

She could never repay this man for helping her to believe that.

"Nay, Aislann, you're a woman. A woman of rare grace and beauty. 'Tis there your power comes from, not from sorcery. Aelfric was simply too weak to face that."

Aislann slowly raised her head. "And what about you, Lyon of St. Vaux?"

The Norman's eyes darkened. Heat licked through him as he stared upon her trembling lips. She was all woman, all that he had ever wanted in a wife. She was fire and courage, suppleness and strength. Yet honor forbade that he touch her now, while the stain of Aelfric's lust was still so fresh.

"I?" Lyon made a ragged sound. "Sometimes I am not sure. Now let's find that basket of yours and get you back to the castle."

Aislann stopped him. "You truly do not fear me?"

Lyon dragged an unsteady hand through his long hair. "By all the saints, do I look like a man who is frightened?" He caught her close and slid her against his aroused body. "Does this feel like a man who's frightened, my lady?"

Aislann gasped. An insidious heat uncurled through her as she felt the nudge of Lyon's arousal at her belly.

It was true then. He did not fear her. He had never believed Aelfric's wretched lies.

Wonder filled her. With it came a wild, heady freedom such as Aislann had never known before. With such a man as this many things were possible. Perhaps everything was possible. "Then why are you leaving?"

Very carefully Lyon put her from him. "My lady, we must go. Otherwise tongues will soon begin to wag."

Aislann blinked. He was protecting her! She who was naught but a wretched Saxon, a woman who had taunted and disobeyed him at every opportunity.

"I—I am not ready to go back," she said softly.

St. Vaux's brow arched. "Indeed. And why not?"

"Because my skirts are torn and my legs caked with mud." As she spoke, Aislann's gaze rose from Lyon's hair-dusted chest to his lips.

They were full and hard.

Aislann wondered how they would feel upon her hair. Upon her mouth. Upon her—

Color flamed across her cheeks. "I couldn't possibly go back yet." As if to prove her point, she raised her skirt and displayed mud-caked thighs.

Lyon swallowed audibly. She was all grace, all sleek skin. By Heaven, he wanted her, wanted all that fire and softness wrapped around him.

It required a vast struggle, but he forced himself to turn away. "Very well. Clean yourself and I shall keep watch from the shore, lest Aelfric decide it is safe to return."

Aislann gnawed at her lip. This was not what she had had in mind. She could not let it end this way, with so much unfinished between them.

She sat on a boulder by the river and raised her skirt, scooping water over her leg. She worked slowly, knowing Lyon could see every move. And she gave him a great deal to see.

One leg done, she turned to her shoulder. His brooch was of a sort Aislann had never seen before, and the prong would not budge. "Can you help me with this, my lord? I do not think I can manage it."

The Norman did not move. His face might have seen carved from the stone that formed his keep. "Try again. It is not complicated," he said hoarsely.

Instantly Aislann understood. He did not dare to approach her. He was not indifferent, but quite the opposite.

The knowledge made her smile deep inside, made heat pour through all the secret places in her body. "It's no use, my lord. I fear it eludes me."

With a muttered curse, St. Vaux knelt behind her. Keeping as much distance as possible between them, he attacked the brooch and the folded cloak it secured.

In the process his hand grazed her breast. His thigh brushed her hip. He tensed with the rush of pain-pleasure that swept through him.

At the same moment Aislann turned and stared full into his eyes. Her lips were soft, parted, faintly trembling. There was a world of wanting in her lovely green eyes.

"Aislann, no. You don't understand. I cannot touch you, not today. Not after—"

Her only answer was to bring her hand to his neck and trace the ridge of his jaw. In those silent, heated seconds Aislann found she wanted nothing more than that he touch her. That he kiss her, long and deep and hungrily. And that she do the same to him.

"Lyon? What if I—" She swallowed. "What if I wish for you to—to touch me? As a man touches his woman? I know there are other women, women grand and rich who claim your affection, but now, just for now, I would like to know your touch."

Lyon gave a ragged groan. She couldn't know what she was saying. Her breathless admission made his blood roar in a wild song of triumph. If only things were simpler. If only he were different.

But things weren't different and his honor could not be swept away so lightly.

Lyon froze as her fingers combed through the golden hair at his chest. His breath caught as her thumb teased the edge of one flat male nipple.

He drew a ragged breath.

"But perhaps you don't care to—that is, perhaps you do not find me—"

Lyon caught her hand and crushed it against his chest. "By all the saints, woman, you drive me to madness! I would have you instantly were things different between us! But not today. Not while you bear the memory of Aelfric's violence."

Aislann's head slanted back. Her eyes were liquid, haunted. "Perhaps now is when you should press me, Norman. Now, while I wonder if there is nothing more between a man and a woman than this savagery?"

"There is much more," Lyon said hoarsely.

"Then I would know it, Lyon of St. Vaux. And know it from your hands only," she whispered.

Lyon felt as if the world were falling apart beneath him. He felt lust. He felt jagged passion and blinding tenderness. He felt joy and awe, along with sorrow that Aislann had ever known such cruelty at a man's hands.

Most of all he felt the weight of honor, an honor that had carried him through years of wandering and war. He could not turn his back on that now.

Especially not now, while she was so vulnerable.

His hand slid into her hair. With his other he eased her chin upward. Her eyes were moss green, uncertain, yet full of determination.

They made him understand that this woman was as much a warrior as he was.

He was still struggling to explain when she stepped back. The brooch pulled free and his cloak fell from her shoulders. Her torn gown followed, sliding downward and snagging at the full curve of her breasts.

"Aislann, don't." Lyon's voice was raw as his control shredded away to nothing. He reached out to stop her, hands unsteady.

But Aislann did not wish to be stopped. She felt his fingers tremble. Was it this way between a man and woman then? Was there a sharing of strength and weakness, of hunger and giving?

She had to find out. Something told her if she

did not find out now, she might never have another chance.

Her gown fell lower. Lyon's eyes locked upon her breasts. He groaned as the linen slid down to reveal tight, dark nipples as sweetly tempting as berries.

"As God is my witness, you are a woman to steal a man's heart! But you don't understand—"

"I think I do understand, Norman. It is you I want. Perhaps it has always been so, for never has a man touched my heart or blood as you have." Her gown glided down over her white stomach.

The sight made Lyon's blood hammer.

"If not you, it will be some other man," Aislann lied desperately. "I must taste a joy to blot out the memory of Aelfric's savagery."

"Never! No other man shall have you! You are mine, Aislann. You will always be so."

He caught her shoulders. Almost without will or choice, his head fell, his lips curving over her supple skin. Groaning, he possessed her, until Aislann's head fell back and she moaned softly.

For answer Lyon eased to one knee before her. Her gown slid to her hips.

He stared upon her beauty, feeling it pierce straight to his heart. Triumph, possession, all were forgotten. All that was left was hunger—and a desperate urge to protect Aislann, even from herself.

Lyon vowed to make her cry out his name in joy when she tasted her first passion.

Her body smelled like lavender and moss, like woman and cool water. Lyon tongued his way to her waist and felt her shudder as he coaxed open her thighs.

"Lyon?" Her voice was high, ragged.

"Hush, beauty. Hush and let me love you as you were meant to be loved. As I've waited all my life to love you."

"But—" And then Aislann's voice caught. She felt

him move against her, felt his lips ease against her soft heat, finding her fire and sweetness.

She shuddered, her hands caught at his shoulders.

Lyon's hard fingers circled her hips, holding her against him while wall after wall of fire broke over her.

Aislann gasped, feeling as if she were caught in a stranger's body, feeling as if she were being torn inside out.

But Lyon was there, holding her, stroking her, never leaving her. And the fear passed, leaving only wonder and a sharp, aching joy.

And then she felt him slide deeper, felt his calloused fingers open her to his sweet possession.

A cry tore from her lips. The world seemed to flash and shudder before her eyes. "Lyon, I can't—" But even then he did not release her. Her torment grew as he drove her, blind and restless, toward something she did not know or understand.

"You are mine, my rose. Bound by laws older than man. Now and forever."

At the tremor in his voice, the need that broke his words, Aislann felt her blood churn to a fury. His, forever. How much she wanted that.

He caught her, teased her, possessed her in ways beyond her imagining. She shuddered against him, breath ragged, offering him her very soul.

"Lyon, it's too—" Her breath caught. "I can't—"

Her body tensed. Colors coursed through her, while sound played before her eyes. She cried out and felt him catch her, felt him shudder as the thunder in her blood built to a roar.

He whispered her name and his hands went rigid against her, as if with pain. "My rose, my sweet, wild rose. Again—say my name again!"

He found her sweetness once more, even while she

shuddered in splendor. And once again she was pulled free, flying blind, his name a breathless cry upon her lips.

To Lyon the sound was sweet, infinitely sweet. Never before had a woman moved him as this woman did. He caught her knees as her legs gave way and with a ragged smile eased her back against the cool moss and soft spring flowers.

His now, she could belong to no other, nor could he. Fate bound them, even though their people were enemies.

Aislann's eyes had just fluttered open when Lyon heard a cry from the far bank.

Frowning he eased above the reeds bordering the river.

Hugh appeared, looking very worried. "Lyon? Is everything—"

"Fine," Lyon snapped, cursing the gruffness in his voice. "The Saxon woman has gone upstream to pick herbs. Send someone to see that Aelfric has left my lands, Hugh. Then leave me. I wish to bathe." He raised a hand as his knight began a question. "Now, Hugh. And I do not wish to be disturbed again."

After a moment FitzRolland shrugged and turned away.

When Lyon looked down, Aislann was staring at him, her cheeks flushed crimson. The Norman cursed inwardly. If only they had not been disturbed.

"What I did—the things I said—" She swallowed. "It is shameful, unforgivable."

"Nay, lady," Lyon said softly. " 'Twould be unforgivable if you did not. I would have you so always, flushed from my loving."

Aislann's eyes widened. "But you did not— that is—"

"Ah, but I will, my rose. And you will want me again when I do."

Her lips trembled. "I already do, my lord," she said softly.

Lyon groaned. He was dying, there was no doubt of it. But still he held back. "You are sure? In spite of Aelfric's savagery? I would give you whatever time you need, my beauty."

"It is not time that I need, Norman." Aislann's hands circled his neck. " 'Tis you that I need. Kiss me, Lyon," she whispered.

Lyon grimaced. The word pain took on new meanings as her silken breasts brushed his chest. "Aislann, you don't have to—"

She didn't listen. Wriggling beneath him she found the curve of his collarbone. She nibbled the center of his chest and licked the male skin half-hidden beneath a swirl of soft hair.

Lyon tensed and instantly Aislann went still. "I pray I did not hurt you." She swallowed. "That is, I'm sorry if I—"

"Sorry?" Lyon growled. "Please God, you will not stop, woman!"

Her eyes widened. "But the pain you spoke of . . ."

Lyon laughed grimly. "Would go far worse with me if you stopped, my beauty."

Aislann's eyes took on a reckless gleam. "In that case . . ." She gave a soft ragged laugh and brushed her palm across his rock-hard stomach.

Lyon groaned at her innocent exploration. And he felt joy, a joy so fierce it frightened him, for he thought the pagan gods of this place must surely snatch it from him.

And then he felt her soft hands slide across his thigh and brush his hardness.

"Aislann, no." His voice was rough, tortured. "Any more and I won't be able to wait."

She paid no heed. Again she skimmed the fascinating length of him.

He snagged her hand and held it still.

"Why?" She frowned up at him, a faint flush on her beautiful cheeks. "It is only what you did, the way you touched me when I—" She swallowed, unable to finish.

Lyon laughed jerkily. "Because I want to be buried inside you—deep inside you—when I bring you passion again. Any more of that and I'll find it impossible."

She didn't understand. Lyon felt a wave of tenderness at her confusion. With a dark laugh he caught her close and twisted them over as one, until he was cushioned by soft moss with Aislann's hair spilling in a red-gold veil across his broad chest.

He caught the tip of one rose-red nipple and worried it with his teeth.

Instantly Aislann gasped and pushed softly against his chest. "No, Lyon! Not until I—"

Lyon slid his hand between them. Her thighs opened with perfect ease. He groaned as he found her softness and eased inside. By the Saints, she was tight. He would have to go careful with her, lest he tear her untried flesh.

But the woman above him had no similar ideas. She tugged at his shoulders, making soft breathless moans as his fingers teased her heated skin, easing ever deeper.

Lyon gritted his teeth, fighting his response to the breathy sounds she was making, feeling her hands drive him mad.

He rolled again, catching her beneath him. Holding her still, he eased his manhood slowly against parted flesh. Moving gently, he slid to touch her maiden's barrier.

"Aislann, I fear this may hurt, just for a moment. It is necessary. I must—"

Her eyes opened, dazed and yearning, and she nodded solemnly. "I am sorry if it must hurt you, my love. You have been hurt far too much already." Her fingers swept his chest, silver with the scars of a hundred battles. "If you do not care to continue, then truly I shall understand."

Her words ripped the heart from Lyon's chest, the breath from his throat. She thought that he must suffer! And she worried for the pain it would cause him.

He wasn't sure whether to laugh or cry. An ache invaded his heart, an ache that had nothing to do with lust and everything to do with vast, blinding tenderness.

With love.

The thought left him speechless.

It also left him unsure how to proceed.

"I'm afraid, my love, you don't quite understand. That pain I mentioned?"

"Yes?" She arched, instinctively trying to draw him deeper.

" 'Tis not . . . for me, Aislann. Would to God I could make it so."

"Then—" Aislann's eyes widened. "Oh! I see." Her cheeks flushed crimson. "How great a fool you must think me!"

"I think, my sweet, that you are the most beautiful creature I could ever hope to know and love." He cupped her cheek gently, fighting back his desire. "You understand me now? That there will be pain for you, though only briefly?"

"But you will find pleasure in this, will you not?" Her eyes were anxious.

"Very great pleasure, little one." Lyon ground his teeth together tightly. All this talk of release and pleasure was a torment. And her worry about him—

well, it nearly unmanned him. No other woman had ever shown the slightest concern about him at such a time. In this as in all things she was extraordinary.

"I am prepared, my lord." Her chin was firm. "You may begin whenever you wish."

Lyon restrained an urge to chuckle. "Lest I forget, you will find pleasure in this thing, too, my love. It may simply take a few minutes of adjustment, that's all."

"Shall I?" Her gaze was totally honest. "But I thought you said—"

Lyon groaned inwardly as her hips moved, easing him deeper inside. "As I live and breathe, I swear it. Unless I die first, that is."

"Oh! You are in pain?"

"Endless, aching pain."

"Then by all means, let me move away from you until—"

"Move?" Lyon let out a growl. "Move one inch and I shall certainly die!"

Aislann frowned. "I fear I am most terribly confused, my lord. If you are in pain, why do you—"

Lyon slid his hand between them, parting her silky petals. "Never mind," he said huskily. "Soon enough you'll understand."

And soon enough she did.

His intimate caress made her whimper and shove restlessly against him. She was ready, Lyon knew. Waiting would change nothing.

In one swift thrust he pierced her maiden's barrier. Almost instantly he came to a halt, grimacing as he felt her tense beneath him. "Aislann?"

Silence. Then a quick, ragged breath. "It was indeed . . . rather uncomfortable, my lord. You are so very—large, you see. And I fear I must be unnaturally formed."

"There is nothing at all wrong with you, mignonne. *You are perfect. It is just that this time is your first. It is always so for a maid."*

"Have you . . ." She bit her lip anxiously. "That is, have you found your pleasure yet, my lord?"

Her innocence delighted him as much as her sensuality entranced him. "Not yet, my little love. But I assure you that when I do, you will know it. But first I have something else to attend to."

"No more military matters! Not now, Lyon."

Laughter rumbled from his broad chest. "No, not military matters, my beauty. It is matters of the heart that concern me now. And matters of your pleasure."

"M-my pleasure? But I thought—that is, I already—"

"That was one sort of pleasure, but there are many other sorts, as you shall soon discover."

"And . . . you mean to show them to me?"

"I devoutly hope so." Lyon began to move inside her, slow and powerful. "A pleasure that will bring us as close as two people can be, my heart."

Aislann gasped at his knowing movements, feeling flames burst within her anew.

"It is good?"

She blinked. "Shockingly so."

St. Vaux gave her a dark smile. "Oh, I haven't begun to shock you with the ways I mean to love you."

"Perhaps it is better if I do not know," Aislann said huskily, raising her hips to meet him, delighting in the long silver slide of friction as their bodies met. "Perhaps you could . . . show me instead."

Lyon found the idea irresistible. "Very well, little one. I trust you are paying attention?" He could not resist this one tiny goad.

She smiled at him through her lowered lashes. "Quite, Norman. Every single inch of me."

Lyon groaned. Her innocent abandon was the last straw. He caught her hips and drove deep inside her, feeling her shudder and then the velvet ripples of pleasure where their bodies met hungrily as one.

"Lyon, I—I love you!"

The hardened warrior swallowed, feeling his heart twist at her ragged cry, feeling himself bound to her with bonds of gold.

"And so do I love you, my rose." As he said the words, the Norman knew they were true. Absolutely and irrevocably.

Lyon gave her every part of himself then, all his joy and sorrow, all his bitterness and regret. He gave her all that he was and yearned to become, holding nothing back.

And she was there to hold him, her fingers buried deep in his hair, her white legs wrapped around his.

There beside the silver water St. Vaux caught her close and poured his seed within her. Beneath the hot blue sky their husky cries mingled in joy and discovery.

And as he held her close, Lyon knew that he would never be whole without her again.

He watched her eyes open, wondering at the fineness of her skin, at the faint blue veins visible beneath. He marvelled at the red-gold flutter of her lashes. The emerald sweep of her eyes.

"Lyon . . ." Her voice was slumberous, lazy, dazed with happiness.

"Yes, my sweet. Come close and say my name again, just so." He eased her closer, delighting in her pliancy, her sweet honesty.

Her lips curved. "Lyon," she repeated, running her fingers over his chest and combing through his dense hair. "I feel most delightfully wanton, lying here unclad beneath sun *and sky. Do you realize that anyone might see us?"*

"Ah, but I sent Hugh to fend them off. I am vastly efficient, you see."

"It seems you've taught me your own sort of magic this day, Norman."

"Magic? Me?" St. Vaux's brows rose lazily.

"Aye, my lord. I never thought to feel this way, to know such happiness in a man's arms."

"But you'll feel this way again, my heart. Sooner than you know."

"Again?" Her eyes widened. "Surely not—so soon?" she squeaked.

"Again and again," Lyon murmured against her cheek, her neck, her breast. "For I shall never have enough of you. You have completely bewitched me, Saxon." With a groan Lyon captured her beneath him.

Aislann's head fell back. She gasped as he drove deep within her. "Oh, not again—" Her voice broke.

Lyon smiled wickedly as she arched against him, blind in a new wave of pleasure.

All through the hot afternoon the Norman possessed her, pleased her, lost in the joy of love and the discovery of a woman he had never thought to find.

A pair of curlews trilled overhead and the stream sang out its soft lullaby beside them.

Aislann never even heard.

He watched her from the cliffs. Her horror was real, and it tantalized him. He had known that trancelike state himself, had tasted its ashes and listened to its same voices. To see it in another delighted him.

He watched, eyes distended, nostrils flared as if to drink in every nuance of her torment. That, too, was something he was good at.

But now it was time. He had been interrupted before, down by the ruins. This time she would not be so lucky.

He eased from the rocks and began moving toward her.

Kelly twisted upright, blinking. Voices filled her head and the hot sweet textures of pleasure still coursed through her. The dream left her shaken, caught between past and present, truth and illusion.

Why *her*? Why these images again and again, a story unfolding in such utter depth and clarity? And why did it always feel so personal, as if she herself had already played out every second of it?

She shook her head and stumbled to her feet, almost too tired to stand.

It was then that she saw the shadow slide across the ground in front of her.

Chapter 21

"**Y**ou're shaking! Damn it, Kelly, what happened?"

Not Lyon. Not the enemy.

Kelly repeated the words in a silent litany, trying to force her fear away.

Just a dream . . .

"I—fell."

"You're paste white and you can hardly stand. I want to know why." Dressed in dark corduroys and a soft gray shirt, Burke stood frowning at her.

But Kelly didn't answer. She had felt something else, off where the ground rose in a stony ridge to gray cliffs.

Someone else?

"What is it?"

"I—I don't know." She squinted up at the rugged granite walls. "There, I think."

"There, *what?*"

"Someone. Watching. A—a man, I think." Her hands began to tremble.

"Hold on, Kelly. You're tired. It must be an animal."

"You don't understand. Someone's out there. I can *feel* him!"

"Feel him?"

"Just—just accept it. He's . . ." Kelly frowned, concentrating on the jab of awareness that teased her from the forest. There it was again, coming from somewhere just over the ridge.

She shivered as the images grew sharper. She touched anger and felt the sharpness of fear. The intuition was so powerful it left her dizzy and frightened.

Very frightened.

In the past her intuition had been focused through the safe distance of maps and geographical coordinates. But ever since she'd come to Draycott Abbey, she'd been besieged by a flood of raw impressions—usually when there was no map in sight.

She stiffened, staring into the shadows of the woods. "He—he's there. He's alone."

Burke's gray-gold eyes scoured Kelly's face. "How in hell could you possibly know a thing like that? Damn it, Kelly, no one can know—"

Before Burke could move, a gunshot ripped through the air. Instantly the Englishman drove Kelly down and shoved her behind a moss-covered shoulder of granite.

Another shot whined from the trees, cracked across stone, and sent gray flakes raining down around them.

Burke cursed. "When we get out of this mess, you're going to tell me how you knew that, Red." *If* they got out of this, he amended silently. They could never make Draycott, not with someone trying to pick them off from the closest route. They'd have to try for the river and Edgehill.

"Can you walk?"

"Walk? Commander, I plan on breaking an Olympic record in the two-thousand-meter dash any minute."

Burke gave her a grim smile. "Then let's do it, Professor. Down the bank and into the water. Swim downstream. On the other side there's a trail leading up the hill, half-hidden by a clump of hawthorns. Just follow it north until you get to Edgehill."

"And what are you going to do?"

Burke's jaw hardened. "I intend to have a closer look at our friend over there in the trees."

For a moment Kelly thought about trying to stop him, but a look at his face convinced her not to bother.

She contented herself with whispering, "Be careful," then turned and made her way down the bank toward the water.

Burke took his time backtracking along the ridge. At the very top, he shimmied up a weathered oak tree that Nicholas always boasted was four hundred years old and pulled out a pair of Steiner electronic field glasses.

He scanned the whole valley carefully, working out from the sector where he estimated the rifle shell had been fired. He made out a rabbit and two gray squirrels near the base of the cliffs, but there was nothing even remotely two-legged moving down there.

Anger coursed through him. He was being cornered on his own ground and that left him furious. For a moment Burke thought of rushing the hill just to see if he'd draw fire, but he reluctantly discarded the idea. It would be just what an attacker wanted.

He also had to rule out the idea of staying put and waiting out his enemy. He didn't have the luxury of time, not with Kelly somewhere over the hill trying to make her way north to Edgehill.

Whoever was out there knew this place too damned well.

An insider? Marston or some other person from the village? Burke refused to believe it.

But the facts screamed that someone with an intimate knowledge of Draycott's grounds wanted Burke or Kelly dead. Maybe both of them.

The Englishman scanned the ridge one last time and found nothing but sun-warmed stone and the bobbing heads of a nest of swallows. Cursing softly, he slid down the tree and worked his way back to the river, watching the ground every step of the way. Halfway down the ridge, he saw what he was looking for.

One boot print, just where the granite ridge was broken briefly by a thick covering of moss.

It was the same kind of print he had seen the night Kelly arrived at the abbey.

Burke's face hardened. The bastard was careful, all right. No matter how thoroughly Burke searched, there were no other prints and no clues as to where the man was headed. The granite covered every trace. Of course, if Burke had had more time, he could probably have found a few broken twigs or crushed leaves to help him.

But he didn't have any more time. He had to find Kelly and make sure she was safe. Everything else, even the urn, would have to wait.

It took Burke eleven and a half minutes to cross the stream and cover two miles of dense, hilly terrain. But it wasn't exertion that made his heart hammer as he raced up the final stretch of lawn behind Edgehill's mellow golden limestone walls. It was worry about Kelly.

Had she made it safely? There had been no suspicious sounds and no sign of pursuit. But they were dealing with professionals and with professionals anything was possible.

He ran beneath a canopy of lime trees, each stride long and fluid, his fear growing.

Still no sign of Kelly.

He frowned as he neared the gardening shed, re-created in the shape of a Chinese pagoda. It was one of his mother's designs, part of her obsession with gardening.

Inside the shed something crashed to the ground. Burke eased around the corner and jerked the door open.

Kelly's face, white and shaken, seemed to float before his eyes.

She stood trembling in the shadows.

"Sweet God, Red." In two strides he was beside her, his palms against her cheeks. He was dimly aware that his hands were shaking. "You're safe." He said the words again to reassure himself. "Thank God, you're safe. It's all right, Kelly love. I'm here now."

At his murmured endearment, she began to shiver. He felt the faint ripples run right through his fingers.

Burke pulled her back into the shed, into the cool darkness, into the sweet, musky scent of peat and redwood chips and drying flowers.

"I—I'm having some problems with this one, Michael," she said stiffly. Her eyes were desperate, locked on him as if he were her only lifeline.

Hell, that was fine with Burke. He *wanted* to be her only lifeline. "Tell me, Red," he muttered, sliding his arm around her shoulder. "Tell me everything you're feeling. Holding it in will only make it hurt more." He whispered the words against her forehead, against her neck, against the curve of her cheek.

"Oh, God," she said softly. Her hands clenched. "Oh, God, Michael . . ."

"Go on and let it out, Professor. I'd say you were entitled to a full-blown nervous breakdown about now."

"N-not a big one, but I'm definitely considering a small one." The fine tremor in her hands grew. Only then did Michael see that she was soaking wet, her legs streaked with mud.

"Tell me, love," he coaxed, mouth to her cheek. "Talk to me."

Her forehead slid down against his chest. The shuddering grew, seizing her, convulsing her. He caught her with one arm around her waist and pulled her against him, knowing exactly what she was feeling.

First the terror. Then the adrenaline high. And then the roller coaster plummet, when the body tried to cope.

"He—he was there," she said jerkily. "I saw him. He was watching me. He . . . could have shot us anytime he wanted to. But he didn't. He likes toying with us. He wanted me to know that he will be choosing the moment, and that it will be when it hurts us most."

Michael slid his hands into her hair, trying to make sense of what she was saying. "You saw him?"

Kelly nodded against his chest. "After I crossed the stream the way you said, I looked up and saw his shadow. Twenty yards below where I left you, I think. It was a man. I can't say how tall. He came out only far enough for me to see his outline."

Burke cursed. There *was* a small granite out-cropping near where he'd shimmied up the tree. Someone could have worked his way down there, and it would have been the one spot Burke couldn't have seen, even from the tree.

"You're sure?"

She gave a ragged laugh. "Sure? If you mean did I see him closely, did I speak with him and shake his hand, the answer's no. But he was there, damn it. I *know* it."

"Steady now. This could be bloody important, Kelly. Can you tell me anything else about him? Anything at all," he said urgently.

Kelly fought to calm her racing thoughts.

Like what? she thought wildly. *That he's one hair away from insanity? That he enjoys watching people, picking the moment when he can hurt them most? That he wants to hurt you and me in particular?*

Most of all, Kelly didn't want to think about her instinct that the man in the woods was some-how familiar.

Marston? She ruled it out as too improbable. But that still left a host of other possibilities, considering that half the town of Long Milton had been gathered at the Crown.

Not that Kelly could begin to tell Burke any of this. Her skills, the psychic ones at least, had to remain strictly her own secret.

She sighed. "What did I see? He was maybe a little less than six feet tall. Slender. Definitely male."

"How do you know that?" Burke asked abrupt-ly.

"Because he *felt* like a man."

"I'm not sure I'm following you here, Red."
Burke frowned. "You said he *felt* like a male?
Not that he looked like one?"

Kelly shrugged. "I mean that the way he was
looking at me, my whole sense of being tracked
and watched, all of that felt like a man's doing."

"I see," Burke said slowly. "Anything else?"

"Nothing. No hair color, no facial description,
no clothing style." *And the man in the woods knew
that, too,* Kelly thought. *He knew he'd given me
nothing of real value, just enough to put me off balance.*

Just enough to let me know he was there.

She looked up at Burke. "I'm scared, Michael.
He's out there right now. I—I know it."

Burke twined his fingers through hers, his face
harsh. "He's not going to win, I promise you
that. Besides . . ." He anchored her hands against
the wall. "If you want to worry about what other
people are thinking, start with me."

"You don't think I can do it?"

Michael shrugged.

Recklessly, Kelly stared into those gray-gold
eyes. Frowning, she narrowed her area of attention, focusing.

Focusing . . .

Contact.

It ripped through her, sharp and nearly instan-
taneous. Suddenly she was bombarded with
Michael's thoughts.

Hot, dark thoughts. Thoughts of *him* wearing nothing but cool dark air. Images of herself
spread like hot silk on top of him.

She swallowed, trying to ignore the breadth
of his back, the fluid play of his thighs against
her hips.

Right, Hamilton. Maybe when pigs can fly.

"So what am I thinking about, Professor?"

"R-right now?"

"Right now," he said darkly.

A rumpled bed.

A night of hot, fierce lovemaking.

A tangle of auburn hair spilled across his pillow—hair exactly the color of *hers*. She tasted his hunger, raw and naked. It was the kind a man feels for a woman he's wanted all his life.

Maybe even longer.

Kelly fought an urge to slide down into all that gray-gold hunger and let Michael make his visions a reality.

But it wouldn't be enough. Just as it hadn't been enough before.

The searing realization made her clutch at the rough wood wall. They had been together before. She felt it, dead in the pit of her stomach.

Michael and her. Heart to heart. *As lovers.*

Kelly felt the blood run from her face.

It was all there, dimly remembered. First the dreams of a hard-eyed warrior brandishing a jeweled sword, then the joy two lovers had felt long centuries ago.

And somehow it was all connected, that long-ago love, a priceless sword, and a buried urn that men would die to possess. Blast, if only she could understand the connection . . .

"Kelly?"

"I—I'm not feeling well. Actually, I think I'd better—" She tried to pull away, but Burke tightened his fingers and held her still.

"What's wrong, damn it?"

"Never mind! You can't—*distract* me like this. I've got work to do." Her pulse became a wild, desperate thing.

The shed was pungent with peat and drying herbs. Between them the air seemed to throb, charged with some primal fury.

"What do you *want* from me?"

His eyes were flecked with amber. "*I want everything*, Red. Everything you've got to give. Everything I can take. And I want to give you exactly the same." He watched her face. "Does that scare you? It should. It sure scares the *hell* out of me!"

Kelly felt something break inside her. He spared her none of his fear. He was a very moral man, Michael Burke. And he deserved someone who could be equally honest with him.

The way Kelly could not.

And what about the urn? What if she found it first? How could she possibly lie to this man?

Maybe it was the pain of her own enforced secrecy that made her probe his. "Did you love her?" The words slid out without warning.

"Her?"

"The woman in the fire."

Burke cursed softly. "You don't miss much, do you?"

"Not usually."

"I wanted her. I admired her. Maybe . . . it's the same thing."

Kelly felt his frustration, his uncertainty. And something that felt like guilt.

He laughed grimly. "Who am I kidding? The answer is no, I didn't. Not the way I should have. Not with half of what I feel for *you* after exactly three days. Does that sound crazy?"

"No," Kelly said softly. *Maybe it would if I didn't feel exactly the same way . . .*

Burke's eyes darkened. "If I cared any less, I'd kiss you now, Kelly." His voice was low, unsteady. "I'd touch you and taste your very soul. But if I did—if I started, I don't think I'd be able to stop."

Don't stop, a voice inside Kelly cried. *Don't wait.*

"But one kiss would never be enough for me, Red. Not one night. Maybe not a whole lifetime . . ."

He turned. Before she knew it, she was caught up in his arms.

He carried her into a scene right out of a Constable landscape. They crossed a garden full of herbs and wildflowers, lavender and bergamot and clematis bordered by climbing roses. Kelly's breath caught as she was assailed by a cloud of sweetness.

And then Edgehill was before her, its golden limestone walls capped by a fantasy roof full of gables, pinnacles, and twisting brick chimneys.

"It's beautiful, Michael," Kelly said softly, feeling the beauty of the house overcome some of the afternoon's horror.

Burke looked pleased. "Structures have stood here from at least the eleventh century, but Edgehill wasn't built in its present form until somewhere around 1500. The gardens were expanded around 1760," he added with an undercurrent of pride. "After growing up next to Draycott, I sometimes forget just how attractive this place really is. Here we are."

He took the rear stone steps two at a time and shoved open the door to a vast, sunny kitchen. Hundreds of gleaming copper pots hung from the walls and along the timber beams of the vaulted ceiling.

There was a hushed air about it, Kelly thought, like a room in breathless readiness, just waiting for an evening of magnificent entertainment to begin.

Michael set her down on a polished but much nicked worktable of solid oak. "Sit," he ordered, then disappeared through a vaulted doorway.

He was gone several minutes. Kelly heard him dial a phone and speak swiftly.

When he returned, his hands were full and his face was shuttered. He dropped a pile of cloth beside Kelly and pointed to the carved oak wainscoting.

"See that?"

"What?"

"That nick on the wall." As he spoke, Burke bent before Kelly and began to clean the ugly welt on her leg.

Is he talking to distract himself or to distract me? Kelly wondered.

"Does it hurt badly?"

She shrugged, smiling faintly. "The wall?" she reminded him.

"Nicholas and I were stealing cookies from my mother's Russian chef when it happened. Alas, old Sergei was a genius with food but a man of no patience. It was ignominy enough that he had to stoop to cook such a common dish as chocolate chip cookies. Then he was beset in his kitchen by two grubby schoolboys with a propensity for hiding lizards in his flour tins."

Kelly gave an unsteady laugh. "Michael, you didn't!"

"Oh, but we did. On several occasions, as I recall. At any rate, the skirmish over the cookies was the final insult to poor Sergei. He heaved the whole tray at us, nearly five dozen full. It narrowly missed me and cracked off the wall, leaving that nick. Nicholas had a nasty bump on the knee when it fell onto him. Mother had the man sacked the next morning, of course, but I think it broke her heart to do it. No one else could make *Baba au rhum* the way Sergei did, so she always said."

Kelly found herself smiling wistfully, thinking about the boy who had stood in this kitchen all those years ago. How she wished she had known Michael then, as a restless, incorrigible, wonderful child.

Smiling, she ran her hand along his jaw. "I'll make you chocolate chip cookies anytime you like, Commander." She didn't tell him it was just about the only thing she could make.

Burke's eyes darkened. "Right now, Red, the one thing that looks good enough to eat around here is you," he said roughly.

His words made her cheeks burn.

Turning with taut grace, he held up a fine paisley dressing gown. "Into this," he said gruffly. "You're soaked."

Kelly looked at Burke's face, at the harsh lines etched there, then slowly raised her arms and stripped off her sweater.

A muscle flashed at Burke's jaw. His eyes burned with the need to touch her, but he refused to yield to that desire. Grimly, he tugged the paisley gown closed around her shoulders, then began to unbutton the small shell fastenings on the front of her skirt.

A soft, hungry sound skittered from Kelly's lips. The gown slid down around her shoulders. A moment later her challis skirt pooled to her hips.

"Damn it, Red, I'm trying to *dress* you here."

"Maybe I don't want to be dressed."

"Kelly." It was protest and painful praise, and it told her he liked every inch of what he saw but he wasn't going to do one damned thing about it.

Kelly slid from the table, her eyes huge. "Michael . . ."

The paisley gown fluttered off her shoulders, framing her ivory throat. Then it hissed to a pool on the floor.

All she was wearing beneath it was a single-strand pearl necklace and a lavender stretch lace teddy that would probably have been outlawed in a dozen conservative third-world countries. The lace cupped every satin inch of her, making her look more naked than if she *were* naked.

"Sweet God, *don't*." Michael bent and grabbed for the silk, his breathing harsh. "It's not going to be that way, damn it. Not fast and easy."

Once again Kelly found herself marvelling over the strength of his jaw, the stubborn set of his lips. She couldn't forget how he'd looked stretched out beside the river. Nor could she forget the dream she'd had afterward, a dream that felt like far more than a dream.

Standing before him, she relived those exquisite, tormenting images, every touch of Burke's fingers reminding her of the blinding heat of a warrior's possession.

No matter that the warrior had died nine hundred years before.

Maybe it was the memory of all that heat and love that made her so reckless. Maybe it was the fear that she was slipping over the edge of sanity this time.

Or maybe it was simply the honesty in Michael's eyes. The need and heat she saw there warned Kelly that if she kept on the way she was headed, things were going to happen— things that they might both regret.

No way. Kelly was certain she'd *never* regret this.

"Look at me, Michael," she said huskily. She ran her thumb over his stubborn jaw. Her other hand slid into the dark hair at his neck. "What a nice name. I've always thought that a woman should know the name of a man she's about to go to bed with."

Burke cursed softly. "It's the wrong time, Kelly. The wrong place. There are still too many questions . . ."

"Not for me there aren't."

She eased into the heat of him, the rigid, unyielding line of him. "I have no question at all about this," she murmured, pulling him down to take her kiss. "In fact, it feels like just about the most natural thing I've ever done."

When she ran her tongue over his mouth, he cursed.

When she eased past his lips, he groaned.

When she feathered his tongue with hers, he shuddered.

And then his hands were molding her, his lips harsh to her brow. "God, I thought he'd got you. I thought I'd never see you again." Burke pulled her against him, anchoring her hips with his big, strong hands, locking their urgent bodies together.

"I don't care about tomorrow, Michael. I just want now. I just want you, deep inside me." With trembling fingers Kelly caught the fine cotton of his shirt and shoved it over his tense shoulders.

Michael's eyes were dark and bottomless as she touched his chest. "Deep inside you is exactly where I'd be right now if things were different. But they aren't, Kelly. Right now you don't know *what* you want."

"I know I don't want to die," she said unsteadily. "And I know I don't want to leave you. Not now, when all I can think about is the hatred I felt out in that forest."

Burke frowned. He started to ask a question, but was interrupted by the sound of a door opening somewhere in the front of the house. Feet hammered over bare marble floors.

A moment later a booming male voice echoed down the corridor. "And here we are. Step inside, please. Closer, that's it. We will begin with the kitchen and servants' quarters today, so that you have an idea of how a great house was run from the downstairs up."

The voice moved closer. "I must confess that Edgehill, though not so grand as its neighbor to the south, has always been my favorite house in the county. Come right this way, please. I promise that you are going to enjoy what you see next."

Chapter 22

*B*urke cursed softly as a score of feet click-clacked over marble. "Damn it, today's the first Tuesday of the month. That must be Marston's brother and his bloody tour."

"Tour?" Kelly said, unsteadily.

"The Heritage Club. Every month they offer a cultural tour of Edgehill," Burke said grimly.

He stared down at Kelly's half-naked body and then at his own obvious dishevelment. Cursing sharply, he grabbed Kelly's hand and dragged her toward the doorway.

Twenty feet away a score of tourists ranged around a row of portraits, leaving no hope of escape.

"Bloody hell. We'll have to try the still room." Burke pulled Kelly around a huge open range and beneath a small archway.

The still room door was closed and locked. Down the hall the footsteps hammered closer.

"Over here," Kelly said breathlessly. Driven by intuition, she tugged Burke into a small alcove. There, hidden behind a painted trompe-l'oeil scene of a garden window, was a narrow door.

"Of course," Burke muttered. Then he frowned at Kelly. "But how did you know there was a linen room back here?"

"Just lucky, I guess," Kelly said swiftly. But of course luck had had nothing to do with it.

Intuition had.

Burke started to say something else, but Kelly dragged him inside and tugged the door shut behind them. They barely managed to wedge themselves between floor-to-ceiling shelves piled high with stacks of pristine damask and lace-edged linen before the tour group filed inside.

"Now then, here are the kitchens. You will observe the high vaulted ceilings, which hint at the house's monastic origins."

"Rot," Burke said softly, dismissing this bit of misinformation even as he tried to dismiss the effect of Kelly's thighs pressed against what was rapidly developing into a tremendously painful erection.

"Legend says that Elizabeth I and Bess of Hardwick slept in the house (not at the same time, of course), and that one of the queen's rivals was murdered here."

"Poppycock." Burke twisted slightly, but he and Kelly were wedged chest to chest between gleaming, lavender-scented linen.

He wasn't going to get a blasted shred of relief.

"Someone's robe," a voice said.

"Someone's shirt," another voice said.

Giggles swept through the group outside the door.

"No doubt the commander is in residence," the guide said briskly.

"And I'll just bet he's not alone," someone else said knowingly.

The tour guide cleared his throat. "That will be quite enough. Commander Burke's reputation, although extremely, er, shall we say . . ."

"Notorious?" someone suggested.

"Passionate?"

"How about a blisteringly hot operator between the sheets?"

The guide made a clucking noise. "Nonsense. The commander is simply a very attractive man who has yet to find a woman worthy of him. And as for these . . ." Fabric hissed past the door and *thwumped* against wood. "These are simply the signs of an age-old problem, and that problem is not Commander Burke's moral character but rather the difficulty of finding good servants."

Kelly tilted her head back. Her eyes took on a reckless gleam. "Notorious, are you?" she whispered, running her hand along one flat, hair-swirled male nipple. "A blisteringly hot operator between the sheets, no less?"

"No you don't, Red," Burke growled as she fitted herself closer and traced his ribs.

He went rigid, his muscles bunched and knotted beneath her questing fingers. He was warm and big and the hair on his chest had the most intriguing sort of swirls, Kelly decided.

She opened her mouth and eased her lips over the same area.

Burke's fingers locked in her hair. He groaned when she found her target.

"What was *that*?" a voice outside demanded.

"Just the house settling, no doubt. These old houses are often a chaos of different structures laid down at varying periods. It creates a tremendous architectural strain where the various renovations overlap. Although," the guide confided, lowering his voice, "Edgehill *is* said to be haunted. Many residents have claimed to see a knight galloping along the cliffs known as Lyon's Leap."

Kelly drew her tongue slowly down the center of Burke's chest, smiling as he shuddered against her. Smiling because right now she didn't give a hoot about ghosts or forests or a madman who liked watching his prey squirm on a hook.

Sunlight fell through the linen room's single window, painting Burke's hair with glints of copper and gold and deep blue, firing his body a warm, supple bronze. Kelly knew *this* was all she cared about.

"You're lovely, Michael. But you've got too many clothes on," she said huskily, searching for his belt.

"You're playing with fire, Professor. I just hope you know that."

"Fire is exactly what I had in mind," Kelly said, her voice like hot silk.

Outside, the group clattered dangerously close.

Burke's eyes probed Kelly's face. He fought to control the desire fast slipping past his control. "Are you sure, Kelly? Completely sure?"

"Totally. Now how about some help here?"

His hand slid behind her and twisted the key in the lock a split second before someone outside tried the door.

"That's odd. This linen closet is always open. Ah, well, suffice it to say that at one time Edgehill possessed over four thousand tablecloths totalling over six miles of damask and custom-woven Irish linen. The parties held here over the years have also become legendary. For example, in one evening alone nearly ten thousand bottles of champagne were consumed. Coincidentally, that same night Lillie Langtry is rumored to have posed *au naturel* in an after-dinner tableau attended by four kings, two heads of state, and several royal princes."

"Ten thousand? That figure's way too large," Burke muttered.

"Wonderfully large," Kelly agreed, her fingers sliding over his thigh, feeling rigid muscle strain against her.

"And getting larger every second," Burke growled.

"Now we'll have a look at the bedrooms."

"The bedrooms sound good to me," Kelly said huskily.

Outside the tour group clattered through the kitchen and back out into the hall.

Burke's eyes glittered gray-gold, promising sweet vengeance. "Forget it, Red. We wouldn't make it half that far," he growled, tonguing one berry-red nipple that thrust with startling vigor against the fine lace of her teddy.

Kelly gasped. Fire licked through dozens of hidden, aching places. Blindly, she fumbled for his belt buckle.

Cursing softly, Burke pushed her hands away, intent on finding the snaps on her teddy. "Damn it, how do you open this thing?"

Kelly shuddered, past coherence, past anything but pleasure as his hands slid over her. "I don't— that is, there are—"

Groaning, Burke simply caught her ankle and tugged it up onto the ledge beside him. Swiftly, he nudged the lace aside and found the sweet heat he was looking for.

Kelly gasped as he parted the hot wet silk of her.

"Sweet Lord, Kelly. We'll burn each other up!"

"Michael, please!" Her voice was choked.

He slid a second finger inside her, slow and exquisitely thorough, smiling darkly when he saw a look of blind wonder flash over her face. "Now, Kelly. Let me feel you burn, love."

She cried out, nails digging into his shoulders.

She clenched around him. He felt pleasure slam through her. God, she had to be the most responsive woman alive.

Then her eyes opened. Their glittering blue lights reminded Michael of the crystal waters of a Tahitian cove he had once sailed right after a hurricane.

He would take her there, he decided. There and a thousand other places he'd always loved. He would share all his tomorrows with her. In dawn and darkness, in joy and sorrow they'd be together.

He had an inkling then, the jabbing sense that somehow in another place and time he had seen and touched her this way before. Something told him that then too she had been the whole universe to him, but somehow he had lost her.

It was not going to happen to them this time.

Kelly stared at him. Her cheeks filled with color.

"Beautiful," Michael whispered, finding the tiny snaps and nudging them free.

Every movement made her shiver.

Then the lavender lace went flying and it was Burke who gasped, taking in the creamy length of Kelly's body and her high, thrusting breasts.

"Now, Michael," she said urgently, pulling him to her.

A zipper hissed. Flannel and cotton went flying.

And then, blessed heaven, the glory of skin, only skin. The wonder of heat on heat, need to blind need.

"Now," Michael agreed harshly. "Oh, God, Kelly, right now, let me have you. Let me have *us*."

"Yes," she gasped, as he cupped her hips and brought her against him. "Now. To hell with tomorrow. All I want is *this*. With you."

Her husky entreaty shattered the last of Burke's control.

In one fluid movement he trapped her hips, shoved her back against the polished door, and plunged inside her.

Kelly cried out. He was huge and hard and the pleasure of it nearly drove her over the edge again. "Michael, it's hot. You're—so perfect." She rocked against him, wanting him even deeper.

He shuddered at every silken movement. "No, not perfect, Red. Not quite yet. But it's damned well going to be."

He watched her face as he moved inside her, loving it when she gasped and moaned his name, fired beyond words when she arched against him, driving him closer.

He made a decision then. A decision that involved not pulling out of her and putting on what he'd shoved into the pocket of his trousers. What need was there for protection when he planned on spending a whole lifetime with this woman? Giving her his name and his children had to be one of the highlights of the new lifeplan Burke was rapidly discovering.

But for one raw moment the ex-Royal Marine knew a nagging fear. Would he be able to please this lovely, fragile woman? Dear Lord, would he be able to hold back long enough to keep from hurting her this first time?

And then the worries simply melted like rain on desert sand. All there was to think about was Kelly, hot and soft and so incredibly tight that he thought he'd die of the pleasure she was giving him.

But not yet, Burke thought.

Smiling darkly, he pulled away, parting her heat with his fingers.

"Michael—oh, God, it's too soon. It's too much." She pushed against him with blind urgency. "I can't possibly—"

Before she could finish he thrust home inside her. Eyes dazed, back arched, she cried out and clung to him, her nails digging into his back.

He felt the tremors seize her again.

Long moments later, her eyes fluttered open. They glinted up at him, luminous, chiding, full of love. "Four thousand tablecloths. I'm *very* impressed, Commander," she said throatily.

They both knew she wasn't talking about tablecloths.

"Impressed? Just wait," Burke warned hoarsely.

White linen tumbled to the floor and Kelly followed it down, anchored tight in Burke's arms. The air was lush with the fresh smell of lavender and sun-dried cloth as he tugged open a square of heavy white damask and pushed her down against it.

They filled the whole floor.

Kelly stared up at him, suddenly serious, fingers curled weakly around his neck. "Michael, that was—you were—" She colored slightly. "Absolutely . . . amazing," she finished, breathless.

"Red?"

"Y-yes?"

"That wasn't amazing."

"It wasn't?"

"No," Burke whispered, groaning a little at her beauty, at her infinite giving, at her lush generosity where she cushioned him against her. He shook his head and smiled grimly. "Hell, no, *this* is amazing."

He gripped her knees and pushed deep within her, driving her down hard into the crisp white damask.

Hot, wet skin parted and slid and folded around him.

She whimpered, clinging tight along the rigid length of him. Burke nearly died with the pleasure of it.

Then there was only Kelly, only the little choked sounds of her pleasure, only her hands holding him tight as the blinding waves of pleasure exploded through her yet again.

And this time Burke let himself go, following her down blindly through pleasure's hot, dark gate. Her name was on his lips as he fell; her face was in his eyes as he watched a lifetime of mornings rise up before him, mornings of sunlight and laughter where his bitter past and all his dark nightmares held no more power to harm him.

She had done that, with her husky laugh and her stubborn courage and her gentle, loving fingers.

Burke knew he was going to spend at least the next hundred or so years trying to thank her for it.

If she didn't kill him with pleasure *first*, that is.

*   *   *

"M-Michael?" She sighed and stirred weakly.

Burke felt the tiny kiss planted on his neck. He smiled, easing his fingers through her warm hair. *"Hmmm?"*

"You were right . . ."

"I was?" He felt her nod against his chest. He held her gently, fingers tracing soft circles against her love-warm skin. "About what?"

"About that. *That* was absolutely amazing."

He laughed softly and pulled her head into the hollow of his neck, awed by the perfect way they fit, amazed by how familiar it felt to hold her just like this.

As if they'd been lovers forever rather than barely one hour.

And then Burke smiled darkly. She thought *that* was amazing?

He decided not to tell her what he had planned *next*.

They finally made it to the bedroom. Behind them the damask was dumped unceremoniously, their clothes a forgotten tangle on one of the kitchen tables.

They fought their way over the satin quilt and laughed their way from one end of the huge featherbed to the other, drunk with love and the reckless joy of discovery.

Neither lost a battle in that big old bed. Both of them won the war.

Afterward, Burke pulled her close and slid one hard hand across her stomach. Just that way he stayed, watching her fall asleep in his arms, wondering once again how she could possibly feel so achingly familiar . . .

*   *   *

The sun was sinking over the hills above the castle when Lyon tugged on his clothes and turned to wake the woman asleep beside him.

She came awake with a start.

A most becoming flush stained her cheeks when she discovered that his hand was wrapped possessively around her breast. "Lyon ? Why are you—" Recollection stirred. Her blush grew flame-bright.

"Precisely, my lady. I see your memory has returned."

"I wish it had not."

"Is that a complaint? You did not complain so an hour ago, woman."

Aislann gave his chest a playful nip. "And you are no gentleman to remind me."

Lyon sighed, wishing they could stay by the river forever, legs entwined, bodies soft with surfeit. But they could not. It was late and Hugh would be returning soon.

"Come," he said, slipping Aislann's gown over her head. "We must go. It will soon be dark and I mean to take no chance on Aelfric's return."

At that word, a shadow crossed Aislann's face. Lyon cursed. "Forget him, my heart. The man will not harm you ever again. As I live and breathe, I swear it."

He spoke fiercely, with a possessiveness that was entirely new to him. And with his arms wrapped around her shoulders, Aislann felt cherished and wonderfully protected.

Most of all she felt loved. In a way she'd never thought to know. Her hands brushed his cheek for a moment, and then she stood up and tugged on her tattered gown.

"Let me help you," Lyon said gruffly. He arranged his cloak over her torn bodice and fitted his silver

brooch atop the folds at one corner. "There. You look quite the wild princess again. As beautiful as a witch caught at her dark enchanting."

He cursed, seeing pain darken her eyes at his thoughtless phrase. "Forgive me for a witless fool, my love. 'Tis not true, you must know that by now."

Slowly Aislann nodded. Her eyes found his, full of wonder, full of joy. "I do know it, Lyon. You have made me believe it."

Lyon groaned, wishing it were night that he might take her against him again in love.

But there was no time.

"I am glad to hear it, mignonne. And I would to God that we could stay here forever, but we cannot. I must meet my chamberlain and I fear the king's representative cannot be put off any longer. Then there are cases to be heard, disputes to be decided—"

Aislann cut him off with a finger to his lips. "There is naught to explain. You are who you are. And I—" Her eyes glistened. "I shall be waiting at the cottage whenever you can come to me."

"It shall be as soon as I can manage. Until then I'll send Hugh with you. Tell him whatever you need and it shall be brought."

"You are too generous, Lyon. The Saxons will resent it. Your own people will dislike it even more."

"Then the devil fly away with all of them," Lyon said crossly. He did not care to be reminded of all the things that separated them. He pulled her close for one last, hard kiss that seemed to go on forever.

Yet ended far too soon.

When he let her go, her eyes were dark with passion, hungry with need—just as his own were, Lyon knew. He stifled a curse and pushed her toward the path that led up to the castle. "Go now. Any more *and I'll never be able to take my leave of you! I'll give you ten minutes before I follow, just in case anyone is watching."* He thrust her basket in her hand. *"And take these. You were here to gather herbs, remember?"* Lyon caught up a handful of limp plants and dumped them into her basket.

Aislann laughed raggedly. *"I fear I forgot entirely."*

"You compliment me well, my lady." Lyon slanted her a wolfish smile.

"But these are weeds not herbs, my lord!"

"They will do well enough, woman. Now go." With every minute Lyon felt it grow harder for him to let her go.

At the top of the hill she turned. For a moment her slender body was silhouetted against the glow of the setting sun. *"You have my heart, Norman. I had not thought to give it, but today it is done. I pray you will guard it well."*

The soft words drifted down to Lyon, carried on the spring wind.

"Aye, I will remember, my rose."

And so he would. He would guard her heart well. With his life. With his very last breath.

And maybe even beyond.

Beneath the azure sky the summer wind blew free. It skittered across the valley, whispered through the maple trees, and teased the ferns beside the Witch's Pool. Somewhere nearby, where the moat gurgled lazily and bees droned among the roses, two voices seemed to rise, little more substantial than the wind's soft sigh.

"They are safe?"

"I . . . I don't know."

Two figures took form, shimmering and translucent in the golden light that haloed the moat. The man was broad-shouldered, clad all in black except for the lace fluttering at his wrists and collar. The woman beside him shone like the sun itself, her cloth-of-gold sleeves fluttering in the wind.

Around them there was no sound, no disturbance to mar the day's drowsy peace.

The guardian ghost of Draycott Abbey frowned. "They have left my land. My power can pass no farther."

His companion studied him silently, her dark eyes full of misgiving. "What are you saying, Adrian? Surely it cannot be so bad as that."

The Draycott ghost looked down at the woman beside him. His hands moved gently to cup her cheek. "My power has limits, my love. You must have known that."

"But Adrian, these people hidden about the estate—these weapons everywhere. And what about the other one, the one with the cold, angry eyes?"

"Yes, I know, Gray. I feel him clearly. But the time is not yet right. His plans are not chosen. Until he has made his choice, we can make no move against him."

"It's dreadfully unfair. The abbey and all its occupants are in danger and we are unable to do anything to help!" The woman beside him moved closer. "Adrian, I—I begin to grow frightened."

He knew the seriousness of the threat then. Never before had this woman flinched at rankest treachery or mortal danger. Never had she retreated, not even when a madman had dogged her steps.

Not even in death itself.

Adrian circled her shoulders. He sent out his love to surround her.

"Is it the urn? If that's so, Adrian, maybe we can—"

He ran a hand gently through her hair. "No more questions."

"But—"

"*Shhh.* I'll find a way, never doubt it. Just as you must never doubt the strength of my love for you."

"What are you planning? I want to know, Adrian. I *insist* upon knowing!"

"I? Planning something in secret? Really, my heart, you are turning shrewish in your old age."

"Shrewish? Old age! Why you—" Her face paled. "You're just trying to distract me. I won't have it! I demand to know what rash thing you're planning."

Adrian pushed his worry away, buried it deep where her clever mind couldn't ferret it out. "All of my plans involve *you*, my heart. I'm afraid I'm quite besotted."

"Cad." Her hand cupped his cheek. "As if I can't read you like an open book by now. You know, if I did not love you so very much I would grow angry at your high-handed ways, my lord."

A thrush called merrily from the coppice as Adrian covered her hand with his. "Do you? Love me?"

"You know it full well."

His face was suddenly hard. "Then show me, sweeting. Show me now."

"H-here?"

"Who is there to see us?"

"But it is barely midday!"

Adrian's dark brow quirked to a slant. "So?"

"So—it is most improper. It is entirely scandalous. It is—"

"Delicious." His fingers eased into the opening at her neck and slowly traced the curve of her breast. "Quite sinfully enticing. I've been able to think of nothing else since I watched you bathe in the Witch's Pool. You were . . . remarkable."

His companion's cheeks took on a becoming hue of pink. "Really, Adrian. You are the most *insatiable* man."

"With you about, I can be nothing less, my dear."

"Adrian, no. We must not—"

But it was too late. His fingers had found her warm, budded nipple. He smiled darkly, feeling a shudder go through her. "As beautiful as the first time I saw you, love. All those lonely months ago . . ."

"You'll never be lonely again," she whispered fiercely.

Her head fell back. His lips feathered down the curve of her throat.

"Yes, love. Whisper my name. Whisper all the ways you want me to touch you. And I shall give you every one," he said hoarsely, as golden silk rustled to a luminous pool at his feet. "Most certainly I shall please you. But not nearly as much as *you* please me."

Even the thrush ceased its wild song as the two bodies began to glow, as light leapt up and played around them and they became one.

Chapter 23

She stormed into the house like a tiny whirl-wind, which was exactly how she did every-thing.

Her white hair was pulled off her brow in an exquisite chignon that showed her fine, high cheekbones. Her suit was what she called the last of the *real* Chanel (pre-Lagerfeld), and her huge quilted leather Ferragamo bag was stuffed full of baguettes, *crème fraîche*, and freshly cut herbs and roses from her garden.

"Mikhail, where are you? I know you're here, so there's no point in hiding."

She stamped her foot when there was no answer. Dumping bag and purse, she started for the kitchen.

In the middle of the floor she stopped, frown-ing down at the paisley silk gown and man's knit shirt tossed on a wooden worktable.

Ten feet away lay a tangle of her best table-cloths, topped by a pair of trousers. Her *son's* trousers, unless the marchioness missed her guess.

And alongside the trousers lay an angora

sweater, a woman's floral skirt, and a very fetching lace undergarment.

A look of pure wickedness flashed through the woman's keen gray eyes. Eyes that looked remarkably like her son's, although Michael Burke was some thirty years younger.

This time when the Dowager Marchioness of Sefton started for the stairs, she was careful not to make a sound.

She heard the noise of muffled laughter before she'd even rounded the second floor landing. Carefully she followed the sound to her son's room.

That he was with a woman did not surprise her. He was a man of deep passion. She had raised him to be so, for it was much a part of their Russian blood.

But that he should bring a woman *here*, to Edgehill, surprised her greatly. She knew for a fact that he had never done such a thing before.

Which meant this one was different.

Thinking swiftly, she slid out of sight and watched. Ah, but this woman was fine, all laughter and shining eyes. She reminded the marchioness of a *rusalka*, the water spirit of her Russian childhood, a fairytale creature of silver and shadow.

So, my Misha, you have fallen at last. The white-haired woman smiled. Perhaps she was going to have a grandchild to dandle on her knee after all.

"No more, *drushka*," the hoarse voice warned.

Kelly inched closer, kissing the beautiful planes of Michael's face. Smiling slightly, she moved down to his collarbone. As she did so, she managed to slide her thigh across his hip.

"Kelly, we must eat. We must talk. We must . . ." His breath hissed out in a sigh.

"And then?"

"Then we must go back to Draycott Abbey."

"Pooh." The russet-haired American turned her head away and feathered a line of kisses along Burke's strong, corded biceps.

His fingers tightened in her hair. He studied her, his expression a blend of tenderness, desire, and acute frustration. "My sentiments exactly, but it must be done. After the sword is found, things will be different. Then we'll have all the time in the world, my love."

"I don't want all the time in the world," Kelly said huskily, brushing her tongue over his ribs and down onto his flat stomach. "I only want *now*. Right here with you."

Burke groaned as she caught the edge of the sheet and slid it lower with her teeth, down over muscles that were screaming for all the same things she wanted.

But they couldn't have them. Not until this mystery of the urn was solved. Not until Kelly was out of danger.

Abruptly Michael felt Kelly stiffen. "What is it, Red? Tired of me so soon?" He couldn't see her expression.

The woman curled against his chest swallowed.

Michael followed her gaze. A slender figure in a fuchsia Chanel suit with gold braid stood staring at them from the doorway, a smile playing over her perfectly glossed lips.

"Mother!" He was on his feet in a second, jerking the sheet up around Kelly and then struggling to find something to cover himself.

Unfortunately, blankets and coverlet had all gone flying in the reckless pleasures of the prior hour and Kelly now had the only remaining cover.

Cursing, Michael grabbed a pillow and shoved it before his lower body. "What in heaven's name are *you* doing here?"

"I live here, Misha. You might perhaps remember that?" The regal figure moved gracefully into the bedroom and held out her hand to the red-faced woman in Michael's bed. "I am Lady Sefton, my dear. My son appears to have forgotten his manners, it seems." She frowned thoughtfully. "I do not think that we have been introduced."

"Kelly," the woman in the bed croaked. "Er, K-Kelly Hamilton."

Michael's lips took on a faint curve as the humor of the situation began to assert itself. "*Professor* Kelly Hamilton, that is. Please meet my mother, the Dowager Marchioness of Sefton."

"How lovely. You are a professor? Naval science, no doubt. Or perhaps petrochemical engineering. You young women of today are all so stubborn and independent."

"Actually, my degree is in archeology," Kelly managed to answer.

"But how fascinating. You must come and tell me exactly what that means."

"Do forgive me for my rudeness, Mother," Burke said dryly.

"Forgiven." The woman gave him an airy wave. "I have grown quite accustomed to it, I'm afraid. Now, my dear, you must come downstairs while I make up a pot of lovely Darjeeling and lemon slices. Then we shall talk. Oh, about everything." She held out her hand to Kelly, who found no choice but to hike the sheet around her chest and slide to her feet.

"Don't worry about my son," the marchioness said, her eyes twinkling as she studied the pillow still clutched to Burke's lower body. "The boy has always had overactive hormones, I fear." She looked searchingly at Kelly for a moment, then brushed her cheek. "Yes, very like a *rusalka*," she murmured.

"Mother, what in heaven's name are you planning?"

"None of your business," came the curt reply.

"Michael?" Kelly asked faintly, entirely bewildered, her face most becomingly flushed.

Burke laughed softly, as usual completely outgunned and outflanked by his mother's sheer imperiousness. "It's all right, Red. I'll be right down."

"Take your time, Mikhail."

Pulled inexorably forward by the marchioness, Kelly wobbled toward the door, her linen sheet billowing out behind her.

Burke shook his head and hurled his pillow against the wall.

"And then I told the man he could take his Maserati and his caviar and his depressingly ugly Patek Philippe watches and toss them right into the Seine." The marchioness laughed softly. "He was most astonished, I assure you. No one had *ever* turned him down before."

Kelly sat nursing her tea, overwhelmed even as she was utterly charmed by the slender woman bustling through the kitchen.

"Now where are the knives? Oh, yes, right here." A cleaver appeared and the marchioness murmured beneath her breath. "I really must begin taking an interest in this kitchen. There is no logic to any of it. Of course it has been that way ever since Sergei left."

Kelly smiled, "I've heard about Sergei."

"The man was a positive genius. And his *Baba au rhum*." The marchioness shook her head, sighing. "Unfortunately it became necessary for him to leave. One does not take risks with one's children," the older woman said, suddenly serious. "You *do* agree with that, do you not, my dear?"

Kelly felt the sharp gray eyes assess her. A test.

She nodded. "I can't speak from personal experience, however."

"Ah, well, there will be time enough for that," the marchioness said, nodding. Then, as she saw uncertainty flash through Kelly's eyes, "And you might as well know the truth. I went up there quite on purpose to meet you. I am delighted that my suspicions were correct. You are quite special. And since you are clearly desperate to ask but afraid to phrase the question, my son has never brought a woman home to Edgehill before. I am enormously happy that you are the first." She set a bowl of red damask roses down before Kelly and inhaled deeply. "And I hope you will be the last," she added meaningfully.

"You are . . . very kind."

"Nonsense. I am simply being selfish. Thank you for bringing my son back here to Edgehill. Back here to *me*."

"But I didn't . . ."

"Oh, but you did. You made him whole so that he was able to return. It has been years since we've shared a civil word, you see."

"What—happened?"

"What happened? We had an argument, Miss Hamilton. A very bad argument. After that my son never spoke more than a dozen sentences to me. Not until today."

Kelly yearned to ask more, but did not. This would be for Michael to share with her if he chose.

"Yes, I am very selfish. I grow impatient waiting for a grandchild, you see."

Kelly's face flushed crimson.

"Forgive an old woman's plain speaking, my dear. My friends indulge me too much, I fear."

"No—it's not that. It's simply that we—that Michael and I—"

"There is no need to explain. My son is as passionate as he is honorable. If he brought you here it is for a reason. He has never been a man for casual *affaires*, I assure you."

A male throat was cleared from the doorway. "Your son also has excellent hearing," Burke said dryly, now dressed in a white shirt and deep charcoal flannels. "He would also greatly appreciate it if you ceased to refer to him in the third person, Mother."

"Of course, if you prefer it, my love," the marchioness said, entirely unmoved.

Burke sighed. He had just showered and his dark hair was slicked back, glistening with water. Kelly thought he looked dangerous and too handsome to be real.

Her eyes told him as much.

His eyes told her roughly the same, only they did it with a far more blatant sexual hunger.

Kelly felt her cheeks grow hot again.

"She does blush a great deal, doesn't she, Mikhail," the marchioness said blandly. "I don't believe that any of your others did." And then, before her son could protest, "Now do be a good boy and make us some cucumber sandwiches. I'm all thumbs in the kitchen, as you know."

Once again, Kelly was struck by the absurdity of the situation. At least she was dressed now.

She sighed and decided there was nothing else to do but go with the flow. "Michael, you didn't tell me you could cook."

"There are a lot of things I didn't get around to telling you, Red," he said huskily. After one dark, heated look, he turned and began assembling ingredients from the state-of-the-art sub-zero cooler opposite the worktable. "We *were* rather rudely disturbed," he muttered.

His mother smiled hugely, looking like a cat contemplating a very large bowl of cream.

Kelly watched, entranced, as Michael juggled wafer-thin slices of bread spread with cream cheese into fine sandwiches, neatly ringed them with cucumber wedges, and capped the arrangement with a cucumber carved in the shape of a perfect rosette.

"Most impressive, Mikhail." The marchioness sampled a wedge, her expression critical. "A pinch of dill would improve the flavor, however. I grow it fresh in my own garden, of course," she explained to Kelly, who could only nod as if she held this kind of conversation every day.

"Eat, Professor." Michael bent across the table, looking at her with unmistakable tenderness. He pushed a sandwich wedge into her unsteady fingers. "After this afternoon's . . . exertions, you must be famished," he said huskily.

Again the flush.

The marchioness chuckled. "Really, children, you do make one feel so appallingly *old*."

"Oh, no, you're not old at all. You're—you're wonderful!" Kelly blurted. "I mean, I only hope I have half your grace and vitality when I'm— that is—"

Burke put her out of her misery. "She knows exactly what you mean, Red. She simply delights in embarrassing people. Don't you, Mother?"

The marchioness spread her hands elegantly. "There is so little else to amuse me these days. All my friends have moved away to Carmel and Provence and Capri . . ." She took another bite of her sandwich and nodded thoughtfully. "Yes, these are very tolerable, Mikhail. But do not tell me you learned this at Sandhill." She held up the carved rosette. "Nor *this.*"

Burke braced his elbows on the table, enjoying the sight of Kelly, flushed and smiling. He was also, strangely enough, enjoying being here with his mother—sharing his happiness with her. "I picked that up in Hong Kong from an ancient Shanghainese painter who'd learned it in Tokyo from the emperor's personal chef."

His mother shook her head, eyeing the nick on the wall with regret. "Poor Sergei. Now there was a chef. If only he'd had a better temper." Abruptly she frowned. "Whatever were you doing in Hong Kong, Misha?"

Burke shrugged. "Some shopping. Some business." His eyes darkened for a moment. "Some recovering."

Seeing pain flash through his eyes, Kelly reached across the table and took his hand in hers. "Welcome back," she said softly. Tenderly.

Burke realized then that he *was* back, feet securely on the ground, mind balanced and heart happy as they hadn't been for years. Maybe forever . . .

"Thanks, Kelly. It's damned good to be home." After a moment Michael looked at his mother, including her in the look. "Do you know, Mother, I feel I'm starting to understand a lot of things I never did before."

The older woman's face softened, and she rose to her feet. "I'm very glad to hear that. But really, some wine is in order. A Côte de Nuits Romanée St. Vivant, I think. Or perhaps you'd prefer champagne."

"No wine," Michael said flatly.

"But surely—"

"No, Mother. It's not safe. I need a clear head."

The marchioness's eyes darkened. Fear flashed over her regal features. "Oh, no, Misha," she said huskily. "Not the danger again. Not with this nice young woman. You told me it was over. After you came back the last time, so terribly hurt, you told me you were done with all that." She caught her son's hand tightly.

In that unguarded moment, Kelly saw the woman's careful gaiety and bravado wiped away, leaving only a mother's ravaged eyes, eyes that had too often watched a son set off for places from which he might never return alive.

Michael dropped a kiss upon her brow. "It's nothing, Mother. I'm—taking some medicine that doesn't mix well with alcohol. And Kelly doesn't drink," he added smoothly.

But not quite smoothly enough.

The marchioness's shoulders stiffened. "If you choose to lie to me, my son, so be it." She turned away and gathered her jacket and bag. "I do not have to like it, however. Nor this unrelentingly dangerous work you refuse to give up. And I can't sit and wait, always afraid they'll bring you back to me in bandages like they did last time. Or that maybe this time they won't bring you back at all . . ."

Her voice broke. She caught a quick breath, gave a last look at Kelly, and brushed her cheek. "Be careful, young woman. Be very careful with this damnable son of mine . . ."

The marchioness looked at Michael then, her eyes haunted, her lips tight with the effort to hold back tears. "May God protect you, Misha." She said something in Russian, low and hoarse.

And then she was gone, as mercurial as the storm winds she so resembled.

Burke cursed softly.

"What did she say?"

"*Nyet vikhadah.* 'No exit.' " He stared at the doorway where the countess had disappeared. "She might be right."

Somewhere in the house a phone rang. Burke let it ring.

"Hadn't you better . . ."

"Why? It will only be more news, almost certainly bad. They'll find me soon enough without my answering."

After a long time the ringing ceased. Burke pulled Kelly against him, his jaw rigid. "I'd like to stay here forever, Red. I'd like to make the world go away." His fingers tensed. "But I can't. I've got to leave here and take you with me. And out there will be more of the same, more of the questions, more of the danger—"

She covered his mouth with her finger. "I knew what I was doing, Michael. You never lied to me." *Oh, but I have lied to you,* she thought. *And even now I withhold my secrets . . .*

"I wish that made me feel better. I wish that made you safer. But it bloody well doesn't."

"Then we'd better get it over with. Maybe then . . ."

He caught her close and pressed a hard, searching kiss against her yielding lips. He took all of her, hungry and open-mouthed, a man driven.

And then he pulled away. The telephone began to ring again.

When Burke walked away he didn't look back.

Kelly watched him, her pulse hammering. Then she felt it.

Danger. It was lapping all around her, smooth and silent.

She locked her fingers to her head, fighting the blackness of it, but there was no use. It was like shoving back water with a sieve.

Him. He was waiting. It felt, suddenly, as if he'd been waiting forever. Watching. Hating them . . .

"My lord, you are not listening. This is the new chain mail you ordered. I must fit it before I can—"

Lyon sighed and looked up from his scrutiny of the dark hills. As he stood on the high tower, the wind ruffling his hair, his chief armorer studied him expectantly.

So had his time passed for two days, ever since his return from the river, one pressing duty after another.

Then had come the evenings.

Villeins with quarrels over grazing rights. A knight pleading family illness to return to Normandy. The bishop requesting a meeting to discuss a donation for the new abbey. On top of all that, a messenger had come from William. Lyon's presence was required two days hence at court.

"And what am I to do about the new sword, I ask you? Decent materials are not available in this

godforsaken place, nothing like the magnificent St. Vaux weapon you carry at your side. I fear I shall have to—"

Lyon barely heard. From the top of the keep he stared out at the darkness to the south. And he thought about the nights.

The long, terrible nights.

In the nights had come dreams, dark and confusing. They seized him and shook him awake, wild-eyed and sweating.

Terrified.

Of what, Lyon could not say, except that he was certain the danger involved Aislann.

Now as he stared out over the great forest he fancied he could almost make out Aislann's cottage and the great oak that grew beside it. Was that a rushlight candle shining in her window? Or was it the flame of her cooking fire?

Did she wait for him even now?

Desire stabbed through him at the thought. How he wished he could be there to roll in the sweet straw, to feel her soft hands upon him.

"My lord?" Now the chamberlain, too, had come in search of him. "The king's messenger awaits below. Shall I—"

"Yes, yes!" Lyon said impatiently. His hands clenched to fists. "Tell him I'll be down shortly."

The chamberlain nodded and backed away quickly.

The old armorer chuckled softly. "You've the very devil of a temper this day, my lord. The last thing you want to hear is me ranting on about armor, I warrant."

Lyon gave his retainer a crooked smile. "All too true, old friend. Do as you see fit about the pommel and hilt. I would have it heavy but well balanced, with the decoration we discussed. But now—" His eyes sought the faint light beneath the great oak tree. "Now I must go."

The armorer gaped. "But the king's representative—"

Even Lyon's hunting dogs looked up at him, their eyes dark with censure.

"Let them all wait!" Lyon muttered, grabbing up his cloak and striding toward the stairs.

Lyon spurred his horse forward through the midnight trees, taking the narrow path much too fast. Branches struck his face, thorns clawed his hands, but he paid no heed. All his concern was for Aislann.

All evening he'd felt a strange uneasiness.

Suddenly he was desperate to be sure she was safe and well. To kiss her, to touch her, if only for a few moments . . .

He cursed as a vine caught at his cloak. No moon tonight, damn his luck! And the gorge would be coming up soon.

He slowed his horse. He could just make out the dark outline of the gorge. Any farther and he might have missed it.

The Norman shivered, imagining the screaming plummet to the rocks below. He backed his horse up, murmuring softly, and then hammered forward.

In one smooth stride they took the black abyss. For the first time in weeks Lyon felt free and he laughed aloud with the joy of it.

And then the clearing was before him. The wind whispered through the leaves of the great oak. As Lyon tethered his horse, Hugh appeared from the shed behind the cottage.

"She is safe?"

"Safe within, my lord. Sleeping, I would think. She's been quite restless today." Hugh gave Lyon a sideways glance. "Just as you appear to be, my liege." The knight looked concerned. "More dreams?"

"What do you know of my dreams?"

Hugh shrugged. "Even here, gossip travels. And I was beside you in Damascus and Sicily, Lyon. I share those dreams."

Lyon shuddered, remembering the heat, the smell of the dead and dying beneath the desert sun.

Yes, his dreams were dark, but he did not tell Hugh that his worries were different now. They all centered on Aislann and his growing fear that he would not be able to protect her.

Lyon covered his fear with a dark laugh. "Aye, I've been cursed with restlessness, my friend. So much that I've alienated old Buttrick, the armorer, and my chamberlain as well. As for the villeins, they think me possessed. But I'm here now at last." He started for the door, only to turn back as he felt Hugh's hand upon his arm.

"My lord—I would speak with you."

"Swiftly then."

Hugh frowned. "I have heard things, Lyon. Rumblings. Complaints. The men grow lazy and gossip like old women. It's all nonsense, of course, but . . ."

"But what?" Lyon bit back his impatience.

"They talk. And often it is about Aislann. They say she's . . . a witch. That she has cast a spell over you."

Lyon cursed. "I'll run them through before the sun rises! I'll not have my woman made mockery of."

"I'm afraid the gossip will not be tamed so easily, Lyon. It is not a random thing, but set about most cleverly."

"By whom, damn it?" Lyon stared at the cottage, willing the danger away, willing the whole world away so that he could be alone with the woman he loved.

Just for a while. Was it so very much to ask?

"I cannot be sure. The Lady Vivienne?"

"Gone."

"Gone but not far, I'll wager," Hugh muttered. "The woman was ever too full of schemes. She is damnably close with the bishop, by the way. I would go careful there, if I were you."

Lyon cursed silently at this new complication, but he refused to take Hugh's warning seriously. There was nothing Vivienne could do, nor even the bishop. Here on this land, he was lord and master.

Lyon studied Hugh. "Advice, my friend?"

The knight clasped his shoulder. "Mind your step, my lord. And I shall mind your back. Just in case."

She was asleep. Her hair was a red-gold pool, lit by the dying flames. She murmured softly, warm and safe in the furs that Hugh had brought her from the castle.

The fire cast a soft glow through the cottage as Aislann drifted from dream to dream, from kiss to kiss, always locked in Lyon's arms.

Softness feathered across her nose. She sighed and turned to her side.

Again it came, atop her cheek this time.

Aislann made a sound of protest and brushed at her face.

Soft lips circled her ear. Soft fingers slid over her hips and lifted the silk chemise Lyon had sent with Hugh.

Aislann's body recognized Lyon before her mind did. Her arms softened, turned, sought his strength.

She was yielding, restless, by the time her eyes opened in recognition.

"Lyon? 'Tis truly you?"

"Here at last. Forgive me for being so late, my love. I could not get away sooner."

"No matter. You are here now. I've cooked a plump hare. And I have wine and bread if you—"

Lyon caught her hand and slid it around his neck. His smile was fire itself. "I have no need of bread or wine. Only of you, mignonne." His fingers anchored her cheeks. "And I need you most desperately. Now."

Aislann felt the heated thrust of him. She gave him a sidelong glance. "So I observe, my liege. You are most awesomely large."

Lyon groaned. He caught her hands against the soft furs and slanted his body over her, kissing her hungrily. His thighs moved against hers.

She was red and gold in the dancing firelight, all softness and woman against the fine furs.

His desire, long simmering, exploded into red-hot demand.

But a sudden thought made Lyon freeze. "You are well, my lady? Your . . . pains have gone?"

"Pains, my lord?"

"You were small and tight. You must have had some pain, my love."

Aislann flushed. Lyon thought her breathtaking at that moment and wondered how he had lived twenty-five years without her. "Tell me, Aislann. I do not wish to hurt you."

She avoided his eyes, toying with a fold of her chemise.

Lyon felt the cold rush of fear. "Aislann? Are you ailing? Dear God, why didn't you tell me sooner?" he bellowed.

Her gaze shot up to his. "No—that is, I vow, you need not—" Her face flamed.

"I need not what, woman?"

"Be concerned with hurting me."

Lyon's eyes narrowed. He fought to see if she was lying.

And then the restless slide of her hips beneath him told Lyon all he needed to know.

"Aislann." He nuzzled her breast and freed it from her furs, an exotic crimson bloom that budded only for him.

His hands combed through her red-gold fleece and found her heat.

She was sleek, on fire. For him.

Groaning, Lyon slid his fingers deep, delighting in her breathless cries, in the tiny marks her nails made against his shoulders.

And then she arched against him, crying his name raggedly.

He waited until her eyes opened, until the tremors had crested. Then he slid his chausses free and lifted her hips to meet his fiery thrust.

Her eyes widened. Her body began to tremble anew.

And this time Lyon held her close, feeling their hearts pound as one while desire poured over him in waves of black and dancing silver. In that moment, his dark dreams faded. All he saw was Aislann's sweet passion; all he felt was her rich yielding.

It was all he would ever need, the great Norman warrior thought as the sounds of his own joy mingled with hers.

He came to her again and again that night.

Wild as woodland creatures, they tumbled and slid across the firelit furs, across the fragrant herbs of lavender, mint, and rosemary that Aislann had scattered upon the bed.

Lyon was urgent, driving, and Aislann nearly as reckless as he. Around them they felt the webs of hatred and betrayal growing.

"This thing we feel cannot be wrong, can it, Lyon? Surely something that feels so perfect could not be wrong."

"Nay, my heart. It is all the best of man and woman. All the best of you and me that we share."

Aislann sighed. Her fingers brushed across his thighs. "Then show me, Lyon. Now. I fear you have made me most shameless."

Lyon groaned. "With all my heart, I'll show you, love. Right now."

The little cottage echoed with their laughter and their breathless passion. Outside, the oak leaves seemed to hum and sigh, sharing that sweet passion.

But even passion could not hold back their dark, unspoken fears.

Both of them knew that morning would come far too soon. And when it did, the world of kings and men and war would tear them apart once more.

So Aislann and Lyon were careful to conceal their fear and regret. Heedless in their pleasure, they wanted their last hours together to be unmarred by sadness or shadows.

"You are too kind in your offer of shelter on my journey, Monseigneur." The Lady Vivienne's eyes were soft, glittering. Enticing.

The bishop inclined his head graciously. "It is only meet and proper, my lady. But St. Vaux must be mad to send you off without proper escort." He frowned. "And in such frightful weather. I hate this country's constant rain."

The Frenchwoman considered her next words carefully. She did not dare to go directly against Lyon's orders. Still, a clever woman always had ways to bend the truth.

She gave the bishop a carefully tremulous smile. "Lyon is overburdened with the running of his lands. He gave the order carelessly, I fear."

The bishop's fingers drummed upon the carved arm of his great chair. "He is a man given to carelessness, I think. He may find it costs him sorely one day."

"Ah, but I fear this Saxon is to blame." The Frenchwoman gave a dramatic sigh. "The woman is said to be a witch. Even her own people fear and shun her. And now she has set her eyes on Lyon."

The bishop scowled. "I know of this creature. She shows none of the proper fear and respect that a believer should." He looked thoughtful. "And you say that she and Lyon . . ." He let his words trail off discreetly.

Vivienne smoothed her satin skirts. "They have been seen together often, Monseigneur. He grows quite besotted with her. I would not mention this to anyone other than you, but with my own eyes, I watched the Saxon fashion a figure in his likeness and hang it upside down while she chanted her godless spells."

The bishop pushed to his feet and crossed himself. "She dares to flaunt her dark arts so openly? Something must be done about this spawn of the devil!"

Behind him, the Lady Vivienne sat back in her chair. She smiled coldly into the shadows. How easily men were manipulated.

Now her careful plan was set and would soon move to its satisfying end. She would have revenge on St. Vaux at last.

* * *

He was watching when they came out of the house.

He inched down between the fluffy linden fronds and levelled the sight until Burke was caught within the crosshairs. His pulse took on a delicious hum as he tasted the power of the kill.

So easy.

One movement, clean and swift.

The bitch had been with him. It sickened him, their laughter, their constant excuses to touch each other. He had watched them through the window after the tour had gone upstairs.

He could almost smell the odor of their rutting.

Now there was no choice. He would have to kill Burke. Then the woman. But with her, he would take his time.

Maybe after that the voices would stop.

He nudged the sight higher, finding the center of Burke's forehead. Very carefully, he began to squeeze.

Kelly felt it as soon as they crossed the gravel drive. He was out there and he was watching. She felt a stab of warning.

Dear God, no! Not Michael . . .

Screaming, she rammed into Burke with her whole weight.

She saw his face crease with shock and then the ground rushing up to meet them.

Even before they hit, a twelve-gauge shell exploded into the earth behind them.

Chapter 24

*E*verything after that became a blur.

Somehow Burke grabbed her and hauled her to the far side of the Land Rover. He swung open the door, crawled inside, and yanked her in behind him.

"Close it and lock it," he growled. "Thank God I phoned Ross to bring over the car. I've got reinforced seat frames and bulletproof glass in these windows. Let the bastard try and shoot through that."

He jammed in the key and gunned the motor to life, then exploded into a 180-degree turn that slammed Kelly against his side.

His other arm came up to grip her as they thundered off toward the rear of the house.

He shoved his foot to the floor and sheared through a line of roses without blinking.

Kelly was frightened then, frightened as she never had been before. Because in Michael's eyes she saw the eyes of a killer.

"Do you want to tell me how you knew he was going to fire?" Michael's face was tight. They hadn't said a word since leaving Edgehill.

Kelly looked up at him, her eyes brilliant with tears. "I . . . can't tell you that."

Burke felt something break inside him. There was danger all around them and he couldn't fight it without answers. "Damn it, Kelly, answer my question!"

But the truth was something Kelly Hamilton had driven so deep that she wasn't sure she could recognize it anymore. "I—I felt something out there, that's all."

"You *knew* he was going to fire?"

"I wasn't certain. I'm still not sure exactly *what* I felt." She took a harsh breath and looked off toward Edgehill's golden walls, glowing above a bank of trees. "It's like that sometimes."

"I must be stupid, Kelly. I'm not following you." Burke's voice was very grim.

The sight of his fingers clenched white on the steering wheel was what finally changed her mind. She'd had enough with lying. She wanted this time to be honest. She loved this man and wanted a life with him, a life that had to begin right now, based on complete honesty.

If he believed her, fine. If not . . .

Kelly didn't let herself think about that.

"Michael, something happened to me five years ago, something that changed my life. There was an accident. I—I nearly died." She gave a mirthless laugh. "In point of fact, I *did* die. For two and a half minutes I flatlined right off the monitors." She didn't look at him, afraid if she did she wouldn't have the courage to finish. "But the marvels of four hundred watts of direct current counter shock straight to the heart brought me back. I was in a coma for a while after that. When I recovered, I was—different."

"Different how?"

"I . . . I can't tell you that, Michael. But some part of me died in that ambulance, and I'm not sure whether the part of me that's left can feel and dream and hope anymore. I thought so, back there with you at Edgehill. Now I'm not so sure. And all the time I know a man is out there watching. Waiting. I can feel him right now . . ."

"That's *impossible*, Kelly."

"Is it?" Hot tears burned down her cheeks. "Is it, Michael? Then how did I know where to find that linen room?"

"I don't believe this!"

"Few people do." Her hands clenched together. "I thought you might be different."

Burke slammed the car into neutral and caught her shoulders. "Are you telling me that you can read other people's thoughts?"

"Sometimes. Not usually. But since I've come to Draycott Abbey, I've been positively awash in impressions."

"I can't believe this." Burke jammed a hand through his hair. "You can—*feel* this man, too?"

Kelly nodded.

"You think what he's thinking?"

"Sometimes."

"Damn it, what's he thinking now?"

Kelly shivered, not wanting to pick up that cold trail of anger. But she did it. Because Burke asked her to.

She shuddered at what she found. He was close, very close. He could have been anyone of the faces at the Crown. He could even have been on the tour at Edgehill.

Kelly's fingers began to tremble. She forced herself to hold the contact, even though it left her weak and sickened.

He had killed once. And he—

She caught back a sob. "Michael, oh, heaven, isn't there any way to stop him? He's close, so close. And he's going to kill again very soon."

"I hope you're wrong about this, Red." Burke pulled a mobile phone from beneath the seat and jabbed out a set of numbers. Then he slammed the Land Rover into gear and raced the last half-mile toward Draycott.

As they jolted out of the woods, Kelly saw two cars parked in front of the little bridge over the moat.

One of them was an ambulance.

Professor Cedric Bullock-Powell sat up with a shout.

It was exactly what he'd been searching for. He had just been too stupid to think of it sooner.

Draycott! He'd done a dig there himself forty-five years ago, fresh out of Oxford. And the last viscount had loaned him an old family chronicle to help with his research. Now where in heaven's name had he put those notes?

He dug through the newly sorted papers on his desk, scattering them right and left in his haste. There had been an addendum in medieval Latin, as he recalled, something hastily added generations after the original chronicle was complete.

Finally in a box shoved to the back of his dusty attic the professor found what he wanted. Inside a worn brown folder tied with threadbare cotton string were preserved all his notes from Draycott Abbey! He recalled that he had even added a hand-drawn map, laboriously copied from the fragile parchment pages of the old chronicle.

Now, however, the map appeared to be missing. Blast! There had almost certainly been something about a "hill of light" by a "stream of gold." Both could have described where a jewelled sword had been hidden in a time of danger and unrest.

At least his record of the chronicle was intact.

Angling his reading glasses, the old scholar studied his spindly handwriting, set to paper almost half a century before. He began a laborious translation, mindful of how much he had always detested his Latin, even as a schoolboy.

And as he read, his sense of uneasiness grew nearly suffocating . . .

I, Brother Geoffrey of Kingston, do add these words in haste as my time of dying grows near. The sky has burned blood-red for three nights and to me this hangs as a grave warning. God grant me forgiveness for concealing this dark tale all these years. Now, as I face my Judge and Maker, my conscience grows full heavy and I must set down the truth for those who will come after.

On a stormy night much like tonight did the knight St. Vaux come to me to offer confession. Dusty and weary the man was, but in his eyes shone a great light such as I have not seen in many years. He told me a tale then, a tale of greed and courage, of trust and betrayal. And he told me, too, of his father's sword, passed down to five generations of St. Vaux men, but now gone, lost to a wolf concealed in the stately robes of the church.

I quake even now to remember. And yet the evil one must be named, though his name is so powerful that I dare only whisper it. But judgement grows near and I must speak.

The man I name is the Bishop of Kingston. Ermine-clad, of proud mien, he holds the king's ear. Yet did this same bishop betray all laws of man and God to seize St. Vaux's woman and his precious sword. Murder was the bishop's goal and murder would have been his outcome had not one of St. Vaux's knights given his life to foil the plot.

But sword was lost and lovers torn apart. Ever since that night, St. Vaux has wandered, searching for the two treasures he was never to see again. He told me that in a dream he had seen the woman he loved carrying his great sword and he vowed he would search for her until his last breath.

Maybe even longer.

I crossed myself at this blasphemy, but the knight was transfigured. And maybe there is more of God in this world than my poor imagination comprehends.

Through the long night he shared my simple fare and sat by my fire, telling of deeds long past, of love most rare.

With the dawn he was gone, leaving behind nothing but a map by his own hand, which he consigned to my protection. There, he told me, hidden in the "Hill of Great Light," his sword would one day be found. Only the hand of someone whose love was true could raise it from its place of hiding. Here too do I copy the map that St. Vaux left for me.

For many days this tale haunted me. Now, though my hand trembles, I set down this account of the bishop's greed. Every word is as St. Vaux told, so do I swear.

I pray that the knight's soul may find surpassing peace in the arms of the woman he lost

*so long ago. And I pray that his sword will be
returned to him somewhere, through the infinite
mercy of God. In some far time and some distant place.*

*But now my breathing grows shrill. Darkness
drifts around me and I grow fearful.*

*Praise heaven, a light. How clear I see it
now—*

The professor was quaking with excitement as
he stared at the last trembling lines of Latin, followed by a slash of ink where the dying monk's
quill had dropped from his hand. The man had
told his tale just in time, it seemed.

Kelly would need to know immediately. There
was little doubt that her sword was buried at the
"Hill of Great Light." The site was near the old
Norman ruin, he recalled, not far from the cliffs
known as Lyon's Leap.

Named after the knight St. Vaux, no doubt.

He smiled as another part of the puzzle fit into
place.

But the professor's worry returned when he
picked up the phone. The story had left him
shaken, almost as if the characters in the tale
were somehow familiar to him. Nonsense, of
course. Yet he could not shake his uneasiness.
And now he had lost the map.

Suddenly he found himself praying that he
would not be too late.

He moved back into the shadows and flipped
open the map.

It was perfectly rendered, every detail clear
even after forty-five years.

Trust the old man to be careful about such
things.

Then he frowned. The bloody names were of no use, rendered in some ancient tongue. No matter how he struggled, he could make no sense of them.

He cursed. There was no more time.

Besides, *she* would know.

He smiled coldly, thinking about her face when she saw him.

Then his pleasure was cut short. Humming filled his head. No, not the voices! Not now! It was all her fault. He never could keep his head, not while she was about.

First he'd stolen, then he'd lied for her. Now he'd killed. And it was all *her* fault.

She would have to die.

It was the only way to make the voices go away . . .

Burke cursed as the stretcher was carried out. He recognized the face as James Herrington's. A bloody good man.

At least, he'd *been* a good man.

Now he was dead. He had two children waiting at home, one barely a month old. Neither was going to grow up knowing his father.

Burke turned, his eyes icy with a need for revenge.

"Michael?" Kelly whispered, her face haunted as she watched the stretcher being carried away.

Burke drew his arm around her stiff shoulders. "Come on, Red. There's nothing more for you to do out here."

"Dear God, that man died because of me!" Kelly's face was sheet white and her fingers were shaking. "He followed me out to the stream this morning. He was *protecting* me. And now—" Her voice wavered, broke.

They were in the sun-filled study overlooking the moat. Damask roses floated in crystal bowls and were reflected in a pair of carved gilt Regency mirrors opposite the open French doors. The chairs were eighteenth century, covered with tufted silk and crimson tassels.

Kelly saw none of it, only darkness.

She caught a raw breath. "I've got to do *something*, don't you see?"

"The best way you can help is by staying right here, finishing this glass of brandy, then going upstairs to rest until Marston brings you something to eat." Burke curved his hands around her cheek and frowned. "It's too deep now, Kelly. Too bloody dangerous for an amateur. Don't worry, we'll get the man who did this to young Herrington. Even if it's the *last* thing I do, I'll see to that."

"Don't say that, Michael. He's clever—*very* clever."

"Don't waste your worry on me, Kelly. I can handle one psychotic killer just fine. But you're to stay here, understand? If what you say is true, he'll be watching and you'll be his first target."

"What about *you*? He wants you, too!"

"And he's going to get me," Burke said darkly. "Clear as day. A perfect bloody target. Only I'm going to set a few traps for him first."

"But I could—"

"*No.* I won't take any more chances with your life. I was a fool to let you stay here. I should have made you go long before things got this dangerous."

Desperation make Kelly reckless. She couldn't face the thought of Michael going unprotected to face a madman's bullet. "Michael, listen to me. I know everything, even about the urn. It—it's why I was sent here, not for the sword."

He didn't move, not even one muscle. But it was clearly a struggle.

Don't hate me, Kelly prayed. *Don't let it be too late for the truth.*

"Urn?" His voice was carefully neutral. "What urn?"

"Michael, I know *everything*, don't you see? I knew from the start. I was sent here to find it." She swallowed. "To find it before you could."

His face went grim. "Who sent you?" he growled.

"An American. Someone who does the same kind of work that you do. In fact, you're on the same team. Or almost so."

"There's no such thing as *almost*, Kelly. Not in the world where I live. I want his name. Then we're going to call him."

A knock echoed from the door. Marston appeared, looking worried. "Excuse me, Commander, but there is a gentleman—"

"Never mind, Marston." The butler was politely but firmly moved aside by a tall man with iron-gray hair and an undeniably military bearing.

"What now, Ross?"

"I've just received word that Professor Bullock-Powell is on his way up. He says it is most urgent that he speak with Miss Hamilton."

Burke cursed fluently. "The less people we have here the better, Ross. We've got a crazed killer hidden somewhere out there in the woods and a priceless—" He caught himself just in time. He didn't yet want Ross to know about Kelly's astonishing revelation. And that meant he couldn't mention the urn. "A priceless artifact hidden somewhere on the grounds. Yes, definitely the fewer people the better."

"The man was *most* insistent."

"Very well, let him in. But not for long." He stared at Kelly. "And you're *not* to go outside."

He didn't wait for her nod of agreement, which was just as well since it didn't come.

Burke didn't notice. Ross had moved closer, looking anxious. His voice was low, but Kelly was able to make out what he said.

"It's Thorpe. He hasn't reported in since two o'clock," the older man said bluntly.

Kelly listened to the clatter of walkie-talkies as Michael disappeared down the hall.

She stood at the French doors, forcing herself to stay calm even as she wondered if another man had been killed. Somehow she had to help, whether Burke liked it or not.

There was no doubt now that her intuition had been correct. The man outside had killed once and would kill again if he wasn't stopped. Somehow Kelly had to find the urn. Now, before anyone else was hurt.

She turned and paced the floor, thinking feverishly. The answer had to be right in front of her, if only she could see it.

If only she could turn off her logical mind and *feel*.

Her toe struck something. Frowning, she picked up the leather-bound copy of the Draycott chronicle. Odd, she hadn't seen it lying there on the rug earlier. Idly, she turned the pages, going through the problem one more time.

The sword was buried. The urn was buried with it.

If she found the sword, she found the urn.

But where was the sword? In the ruins? Near the stream? Somewhere near Lyon's Leap?

Then she saw it. The page had seemed nothing but an oddity at first, full of another of the superstitions that medieval chroniclers delighted in recording, even while they made light of them.

But now Kelly looked again. With her heart this time, not her head. *Feeling,* not thinking . . .

The words were crammed low in one margin, written in a fine, spidery script unlike the rest of the book. And as Kelly translated, her heart began to pound.

Here do I rest, caught between darkness and daylight.
Hidden between yesterday and tomorrow.
Only a woman's love can find me.
Only a warrior's hand shall call me forth and make me whole once more.

Kelly sat down slowly, her eyes fixed on the fine script.

"Caught between darkness and daylight"—did that mean hidden? Hidden in water or some perpetual twilight? Somewhere in the shadow of the old ruins, perhaps?

Kelly's fingers froze as awareness flashed through her.

In a cave!

She remembered that there had been a cave mentioned somewhere in the chronicle. Flipping carefully through the fragile pages, she finally found the passage.

A worker did die today, crushed in a fall of rock beside the quarry near Lyon's Hill. His family

*was recompensed with a plot of land for their use
the rest of their days.*

*His bloody body was found inside a cave opened
by the falling rock.*

*The workers were fearful at first. They spoke
of some ancient curse upon this hill. They do say
that a knight rides the cliffs, searching for a treasure taken from him by treachery and deceit.*

*It is naught but empty talk of course, but to
appease their fear we have closed off the cave
and the abbot has held a rite for the fallen worker.*

*Though they grumble, the men have gone back
to work. I will allow no more talk of lost swords
or a "Hill of Great Light." Next month we will
move the quarry south toward the lower end of
the cliffs. There is fine stone there, enough to
build ten walls.*

*And I have ordered that anyone spreading
tales of swords and ghosts and hidden treasure
be dismissed instantly.*

Kelly stared at the entry in the chronicle, her
heart pounding. The sword *had* to be buried near
that old quarry. The legends about the "Hill of
Great Light" confirmed it. She had seen the marks
of chisels high on the cliffs and knew roughly
where the site was located. Now all she had to
do was find a cave, a cave half-hidden by fallen
stone.

The urn would be there with the sword. She
could feel it clearly. And with the urn restored,
she and Michael would finally be free.

But she had to act now. There was no time to
convince Michael that she was right.

Because Kelly had seen something else in that
momentary flash of awareness.

When the killer struck next, it would be against Michael.

Her instinct of danger was confirmed a moment later by the low voice behind her.

A voice from her past.

A voice from her nightmares.

"I've been waiting for you, Kelly."

Chapter 25

*K*elly froze at the low, snarled words. Around her stone and wood bled away into darkness and throbbing pain.

No, not him. Not here. How did he get in?

"What, not going to say hello?" Hard fingers circled her throat and tightened. "A pity. I always thought the two of us were such good friends."

Kelly swallowed, fighting her panic and shoving at the taut fingers. "Friends? You have a warped idea of friendship, Trevor. The only thing you've ever liked was your own image in a mirror and all the ways you could think of hurting people."

"How well you understand me, my dear." The white hand caressed her cheek in a parody of tenderness. "You are still very beautiful, even after the accident. How long has it been? Four years?"

"Five," Kelly said harshly, digging at his fingers. She thought of calling for Marston or Burke, but decided this was one battle she'd put off too long. She would face Trevor by herself. Maybe that was the only way she could heal the old wounds. "Five years, four months, and six days." She stared with undisguised contempt at the man who had caused the "accident" that had nearly killed her. "But who's counting?"

"Always ready with a quip, aren't you, love?" Cold blue eyes measured her face. Kelly wondered that she had once been attracted by Trevor's handsome features. Now all she could see was pale eyes and a mouth that was both weak and singularly cruel.

"How flattering of you to remember."

"Oh, I remember a great deal, Kelly. More than you might imagine."

"Too bad you didn't remember to phone for an ambulance that night after you pushed me twenty feet from the top of the dig site."

Trevor merely shrugged. "I hadn't meant for it to happen. Still, I couldn't take a chance on being found nearby. My father would have cut off my funds."

Kelly laughed bitterly. "Do you know, you aren't even worth hating, Trevor?" She frowned. "How did you find me anyway?"

"My father, of course. The old man knows everything and everyone in the rarefied world of archeology." The cool blue eyes narrowed. "He never could hide his disappointment with me, did you know that? All he ever talked about was the hotshot American who did everything faster and better than any of his other students. You, Kelly."

"I'm not interested in ancient history, Trevor."

Cedric Bullock-Powell's son smiled thinly. "Oh, but I think you are. I think ancient history is *exactly* why you're here."

Something in his eyes made Kelly shiver. "Go

away, Trevor. Otherwise I'll call Marston to throw you out."

"I think not, my dear. Not until I finish what I didn't get to do that night five years ago."

Something snapped inside Kelly then. She slapped him, putting all her rage and disgust into the blow. She had the pleasure of seeing Trevor reel away, cursing.

"You foul little tart," he hissed, shoving her against the sunlit wall. "You're going to pay for that. This time you're not going to get away from me. Not you—not your filthy lover either."

Kelly felt his hatred, cold and razor-sharp. His eyes were just as emotionless as they'd been five years ago when he'd come to the site with two friends.

The night he'd followed her, mocked her.

The night he'd tried to assault her, then shoved her twenty feet off a ruined wall.

Now she stared at him, marvelling that she had no fear. His eyes were puffy. Alcohol? Drugs?

It didn't matter. Her past was swept away, healed in the love she'd found in Burke's arms. Trevor Bullock-Powell was no more than a pest to her now, a nagging insect with no power to harm her.

He had ruined her career and very nearly killed her five years ago, but he wasn't going to do it again.

"Forget it, Trevor. If you touch me again I'll call the police. And *this* time you can be sure I'll tell them everything—including what I chose not to tell last time."

"But you won't call them, Kelly. You *can't*." He eased a pistol from his pocket. "Because if they come in here, they're going to die. Just the way that nice young James Herrington did."

She swallowed, unable to believe what he was saying. Then the terrible certainty of it struck her.

Trevor. *Trevor* was the one.

"And now all that training of yours is about to pay off. Because, my dear, you're going to find that urn for me."

"How did you find out about the urn?"

"The same way I learned everything else. Yes, I'm going to be very, very rich. So rich I won't need you or anybody else." His lips curled. "Not that you'll be around then."

"You're sick, Trevor. What you need is medical help, not more money you'll just burn through."

"Don't tell *me* what I need," he snarled. "I'm fed up with people telling me they know best. I'm tired of the voices telling me what I want—what I need." A vein pounded at his forehead. "No more advice! And no more *voices*, damn it."

Kelly felt a jab of panic as she stared into his mad eyes and slack mouth. "No, no more voices," she agreed softly.

The cold metal slid against her rib as Trevor tossed a yellowed parchment sheet onto the table. "If you're so smart, read that," he snarled.

It was a map of Draycott lands, probably about nine hundred years old judging by the inscriptions, a blend of Norman French and medieval Latin. Kelly's breath caught as she saw the exquisitely drawn curves of the old castle. And there, too, was the Hill of Great Light, beside the cliffs marked Lyon's Leap.

But she kept all expression from her face. She wasn't about to reveal anything important to Trevor. She simply shrugged. "Read it yourself."

"You want to do this the hard way? Shall we stand here and wait for your lover to walk in so I can put a slug into his head?"

Looking into Trevor's cold blue eyes, Kelly had no doubt that he would do it. Frowning, she picked up the map. "Very well, this part is . . . a quarry. Over here is something called Lyon's Hill. And this blue area is described as a—a Hill of Great Light. Whatever that means."

As she spoke her fingers tapped the page, but she was careful to reverse the true locations. Trevor would be searching for the sword in the quarry instead of its true location.

"Well done, Kelly. Now you're going to come along with me. I wouldn't want to find out that you'd lied to me, my dear." Trevor pocketed the fragile map and shoved her toward the door.

Kelly couldn't fight him, not with a loaded pistol jammed against her side. But maybe she could distract him. "How did you find your way around so well, Trevor? You must have eluded two dozen men out there."

"You forget who my father is. Cedric has worked on every important site in Britain, and Draycott Abbey was one of them. I found his old field notes. Most thorough, I assure you. They told me all I needed to know about the Hill of Great Light, which is, of course, where the sword is buried. They also contained this copy of an ancient map of the site. Very useful, wouldn't you say? It also gives the location of several old tunnels that allowed me to come and go at will."

Kelly hadn't noticed the tunnels. Only a madman would have dared use them. "That's *suicide*,

Trevor. Without proper restoration a tunnel that old could cave in at any moment."

"Ah, but that didn't happen. Being careful is something I've learned to be very good at, Kelly, my love."

"Don't call me that. I'm not your love. You never liked me at all, Trevor. I was just a way to get back at your father."

"Perhaps. But I was intrigued by you and that is probably even more exciting." The steel muzzle prodded at her back. "That's something else we're going to find out very soon."

Then Kelly's breath caught. She turned, her face white as she saw Burke appear in the doorway. He stared first at her, then at the man right behind her.

"Damn it, Kelly, I told you to—"

"Do come in, Commander. I was wondering how long it would take for you to get here."

"Take your hands off her." Burke's voice was stony.

"I think not. Miss Hamilton is helping me."

"Not anymore she isn't. Step away from her," Burke ordered, his voice deadly. Now a pistol gleamed in his fingers.

But Trevor Bullock-Powell only laughed. He jerked Kelly sideways, allowing Burke to see the snub-nosed black .357 Magnum levelled at her back. "And *you* will be helping me too, Commander."

"What do you want?" Burke said slowly.

"First the gun on the table."

The weapon landed with a clatter. "What now?"

"Next the men outside get pulled. Every last one of them, including Inspector Ross. And don't try any games, Commander, because I know *exactly* how many there are and what they look like." Trevor smiled thinly. "I even know how they like their tea."

"Congratulations. Now you can open a tea concession," Burke said harshly.

Trevor jammed the pistol against Kelly's back. "Do introduce us, my dear."

"Meet Trevor Bullock-Powell, Michael."

Burke frowned. "You're *Cedric's* son?" His voice was tight with disbelief.

Trevor heard it, too. That flat disbelief was something he'd heard all too often in his life. "Exactly. I can see you asking yourself how such a brilliant man could have such a misbegotten son." His eyes darkened as Burke didn't answer. "Go on, say it. Don't make the mistake of treating me like a child, Commander."

Burke angled his shoulder against the wall. "All right. How *did* such a brilliant scholar sire a misbegotten little shit like you?"

Kelly felt fury whip through Trevor. What was Michael up to?

Trevor's hands were shaking as he stared at Burke. "For that you're going to pay, Commander."

"What do you want with Kelly? Let her go and I'll get the men taken off. Then you'll have a clear field."

Trevor laughed. "Oh, I think not. I am not quite so foolish as that, Commander. Kelly is going to help me find that urn you've been looking for. Then she's going to be my ticket out of here."

Burke's expression didn't change. "Why take her? I'm worth a lot more to you as a bargaining chip with the men outside."

"Nicely done, Burke. You almost begin to interest me. But no, it's Kelly I want and Kelly I'll have. Along with the urn, of course. Besides, we have some unfinished business, don't we, my dear?" His eyes half-closed as he studied Burke. "I think I'll make you listen when I hurt her. You'll hear every little whimper and scream when I teach her the things I should have taught her five years ago."

Burke's eyes never left Trevor's face. "And just when was that, Trevor? At the site where she was hurt? You were seen leaving abruptly, you know. Questions were raised, but nothing could be proved without Kelly's testimony. And for some reason after she recovered, she wasn't interested in bringing any charges."

He knows, Kelly thought. *He's known all along.*

"Very good, Commander. Too bad you didn't work it out a little faster. Yes, Kelly turned unaccountably stubborn that night. I simply did what it took to teach her a lesson."

"You nearly killed her," Burke said tautly. "What fun would you have had with her dead?"

Trevor's eyes glinted. "Oh, but I didn't kill her. I only made her suffer, just as she had made *me* suffer. She and all the others."

Burke raised a lazy eyebrow. "Others?" His voice was carefully casual. "Don't tell me you've made a practice of this."

"Enough, damn it! You're not getting inside my head. I'm done with all that." Trevor jerked Kelly close and began backing toward the door. "Now get on that two-way and call off your men. Otherwise you're going to watch Kelly take a slug right through her chest."

Burke reached in his pocket and removed a matte black two-way radio. "Ross?"

"Right here."

"Listen carefully. I've got our man in here," Burke said tautly. "He's got Kelly and he's calling the shots. He wants all the security pulled."

A hesitation. "Burke?"

"He's got the gun, Ross. Just *do* it."

"Affirmative." The radio carried the sounds of Ross's shouted command. "What else?"

Burke stared at Trevor, his eyes expressionless. "You heard the man. What next?"

"What happens next, Commander, is that Kelly and I take a walk up the hill. She gets me my urn and we finish a little business. Then, if you do everything just right, I let her go and leave."

He's lying. Kelly felt the knowledge slam through her. Trevor had no thought of letting her escape.

She turned wild eyes on Burke and shook her head, very faintly.

Burke saw. A muscle flashed at his jaw. "How do I know you're telling the truth, Trevor?"

All this time he had been holding down the transmit button. Outside Ross would hear every word.

"Very nice, Commander. But it will make no difference. One move against me by your Inspector Ross or anyone else and Miss Hamilton dies, understand? I'm sure she's told you I'm crazy. She's probably right. I'll do anything at all to get what I want. And I doubt you'd care for another dead woman on your conscience." He smiled thinly. "Oh, yes, I'm very thorough. I know all about your past. That's why *I'm* going to win and you're going to lose."

Outside doors slammed. A half-dozen cars moved slowly down the drive. Trevor nodded. "They'd better all be there. I'll know if they're not. And now it's time for us to take our walk, Kelly." He pulled a small two-way transmitter from his pocket. "You'll be able to listen on this, Commander. Officer Herrington was so obliging before he died. Now take it and get into that closet." Trevor made a jabbing motion toward an oak door at the opposite side of the room. "And don't expect any help from that officious butler. I've put him where he won't be interfering with my plans."

"Damn you," Burke hissed. But he knew he was powerless as long as Trevor held Kelly captive. Grimly, he did as ordered. The lock was solid iron and built to last.

"Enjoy the performance, Commander. Then come and get us. Oh, I'll leave the key right here on the other side of the lock just where you can reach it—if you can break down two inches of solid oak, that is."

The door slammed shut to Bullock-Powell's jeering laughter, and Burke was left in total darkness.

Miles O'Halloran frowned out at the passing Sussex countryside. It had just begun to rain.

He hated driving on the left. He hated English food.

But most of all he hated the incessant English drizzle.

He slowed, watching for the roundabout and the narrow gravel turnoff to Draycott Abbey. In the heavy, drumming drops he nearly missed the turn.

He was tired and cold and wanted nothing more than to have the whole business done with, but things were in chaos over here. His people had been unreliable, and Kelly had failed to make contact the way she was supposed to.

Abruptly the abbey's granite walls slid into view, faintly menacing.

Frowning, O'Halloran gunned the motor and wondered what new problems he would find waiting for him at the abbey.

Burke's set hissed to life less than five minutes later.

"Are you listening, Commander?"

Burke jabbed the transmitter control. "I'm listening, you bastard." He flinched as he heard the crack of a palm, then Kelly's gasp, swiftly muffled.

Trevor laughed softly. "Say hello to your lover, Kelly."

"Michael, be careful! He's left—"

Trevor's hollow laughter cut into the line. "Now, now, no clues. It would hardly be sporting to reveal all our little secrets, my dear. Let the commander find them for himself."

The radio whined, then fell silent.

"Trevor! Let her go, damn you!"

No answer.

Burke hadn't expected any.

"What do you mean, I can't go up?" Miles O'Halloran stood glaring at a grim-faced man with iron-gray hair who claimed to be in charge. "Listen, Mr. Ross—"

"Inspector Ross. And the answer is still no."

Cursing softly, Miles flipped out a badge and shoved it before the man's face. "Does this change things just a little?"

Ross frowned. It looked official enough. And if it was . . . "We've got a problem up at the abbey. Commander Burke has ordered everyone off. I can't reverse that order without proper clearance."

"Then get it, damn it. Kelly Hamilton is up there and I want to see her."

Ross's face gave away no secrets. "She is working with you? Perhaps you would explain your connection with Miss Hamilton—since I take it you are *not* an archeologist," Ross added flatly.

"I'll answer questions when I'm certain that Kelly is safe."

Ross shrugged. He could play the game too. Amazing how long a call to London could take sometimes. "Very well, Mr. O'Halloran. If you'll have a seat in the car, I'll do what I can. But it may take some time," he added blandly.

"You'd better hope it doesn't, Ross," Miles snapped.

Burke had just unscrewed the housing at the back of the radio when it hissed alive again.

"Commander? Managed to break through the door yet?"

Burke didn't answer immediately. He decided Trevor could sweat a bit.

"Burke, answer me, damn you!"

Burke just kept working.

"Very well, Commander." Burke heard Trevor turn away for a moment. "You talk to him, Kelly."

And then he heard Kelly's voice, tight with what he prayed was tension and not pain.

"Michael, we—we're going to find the urn. He took a map from his father. I think the sword is—"

"That's just about enough, I think. Until next time, Commander."

Burke scowled at the radio, cursing the darkness, cursing his fingers that slipped again and again and cursing Trevor Bullock-Powell. Finally he eased off the radio's metal housing and looped his belt around the flat plate, praying that Trevor would not contact him again until he was done.

The plate slid neatly beneath the door. He checked the belt, made certain it was secure, then unscrewed the flexible antenna from the top of the radio. The antenna fit perfectly into the hole on the lock. Now as long as he had judged the distance properly . . .

He jabbed the antenna forward. The key slid free. A moment later it clattered down, striking metal. Carefully Burke reeled in the radio plate and searched along its edge in the darkness.

The key was balanced dead center on the plate.

Sighing with relief, he fit the key in the lock. The metal bolt slid free and the door creaked open.

He ran up the stairs, radio clutched beneath one arm, antenna beneath the other. He stopped in his room and contacted Ross on a separate transmitter secured with random frequency scrambling fifty times per second. Let Trevor try to tap into *that*, he thought grimly.

"Ross, this is Burke here."

"Damn it, Burke, where've you been? I've been trying to get you for—"

"I was out of commission, I'm afraid, but there's no time for explanations. Trevor Bullock-Powell's got Kelly and I'm going after him."

"Trevor . . ." Ross's voice was tight with disbelief.

"Precisely. Everyone is to stand off until you

have my order. Do you have that, Ross?"

"Understood," the older man answered tightly. "I don't like it, but I'll do it. Meanwhile, I've got someone who claims that he works with Kelly threatening international repercussions unless I—"

"He claims *what?*" Burke's face hardened.

"That he works with Kelly. He's got top-level clearance along with a few things even *I* haven't seen before. Damn it, Burke, you never told me that Kelly Hamilton was part of an intelligence network."

Because I didn't know she was. And even when she told me I didn't believe it. Not until now. "Maybe she is and maybe she isn't," Burke said grimly. "There are a lot of things here that don't make sense, Ross. Until we get them sorted out, let's keep it tight. No one comes up here and no one goes out, understand?"

"Copied, Commander."

"Good."

Abruptly the voice on the radio changed. "Commander Burke? I *must* speak with you. I've found something that might pinpoint the location of that sword Kelly is looking for. You must let me—"

Burke heard the sounds of scuffling. "Ross? Who in God's name was *that?* It sounds like a bloody soccer match gone out of control down there."

"Sorry, Commander. That was Professor Bullock-Powell."

"Good God, don't tell him about his son. Not till we have everything clear."

"Understood. Meanwhile, he's found some old notes that mention where the sword might be hidden."

At last a bit of luck, Burke thought. "Put him on then, Ross."

Two minutes later he was heading through the woods toward Lyon's Leap. It wasn't much to go on, but the professor had given him his first solid clue since this whole bloody mess had begun.

Burke prayed it would be enough.

Chapter 26

As the sun sank toward the horizon Burke darted through the woods, keeping to trails that he and Nicholas had followed since they were boys. Only now the game of hide and seek was brutally *real*.

The rain had stopped. Bars of sunlight filtered down through the great oaks, glistening off water drops scattered over the ground like great, liquid diamonds. The woods were utterly quiet.

Too quiet, Burke thought, replaying Kelly's terse comments in his mind, certain she'd been trying to warn him of something.

And then he saw it.

The wire was fine-gauge steel, stretched knee-height and nearly hidden in the foliage. It could easily have knocked him flat.

Bending down, he tracked the wire into a clump of azaleas.

There it wound upward, only to slide with lethal accuracy around the trigger of a braced and fully loaded HK-91 submachine gun.

Carefully Burke detached the cable and emptied all the rounds.

This must be what Kelly had been trying to tell him. No doubt Trevor had set other, equally dangerous traps for him ahead.

Burke continued north, feeling sweat bead across his forehead.

Kelly's eyes were tense with strain as Trevor shoved her along the muddy path. She had done what she could to confuse him, reversing the location of the quarry and the sword site. Now all she could hope for was a chance to break free.

But with a gun at her back, she'd have to pick her moment carefully.

Abruptly gunfire exploded over the far side of the hill. The forest silence was shattered as a flock of greylag geese rocketed upward in a frantic flight.

Trevor jerked her to a halt, his pale eyes glittering. He jabbed at the two-way radio. "Burke?" His voice was taut with excitement.

No answer.

"Burke, are you *there*?"

Still no response.

Trevor pocketed the radio slowly. "I'm afraid that was the last of your poor, inept lover, Kelly. It seems the man wasn't quite as smart as he thought he was."

Kelly squeezed her hands to fists, trying to ignore Trevor's gloating triumph and the brutal evidence of her own ears. It couldn't be true. She refused to believe that Michael was lying dead on a muddy path right now.

She turned wildly, intent on going back, but Trevor's fingers locked onto her arm. "Not yet, my sweet." Cold steel prodded her back. "Not until I have the urn."

Not even then.

Biting her lip, Kelly shut her mind to Trevor and to her own fear, searching, hoping . . .

Finally she found it.

Fierce determination. Grim haste. A primitive, pounding need for revenge.

Michael.

She bent her head, knowing she couldn't hide the joy that lit her up inside like Fourth of July fireworks.

Looking away, she surveyed the hillside, hoping she could carry off her deception until Burke found them. Meanwhile, she forced herself to reach out and probe Trevor's intentions.

His first priority was the urn. And then?

She frowned, seeing that, too. He was going to arrange for her to take a tumble from the top of the cliffs.

And this time he meant to see that the fall was fatal.

Had Trevor turned then, he would have noticed her sudden pallor. But he didn't. All his attention was focused on the granite cliffs that had just come into view.

"Perfect timing, my dear. That, unless I am mistaken, is exactly what we have been looking for."

The second trip wire had been well hidden.

Trailed through the lacy fronds of a row of ferns lining the path, the fine steel was little more than a faint blur against the forest floor. A man moving quickly would never have noticed it.

Not in time, at least.

When Burke had slid to the ground and carefully tugged at the concealed wire, gunfire dug up the narrow path.

He'd counted ten seconds before the two-way hissed to life.

He was ready with his receiver. When Trevor transmitted, Burke calculated the direction and distance of the signal.

It was closer than he'd thought. Due north at barely three-fourths of a kilometer.

As he melted back into the forest, Burke let Trevor eat static.

They were nearly at the edge of the old quarry when Kelly saw the fissure in the rock. It was covered by vines and ringed with shadows, suggesting an opening behind the foliage.

The cave?

Kelly felt her pulse pick up. She was careful to look away before Trevor could notice her interest. "Let me see the map again," she said curtly.

She knew it would be a waiting game now, and whoever had better timing would win.

"Awfully helpful, aren't you, all of a sudden? Maybe because your lover just bought it with two rounds in his chest."

"Shut up, Trevor! All I want is to find that urn and get away from you. The urn sickens me almost as much as *you* do."

He laughed coolly as he handed her the yellowed sheet of parchment.

Kelly made a great pretense of studying it, all the while thinking frantically. If she was going to try to escape she would have to do it soon. Trevor was going to discover her deception before long.

She pretended to study the map, then looked up the slope, searching for a place that would offer her even a few seconds' protection.

Abruptly Trevor pulled her to a halt. He drew out another piece of steel wire and eased his pack to the ground, keeping his pistol trained on her all the while. "Just in case," he said coldly.

Kelly knew the process perfectly by now. Her only opportunity for flight would be when he bent to connect the wire to the trigger.

She shot one last glance upward, memorizing the boulder-strewn slope.

The moment Trevor bent low, she bolted forward and disappeared behind a shoulder-high ridge of fallen granite.

Burke was circling up the hill, slow and silent, when he heard gunfire and the shrill cry of a woman in pain. It came from due north, where the path zigzagged up to the gorge.

Kelly!

He hammered forward.

This time he made no effort to conceal his presence.

Blood oozed from Kelly's arm. One of Trevor's bullets had sent a sliver of granite raking into her skin. Nothing dangerous, but the pain was searing.

She fought down her pain as she dug at the vines trailing over the cliff. Sure enough, they covered an opening in the stone face.

Ignoring Trevor's curses, she ripped the foliage away from the cave entrance, clearing away just enough space to be able to enter the cool darkness. Trying not to think about any four-legged residents who might resent her intrusion, she tugged the vines back over the opening.

Then, standing in the darkness, she reached out for Trevor.

She touched his fear and his fury. And with it came the hint of voices, carried over a vast distance of time.

Kelly shivered, feeling the hairs at the back of her neck rise.

Voices . . .

And with them a flood of haunting memories.

"Aislann," she whispered, feeling the fear of a long-dead woman tighten her throat. Touching the fire of a love that would not die.

And then she knew.

The sword was very close now. Memory churned within her, setting her mind aflame. She turned and followed the wall of the cave back into blackness, driven by an intuition she could not explain.

Twenty feet back, near the rear of the cave, she stopped and began digging. Finally she found what she was looking for, half-hidden beneath a mound of dirt and fallen gravel.

Her breath caught as she touched the cool blade and traced the vast unfaceted emerald on the beaten silver pommel. Even in the darkness she could envision the sword, its crossguard agleam, the emerald surrounded by a sunburst of garnets.

The sword of St. Vaux, passed down through five generations of warriors.

She remembered the words in the old book. "Caught between darkness and daylight. Hidden between yesterday and tomorrow. Only a woman's love can find me."

She had done it, Kelly thought.

A whisper of sound teased her senses as she smoothed her hand over the great pitted blade, feeling time bend and shift around her.

The voices grew louder . . .

The warrior St. Vaux coaxed her awake with warm fingers and softer kisses. As the sun cleared the treetops, he brushed her hair gently with a fine hardwood comb he had brought from the castle.

It had belonged to his mother and now it was to be hers.

Aislann frowned, her eyes the deep green of the forest. "What is it, Lyon?"

The Norman sighed. "I must leave you, Aislann. The king has sent his messenger. Some problem requires my presence at court and there is no avoiding it without grave displeasure to my liege."

Aislann shivered. "So soon?"

Frowning, Lyon pulled her close. "I'll be back, I swear it. Two days, three at most, and then I'll share your bed again, my rose."

Then he held out his sword to her. Its long polished tang was etched in gold and a sunburst of garnets gleamed around its pommel.

"It—it is beautiful, Lyon." Her voice was awed. "It is a thing of vast power."

"For you, Aislann. It is my most prized possession, passed down among my family for generations. Guard it for me and know that I will return for it—and for you—no matter what might bar my way."

Aislann gripped the hilt with trembling fingers. "It will be safe with me, my love. I shall await you here, here in this cottage beneath the great oak tree where the red rose twines. I shall always be waiting."

"And here I shall find you," the Norman said roughly, feeling his heart twist in his chest. "No matter what

comes between us. No matter what danger. Do you believe me, my love?"

She nodded even as tears filled her emerald eyes.

Lyon turned away swiftly and caught up his cloak. To leave her brought a pain such as he had never known.

But he could not stay. Their time had run out. To disobey William would bring certain disaster.

He slid his fingers through her hair and pulled Aislann close. He inhaled the scent of her, all lavender and violets and woman.

Lyon would remember that smell forever.

Two days passed, and then another, but Lyon did not return.

Restless, distracted, Aislann forced herself to concentrate on her work, sorting her herbs and laying them out to dry. When she was finished, she told Hugh she must go in search of more.

He insisted on following her, awkward and good-natured as a boisterous dog. He even tried to help her, dropping as many flowers as he found, though Aislann was careful not to tell him that.

She only laughed and told him he would make a very poor sort of healer. To this, Hugh responded that she would make a very poor sort of knight.

Finally the sun sank down into the valley and the time Aislann most feared was upon her. In the dark hours of night she could think of nothing but Lyon's arms, nothing but how they'd laughed and loved in her little cottage.

He'll be back, she told herself as an owl cried somewhere in the night. He'll be safe, she thought fiercely. And he'll soon return. He's promised me this, after all.

But the flickering lights of the fire whispered another story. Each spark hissed to her of betrayal.

* * *

Hugh was making up his pallet in the shed when he heard the low snap of twigs. He caught up his sword and listened.

Lyon? Back already?

He waited, ears focused on the night.

Again came the muffled snap, the crunch of leaves.

He peered through the weathered planks, cursing the fact that there was no moon.

From the darkness came a low sound. It was like the cry of an owl, except that Hugh knew it was too soft for that.

No, this was a man imitating an owl.

He felt the fine hairs at the back of his head prickle and rise. Another cry came, this one from the far side of the clearing. How many were there?

His fingers tightened on his sword. Thank God, no one knew he was here. He would have to circle around and take them one by one.

The Norman had just turned back for his tear-drop shaped shield when a shadow leaped from the doorway. The iron club smashed down against his forehead before he even saw it.

Aislann heard the door creak open. She spun away from her cooking fire, a glow of delighted surprise upon her face. "Lyon? When did you—"

Her words died in her throat. She saw the glittering eyes, the cheek marred by an angry scar. The face dark with a mix of hatred and desire.

"Aelfric! What are you doing here?"

"You expected your Norman lover? But St. Vaux has gone north and will not return for some time. Perhaps not at all, if these bandits flooding the country-side should happen upon him." The Saxon gave a shrill laugh. "And that gives us more time to become comfortable, my love."

He kicked the door shut behind him.

Aislann fought a wave of fear. Dear Lord, where was Hugh?

Aelfric's eyes narrowed as if he'd read her thoughts whole. "You wonder about FitzRolland? He was easily taken, I assure you. In his weakened state he put up very little fight. Now he lies bound and bleeding at the bottom of the gorge, where I had my men toss him. So you can expect no help there, my sweet Aislann."

"You are an animal!" She ran at Aelfric, her nails meant to slash his face.

He caught her arm and wrenched it sharply behind her until Aislann went pale with pain. But even then she did not cry out. She knew her cries would only amuse him.

"Very brave, my sweet. But the night is young and we shall soon see just how brave you are."

He dragged her to the door, kicked it open, and pushed her outside. Aislann saw the light of a dozen torches flickering in the woods.

It must be the villagers, she thought wildly. They would help her! A cry rose to her lips, only to be bitten off a moment later as Aelfric laughed harshly beside her.

"Don't look to find help from them. They fear and hate you despite your healing skills. Yes, they've come here tonight on a different errand, my sweet: to rid this place of the workings of the devil and of the devil's handmaid. In short, to rid themselves of you!"

Aislann flinched before the madness in his pale eyes. As his wild laughter rumbled through the darkness, a score of torches filled the clearing before the little cottage.

Lyon, my love, where are you? she thought wildly.

*   *   *

Lyon jerked awake in his bed in the small, smoky inn.

He stared out into the darkness, seeing the flicker of torches as a group of drunken revelers made their noisy progress through the crowded streets. Fear bit through him. Something about the dancing light and the drunken laughter. Something he should know . . .

Suddenly as if in a dream he saw Aislann, her eyes wild with fear. He heard the thunder of footsteps and shrill laughter. And then her ragged cry.

He jumped from his bed and threw on his cloak. The startled innkeeper watched him hammer down the narrow steps and run for his horse.

"But my lord, your account! You are already paid for the night!"

Lyon didn't even hear him. He pounded from the inn yard, his cloak sweeping wild about him. King, court, and country be damned! Aislann needed him more; he could feel it.

But as he rode through the smoky streets, the Norman was gripped with a terrible premonition that he was already too late.

They swept through the cottage, taking everything of value. Aelfric claimed the valuable furs for his own and ordered every bag of herbs slit and dumped upon the fire. Everything else was ripped or claimed by the sullen mob.

And then came what hurt Aislann most. Cheering, they seized her precious red roses. One by one, they tore the vines out by the roots and broke them into jagged pieces, even the Damascus rose that bloomed but once each midsummer's eve.

"You'll have no joy of this, Aelfric. Soon they will see your madness just as I do."

"Silence!" he screamed.

Fear gripped Aislann as she stared into his blazing eyes. *Lyon, where are you, my love?* She clenched her hands, fighting to remain calm.

Aelfric nodded to one of his sullen companions to watch her while he joined the group milling about the glade.

They were gathering wood, Aislann saw in horror. Wood to make a fire. A vast fire . . .

She bit down a sob as she heard a low whisper behind her.

It was Hugh. "I have a knife. Come closer, and I will try to cut you free."

Aislann felt metal brush against her wrist, then the sweep of a rope falling free. Her ankles came unbound next.

"When I tell you, run. I will hold them off as long as I can."

"But Hugh, you cannot! You are wounded yourself and they will—"

"There is no time for arguing, woman! Go now. They are not watching."

Still she hesitated. She could see that Hugh was bleeding, his tunic slashed through from shoulder to ribs.

"Go!" he hissed.

At that same moment Aelfric looked up, his eyes bright with hate.

He saw her.

"The witch is escaping. After her!"

Aislann ran for the forest. Shrubs slashed at her feet and vines caught at her skirts. She pulled the worn linen high and ran breathless and blind.

All the while she heard them coming, close behind her.

The forest was full of their shouts, and their torches lit the darkness, making the tree trunks dance like demonic shadows.

Gasping, she found the narrow cave entrance and dug away its shielding wall of vines and elder boughs. She had always kept her most precious herbs here, along with the wild roses she cut for drying. Here, too, she had hidden Lyon's great sword, to safeguard until his return.

Crouching low, she shoved through the narrow entry.

They would not know of this place. She had kept it hidden, covered with trailing vines and leaves. And even if they followed her here, they would do so at their peril, for the gorge lay like a great black maw only a few yards to her right.

Carefully, she pulled the foliage back in place, covering the opening.

Outside the men's shouts grew louder. She heard Aelfric's sullen curses, followed by the shrill laughter of a woman. A torch lit the darkness, then another. They were coming—coming for her.

Pain shot through her wrists. She caught back a sob, braced her hands against the damp stone walls, and held her silence. There was nothing she could do now but wait—wait and pray that Hugh was safe and Lyon would make his way back to her.

Before it was too late . . .

Voices.

They reached out to her over time, those voices. Their hold was strong, even as Kelly jolted back, blind-eyed and heart racing into the chaotic fringe of the late twentieth century.

She understood so many things now.

Michael. The warrior she had loved so long ago and then lost. She, the Saxon who'd pledged her heart and fealty to a man her own people reviled as an invader.

Kelly felt her hands shake. Carefully, she set

the sword back against the ground. As Aislann, she had hidden it here to safeguard for the man she loved. And here the weapon had lain for nine hundred years. She could not let its beauty be shattered now.

And then she felt the outline of another object, cool and smooth beneath her fingers. It was a circular shape, made of hammered metal. Kelly lifted it slowly, feeling death clinging close to it.

She knew that this was the urn Miles had sent her to find.

She did not dare to touch it with her mind. Too much darkness hung about it. Too much madness.

She slid the urn back against the ground and moved toward the mouth of the cave.

Her face resolute, she waited. Michael would come.

Burke saw the shadow twenty feet below the crest of the hill, well concealed by a tangle of brambles, wild roses, and dwarf hazel.

Not Trevor nor anyone else he knew. Damn it, what was a stranger doing here?

Abruptly Burke's radio gave a short whine, a signal from Ross.

"Yes?" Burke spoke softly.

"Sorry, Commander, but it's this man O'Halloran, the one who works with Kelly. I'm afraid he's cut line and is headed your way. And he's one bloody slick customer." Ross's voice hardened. "Took out two of my men to do it, damn his godless heart."

Burke thought about Kelly. He thought about lies upon lies and a web of danger so vast he was only now beginning to understand it.

"Burke, do you want us to—"

"No. I'll manage O'Halloran just fine."

The radio hissed off as the shadow began to move.

Burke eased low and watched, feeling a whole lot of things begin to fall into place. Unfortunately, none of them boded well for Kelly.

Chapter 27

Kelly inched toward the cave mouth, trying to see past the foliage. She had no idea how long she'd been waiting in the darkness.

But Michael would come. *Was* coming, even now. She felt the force of his determination, so familiar that it raced through her like the rush of her own pulse.

"Kelly?"

She heard the low rustle of feet just outside the cave entrance.

"You don't have to hide. Not anymore. It's only me."

Miles? What was *he* doing here?

She started forward, relief pouring through her, when some indefinable instinct caught her back.

Safety. So close. All she had to do was call out.

But Draycott Abbey had taught Kelly many things in the last few days and not the least of them was to begin trusting her own heart and listening to its low whispers even when her head argued otherwise.

It was her heart and not her head that she used now, probing a person she had always called a friend, one she had trusted with her life.

It was a trust betrayed, she sensed now. She could see Miles clearly in her mind. He was staring at the cave, looking the same way he had when he'd watched the villagers ransack her cottage and kindle their bonfire.

Nine hundred years before.

As the Bishop of Kingston, proud of mien, grand of person. A wolf without a heart.

She shuddered. The whisper of evil touched her, carried down through the vast corridors of time.

So Miles, too, was part of this great subtle game. She remembered the bishop's face. It had been different then, but the eyes were strangely the same.

Were they bound to replay this cruel contest through to its harsh end?

"I'll take you away. Someplace safe, where no one can harm you. You trust me, don't you, Kelly? Haven't I always taken good care of you?"

There was something compelling about his voice. It called to her, seductive in its offer of safety.

"Just make a sound, my dear. I'll find you. And then we'll go help Burke. We wouldn't want to leave him to face Trevor all alone."

Kelly flinched, her hand scraping the rock wall. How did Miles know about Trevor?

The footsteps stopped. "Kelly? Is that you?"

Her fingers clenched. Through a break in the foliage Kelly could see Miles crouching only a few feet down the hill, scanning the granite wall.

Not a friend but a cold professional who would manipulate anyone for his own ends.

Just the way he'd manipulated *her*.

"You might as well come out. I *know* you're in there."

Hidden in the cave, Kelly felt fear stab through her. He was close, so close. The whispers were insidious, unrelenting, but Kelly kept her silence.

"Don't make me come in and get you, Kelly." A twig snapped. "Just one sound. Then I'll find you and take you away from here, I promise." Abruptly the voice changed. Grew hard and cold. "I'll find you, of course. And when I do, it will be worse for you—and for *him*. Spare yourselves that." Miles cursed. "The shot Trevor fired the night of your arrival was only to frighten Burke and throw him off guard. *This* one won't miss."

Kelly didn't move, didn't even breathe.

And then she heard a sharp cry outside.

Michael. He was calling her, running straight toward Miles.

Kelly moved by sheer instinct, desperate to save the man she loved. "*No*, Michael!"

It was exactly what her tracker had been hoping for. At the sound of her voice, Miles jumped forward, weapon in hand. It took him only a few seconds to find the cave mouth once he knew where to look. Cursing, he stripped vines and foliage aside, freeing the entrance.

His face was harsh with triumph. He caught her arm and jerked her from the cave. But Kelly had time to shove the old sword back into the shadows alongside the urn.

"Let her go, Miles." Burke was standing ten yards away, legs braced, a laser-sighted crossbow cocked in his hands. "The game's over and you've lost."

"There you're wrong, Burke." Miles shoved

Kelly before him, his pistol digging into her back. "Everything I need is locked inside this clever little brain of hers. She's psychic, did she tell you that? And she's not here searching for any sword. All along she's been after the urn. Made you look a bloody fool, hasn't she?"

"I doubt that Kelly knows *what* she's looking for or who she's working with," Burke said brusquely, his eyes on her white face. "I think she's been manipulated by pros from the very start. Her only mistake was to trust a piece of scum like you. Who *are* you employed by, one of Trang's people? Or someone who wants to pick up Trang's pieces in the Golden Triangle and make a neat new drug kingdom of his own?"

Miles laughed coldly. "I work for myself, Burke. Strictly an independent subcontractor, shall we say. And right now a certain party has offered me a cool ten million for that urn. Microfilm intact, of course. I'd be a fool not to turn it over for money like that."

"You *are* a fool, O'Halloran. No matter how you look at it," Burke spat. "But as it happens, *I* know where the urn is. Let her go and I'll—"

"Forget it, Burke. If you'd discovered that urn, you would have reported it to Ross. Or to Nicholas Draycott, at least." He laughed as he saw Burke's face harden. "Oh, yes, I've been monitoring your calls. It's simple enough to arrange, given my position."

"What about Trevor?"

"Very good, Commander. Yes, Trevor had his uses. Unfortunately, he has always been rather unstable. Voices and all that, you know. That little trick with the car was his idea. The man ceased to be an asset to me when he stopped taking orders." Miles smiled thinly. "He has now gone over the edge—quite literally. His body is lying at the bottom of the gorge right now."

"My, my, whatever happened to honor among thieves?"

"Honor is a vastly overrated commodity, as I'm sure you know, Commander. It certainly won't buy me the kind of life-style I intend to pursue."

During this angry exchange, both men seemed to have forgotten about Kelly. Now she interrupted, her face defiant. "How do you know that I *didn't* find the urn, Miles?"

"Kelly, *don't.*"

Miles went rigid. "Tell me, damn it! Did you find the urn or not?"

She nodded. "Eighteenth century and inlaid with precious gems. Hammered gold in perfect ovoid. A real museum-quality reliquary urn all right."

"*Where?*" Miles's voice was a flat hiss.

"I—I'll have to show you." Instinct guided Kelly now. She had finally learned to trust this unpredictable gift of hers. "I'm not certain that I can describe it."

Miles's grip tightened. "Move, then. And no tricks." He turned to glare at Burke. "The same goes for *you*. One move and she takes a bullet, point-blank to the neck. Understand?"

Burke gave a grim nod. Miles left him no choice.

O'Halloran backed up the hill, careful to hold Kelly as a shield between himself and Burke's crossbow. "Where is it?"

"In the cave, of course. I expect the viscount must have visited it once as a boy, then forgotten it until he was programmed to find the safest spot for the urn."

Miles laughed harshly. "By God, you really are something, Kelly. Without that damned sight of yours, I never would have found the urn."

"Trevor figured out the location from his father's field notes. Thank him for narrowing the search." By instinct, Kelly moved as slowly as possible, pretending to stumble several times.

"Hurry up, damn it!"

The cave stretched dark before them. Kelly pointed. "It's in there."

Miles shoved her forward. "Go on in. And no tricks. At this range I could hit you even in the dark."

Kelly slipped into the cave. Bending down, she groped along the ground until she found the cold metal vessel. She shuddered when she brushed it, flinching as if she had touched something very evil.

When she turned back toward the opening, she saw the sword lying where she had shoved it.

Again the glimmer of intuition.

"Kelly, get over here, damn it!"

Quickly she worked the sword beneath the waist of her skirt, then pulled her sweater down until blade and pommel were completely covered.

"What's taking you so long?" Miles demanded harshly.

"I—I'm right here. It took me longer to find than I thought." Holding the urn before her, Kelly walked outside. As she did, a bar of sunlight struck the burnished gold, illuminating the jewels encrusting the lid.

Miles cursed softly. "You really did find it," he whispered. "I always knew you saw too much to be trusted. It was only a matter of time before you locked onto my own little masquerade, no matter how carefully I blocked it from you."

"You've got what you want, O'Halloran," Burke shouted, striding uphill. "Let her go. She's no more use to you now."

"Ah, but I'm afraid you're wrong. Kelly is going to get me out of here." Miles grabbed Kelly's shoulders and shoved her down the hill, careful to keep her between himself and Burke.

"It won't work. I'll follow you. If you touch one hair on her head, I'll find you and—"

Miles laughed harshly. "Empty talk, Burke, and we both know it. Now get back and let us pass. Unless you want something to happen to her. I don't really mind one way or the other."

Grimly, Michael did as he was ordered. At the same time he held his bow level, hoping for any chance of a clear shot at Miles.

But O'Halloran was clever. He kept Kelly locked before him every step of the way.

Kelly, however, had her own plans.

She caught Burke's eye, then looked down at the urn. When he nodded, she swayed slightly, then tossed the urn into the air. It clattered down and bumped over the ground, gaining speed as it rolled toward the gorge.

With a clear clang the urn struck granite, then toppled to the cliff edge, where it balanced precariously.

Cursing, Miles leaped out after it. Burke moved too, but O'Halloran spun about and yanked Kelly before him just in time. "That little trick just cost you Burke's life," he hissed.

His pistol levelled on Burke's chest.

And then sunlight glinted off gilt bronze and

etched silver. The great blade of St. Vaux swung up from Kelly's side and slammed into Miles's knee at the same moment he fired. The blow threw him off balance and the bullet cracked off a tree to Burke's right.

Again Kelly swung the heavy blade, this time catching Miles across the ribs.

"Damn you, Kelly!" With a growl of rage, Miles grabbed the sword and sent it flying. For a crazy moment the great blade spun tang over pommel, jewels aglint and metal gleaming. Then it clattered down and disappeared into the gorge.

But Burke was already diving forward. He caught Miles with a savage right hook to the jaw. Miles's pistol went flying, kicked from his fingers, and Burke sent him stumbling backward with a furious blow to the chin.

"I should shoot you right now, O'Halloran. By God, I'd enjoy that. But I'm going to enjoy rearranging your face first."

Miles looked down, searching desperately for his pistol, only to find that Kelly now had it clutched in her hands.

Cursing, he caught up a stick and slammed it against Burke's hip. Burke didn't even flinch.

Then his hands were against Miles's throat. His grip tightened. Fury darkened his face. Beneath his crushing fingers, Miles's face went pale and mottled. He began to choke.

Burke shook himself, struggling back from the darkness.

Slowly his fingers slid free. He watched Miles collapse in a slump before him.

What was happening here? Burke wondered, staring down at the man lying against the grass. He looked at his hands. At the hands of a stranger, seen through the *eyes* of a stranger. Something told him that this was a fight that should have ended centuries before.

He turned to Kelly. She stared at him with tear-filled eyes, then ran across the grass and flung herself into his arms.

Bending his head, Burke kissed her hair, feeling as if he were awakening from a terrible dream.

Her eyes reminded him of that Arizona sky of hers. They burned into his face, into his very soul, giving of herself freely, giving all that she was and hoped to be. And asking—no *demanding*—all the best of him in turn.

And Burke gave it. Willingly. Completely. Knowing there would never be anyone else for him but Kelly.

Behind them wild laughter echoed over the slope.

Conscious now, Miles O'Halloran staggered to his feet. "I'll have it yet, damn you both!" Cursing, he stumbled toward the ridge of stone where the urn lay glinting at a slant.

"Stop, man! Be careful of the—"

"Fools. All of you, fools! The urn will be mine. And then I'll—" Smiling grimly, Miles grabbed for the lost urn, but his foot twisted and he shot forward.

Cursing, he clawed at thin air.

A moment later the urn crashed over the edge of the cliff, and O'Halloran went with it.

"The urn!" Burke felt a terrible wave of fear. He spun about, dragging Kelly behind him.

They had barely made the middle of the hill when a metallic clang echoed up from the gorge.

An explosive boom ripped the air, rocking the ground.

Burke shoved Kelly beneath him, covering her

with his body as the blast tore over them, sending down a wild rain of rocks and torn branches.

It seemed that hours passed before the stones settled and the smoke finally disappeared.

Burke raised his head cautiously. "Kelly?"

Her head rose. Her beautiful cheeks were smudged with leaves and dust. "I'm fine, my heart. But you covered me with your body. Were you hit? Are you—"

Burke answered her with a ferocity that stunned even himself. His lips crushed hers, sealing out words or speech, binding his body to hers forever.

Kelly's arms slid around his neck. "Michael?" Her voice wavered for a moment. "The sword. It—it saved us . . ."

"So it did," Burke said softly, feeling as if a ghostly hand had reached out from the ashes of time to offer its protection to the two of them.

Not that he understood it. Perhaps he never would.

But feeling was enough.

At that moment shouts came from down the trail. "Burke? Good God, are you two all right up there?"

Burke recognized that gravelly voice. "I'm here, Inspector." He looked at Kelly. "We're both here."

Ross charged into the clearing. He stared at the broken branches and the now jagged cliff, where a wedge of granite had been torn away by the explosion. "Good sweet heaven, Burke, what's been going on up here?"

"It's rather a long story. You'd better have someone look at him first." He nodded toward the still-smoking gorge. "When the urn went down, I'm afraid that O'Halloran went with it. He also said that he'd dealt with Trevor. You'll probably find his body somewhere at the bottom of the gorge."

"Lovely fellow," Ross said grimly.

The inspector crouched gingerly beside the cliff as two other officers panted into the clearing. When he stood up, he shook his head. "Whatever was down there is gone now." He frowned, seeing Burke pull Kelly close and set off to the north. "Burke? You can't leave yet! Have a heart. I've got a report to complete that's probably going to take me the best part of the next five years. I'll have to account for equipment loss and damages and overtime costs and—"

"You'll have to manage by yourself this time, Ross. I'm no longer employed. Pass that along, won't you." Burke looked down at Kelly. "Where to, Professor? Tahiti? Venice? I'd even like to see that red rock desert of yours."

"Home," Kelly said softly, touching his cheek. "To that big bed in that lovely room in the wonderful house where you grew up."

Michael smiled. "Your wish is my command, Red."

They had one hour and fifty-three minutes of glorious peace before the door knocker boomed.

They ignored it.

They were still sitting, fingers twined, in Edgehill's sunny kitchen when Marston appeared a few minutes later, impassive as ever. His hands were filled with baskets of food.

"Pardon, Commander, but I brought a few things for dinner."

"Marston, this goes far beyond the call of duty."

The butler gave no notice, intent on unpacking

the baskets that were issuing forth mouth-watering aromas. "I thought perhaps a cold asparagus soup to begin, followed by salmon with lime sauce and braised new potatoes. I've prepared orange trifle for dessert, along with a chocolate mousse. Dom Pérignon is chilling on ice."

Burke shook his head. "You are seriously disrupting my life, do you know that, Marston?"

Kelly couldn't hold back a soft laugh.

The butler unbent so far as to smile faintly. "I trust you will survive, Commander. It seems that you always do."

"Oh, I have every intention of surviving, Marston." Burke looked down at Kelly and raised her fingers to his lips. "Now where were we? Oh, yes. I was asking you to marry me and you were busy not answering."

"Michael, that's not the way it was. It's just that . . ." Kelly flushed, glancing over at Marston, then back at Michael.

"Don't mind Marston, my love. The man can't hear a thing, right, Marston?"

"Deaf as an old seaman, Miss Hamilton," the butler said cheerfully, arranging food and china and silver.

"Michael, you're impossible. *This* is impossible. We've spent exactly three days together—"

Michael interrupted with a wolfish smile. "And we loved every minute of it."

"Yes, but you know next to nothing about me."

"Except that I love you."

"You're being unreasonable!"

"Bloody right I am. And I mean to continue being unreasonable until I have your answer."

"I love you," Kelly said softly. "I want to spend

my life with you. But I just want *you* to be sure before—"

"I *am* sure, woman! Tell her I'm sure, Marston."

The butler turned, his eyes twinkling. "He is entirely sure, Miss Hamilton. I vouch for the fact. Though of course I can hear nothing."

"Yes or no, Kelly? Make me an honest man so that Marston isn't put to the blush."

Before Kelly could answer, a new voice echoed down the hallway. "Michael? Kelly? I phoned Draycott and a nice man named Inspector Ross told me you were here." The Dowager Marchioness of Sefton stood framed in the doorway, regal in a lime-green wool Balenciaga sheath with matching jacket. "He was quite right. Ah, Marston, I see you were able to arrange the salmon. You really are a marvel. I must try to lure you away from Nicholas. Now, what about that bottle of Dom Pérignon?" She bustled to the table, looking at Kelly. "Well, have you answered him yet, my dear? He'll make you an unmanageable husband, but I do so want you in the family that I'm going to badger you until you accept, I warn you."

Michael looked offended. "I really think I can manage my *own* proposing, Mother."

"Nonsense. Look what a hash of it you've made so far."

Kelly shook her head and then slipped her arms around mother and son, her eyes alight with love. "The answer is yes, since you're foolish enough to want it. And I love you both."

Behind them Marston smiled. "Dinner is served," he intoned formally as he popped the cork of the now perfectly chilled Dom Pérignon and began filling three glasses.

Epilogue

"**M**ichael?" The voice was tense with barely suppressed excitement. "Blast it, man, where are you?"

Footsteps hammered through the courtyard. A moment later the great oak doors of Draycott Abbey burst open with a cheerful creak of wood on metal.

"Welcome back, my lord!" Marston was beaming, dignified in black worsted and bright green running shoes.

The twelfth Viscount Draycott laughed and shook his head. "Ah, Marston, I'm delighted to see that *you* haven't changed."

"I should hope not, my lord. Ah, there is the viscountess now. Looking entirely radiant, if I may say so."

"Of course you may say so, you charming man." The viscount's American wife smiled up at the beaming butler. "And here's someone else who's waiting for compliments." As she spoke, Kacey Mallory Draycott shifted the bundle in her arms and slid back one corner of the linen blanket that seven generations of Draycotts had used to welcome their firstborn home to the abbey.

A perfect oval face peaked out from beneath the fine embroidered linen, all pink cheeks and keen sapphire eyes.

"She's got your mouth, my lady. And I believe she has a touch—yes, just a touch of Draycott stubbornness about her chin."

"Which means she'll lead us a fine dance, no doubt," her father muttered. But Nicholas was beaming and his smile held the glowing contentment of fatherhood.

"Come in, come in," Marston urged. "I've lit a fire in the study and tea will be ready directly."

The viscount frowned. "Where is Burke?" he asked, looking about. "Don't tell me he's run off again!"

A smile played about Marston's mouth. "The last I checked, Lord Burke and Miss Hamilton were poring over some old volumes in the library. At least," he said dryly, "they were trying very hard to give *me* the impression that that's what they were doing."

The viscountess eased closer to Marston, beset with curiosity about her husband's friend, a man she had heard much about but had never met. "Is he happy, Marston? Is she good for him? He's had a foul time of it, you know."

"I would venture to say that Miss Hamilton is exceedingly good for him, my lady."

"Is she, by God!" Nicholas snorted. "Blast it, we've been out of touch for only two weeks and everything's topsy-turvy. And the bloody man's told us next to nothing!"

The butler's eyes held a secret glint. "I surmise that Lord Burke is happy. Blindingly happy, in fact. But then you must decide for yourself. Meanwhile, I shall fetch the tea before it cools. Might I suggest some of my black forest soufflé and a nice Moët et Chandon '97 to go with it?"

His eyes met the viscount's.

Nicholas Draycott gave a soundless whistle. "*That* serious, is it?"

"I have every expectation of its being so."

Draycott shook his head as he watched the butler pad off to the kitchen, humming softly and quite off-key. "There'll be no living with the man now, you know. I expect he hasn't had so much fun in ages!"

His wife laughed. "I suppose you can't blame him, my dear. To be right in the middle of a mystery, after all!"

"Well, we've been living in virtual seclusion. Burke owes me some answers and I mean to have them. What the devil went on here while we were gone, aside from an explosion that rocked half the gorge? What happened to that urn? And what about that sword everyone was making such a fuss about?"

His wife put her hand gently on his sleeve. "All in good time, my heart. Let's not press them first thing, shall we?"

Lord Draycott sighed. He studied his wife lovingly. "You're right, of course. You always are."

"Oh, not always. I wasn't right the first time I came here. And I certainly wasn't right to ignore you when you warned me to be careful." Her blue eyes darkened. "My foolishness nearly cost us both our lives."

"Done and forgotten, my love," her husband whispered. "Besides, something tells me that this little bundle is going to keep us far too busy to think about the past."

Right on cue, Cecily Austin Mackenzie Draycott smiled and cooed softly, wrapping her tiny fist around her father's strong fingers.

"You see? An out-and-out charmer and her barely two weeks old. Lord, I can see it already. A few more years and she'll be knee-deep in scoundrels. I'll have to *beat* them away with sticks!"

"And you'll be loving every minute of it," his wife said softly, a smile in her eyes.

Nicholas gazed down at his daughter and nodded, entirely besotted. "You're right, my love. So I shall."

"You see? It's *perfectly* formed, just as I said. Long. Good definition. Powerful. Just look at those lines."

A low masculine groan came nearby. "You're killing me, Red. It's nothing short of cold-blooded, premeditated homicide."

"But I haven't even got to the exciting parts yet. Especially here. Just look at that proportion. I'm itching to run my fingers along it. How else can I get the sense of its strength." Kelly paused. "Michael? What are you doing?"

"Doing? I'm dying. Melting. Going thermonuclear. But do go on, love. Don't let that stop you."

"I might stop, but only if you promise I don't have to drive to my wedding in that wretched, noisy car of yours. Michael, no. I—oh!"

Husky female laughter rang out, echoing through the open French doors facing Draycott Abbey's silver moat. Behind a mahogany bookcase two pairs of legs were visible, outstretched on the rich Aubusson carpet.

At the sound of that laughter the moat seemed

to tremble and the wind ruffled the roses, as if in silent salute.

To lovers.

To happiness.

To *life*.

Kelly looked up innocently from the open pages of *The Geological Formations of the Sussex Coast*. She lay crosswise to Michael's prone body, her chest nestled across his waist as she thumbed through the thick volume. Her lips were red and very well kissed. "I had no idea you liked geology so much, Michael. You should have told me sooner."

"I don't."

"No?" Kelly turned a page, brushing Burke's thigh in the process. "But, Michael, this is fascinating."

The Englishman's teeth grated together. His eyes promised vengeance—and exquisite pleasure—for what she was doing to him.

Kelly reached for another book, her breast brushing against his arm. "Oh, Michael, just look at this one. It's another one by William Smith. *Order of the Strata and their Imbedded Organic Remains*. And look, it's a first edition of 1799!"

"That exciting, is it?" With one quick movement, Burke caught the book and slid it beneath him. "The organic remains of Sussex? In a few minutes that's what I'm going to feel like."

"Give it back, you wretch! That book is a classic! And William Smith is—"

"I suppose *his* structures are good too. Long. Well shaped?"

Kelly looked confused for a moment. Then her cheeks flushed as she grasped Burke's innuendos. "I was speaking about science, and well you know it."

Burke's eyes darkened as he toyed with a strand of her hair. "What would you pay to have the book back, Professor? I might be open to negotiation."

Kelly gave Burke a slow smile. "I take it a personally guided tour of the Sussex coastline isn't exactly what you had in mind."

"Too bloody right."

"A firsthand look at some amazing limestone structures near Edgehill?" As she spoke, Kelly eased closer, her soft stomach angled over his rapidly hardening masculinity.

Sweat broke out on Burke's brow. "Not even close."

"Hmmm." Kelly ran her finger along the rim of Burke's ear. "Am I getting . . . warmer?"

Burke swallowed. "Any warmer and you'll have me in a puddle right here on the floor."

Kelly closed her eyes and pretended to sigh. "I can't imagine what would interest you then. I've mentioned everything that I—"

With a growl, Michael rolled over and caught Kelly beneath him. "Not stratigraphy. Not ancient grave goods. Not even Norman swords, temptress." His eyes lowered to her sweater. Her breasts were outlined with lovely clarity against the soft wool. At Burke's dark scrutiny the crests began to tighten.

Kelly gave a wriggle. "Let me up."

"Not just yet, I think," Michael murmured. His fingers swept gently over her soft curves. "Not until I get you to make that funny little noise."

"W-what funny little noise?"

"That one. The one in the back of your throat. The one you make when you get excited."

Hectic color flared on Kelly's face. "I d-don't! I never—"

"No?" Michael's brow rose. He circled the hungry skin already tight with arousal. "Now let me see . . ."

"Michael, you *can't*! Not here. What if Marston—"

"Marston's busy making tea." The Englishman's fingers eased apart. His mouth took their place, gentle and stroking against the whisper-thin angora.

"Oh, no—don't." Kelly's voice broke again. "Please, Michael . . ."

"Ah, *drushka*, there it was again, that husky little sound. It does utterly amazing things to my lower body, did you know that?"

Kelly's eyes darkened with passion. *He* was doing pretty amazing things to *her* lower body right then. "It does?"

Burke's fingers eased beneath the warm angora. "It does," he murmured wickedly. "By the way, I hope you won't expect me to give up my job after we marry."

"And what exactly *is* your job? I don't believe I ever found out."

"Why, harassing beautiful American scholars who come down to visit Sussex, of course."

Kelly's eyes glinted. "Consider yourself fired, in that case."

"Now why would you—"

She cut him off with a mock right jab to the shoulder and a left to the ribs.

And a hot, slow, and utterly abandoned kiss to the neck.

And the chest.

And the skin she slowly bared just above his waistband.

Groaning, the Marquess of Sefton subsided without a contest. "You win, Red. Consider me unemployed. Need a helper on your digs? I'm told I'm very good with my hands."

Kelly's eyes narrowed. "And who told you that, Englishman?"

"Oh, any number of people. You see, I'm far more capable than you credit me for."

Suddenly Kelly's laughter died away. "I didn't say you weren't capable, Michael. In fact, as I recall I said that if you were any *more* capable, we would *never* get any work done today." She pressed a line of kisses across his chest.

Burke's eyes darkened. "Truce, Red. Otherwise, I'll be nothing but porridge when you're finished."

Kelly's brow arched. "But I never *shall* finish with you, Michael. I thought I'd made that very clear." Her eyes turned serious, glinting with love. "I'll be there to kiss you awake each morning and torment you to sleep each evening. Just like last night. Do you remember how the moon hung silver overhead when we walked back from Edgehill? The air was so warm that I just had to test the water in the Witch's Pool."

"Remember?" Burke groaned. "Which part? When you called me a stuffy old aristocrat? Or when you dared me to join you in a moonlight swim? *Sans* clothes, naturally."

"Naturally."

Burke's fingers slid into Kelly's hair. "Oh, I remember, hellion. It's something I'm not likely ever to forget." His voice fell. "Especially when you hid my clothes so we couldn't go back right away." He gave a low laugh. "I do believe it was the loveliest evening I've ever had."

A hint of uncertainty flickered in Kelly's eyes. "Do you, Michael? Truly?" She was talking about more than their scandalous midnight swim, and they both knew it. "We're so different. Our lives, our backgrounds are so far apart. I just worry that—"

He silenced her with an open-mouthed kiss to the tormentingly beautiful line of her jaw and nibbled his way up to her mouth.

"Oh, Michael . . ." Kelly's breath slid out on a sigh.

"That's better. I don't want you raising any foolish doubts. Come to think of it, you didn't appear to be protesting very much last night."

Kelly's eyes jerked open. "Are you implying that—well, that I'm—"

Burke's smile grew. "Hot-blooded? Susceptible to seduction?"

"I am *not!*"

"Of course you're not." The Englishman gave her a slow, wolfish grin. "No more susceptible than I am to *you*, at any rate. In fact, what do you say we go back down to the pool? In the daylight I could see you so much better when I—"

A low cough brought them both around. Their faces were faintly guilty.

At the doorway Nicholas Draycott shook his head, trying to look disapproving. "Hard at work, I see, just as Marston told me."

Instantly Kelly jumped to her feet, her cheeks crimson. "Oh, but we were. *Working,* that is. Until just a moment ago we'd been studying your books on Sussex stratigraphy. You have a wonderful collection here, by the way. and then, well, that is—" She cleared her throat abruptly, staring from Nicholas's grinning face to Michael's equally wolfish features.

Her husband-to-be stood up and slid his arm around her shoulders. "Nicholas knows precisely how hard we were, er, *working*, my heart." Burke held out his other hand to his friend. "It's good to see you back, Nicky. I'll be glad to put this place behind me."

"Oh, how can you say that?" Kelly frowned. "It's *lovely* here. And the geological strata are so exquisitely *predictable*! Just yesterday I found two limestone levels running parallel down at the gorge—"

Nicholas Draycott rubbed his jaw. "Geological strata? I'm afraid I'm out of my depth there."

Again Kelly flushed. "Oh, I beg your pardon. Sometimes I do ramble on."

"Nonsense." Viscount Draycott gave her a thoughtful nod. "It's about time I had an expert in to give me some professional advice about this place. Did you have a chance to look at the old Norman ruins south of the gorge? That place always seemed rather unstable. I can even recall my father saying how when he was a boy—"

"Do you *mind*?" Michael glared at his old friend.

"Not at all, Misha," Draycott said affably. "Chime in any time you like. I didn't know that geological strata were in your line though."

Burke muttered something beneath his breath. "I daresay that there are a *lot* of things you don't know about me."

Draycott studied the books littering the library floor. "Such as your interest in first editions? Or were you exercising your skill in page turning?"

Kelly flushed. "Oh, that was because of my hand. I hurt it yesterday when I—"

"There's no need to apologize, Kelly. The man was just being an ass. The way he always is."

Kelly stared from one to the other, biting her lip, frightened by the deep currents of tension and anger that flowed between them.

And then, without warning, Nicholas threw back his head and laughed. Slowly Burke's face curved up in a smile that took ten years off his age.

"I remembered, Misha. About your being there in Thailand and quite a few other things." Nicholas smiled darkly. "Somehow it makes being your half-brother not nearly so painful."

"I'm glad to hear it. I guess I can live with it too," Burke muttered. "There's been enough anger between us."

A soft hand touched Kelly's shoulder.

"Don't mind them," a low voice said. "Let's go and talk, shall we? Just the two of us? I've been dying for a little female company. Men can be so—so redundant at a time like this, don't you think? And I've especially been longing to talk to another American."

Kelly smiled at the golden-haired viscountess and the cooing baby in her arms. "Oh, how beautiful she is! Michael's mother told me she was two weeks old. And just look at those adorable dimples. Is she sleeping through the night yet?"

"Not yet, I'm afraid. But I have hopes . . ."

The two women wandered off through the French doors and out toward the moat, their heads bent over the smiling infant, while the men watched wordlessly.

Nicholas snorted. "Redundant, am I?"

"Afraid so, old man." Burke smiled. "You must be getting old."

"Humph. Just you wait, Misha. You'll get your turn."

Michael looked exceedingly pleased by the prospect. "I certainly hope so. God, she makes me happy."

Nicholas chuckled. "So she's the one they sent to find the sword. Damned smart, she sounded. Did you ever find that sword by the way? When you weren't too busy blowing up half my land, of course."

For the first time Michael's voice faltered. "We did, amazingly enough. But then . . . we lost it. It's—well, it's rather a long story, Nicky. Why don't we go in and have a drink while I tell you about it."

Meanwhile, down by the moat's edge, the two women had found a sunny spot against a rock. For a moment little Cecily Draycott seemed about to cry, then her eyes crinkled and her tiny fist speared at the air.

A moment later soft laughter broke from her throat.

"She does that, sometimes," her mother said softly. "It's almost as if she sees something I can't. Oh, it's utterly silly, of course, but sometimes I almost wonder if . . ." The viscountess shrugged and lifted her daughter for a kiss. "Enough about us. I want to hear about *you*. Just what has been going on here since we left? I know Nicholas has been dying to hear, but that Inspector Ross has been as quiet as the grave about everything."

Kelly settled back in the sun, frowning. "This might take some time, you know. It's, er—rather complicated."

"Fire away." The viscountess's eyes gleamed. "I love a good mystery."

Kelly took a long breath, her eyes on the distant line of trees above Lyon's Leap. "Oh, it was a mystery all right. Sometimes I still can't believe it happened. You see, it all began before I came to Draycott. Back in Arizona, actually. I'd had an awful day and . . ."

"But she *did*, I tell you! That infant definitely *saw* me."

At the edge of the moat, a golden glow drifted over the water. Two figures shimmered into view, their arms entwined.

"Now, now, Adrian. There's no reason to become so excited."

"She did, I tell you!"

"Of course, I agree that it looked that way. And I'll grant you that the sweet child did seem to blink. Even that she reached out her little hand toward you. But you must admit that there could be a hundred different reasons why—"

"Stuff and nonsense, woman. That child *saw* me!"

The woman at his side looked unconvinced. "But how could she see you, Adrian? You told me yourself that you can only appear under special conditions, and then only to the master of the abbey."

"Damned if I know." The man in black fingered the lace at one cuff. "And to think that the viscount's friend Burke is a descendant of the warrior St. Vaux. Quite remarkable." He sniffed. "I never did like the St. Vaux line, however. I shall have to keep a close eye on the man."

"Why is there no mention in the family records?"

"The Bishop of Kingston, my dear. The man was very thorough in destroying every mention of his enemy. But Professor Bullock-Powell will discover all of this in time."

"He will, will he?" The woman's eyes twinkled.

"Of course. You and I will see to that." He shook his head. "They might at least have named her after me," he muttered crossly, his mind fixed back on the youngest Draycott.

"You know they thought of it, my love, but I don't think they liked the sound of Adriana with Cecily."

"Nothing wrong with it."

His companion hid a smile. "But what about your vision? What about the woman with the sword?"

"I believe that problem will soon be resolved."

"How? You said she was—not of this time."

"Sometimes past and present are closer than you think. All it required was a suggestion here and a hint there. Yes, it will soon be taken care of."

"You can be the most provoking man, Adrian! I want to know how you plan to—"

"Later." Abruptly Adrian smiled and tugged her over the grass. "Come with me."

"Where, you impossible man?"

"To the nursery. Cecily will be going up for her nap soon."

"How do you know *that*?"

The guardian of Draycott Abbey looked very smug. "So I can still surprise you, my love. Good. Now do hurry. I want to be there before the precious little child goes to sleep. Then I'll prove it to you once and for all. She *did* see me."

The woman in gold brushed his cheek. "My dearest love, I never knew you were so partial to children."

The abbey ghost gave a low cough. "Hmmm. Well, not any child, you know. Just her. Special, she is. And she *is* the first born, after all," he added gruffly. " 'Tis my duty to keep an eye on her."

The woman nodded soberly. But her eyes, as she followed Adrian up the bank and right through the abbey's gray granite wall, were full of love and complete understanding.

"Do you have everything?" Kelly stood uncertainly above the moat. It was nearly midnight, and the woods were silent. The moon was not yet up, leaving the stars a clear field to blink madly against the velvet sky.

"The whole lot." Michael's voice sank to a conspiratorial whisper. "Whose house are we breaking into, by the way?"

Kelly chewed her lip, entirely oblivious to his joke. "Not breaking in. I rather hope it's the opposite."

Michael shot her a quick look, concern darkening his features. "You mean breaking *out?*"

"I can't really explain, Michael. It's just a feeling I've had, ever since—well, since that day by the stream. It's got to do with my visions . . ." Her voice trailed away.

Michael caught her shoulders. "I believe what you've told me, Kelly. Never try to deny something that makes you very special. Without that gift of yours, I don't know what would have happened at the gorge." He frowned. "But you're saying that it's not over?"

Kelly looked out at the moat, trying to explain the sense of urgency that she'd felt the last few days. "It's almost as if the two of them were still out there somewhere, lost and grieving. So terribly alone. I don't think I could bear to be the cause of that, or to know I'd left them unhappy somehow." She stared up at the tall man beside her, struck as always by the strength in his face. "I'm not hopelessly crazy, am I, Michael?"

Burke slid his arm around her shoulder and planted a hard kiss against her glowing hair. "Not in the least. If you believe this thing, if you *feel* it, then it must be true. I have no doubt of that."

Kelly sighed. "I wish I were so sure. I try to forget, but sometimes in the night, I—I see him. I hear him call out, but he never finds her. And then . . ." Her voice broke.

Michael raised her face to his. "I love you, Kelly Hamilton," he said fiercely. "Because you are what you are. Because you feel what you feel. Do you believe that? If you don't, then we haven't got a snowball's chance in hell of making a success together." There was pain in his dark eyes— and uncertainty.

Kelly sniffed back the beginning of tears. "Badgering me already, are you, Englishman?" Her hand rose to his cheek. "The answer is yes, I do believe you. Sometimes I think your love has been the greatest miracle of my life. And that's why I have to help *them*."

"Then let's do it," Michael said briskly, as if they were off to prune hedges instead of participate in an arcane metaphysical mission.

To rescue two people who had been dead for roughly nine hundred years.

Kelly straightened her shoulders and took the candles from Burke. With slightly unsteady fingers she struck a match and set the first wick aflame. Soon the grassy bank was alive with tiny winking lights, a star-studded sky in miniature.

"Ready?"

Kelly smiled, crouching beside Michael on the grass. "Ready, my love."

One by one they launched the floating candles, watching them rock and sway across the water until the moat was shimmering with light.

As the last candle sailed free, Kelly felt a sudden sense of elation, as if a great burden had been lifted from her shoulders. Why or how, she could not say, but she knew that somewhere her gift had been received.

She brushed away a tear and stood up, holding out her hand to Michael. "It's done," she said softly as their fingers meshed. "Somehow I can feel it. They will be together at last."

Above the dark woods, above the scarred granite of Lyon's Leap, a shooting star blazed into view, burning a silver path toward morning.

Kelly looked at Michael, feeling awe at the vastness of life's patterns and the incredible tenacity of the human spirit. It was a miracle that she had found this man. It was a miracle they had survived Miles's treachery. But then, Draycott Abbey was a place tailor-made for miracles.

She gave a long, glad sigh. "Let's go home now, Michael."

Holding hands, they walked over the abbey's little stone bridge.

Their hearts were far too full for words.

High on the abbey's windswept parapets a great gray cat sat tensely, watching a spark of light arc through the night sky.

He meowed softly, listening to things that others could not hear, seeing the dim glow of a

jewelled sword hidden between earth and old
stone.

Finally content, he twitched his tail and padded off to one corner of the roof. There he circled
once, eased down against the smooth cool stone
and went to sleep.

The great sword lay forgotten in the darkness.

Trapped between mud and stone, its ancient
blade was still, the priceless emerald dark and
unwinking.

But one day jewel and sword would glow
again. The great blade would hum with raw
power restored. And on that day Draycott's very
ground would shake. The sky over Lyon's Leap
would scream and the fabric of time would twist
and reform.

But not yet. For that the moment was not right.

Tonight the earth was quiet, at peace.

And the fabled sword of St. Vaux slept on,
cushioned against Draycott's rich dark earth,
awaiting the day an ancient curse was finally
put to rest.

*He was lost. The wind tore at his gray-flecked
hair and raged through the black trees, bending them
nearly double.*

*Lost, again. No matter how hard he searched, he
never found her.*

*The warrior cried out hoarsely, his strength nearly
gone. It seemed as if he had travelled these dark woods
night and day for months, for years.*

Nay, forever.

*And then, where before there had been only dark-
ness, suddenly there was light. Just a tiny pinpoint it
was, faint and winking. But its glow was warmth and
hope in a nightmare that seemed to stretch on forever.*

"Aislann," he cried hoarsely, gripping the reins and kneeing his steed forward. "Please God, let it be you."

The light grew, became two and then ten. Before him the forest seemed aglow, the only hope he had known for days.

The Norman's hands trembled. He slid from his horse and stumbled over the uneven ground.

Toward the light. Always toward the light.

"Aislann!" His voice was a mere whisper above the storm.

But she heard. A rectangle of light appeared against the darkness. And then her face, sweet, merciful God, her eyes. Her blinding, happy smile.

"Lyon!" She ran toward him, her hair unbound, red-gold in the streaming light, her eyes streaked with silver tears. "You came! Dear God, I waited. Night after night. Praying. Always hoping—"

Her breath caught in a broken sob as his strong hands slid around her, his body hard against hers.

"I came. And now I've found you again. Blessed heaven, the lights—" St. Vaux caught the woman he loved close, lifting her against him as if he still couldn't believe she was real.

"I always lit a light, just as I told you. And I waited, here beneath the great oak, where the red rose twines. It's opened, our rose. Right now the crimson flower lies in bloom. Can you smell it?"

St. Vaux's eyes glinted. "Aye, my love. I smell it. Right now the whole world lies in bloom around us. Cannot you feel that?"

She laughed. "My great, flattering Lyon. I see now how you've managed to steal so many women's hearts."

"But there was only one heart I've ever wanted, love. Only one I fought to keep." He bent his head and whispered against her temple. "Yours forever."

And then he stiffened. His hand slid down across her waist. "Aislann? Sweet Lord, are you truly—"

"Breeding," she answered softly, shy for a moment. "The babe is due in three more months."

With a great cry of laughter St. Vaux tossed her up, only to catch her with a look of anxiety. "Did I hurt you? I didn't think—what about the babe? Are you—"

"We are both fine, you great lumbering Norman." Her green eyes shone. "Now come inside. I think we have a great many things to catch up on."

"Many things indeed," the warrior said softly, his fingers gentle on her stomach, his eyes aflame with love. "Aye, let us finally go home, my rose."

Author's Note

Dearest reader:

All right, I admit it. I just haven't been able to get Kelly and Michael out of my mind! Brash and relentlessly stubborn, this pair was born to strike sparks from the first moment of their meeting. Either they would be deepest friends—or darkest enemies. Thank heavens they turned out to be the first!

Now about that sword.

Swords have been objects of mystery since the first bronze blades were forged almost 5,000 years ago. With the touch of a sword, a man was raised up as a knight and with the breaking of his sword all honor was denied him. It's easy to understand why the heroes of Celtic epic treasured their swords. Beautifully crafted and decorated with rare stones or precious metals, they remind us of Arthur's Excalibur as described by Tennyson:

> *... rich*
> *With jewels, elfin urim in the hilt,*
> *Bewildering heart and eye—the blade so bright*

Such was the magnificent weapon that Kelly found at Draycott. For such a treasure we can well believe that the laws of time and matter might be shifted. Add to this the power of love, undying and unchanged over centuries, and it seems possible—indeed *probable*—that two lovers could defy fate to find a happiness denied them by history long years before.

Aislann and Lyon did. I firmly believe it.

What next, you ask?

I'm delighted to tell you that Kelly and Michael will be back as secondary characters next year when Avon brings you my next contemporary romance, which will also be set at the hauntingly beautiful Draycott Abbey.

The story?

A little . . . offbeat, actually. Picture an island, mist-veiled and beautiful, set like a jewel in the middle of an English valley. Pit a stubborn American conservationist against men who don't know the meaning of the word. Throw in a nasty curse which has veiled the isle in enchantment for roughly 800 years.

Not enough?

Okay, toss in a knight. That's right, a knight. The real, old-fashioned kind, decked out in chain mail, chausses and leather gauntlets. The kind of man who's never heard the phrase "looking out for number one." The kind of warrior who lives by his code of honor and expects to die by it. A man who measures the meaning of his life by the strength of his commitment to gallantry and valor.

A *hero*, in other words. The kind of man who would gladly lay down his life to save a damsel in distress.

Even when said damsel is a self-reliant, self-empowered twentieth century female who has absolutely *no* interest in being saved by any man and can manage quite nicely by herself, thank you.

I think you get the basic idea.

The poor man hasn't got a chance.

I hope you'll enjoy the book which will be coming to you early in 1995.

In the meantime, I'd love to hear from you. If you'd like a signed bookmark and a copy of my next newsletter with information about past characters, upcoming books and historical tidbits, please send a stamped, self-addressed envelope (the LONG kind works best) to me at:

111 East Fourteenth Street, #277H
New York, New York 10003

With warmest regards,

Christina Skye

Bestselling Author

CHRISTINA SKYE

"CHRISTINA SKYE IS SUPERB!"
Virginia Henley

BRIDE OF THE MIST
78278-2/$5.99US/$7.99Can
Urged by a psychic to visit England's Draycott Abbey,
magazine editor Kara Fitzgerald is thrown into a passionate
encounter with one Duncan McKinnon—an encounter laced
with fiery desire and ancient rivalry.

A KEY TO FOREVER
78280-4/$5.99US/$7.99Can

SEASON OF WISHES
78281-2/$5.99US/$7.99Can

BRIDGE OF DREAMS
77386-4/$5.99US/$7.99Can

HOUR OF THE ROSE
77385-6/$4.99US/$5.99Can

Buy these books at your local bookstore or use this coupon for ordering:

Mail to: Avon Books, Dept BP, Box 767, Rte 2, Dresden, TN 38225   G
Please send me the book(s) I have checked above.
❏ My check or money order—no cash or CODs please—for $_____ is enclosed (please
add $1.50 per order to cover postage and handling—Canadian residents add 7% GST). U.S.
residents make checks payable to Avon Books; Canada residents make checks payable to
Hearst Book Group of Canada.
❏ Charge my VISA/MC Acct#_____Exp Date_____
Minimum credit card order is two books or $7.50 (please add postage and handling
charge of $1.50 per order—Canadian residents add 7% GST). For faster service, call
1-800-762-0779. Prices and numbers are subject to change without notice. Please allow six to
eight weeks for delivery.
Name_____
Address_____
City_____State/Zip_____
Telephone No._____   SKY 0797